Praise for
Adelaide

"Wheeler's debut is searingly raw. . . . Her whole soul is poured out onto the pages, and you'll find it hard not to feel your own heart crack and [your] stomach turn as Adelaide tries without avail to win the love of someone who simply can't give it. Wheeler deftly relates Adelaide's journey of unbending friendship, grief, and passion, and for many readers, her tale will strike a resonant chord."
—*Kirkus Reviews* (**starred review**)

"Heartfelt . . . This is a portrait of a woman struggling with her empathic desire to be all things to all people and realizing that she is allowed to put herself first."
—*Booklist*

"Wheeler perfectly captures her protagonist's depression, anxiety, and negative self-talk—not to mention her keen agony of unrequited love—and a solid supporting cast provides Adelaide with ample emotional support. The complex heroine animates every page."
—*Publishers Weekly*

"Poignant."
—*PopSugar*

"A raw and honest look at the complicated web of mental health and modern-day relationships and all their complexities, especially the gut-churning ups and downs of unrequited love and the power of friendships. If you've ever loved the wrong person or the right person at the wrong time, then your heart will ache for—and you'll wish you could give a big hug to—our heroine Adelaide."
—*Serendipity Magazine*

"Genevieve Wheeler perfectly captures the exquisite pain of being head over heels in love with someone whose feelings don't match yours, and poignantly celebrates the people on our journeys who make life worth living. A remarkable debut."
—**Jill Santopolo**, *New York Times* **bestselling author of** *The Light We Lost*

"Emotional and poignant . . . Genevieve Wheeler has made a remarkable debut with her fresh, modern voice. I was charmed. *Adelaide* exposes the raw edges of early adulthood and unrequited love, ultimately showing us that the true magic of life is that it's always worth living."
—**Sarah Addison Allen**, *New York Times* **bestselling author**

"I saw myself and all of my past mistakes reflected back at me on every page. Genevieve Wheeler writes with brilliant clarity and specificity. I feel like I'm longtime friends with every one of her characters. I've been recommending this book to every one of my female friends who knows what it is to love too quickly and too deeply, with the wrong person."

—**Dana Schwartz,** *New York Times* **bestselling author of**
Immortality: A Love Story

"Wheeler's debut is engrossing and poignant, full of grit and vulnerability."

—**Carola Lovering, author of** *Bye, Baby*

"Sharp-eyed and bighearted, *Adelaide* dives headfirst into the tidal pulls of love, friendship, grief, and mental health. Wheeler captures the lively adventures of an American twentysomething trying her best in London with dazzling humor and dizzying aplomb. This is a can't-miss, can't-put-down debut."

—**Beck Dorey-Stein,** *New York Times* **bestselling author of**
From the Corner of the Oval **and** *Rock the Boat*

"*Adelaide* puts the heartbreak of loving the wrong person and the healing powers of friendship on magnificent display. With whimsical prose and a charming London backdrop, this deeply relatable novel infuses even the most painful moments with hope. I savored every single page of this beautiful book." —**Hannah Orenstein, author of** *Meant to Be Mine*

"I fell head over heels in love with *Adelaide.* Featuring an unforgettable main character, this debut bursts with warmth, while offering an unflinching look at heartbreak and mental health. Genevieve Wheeler's writing had me cackling, crying, and nodding in recognition so vehemently that I almost gave myself whiplash." —**Laura Hankin, author of** *One-Star Romance*

Adelaide

GENEVIEVE WHEELER

ST. MARTIN'S GRIFFIN
NEW YORK

Published in the United States by St. Martin's Griffin, an imprint of St. Martin's Publishing Group

ADELAIDE. Copyright © 2023 by Genevieve Wheeler. All rights reserved. Printed in the United States of America. For information, address St. Martin's Publishing Group, 120 Broadway, New York, NY 10271.

www.stmartins.com

The Library of Congress has cataloged the hardcover edition as follows:

Names: Wheeler, Genevieve, author.
Title: Adelaide / Genevieve Wheeler.
Description: First edition. | New York: St. Martin's Press, 2023.
Identifiers: LCCN 2022052674 | ISBN 9781250280848 (hardcover) |
    ISBN 9781250280855 (ebook)
Subjects: LCGFT: Romance fiction. | Novels.
Classification: LCC PS3623.H42966 A73 2023 | DDC 813/.6—dc23/eng/20221122
LC record available at https://lccn.loc.gov/2022052674

ISBN 978-1-250-84280-0 (trade paperback)

Our books may be purchased in bulk for promotional, educational, or business use. Please contact your local bookseller or the Macmillan Corporate and Premium Sales Department at 1-800-221-7945, extension 5442, or by email at MacmillanSpecialMarkets@macmillan.com.

First St. Martin's Griffin Edition: 2024

10 9 8 7 6 5 4 3 2 1

*For my parents, my sisters,
and the many women who held my broken pieces*

Author's Note

This is a work of fiction. As is true in many fictional works, aspects of this story were inspired by life experiences. However, all of the characters, all of the dialogue, and all of the events described in this book are wholly imaginary. No identification with actual, real-life events, organizations, or persons—living or dead—is intended, nor should any such identification be inferred. But the love, the grief, the pain, the joy, the feelings, the feelings, the feelings? Those are all genuine—existing, living, and breathing off-page. I hope those are the bits that feel most real to you, reader. They're certainly the most real to me.

We tell ourselves stories in order to live.
　　—Joan Didion, *The White Album*

I know that that sassy little minx called love will find me
　　when I'm ready, but right now, it's time to write.
　　—Beck Dorey-Stein, *From the Corner of the Oval*

Prologue

The funny thing about hitting rock bottom is that you never quite know once you've reached it. That whooshing, falling feeling never ceases, and at every preceding level you've thought, *This has to be it, right?*

Sitting in a hospital room in Chelsea—drowsily answering questions about her emotional state, her family's mental health history, the exact number of pills she'd just swallowed—Adelaide still couldn't be certain this was it. Rock Bottom. She was waiting for the floor to give out from under her or the ceiling to cave in, for something else to push her further down. *This can't be it,* she thought. It never was. (Though, this was the closest she'd come.)

Celeste was in a chair to her left, a Tesco bag filled with snacks on her lap. She'd met Adelaide at the hospital an hour or so earlier and hugged her in a way Adelaide would never forget, so simultaneously careful and caring. It's a very odd thing to check yourself into the hospital for suicidal ideations—particularly when the receptionist can't quite make out your hushed words (*I. Am. Soo-ih-side-al. Can I just write it down?*)—and Adelaide was immeasurably grateful to have her there. In conversations with hospital staff, Celeste helped her fill in the blanks, out loud and on paper, jotting down her number under "Emergency Contact" without a moment's pause. She was in *Ms. Celeste Mode,* she explained, adopting her caretaking, primary-school-teaching demeanor, feeding Adelaide pretzels and petting her hair in the waiting room.

Did Rock Bottom even permit visitors?

Whatever the answer, Adelaide was relieved to have Celeste by her side, but just beyond this relief sat a swirl of more sinister emotions.

She was sure she'd hit a new low, found a new darkness. Her heart was still graciously beating, and pretzel salt was stinging her tongue, and she didn't want to be alive anymore. Physically, Adelaide was held together— her thighbone connected to her knee bone, and so on and so forth—but internally, mentally, she was a mess of jagged, disconnected pieces, and she didn't believe she was capable of putting herself back together. She didn't want to die, per se, she just wanted to stop existing. Stop being. And, frightening as it was, Death felt like the only avenue by which to get there. A handful of pills and a swig of water and she'd be free—her broken pieces swept up and transferred to another spiritual plane.

A delaide hadn't woken up that morning thinking she would choose it to be her last. The latte to which she'd treated herself had been mediocre at best, and she didn't remember eating anything more than a smooshed granola bar from Pret—far from the Southern feast she'd always joked would be her last meal (mac and cheese and corn bread and fried green tomatoes and a rich chocolate cake, thank you very much). No note was written, no will established, no preparations made.

The sun was surprisingly bright and chipper for a day in late September, clouds politely staying out of its way. Adelaide had the chance to sleep in and sing show tunes in the shower. She got a seat on the Tube and called her mom at twelve thirty, wishing her a happy birthday as she watched *The Today Show* from her home in Massachusetts. Sure, she was still reeling from the breakup, but there was nothing *bad* about the day. Nothing that made an earthly exit feel imperative. It was Moving Day! The start of something fresh! New! Exciting!

But slowly, then in one swift motion—the way anyone and anything unravels—she started to lose her grip.

She picked up the keys for her new one-bedroom flat and noticed the couches didn't match. Her landlord rolled her eyes when Adelaide asked who the electricity provider was (*I'm sorry, what is it that you do? I've never had to explain this to someone before*). Though she'd taken the day off, she still had a mountain of work waiting, and the movers were late, and *Are you sure I can't put art on the walls?* And fuck, she needed to lie down.

It's ludicrous in retrospect—*The couches didn't match and I didn't want to write a press strategy, so I decided to kill myself*—but Adelaide had nothing left in her tank. No emotional reserves to ground her, or push her forward, or remind her that she could mount this anxiety. She checked Twitter to distract herself and saw that *she'd* been honored at the London Book Awards—been recognized, rightfully, by the literary community to which Adelaide so desperately wanted to belong—and she just couldn't do it anymore. She couldn't live.

Adelaide hadn't even realized she'd started crying; she just noticed the raw, stinging feeling on her cheeks several minutes later, looking down to find her T-shirt wet with tears. That's when she filled a glass with tap water, dug through her purse for the emergency stash of Xanax, and started swallowing pills like Smarties.

It's a good thing, really, that she reached this breaking point on her mom's birthday—a birthday that, exactly three years before, they'd celebrated by welcoming Adelaide's nephew into the world. It's lucky. She sat on an undressed mattress with a prescription bottle in one hand, a glass of water in the other—five pills down, twenty or so to go—and thought, *Maybe I should finish this tomorrow. Maybe I shouldn't mark my favorite people's birthdays with my suicide.* (What might have stopped her, had this spiral begun a day or two later?)

Adelaide called a hotline, met the movers, called Celeste. She texted her family, her best friend Eloise. She took several deep breaths and a cab to A&E at Chelsea and Westminster. And she sat in the waiting room, wondering if this, indeed, was Rock Bottom, or if she still had further to fall.

Name?
Adelaide Williams. With an "e."
Williams has an "e"?
No, Adelaide. At the end. A-d-e-l-a-i-d-e. They always left off the "e."
Age?
Twenty-six.
Nationality?
American, but I'm a permanent resident in the U.K. I have my residence permit, if you need it.

That's all right. Occupation?
Communications manager, I do PR for a tech company.
Relationship status?

Celeste and Adelaide exchanged looks. *Single.* She cleared her throat. *Very single.*

At this, the nurse paused, wordlessly willing her to elaborate. Adelaide did not.

She recently went through a breakup, Celeste said. *Really recently. A not-so-great breakup.*

The nurse nodded, scribbling something onto her notepad. She was a curvy woman with purple scrubs, thick glasses, and a Bajan accent. In Adelaide's mind, the nurse was thinking, *Ah, yes, another brokenhearted girl playing Juliet and wasting our time and resources.* She didn't blame the nurse for thinking these things; clearly, Adelaide had the same impression of herself.

She had a Venus symbol tattooed on her middle finger and a cardboard box labeled FEMINIST LITERATURE waiting to be unpacked in her new home. She was prone to intense crushes and loved Richard Curtis films, yes, but Adelaide had never thought herself the type to become swallowed whole by unrequited love. Boys were dumb! She didn't even like them! Women were better, smarter, stronger! Yet here she was in a hospital room, answering questions about her relationship status with a sardonic *Very single,* seemingly incapable of coping with the fact that one boy did not love her.

Was there a Suicide Section in heaven? Adelaide imagined the smoking room of a Tex-Mex restaurant in her hometown—literary greats mingling over ashtrays and red plastic baskets of tortilla chips. Would Virginia Woolf even talk to her if she showed up there?

History of mental health challenges?

Ish, yeah. I was diagnosed with anxiety and depression when I was in high school. Her mom had dragged her to a psychiatrist after her first breakup. Adelaide hadn't slept or eaten in about a month, and as her waistline shrunk, her mother grew concerned. There was a theme here, it seemed. *I've also got some obsessive-compulsive tendencies. Those were kind of, um, triggered today. For lack of a better word.*

Triggered?

Yeah, the new couches in my flat didn't match. The nurse didn't
question this.

Are you taking any medication?

*Just birth control, mostly to treat endometriosis. I also take Xanax on
occasion, like today.*

And how many Xanax did you take today?

I think six or seven milligrams. Not a lot more than that.

All at once?

All at once.

How are you feeling now?

Pretty drowsy, but calm.

Do you have any family history of mental illness?

Uh, yes. Adelaide chuckled inappropriately—when she was growing
up, her family's home phone had a psychiatrist on speed dial.
*Virtually everyone in my family has some form of mental illness,
minus my dad. He's surrounded by crazy women. He was, rather.*

Are you able to share specifics?

*Sure. My sister, Izzy, has bipolar disorder. Holly, my other sister, has
ADD. My mom is clinically depressed.*

Any suicide attempts?

*Several, yeah. Mostly my sister, the bipolar one. Mom on occasion as
well.*

And have you attempted suicide in the past?

*Not really, no. My high school journal entries were pretty bleak, but I'd
never tried this before.*

She appreciated the clinical nature of the conversation. There were
no long *Hmm*s or stretches of painful eye contact, no shrink-like *And
how did that make you feel*s, punctuated by ellipses rather than question
marks. These were clear questions with clear answers, and Adelaide was
relieved they were finite. There was a rhythm to this Q&A that felt
oddly comforting, like a volleying ball or a metronome.

And what made you try it today?

This answer would break the rhythm. The couches, the breakup,
the work—they were all trigger points and catalysts. But the events and

feelings that led Adelaide to this moment had taken far longer than one afternoon to accumulate and combust; they were more difficult to quantify and explain.

Her heart didn't break once. It had broken multiple times over the last year—over the last decade, really—and each time she'd started to put the puzzle back together, to reconstruct her heart and soul with metaphorical superglue, they would shatter again. The pieces were getting smaller, less recognizable, more difficult to reconnect with each blow.

Um, she said. *I'm not even sure how to explain it. It's kind of a long story. A lot of long stories.*

The nurse put down her notepad. *Would it help to talk through it?*

Spring

London, England
2018

One

The skin on my heels is coming off in chunks, and I probably shouldn't have sex tonight, right?

These are the types of things Adelaide shouts across her flat, prompting the kinds of conversations with which Madison, her roommate, quickly had to become comfortable. They'd been loose acquaintances at Boston University—members of the same sorority—but never really spent time together outside of chapter meetings and other mandatory events. Different majors and friend groups and all that. One afternoon, a few years after graduation, Facebook informed Adelaide that Madison would also be heading to the U.K. for grad school, and, *Well,* she'd thought, *I could really use a pal over there.* She dropped her a note and, somehow, convinced Madison to forgo student accommodations and search for a home with her in north London.

Five days before landing at Heathrow, they'd signed a virtual lease for a gorgeous Victorian flat in Highgate—all beveled glass and chipped paint and worn-down, antique furniture—which they quickly decorated with framed posters from flea markets and an abundance of fairy lights. The cupboards were stocked with chocolate biscuits and ground coffee, the windowpanes lined with empty wine bottles stuffed with candlesticks. Polaroids of the two girls in sparkly dresses, winged eyeliner, and cheap faux fur coats covered the various dings and stains on their refrigerator—an appliance that made an unusual whistling sound and might, they feared, give out any day now.

On their first night in the neighborhood, the new roommates had gotten drunk at a local pub populated by dusty leather chairs and old men, eating veggie burgers and giggling from a corner table. The conversation flipped from politically charged ideological discussions to *Remember that girl who got carted out of a frat party on a gurney senior year? That was me!* and *Which Spice Girl was your favorite growing up?* They bonded quickly and easily and thank goodness.

During the first week of classes, Madison attended a yoga session for new students, and—in a twist of fate for which Adelaide would forever be grateful—laid her mat down next to a girl with a faint New England accent and a Boston College T-shirt. *The girl's name was Celeste,* Madison texted. *She was a few years their senior, but had just moved to London for graduate school as well (same uni as Madison, slightly different program), and Would you want to grab a drink with us later?* Adelaide did, indeed.

Just as she'd convinced Madison to move in with her, and just as she'd convinced Madison and Celeste to spend countless evenings at the pub (*To study!* she'd say, grinning), Adelaide had also tricked her roommate into doing a very intense foot mask earlier in the week—something she'd found on a Korean cosmetics site that smelled, alarmingly, of bleach. Now, their feet were essentially molting. At a glance, it looked like Adelaide's legs were attached to two very wide, very pale snakes in ecdysis.

My heels are the same, it's terrifying, Madison said, glancing at the bottoms of her feet and handing Adelaide a mug of red wine (the glasses were dirty, per usual). *You know you don't have to have sex with every guy you go out with, though, right?*

Adelaide laughed. After nearly half a decade of celibacy, she had thrown herself into the worlds of dating apps and one-night stands with force and fervor when she was twenty-two—charming strangers in text conversations and sweaty dance halls on a weekly basis. First in New York, now in London.

Tonight's date would be no different from the rest, she thought. She'd meet this boy and melt at the sound of his accent (Adelaide had been living in London for seven months now, but the novelty had yet to wear off). He'd mock American politics and ask if life in New York was anything like an episode of *Friends.* She'd laugh at his jokes; he'd excuse her clumsiness when she knocked a drink over. At some point, they'd stumble back to one of their homes, have sloppy, mediocre sex, and their fling would be over before the sun was up. It had become a pattern.

The week before, Adelaide had three one-night stands over a six-day stretch. A month or so before that, she made out with two guys in the same evening at a grimy bar in Shoreditch. It had little to do with low self-esteem and everything to do with control. There were few things more intoxicating to Adelaide than locking eyes with a stranger, running her tongue along his bottom lip, and abruptly leaving the bar, or his flat, or wherever when she decided she was ready to go. Adelaide had found agency in her twenties that she'd lacked in her teens (that had been stolen in her teens, really), and she enjoyed using it.

I don't have to sleep with everyone, you say? She took a swig of wine and winked at Madison's reflection in the mirror, then turned her attention to swiping black eyeliner above her lashes. *News to me!*

Madison sat on the bathtub as Adelaide started to iron her hair into long, dark blond, pin-straight sections, chuckling as she watched her struggle to tame her grown-out fringe. They talked about term papers, sailing trips in France this coming summer, and *Oh my gosh, did you see that Marissa and Josh got engaged in Miami? I still remember holding her hair back at Sigma Tau the night that they met.* Eventually, Adelaide poured the rest of her wine into a plastic bottle, ran her tongue across her teeth—*Good?* she grinned at Madison; *Good,* Madison nodded— and tucked her flaky little feet into a pair of floral flats, praying this boy didn't notice their appearance.

The boy's name was Rory Hughes, and Adelaide hadn't yet decided whether or not he was her type. They'd met on a dating app and his photos were mostly out-of-focus group shots (as many men inexplicably featured on their profiles), so she couldn't quite discern what he looked like. Not really. But he'd left little "hearts" on her profile, and he liked the Spice Girls, and the bits of banter they'd exchanged over text had put a smile on Adelaide's face. If nothing else, she was hopeful she'd get a drink and some pleasant conversation out of the evening. And besides, it was best not to sleep with him, anyway—she had papers to finish and exams for which she should be studying. The date would be quick, she told Madison, throwing on a leather jacket.

I'll be home before ten, she said.

(She would not, in fact, be home before ten.)

If one were to cleave Adelaide's adult life in two—like a melon, split clean down the middle—those halves would likely be *Before Rory Hughes* and *After,* a different version of her sitting on either side.

On the Tube en route to their first date, drinking dregs of wine and playing Ginuwine's "Pony" on a loop, she had no idea that this was it. That these were her final moments in this particular body, in this identity. Maybe she would have done something differently if she'd known; maybe not. (Probably not.)

He'd suggested they meet outside the Old Vic, a quick walk from Waterloo station. Adelaide had been to the theater once before, about three years earlier for a performance of *Clarence Darrow.*

(Later, she'd learn that Rory had been there for the same performance—he'd sat in the dress circle, Adelaide had won lottery tickets for the stalls. She'd often daydream about their paths crossing in the lobby that night, the backs of their hands brushing against one another in the crowd. She liked to imagine their lives tied by fate into an inextricable knot.)

She had rolled her earbuds into a neat bundle and tossed them into her bag, wondering what to do with her hands, when she heard a voice say, *Hiya, Adelaide?*

Her body went numb.

Two and a half years before she packed up her Brooklyn apartment and moved into that Highgate flat, Adelaide spent the most carefree semester of her life studying abroad in London. She'd always had a soft spot for the city, having lived on the outskirts for a few years growing up, but she'd never known that a metropolis could become a booming, integral character in your life. Not before then. *It's crazy,* she'd tell friends over Skype. *My baseline emotion is just contentment here. Who knew that was even possible?* Her responsibilities were minimal and Hyde Park was at her doorstep. It was perfect.

At one point that semester, Adelaide threw on a navy dress covered in tiny white anchors and joined her friends at an open-air pub along the River Thames, eyes peeled for the Oxford versus Cambridge boat race. They drank bottomless pitchers of Pimm's and lemonade and basked in that elusive little thing called the sun. Late that afternoon, tipsy and tanned, she saw him.

He was wearing a scarf and a blue button-down and Adelaide loved him instantly—all brown curls and razor-sharp jawline. Like a young Colin Firth. *Stop drooling over that stranger,* her friend said. *You look like a drunken trout.* She closed her mouth and stood up, steeling herself as she strolled over to approach him at the bar—two empty Pimm's pitchers in her hand and no shoes on her feet (they'd been giving her blisters all day).

Hi, she said, tapping his arm. *I'm so sorry, I just. I had to tell you. You look like a Disney prince.*

Oh, um, hi, he said. *That's so nice. Thank you.*

He gave Adelaide's shoulder a friendly pat, then turned back to his group. But she had never forgotten his face.

She told this story over and over again in the years that followed. When Adelaide would joke about her blundering lack of sex appeal and friends shook their heads in polite disbelief, this was the anecdote she would offer up. *See?* she'd say. *I'm the type of person who approaches strangers and tells them they look like Disney princes without shoes on!* It was humiliating and hilarious and very much Something Adelaide Williams Would Do.

She never expected the prince to reappear in her life, patting her shoulder once more and introducing himself as Rory outside of the Old Vic theater.

Adelaide's jaw dropped for a split second. How had she not connected the dots sooner? she wondered. How had she not recognized him from his photos? *Oh my gosh, hi, I'm Adelaide,* she said. *It's so good to meet you! Can I hug you? I'm going to hug you.*

Luckily, magically, Adelaide's aggressively friendly disposition was seen as American charm in London, not a bunny-boiling red flag. The beauty of a foreign accent, really. Rory chuckled and returned the hug, then puffed his chest out a little.

Shall we? he asked.

This was a habit of his. When nervous, he'd puff his chest out like a bird—an effort to seem bold or brave or confident—and say things like, *Shall we?* Adelaide was just so glad to be near him, next to him, with him (with! him!) that she'd melt and oblige each time. He could have asked this question at a cliff's edge—gesturing to a rocky canyon below—and Adelaide would have gleefully replied, *We shall!*

But they weren't at a cliff's edge. Not yet. On this particular evening, he led them to a rickety Italian bar on Lower Marsh Street—one that smelled like roasting espresso and had creaky, wooden tables covered in ring stains. Before their date, Rory had texted to see if Adelaide preferred bustling pubs or cozy spots with fairy lights. She'd opted for the latter and, taking in the setting, was glad of her choice.

What can I get you to drink? he asked.

Oh, anything! I like all alcohol, she said, an unsuccessful attempt to seem nonplussed and low-maintenance.

Rory gave her a funny look but returned a few minutes later with two orange goblets of Aperol spritz, striped paper straws bobbing on the sides. *Cheers,* he said.

She decided not to tell him that they'd met before, to keep that delicious little secret to herself for now, fairly certain he didn't recall.

Rory spent his gap year on a farm in the South of France, he explained. Studied at Cambridge. Worked in law for a little while. He took a year off to do pro bono legal work in Alabama, then spent a few weeks at film school in L.A.—*Just for kicks*—which inspired him to switch fields entirely. These days, he was working for a budding production company, and it was wild how much happier he was making films and shit money, wearing jeans and T-shirts to work instead of stiff gray suits.

She learned all of this as he peppered her with questions about her own life—about the States, her many moves, those months she spent au-pairing in Paris. He asked about her favorite shows on Netflix and the American snacks she missed most, gently teasing when she said she sometimes dreamt about eating Kraft Macaroni & Cheese and gooey summer s'mores and woke up with drool on her chin.

That's not cute, she said. *Let's strike that from the record?*

It's hilarious and adorable, he said. *You are hilarious and adorable.*

They finished their first spritzes. Then their seconds. Then moved on to a shared bottle of the house red. Adelaide had never felt this instantly comfortable with a stranger, let alone one so cartoonishly handsome.

Fuck my feet, she texted her roommate from the bathroom. I'm going to have sex with this guy.

Of course you are, Madison replied. Celeste and I had been taking bets.

Around eleven thirty that night—four and a half hours after they'd met—the bar staff politely informed the pair that they were closing, and *Would you mind if we cleared the table?* They quickly finished their glasses of wine and Rory grabbed the door, leading Adelaide out of the bar and into the open air. She shivered.

Are you cold? he asked.

Just a little, she said. *I'll be fine.*

I would offer you my coat if I had one.

Instead, he wrapped his arms around Adelaide, rubbing her shoulders with the sleeves of his jumper. She was covered in goose bumps and wished she could take her own jacket off, just to feel his hands on her skin. He smelled of pine trees and fresh laundry; being near him felt like Christmas morning.

It's a shame, really, he said, arms still enveloping hers. *This street used to be all independent bookstores and locally owned coffee shops. Now it's Costas and Boots. Gentrification, innit?* Adelaide nodded. *I've only lived around here for two years or so and it's already changed so much. It's sad to watch. This used to be a tea shop run by this lovely older woman. None of the crockery matched and everything was homemade.* She nodded again. *Why am I talking so much about gentrification?*

I watched the same thing happen in my neighborhood in Brooklyn, she said. *It's hard to walk down the street and not think about it all the time. About what it used to be. Oof, capitalism.*

They chuckled and reached the end of the street. *Well,* he said. *I suppose you're going this way.*

Adelaide turned to the station, then turned back to Rory. He pulled her closer by her elbow, tucked his hand beneath her chin, brought her lips to his, and slipped his tongue inside her mouth. And then, she remembers, she was on fire. It was well past eleven at night and the sun must have set hours earlier, but in her memory, standing on that street corner, the sky was bright. Birds chirping, clouds parted, sun shining. It's painfully clichéd, but darkness didn't exist here, not in this little universe Adelaide entered when she first kissed Rory Hughes.

You know, she said, pulling her lips a centimeter from his, *I don't have to go this way.*

He hesitated. *How about this weekend?* he asked. *Are you free on Friday?*

It was Wednesday. She paused, looked up, trying to think through her plans. She and Madison were grabbing dinner with Celeste, but after that, maybe?

Oh no, Friday's too soon, he said. *I'm too keen, aren't I?*

I think I'm free later on Friday, she said. *Let's plan something. Text me?*

Of course I will, he said. *This has been lovely.*

It has been. She paused. *But did you, um, just turn me down?*

He squeezed her hand and crossed the street, winking over his shoulder and leaving Adelaide to wonder if the entire night had been a fever dream. The sky was still bright. She stood there for a second, then reflexively dialed her best friend's number.

Eloise, she said, *I think I just met my soul mate.*

Two

A delaide sat at a table with Celeste and Madison—stacks of sourdough, burrata, and complimentary olives spread between them—and recapped every detail of her date. The questions he'd asked, the stories he'd told, their cosmic connection, and the kiss (the! kiss!) at the end of the night. She'd made a reservation at a bar in Soho, where she'd be meeting Rory in an hour and a half. Her body was buzzing with anticipation and lambrusco.

To Adelaide's love life! Madison said, raising a bowl of sparkling wine.

To Adelaide's love life! Celeste echoed. *And her tits!*

The girls giggled and clinked ceramics. Adelaide was wearing a bra so padded it was practically a flotation device, but it gave the impression that her slight frame was not entirely devoid of curves. Cheers to her tits, indeed.

All American, and all nearing the end of their graduate programs, the girls discussed their dissertations and postgrad plans, talking through job interviews and how in the hell to secure a visa. Earlier that day, Adelaide had gotten an email from Sam, a woman she'd worked with in New York—one of the few account directors who hadn't drowned her in administrative tasks and scoldings—wondering if she was interested in working in the tech space again. She'd been working as the in-house communications director at a start-up called Alliance Technologies and now needed *A solid number two* (unfortunate word choice, Adelaide thought) in the U.K.

The offer came with a cushy paycheck and a Tier 2 visa, but it wasn't an editorial or marketing role at a publishing house—the type of job Adelaide had promised herself she'd land in London, the reason she'd been writing freelance book reviews and roundups all year (for minimal pay). She weighed the pros and cons with her friends, twisting spaghetti around her fork.

It's the age-old choice between love and money, Celeste said. *Only, in this case, it's your love of books, I guess?*

Adelaide nodded. She had the words of Sylvia Plath, Louisa May Alcott, and Emily Dickinson tattooed across her wrists and hip bones; illustrations from Antoine de Saint-Exupéry's *The Little Prince* were etched onto her rib cage; and a tiny peach sat on her left buttock in a cheeky nod to *Call Me By Your Name.*

Books—words, really—were her favorite things, her greatest love, and the thought of working and playing with them each day was thrilling. But equally thrilling was the promise of a secure job and a signing bonus so big she could swim in it, à la Scrooge McDuck.

It's just a lot to think about, she said, her mouth full.

The other girls were balancing similarly heavy choices. Both Celeste and Madison had teaching jobs waiting in the States, but interviews lined up at some of London's most elite preparatory schools in the coming weeks. The grade schools where they'd taught before pursuing their master's degrees had held their positions for the year, but London's indelible charm had rubbed off on both women, it seemed. They were increasingly eager to get jobs on this side of the Atlantic and stay in the city, unwilling to give up its colorful mews streets and tea shops just yet—a feeling Adelaide understood on a visceral level.

There was a lot to unpack.

They paid the check and stayed at the table, nursing the last of their drinks and talking through the myriad decisions that lay ahead. When Adelaide noticed the time, they collectively hummed "Someday My Prince Will Come" as she grabbed her raincoat and started to head out.

Oh, fuck off, she said, laughing. The girls confirmed that her eyeliner was unsmudged and her smile free of pesto, and off she went.

Go get 'em, Adelaide, Celeste yelled after her. *Tits still looking great!*

Just as she had two nights before, Adelaide leaned against the façade of a building and waited for Rory Hughes, still wondering what, exactly, to do with her hands. She'd made a reservation at the Blind

Pig, a sneaky little bar that sat atop London's Social Eating House. The menu was full of pricey cocktails and elaborate illustrations, each drink themed after a different work of children's literature. Like Adelaide, the venue was bookish and dark; it felt like just the place to share a bit more of herself with Rory.

Hey you, he said, grabbing her arm and catching her by surprise.

Oh wow hello, she said. They exchanged quick kisses on both cheeks. *How continental,* Adelaide thought, leading them inside.

Reservation for two under Andy, she said to the host.

It's the name I always give restaurants, she whispered to Rory. *They can never seem to make out "Adelaide" over the phone.* He gave a quick laugh and nodded.

By the way, Andy, he said. *You look extra lovely tonight.*

A moment later, they were tucked into a booth, a server wondering if they had any questions about the menu. Rory asked if he had any recommendations—another habit Adelaide would notice in due course. (She saw it as a polite gesture at first, another way Rory was able to engage everyone around him, even strangers. Only later would she realize it was a symptom of his inability to ever really make up his mind.)

She chose a syrupy cocktail called Winnie the Pooh's Hunny Pot. At the server's recommendation, Rory ordered Paddington's Lost & Found, an amalgamation of citrus flavors and vodka, served with a teensy marmalade sandwich and a note that read, *Please look after this bear.* (Adelaide snagged the note and tucked it into her bag at the end of the night. A little memento.)

Have you seen Paddington 2? he asked. *It's a goddamned masterpiece, I swear to you.*

This prompted a conversation about their favorite films and books, the characters they most adored growing up. Ordinarily, Adelaide offered canned answers to these kinds of date questions—she didn't want to seem too starry-eyed or old-fashioned, so she'd say her favorite movies were *Dead Poets Society* and *The Empire Strikes Back* (not *untrue*) instead of *Funny Face, An American in Paris,* and *Singin' in the Rain.* But with Rory—sweet, handsome, *Paddington*-loving Rory—she felt she could be wholly honest about her hopeless romanticism, her appreciation for old-school musicals.

She described the nights she spent jumping around her bathroom at five years old, imitating Debbie Reynolds's routine to "Good Morning." He smiled. *Singin' in the Rain* was his mum's favorite, he said, though he'd never seen the other films.

You have to! she said. *They're just so joyful and effervescent. Like a bubble bath for the soul.*

We'll have to watch them together sometime, he said.

Adelaide saw his eyes flash again when she started listing her most beloved books. *The Little Prince,* of course (she'd read it more times than she could count). *The Bell Jar* and *Little Women* and *A Wrinkle in Time. Call Me By Your Name. 1984. To Kill a Mockingbird.*

The latter two were some of his favorites as well, he explained, green eyes sparkling. Atticus Finch had long been his hero, and *Did you read* Go Set a Watchman? *It broke my heart.*

Rory shared stories about falling in love with Hugo and Hemingway and Godard at university, about watching *The Princess Bride* over and over when he had his appendix out in sixth form. He talked about reading Harry Potter well past his bedtime and playing cricket with his brothers when they were kids.

Where did you grow up? Adelaide asked, placing a hand on his knee. He looked down, and for a split second, she saw his mouth twitch with a smile.

In Shere, he said. *Little village in Surrey. Not far from Harry Potter himself.*

Adelaide imagined rows of thatched roofs and Tudor-style homes. She thought of front lawns with wishing wells and daffodils planted each spring, not unlike the English town where she'd spent a few years of her own childhood.

And your family? she asked. *Are they still based there?*

Well, he said. *My brothers and I are spread out across London and Manchester. But my parents were Irish, so most of the rest of my family is back in Galway.*

Were, she thought. Past tense.

And you, he said. *Where is your family based in the States?*

Mostly Boston, she said. *We all went to school in the city and my sisters never left, then my mom moved up a few years ago to help take care of my nephew. My dad's remarried and lives in New Jersey with his wife and her daughters now.*

Rory nodded, noting that he'd always wanted to visit Boston and see the *Good Will Hunting* bench (another one of his favorites). *I'll take you,* she wanted to say. *I'll show you the bench and we'll ride in the swan boats and you'll meet my wonderful mess of a family and it will be perfect.*

She took a sip of her drink.

You should go next time you're in the States for work, she said instead.

Aptly, London itself looked like a film set that evening. It had rained earlier in the day—because what else would London do on an April afternoon?—and the warm light of the streetlamps bounced off the wet pavement, filling puddles with an orangey glow. Poofs of vapor rose from steam grates, and it started to sprinkle again when Rory and Adelaide stepped outside (they'd been politely ushered out by the bar staff once more).

I wish I'd brought a brolly, Rory said.

Adelaide giggled to herself, having only recently learned that word.

What? he asked. *Are you laughing at my accent?*

No, she said. *I'm laughing at myself because I'm obsessed with your accent.*

He laced his fingers through hers and, suddenly, whisked her down a side street. It was all so swift, so laughably cinematic—he was wearing a trench coat and his tongue was in her mouth again and how on earth was she supposed to breathe? She tried her best to memorize everything about this moment: The taste of him, like vodka and oranges. The smell of wet pavement. The feeling of brick on her back.

I've been waiting to do that all night, he whispered, his nose touching hers. *Would you . . . Would you like to come home with me, Adelaide?*

Mhm, she said, breathless. She would like that very much.

Rory lived in a house full of very tall boys, not far from London Bridge. A pile of their giant shoes sat at the entryway, over which Adelaide immediately tripped when he opened the door. She caught herself on the banister with a loud *thunk*.

Oh my gosh I'm so sorry, she whispered.

No, Rory said. *I'm so sorry! It's like I set an Adelaide trap.*

He led her upstairs to his tiny, book-filled bedroom. A wall of square shelves surrounded a small fireplace, each cubby overflowing with worn-down hardcovers and faded postcards. (Adelaide didn't know where all of these books and postcards had come from—or who they'd come from, rather. Not yet.) Stacks of paperbacks lined the floors and balanced precariously by his bedside; bunches of theater tickets were pinned to a corkboard by his door. A pastiche of Matisse's *The Fall of Icarus* was framed beside them.

I saw Kendrick Lamar in February as well, Adelaide said, eyeing the tickets. *And* Clarence Darrow, *years ago.*

Oh, I loved that play, Rory said. *My flatmate and I saw it a few times actually. Once on opening night, and then twice more after that.*

I saw it on opening night, too! she said. *I won front-row lottery tickets while I was studying abroad. It was one of my favorite nights.*

How funny, Rory said, hugging her from behind. *The world is so impossibly small sometimes.*

Each time Adelaide returned to this room, she'd scan the tickets for more hints at these magical coincidences. Their seats at Kendrick had been just two rows apart, she learned. They'd both seen *Once* on her birthday in 2015, and they'd watched the same Sadler's Wells production of *The Great Gatsby* (which, they agreed, was a bit too modern for their liking) a month or so after that. Both had been to exactly one game at Yankee Stadium in their whole lives, drinking lemonade from the bleachers on the same sticky evening in June 2016.

It seemed so intentional—the way their lives had been woven together. Like some deity had spent centuries writing their story, meticulously planning the details and paving their paths. But again, Adelaide didn't know all of this just yet. For now, all she knew was that the Disney prince had his hands wrapped around her and there was a chill creeping up her spine.

May I take this off? he asked, tugging at her raincoat.

You may, she said, but that was the only article of clothing she was going to let him remove. For the first time in her adult life, Adelaide decided she wanted sex to be special. She wanted to build a little anticipation before their relationship became ultraphysical.

Do you mind if we, um, don't have sex tonight, though? she asked. *I can't at the moment. You know.*

Adelaide got an injection every few months that meant she hardly ever got her period, but she felt the need to justify her choice not to have sex. Old habits.

Are you joking? he said. *Of course I don't mind! I'm just so happy you're here. Though, I have to admit, your tits look incredible.* Celeste was right! Adelaide chuckled a little.

Yikes, he said. *That was crass, I'm sorry. I don't even know why I said that.*

The credit goes entirely to this bra, she said. *And now I'm afraid the real things will disappoint you.*

Nothing about you could disappoint me.

Rory made cups of peppermint tea, which they drank sitting cross-legged on his bed, whispering and giggling like children. They kissed and cuddled and talked as their noses touched. It was innocent, special—so unlike the interactions Adelaide was used to having with men.

You know, he said, *I think your eyes are my favorite kind. Big and beaming and hazel—they're dreamboat eyes.*

He didn't even realize he was quoting *A Wrinkle in Time,* that Adelaide had read that line as a little girl (*"Well, you know what, you've got dreamboat eyes"*) and thought, *I hope a boy says that to me someday.* Rory was striking every chord, playing her heart like a fucking harp.

When Adelaide finally looked at the clock, she saw it was two in the morning—well past the time she should have gone home. Her final exams started on Monday, and she'd promised herself she would spend the weekend studying (she'd been procrastinating for weeks).

I should head out, she said.

No, he said. *You can sleep here! I can loan you a T-shirt and we can watch* Parks and Rec, *it'll be so cozy. And I'll make us breakfast in the morning!* It was one of her favorite things he ever said.

That's a very tempting offer, she said. *But I really should go home.*

Don't leave, he said. *Please? Let me keep you a little longer?*

She gently nipped at his bottom lip.

I have to go, she said. *But promise you won't disappear after tonight?*

I promise, he said. *Don't you disappear either.* She made him pinkie-swear.

He lent her an umbrella and walked her to the door, kissing her and asking, *Are you sure you have to go?* one last time. She was sure.

Can I walk you to the Tube, at least? he asked. *Or call you a cab?*

She was fine on her own. *Really,* she insisted.

Let me know when you get home safe?

Of course, she said. *Thank you again for the umbrella, and the tea, and the really lovely evening.*

Once she'd turned the corner off his street, Adelaide dialed Eloise again.

Omygosh, Adelaide? Eloise said. *Is everything okay? Isn't it the middle of the night there?*

Everything's fine, Adelaide said. *More than fine. It's late, yeah, but I just . . . I have to tell you more about this guy. Eloise, I've never felt like this before.*

In the months, sometimes even years that followed, Adelaide's mind would return to this night. She would picture Rory quoting Calvin O'Keefe, and stroking her hair, and kissing her in the rain. She'd remember talking to Eloise with her hand on her heart, feeling it thump in her chest, thinking, *This. This is what you've been waiting for. This is the light at the end of a very dark tunnel.*

Adelaide would never be defined by Rory Hughes. He did not construct her character; she did that herself. But to say that this night did not transform her life would be fallacious. Were she to slip into a *Groundhog Day* dream state, this is the day she would choose to live over and over and over again. These were the memories—painful though they were—that she never, ever wanted to forget.

She was always going to jump into this lake, no matter how dark or dangerous it might turn out to be; she was too intrigued by its shimmering surface to even consider turning away. There was no world in which she wouldn't dive headfirst in love with Rory Hughes. This was the only way.

Three

S tudying was impossible. Adelaide sat on the floor of the British Library, laptop on her knees and an iced coffee at her side. (The tables were all taken.) She was staring at a blank Word document, pretending to be capable of constructing a study guide; she was not.

She was tired and lovestruck and playing last night on a loop in her mind. The kiss. The other kiss. His eyes. That smile. How desperately he wanted her to stay the night—no, how desperately he wanted *her*. Adelaide. Full stop.

It was such an unfamiliar feeling.

She took a sip of her drink, rubbed her eyes, squinted at the screen. *Write something,* she told herself. *Literally anything.*

The General Data Protection Regulation (GDPR) outlines six principles with which organizations must comply when processing personal data. These principles include . . .

Adelaide was pursuing a degree in marketing and communications, which—to her chagrin—meant learning to understand regulatory data legislation, statistical analysis, and zero-based budgeting techniques. She'd turned down offers to study global media at LSE and comparative literature at UCL, instead choosing to attend a small business school whose name didn't matter at all. They'd knocked 25 percent off of her tuition price, which Adelaide thought made it all worthwhile—it absolutely did not.

(Months later, when Adelaide would say where she studied, Rory would follow with a quick *But she got into UCL! She's a bright thing.*

It was meant to be a kind, social bolster; instead, it felt like a twisting knife.)

She listed out the principles of GDPR—first on her laptop, then onto flash cards in brightly colored gel pen. She did repeated mathematical exercises, calculating marketing budgets and analyzing conversion rates, cursing under her breath when she got the answers wrong. She recited the elements of the Shannon-Weaver model of communication aloud, brushing figurative dust off of shelves in her mind that she'd largely ignored since undergrad. Intermittently, she would allow herself five minutes to stare at her hands, imagining what it would feel like to floof Rory's hair or trace the squiggly shape of his chin with her thumb.

Her phone lit up, as if on cue.

A little something to get you through revisions, Rory texted. He'd included a picture of a tiny fluff of a Pomeranian. (It looked just like her dog in the States, Puff. *How had he known?* she wondered.) By the way, he continued. Feel free to say no if this isn't quite your scene, but do you have any interest in going to the Globe with me on Friday? As You Like It's on and the weather's supposed to be brill. Let me know? x

Adelaide had grown up watching her big sister, Holly, act on stage, mostly in high school plays and local theater productions. She'd played Sandy in *Grease* and Rosemary in *How to Succeed in Business Without Really Trying* and Rosalind in a summer camp rendition of *As You Like It*. When Adelaide was little and couldn't sleep at night (which was often)—or when their other sister, Izzy, had a particularly violent episode—Holly would read from Charles and Mary Lamb's *Ten Tales from Shakespeare,* reciting the stories at lullaby volume and combing her fingers through Adelaide's hair.

In middle school, her English class started a unit on Shakespeare, and Adelaide had known the answers to every question her teacher posed that first lesson. *Could anyone tell me the three genres in which Shakespeare's plays are most often classified? The number of sonnets he allegedly wrote? The name of his theater in London?*

Tragedy, comedy, history. One hundred and fifty-four. The Globe.

The Globe? she texted. She'd taken tours and read about its roots, but she'd never had the chance to see a performance. No one had ever asked. I've only spent my whole life wanting to see a show there, and As

You Like It is one of my favorites. So yes, I have much interest. All the interest! (And thank you so much for that fluffy motivation, btw!)

I'll book the tickets, he said. x

Adelaide felt like her heart was short-circuiting.

The next few days passed in a blur of flash cards, espresso shots, and phone calls with her old colleague Sam (she was going to be in London next week, and *We'll have to grab drinks and talk through job opportunities, yes?*). Adelaide's five exams were spread out across a ten-day stretch, with the shortest and most challenging scheduled at the tail end. By Friday afternoon, she'd wrapped up three tests, spent a dozen hours cramming for the others, and desperately needed a nap.

Adelaide opened the windows and plopped onto her bed at 1:00 P.M., pulling the quilt above her shoulders and closing her eyes. She was sure she'd be up in an hour or so, but set an alarm for 4:00 P.M., to be safe. She and Rory were meeting at the Globe at six thirty, and she wanted to give herself plenty of time to straighten and re-straighten her hair and . . .

She opened her eyes at 5:30 P.M. on the dot, fifteen minutes before she had to leave for the date. *Fuck.* Her alarm had been set for 4:00 A.M. *Fuck fuck fuck fuck fuck.*

Adelaide splashed cold water across her face and threw on a smattering of makeup, relieved when she drew on the cat eye of her liner with one easy flick. She pulled her hair into a low ponytail and ran a straightener down the ends, smoothing out the flyaways and stray kinks. There were few things that upset Adelaide more than unwanted waves in her hair (a symptom of her obsessive-compulsiveness, she assumed), and she would have none this evening. She tied a velvet ribbon around her ponytail as a decorative touch.

Adelaide stripped down and re-dressed, practically leaping into lingerie that was coordinated, but not matching. (She was hoping to give the very false impression that she'd not given this any thought. *Sex? Us? Tonight? Why, it had never even crossed my mind!*)

Ohmygosh-I-overslept-I'm-going-to-meet-Rory-I-probably-won't-be-home-tonight-wish-me-luck-I-love-you-bye, she yelled over her shoulder.

Good luck, Madison called back. *Break a leg! Or something, I dunno! I love you, bye!*

Rory had gotten caught up at work and was running about ten minutes late, he texted. Adelaide bought them cans of cider at the bar, realizing this was the first time she would be meeting him completely sober. Should she chug this quickly? *No,* she told herself. She didn't need to have a buzz to interact with a handsome man. (Right?)

She leaned against the railing of the riverside, watching the sun slip down the skyline and seep into the Thames, a chilled can of cider in each hand. She exhaled. It seemed trite, but there were moments in which Adelaide looked around and thought, *Holy shit.* She was doing it. She was living in London, and getting her master's, and about to meet a cute boy at the Globe. It gave her the same feeling that came with keeping a friend's secret, with fulfilling a promise.

Her phone buzzed. Standing by the main entrance, the text said. Adelaide inhaled slowly—allowing herself another thirty seconds of silly, saccharine reflection—and exhaled again.

She met Rory by the entrance, handed him his drink.

To the end of the week, he said. *And the end of exams.*

Just about, Adelaide said. They clinked their cans together; the aluminum made a tinkling sound.

By the way, he said, *I like your bow.* He ran his hand beneath her ponytail, sending involuntary goose bumps down her arms.

They collected their tickets and shuffled in. Adelaide looked up and around her, goose bumps multiplying. Their tickets were standing—which was generally Adelaide's least favorite activity (she was prone to sitting down on filthy pavement and Tube platforms)—but she didn't really mind tonight. They made small talk about their weeks; Rory said he'd been home with a summer cold for a few days.

You should have told me, Adelaide said. *I would have sent soup or something!*

You're sweet, he said. He'd had plenty of soup and Inigo Montoya to get him through, but thank you.

The show began.

I t had been a little while since Adelaide last read Shakespeare, she realized. There were bits of dialogue that flew over her head, but she was familiar enough with the plot to catch Rory up at intermission.

I'm glad you're here, he said.

The sky had turned dark by the time the play ended, and Rory suggested they grab another drink or two at a pub down the river. They sat in the evening air, nursing gin and tonics, a handful of stars hovering above them. He asked where she liked to go out in London, and instead of answering honestly (rooftops in Hackney, the Duke's Head on Highgate Hill, grimy dance halls with Motown nights in Dalston), she gave the answer she thought would most appeal to a posh Englishman. Inexplicably, she felt the need to put on a show this evening. To impress Rory, to prove herself.

Oh, she said. *You know, Mayfair and Chelsea and all that.*

(It was the equivalent of saying, *Anywhere that requires women to wear bodycon dresses, strappy heels, and serves twenty-quid vodka cocktails cut with water!* It was also very much the wrong answer to give Rory Hughes, who voted Lib Dem and largely resented his King's School education. She would realize this later, telling him she thought it was one of the cringiest things she'd ever said. *Yeah,* Rory would say, nodding. *That was pretty bad.*)

Huh, he said. *Wouldn't have pegged you for the Mayfair type.*

She watched the black tongue of the Thames lap against the shoreline and quickly changed the subject.

Have you ever thought about going swimming down there? Adelaide asked.

Oh no, Rory said. *That water's filthy.*

I've heard the eels are all high on cocaine, she said. *They have crazy eyes.*

Do you know many eels who don't have crazy eyes?

Third dates were interesting, Adelaide thought, because you're sitting in this odd conversational limbo. You know the basics of another person's life—their hometown, their job, their favorite drink, perhaps—but it's still too early to brush past superficial topics and dig into the grittier details of their character. Her past conversations with Rory had been easy, like spreading warm butter on toast. This evening's dialogue was choppier, a bit crumbly.

What about you? he said. *Would you ever swim in the Thames?*

Only to check on my friends the eels, she said. He laughed a little.

If not swimming with eels, what are the top three craziest things you've done? he asked. *Your best stories?*

She felt her stomach jump. *You first,* she said. Rory told her about the night he and his friend—he coughed, *Ex-girlfriend*—passed by a wedding venue at their university, saw glimpses of a celebration through the window, and decided they were going to gate-crash. They looked at each other, he explained, and decided to meet back in thirty minutes in black tie. They made it about an hour or so before guests started to get suspicious; it was such good fun.

Your turn, he said.

Hm, Adelaide said, brushing past the reference to his ex. *Well, it's not wedding crashing, but. I went to watch the Oxford-Cambridge boat race when I studied abroad over here, years ago. Drank too much Pimm's, was having too much fun. Anyway, I saw this really handsome stranger. And I walked right up to him and said . . .* She could feel her heart in her trachea. *I said, "I just have to tell you, you look like a Disney prince."*

Rory's eyes widened. He didn't say a word.

He did not invite me to live happily ever after in his castle, she continued, a grin stretching across her face. *Can you believe it?*

I, he said. *Um.*

Adelaide took a sip of her drink and winked at him over her glass. She could feel her whole body starting to shake, but tried to keep her hands still. She didn't want to let on that she felt anything other than completely cool and collected, that she was in full control.

This whole time? he asked. *Have you known this whole time?*

Mm, Adelaide said. *Maybe.*

Is this a game show?

She started to laugh. It was crazy, right? Truly mad, he agreed.

I feel like I need another drink, Rory said. *Do you want to grab one here? I have wine back at the flat, if you like?*

Wine at the flat sounds perfect, she said.

They headed toward his place and Rory must have exclaimed, *This is mad!* thirteen times on their walk. Adelaide couldn't stop giggling.

At one point, she made a joke about a statue that appeared to have no arms. He scooped her up and kissed her.

Was it my talk of dismemberment? she asked.

Mm, that's it, baby. He kissed her again. The word "baby" bounced and echoed off the corners of her brain. *I'm just trying to live up to that Disney prince archetype.*

Rory's home included four other boys and just one bathroom, which were not great odds for Adelaide. With a pang of discomfort, she realized she hadn't used the restroom in eight hours (and three drinks). Rory carried her inside and up the stairs, gently tossing her onto his bed, and *Oh my gosh,* she was going to pee her pants.

Another crazy story of mine, she started to say, *is that I once peed in a Pepsi bottle in New York. On a subway platform.*

That's disgusting, he said, sucking on her bottom lip.

Do you, um, know when your roommate will be out of the shower?

Rory popped downstairs to check. Bubs, his flatmate, would only be five more minutes, he assured Adelaide, his mouth returning to hers. (*Bubs?* Adelaide wondered. She didn't ask.)

The shower stopped and she ran to the bathroom, stealing a swig of the boys' Listerine (and, admittedly, a glance at Rory's roommate's abs as he stepped out into the hallway in a towel) just before she relieved herself and washed her hands. Adelaide kept a little sample bottle of perfume in her pocket for occasions like this—something she'd snagged from the Viktor & Rolf counter at Selfridges—and spritzed it between her legs, under her arms, at the nape of her neck. She flipped her hair down and tied it up again, a bit higher this time. It bounced as she darted back up the stairs.

Hi, she said, closing Rory's door behind her.

Oh hi, he said. There were two glasses of wine on his nightstand. *Care for a drink?*

I was actually wondering, she said, sitting beside him on the bed. She kissed his lips, his chin, his neck, ran her tongue along the edge of his earlobe. Her voice dropped to a whisper—*Would you like to have sex with me, Rory?*

In recent years, Adelaide had come to view sex as a fun but fairly mechanical exercise. She enjoyed it, sure, but she rarely felt connected to the men she slept with. Not in any way that wasn't literal, at least. She went through the right motions; she made the right sounds. Eventually, the guy would come, and Adelaide would feel like a retail worker who'd made a sale, glad to be clocking out of her shift.

This was different. Sex with Rory Hughes meant kisses on her nose, her temple, her shoulders. It meant coos and full sentences, the words *Where have you been all this time?* whispered into her hair instead of indiscriminate grunts of pleasure.

Is that a motherfucking Call Me By Your Name *peach?* he asked, his hands on her ass.

Mhm, she said. She was amazed he'd connected the dots.

It's so sexy, he said. He kissed the little fruit tattooed on her left cheek. *You are so sexy.*

Adelaide didn't come (she never did), but her body could hardly stop shivering when they finished. She wasn't cold, but exhilarated. She felt awakened.

Where have you been all this time? Rory asked again. *I can't believe you ever thought I might disappear. How could I go anywhere after that?* She kissed him and agreed to stay the night, to sleep in his T-shirt and his arms, warning she would not look cute in the morning.

I'll be the judge of that, Rory said.

Adelaide slept in short bursts, beaming each time she woke up and remembered where she was, who she was lying next to. Around four or five, they rolled toward each other and had drowsy, wonderful sex again, breathing heavily and drifting back to sleep as the earliest speckles of daylight began to peek through his windows, their legs still tangled together.

Rory's side of the bed was empty when the sun came up. Adelaide grabbed a piece of gum from her bag and rubbed the residual mascara from her eyes. A second later, he opened his bedroom door, plates of toast and teacups balanced in his arms.

I used to be a server, he said, handing her a cup of English breakfast tea and kissing her forehead. *Wasn't sure how you liked your tea, so I made it my way.*

It's perfect, she said, swallowing her gum. *Thank you.*

Good morning, by the way, he said. *You look so nice.*

You're a liar, but I'll take it.

They ate buttery triangles of toast and drank their tea (Adelaide burned her tongue on the first sip, and it took everything in her not to curse and kill the moment). They talked about their plans for the weekend—more studying for Adelaide, Rory was helping a friend move—and laughed about the Disney prince coincidence some more. He asked if she wanted to watch last night's *Graham Norton* from his laptop (she loved Graham Norton—*How did you know?*), but Adelaide said she had to go. Better to leave too early than overstay her welcome, she thought.

So soon? Rory asked.

Just giving you a Saturday morning to yourself before all that heavy lifting, she said, hopping into her jeans and knotting her hair into a bun. *Let me know how the move goes? I hope the sun stays out for you guys.*

She stacked her plate and cup beneath his and kissed him, running a hand through his mess of curls.

Still promise not to disappear? she asked.

I could never, he said.

Thank you, she said. *For everything. Have a great weekend.*

She never did hear how that move went.

Before

St. Marys, Georgia, and Cambridge, England
2009–2010

Four

At sixteen years old, Adelaide Williams was the type of student every teacher both hoped and feared might walk into their classroom. She was bright and curious, eager to participate in class discussions and bake cupcakes for peers' birthdays (her cream cheese frosting was always homemade and often dyed pink). But she was also unafraid to call bullshit.

If one of her instructors started to conflate the conflicts in Iraq and Afghanistan, imply that the civil rights movement ended in 1964, or misrepresent the meaning of the word "feminism," Adelaide was quick to raise her hand and correct their mistake. To their delight, she was sure.

For the same reasons that teachers appreciated (and, at times, resented) her, Adelaide knew why boys were less than eager to reciprocate her compliments and crushes. She was cute and giggly, yes, but she was also staunchly opposed to so many of the things that teenage boys loved: House parties. Cheap weed (any weed, really). Cursing. Sex. Keg stands. And sometimes—well, all of the time—that meant dancing by herself at homecoming. It sucked, but she understood.

Then, in April of 2009, she met Emory Evans.

He had a silly name and a crooked smile and a ukulele he'd play, barefoot and cross-legged, in his friends' front yards. That was how they first met: Emory was strumming a Say Anything song at a birthday party and caught Adelaide's eye, singing the words *I'd walk through hell for you* straight into her goddamned soul.

It was funny—ironic, almost—because he was hell. He was fire and brimstone and pitchforks, a collection of demons in the shape of a red-headed, gangly teenager—demons that would chase her for so much of her life. But all that mattered, in that moment, at that birthday party, was that he was the first boy to ever really see Adelaide. To give her a second glance.

"Let it burn right through my shoes," he sang. *"These soles are useless without you,"* she mouthed back, smiling through the lyrics.

It started with hands held in movie theaters and sticky weeknight drives to get ice cream, with coffee milkshakes shared over center consoles. He brought her mom flowers the first time he came over for dinner—just a few tulips from the grocery store, just enough to melt both of their hearts. Adelaide and her mom had moved to a sleepy town in Georgia about four years prior, shortly after her parents' divorce was finalized and long after her sisters had left for college and boarding school. They had been slow to let others into their circle, but soon, they stretched fresh sheets over the guest bed and welcomed Emory in. (The drive home was *Long,* and it was *So late,* and *There just aren't enough traffic lights in this town, why don't you stay in the spare room downstairs tonight? To be safe.*)

Emory nearly moved into their house that summer, staying two or three evenings a week. He and Adelaide would sneak out to swim and quietly splash in the moonlight, her pool an inky black at that time of night. Wrapped in towels and dripping water onto the carpet of the spare room, they would spend hours whispering while her dog Puff snored, talking about college and Christmastime and *Did you know there were no toilets at the Palace of Versailles until the eighteenth century? We learned about that in AP Euro.*

Time ticked by, pushing them, minute by minute, closer to the future they imagined together. One night, with his hands in her wet hair, Emory whispered that, *Even if I'm not the one who gets to marry you someday, I hope I can shake the hand of the man who does.* At these words, Adelaide felt everything inside her light up.

For years, these were the tapes that played in her brain. Adelaide chose to remember the feeling of his thumb tracing circles in her palm or looping through the damp locks of her hair, the spoken promises he'd never keep. Her mind blocked out the rest. It scrambled the tapes, refused to press Play.

About five months into their Facebook-official relationship, though, Adelaide started to have panic attacks. She'd experienced them in the past—sometimes before flights, or during her sister's episodes, or once, almost comically, at a *High School Musical* concert—but these were different. She never really remembered how they started. She barely realized these panic attacks were happening until they ended, and she invariably found herself lying on the floor, sobbing.

Her brain seemed to jumble everything up, placing some memories in a dreamy fog (the swimming, the whispers, the kisses exchanged in Barnes & Noble) and others (whatever it was that triggered this panic) behind an opaque veil—a veil that wouldn't be lifted for years.

(Eventually, it would all come back in body-throttling waves. Usually late at night, in the space between consciousness and dreaming. Memories would bubble to the surface and seep into Adelaide's psyche, impossible to process and even more impossible to ignore. She would try to sift through them and pinpoint when it changed. To figure out when, exactly, their relationship went from sweet, tender first love to pulled hair and pressure. Immense pressure. Every kind of pressure. She never really made sense of it.)

For now, though, Adelaide was young and in love, and so what if her boyfriend was kind of an asshole sometimes?

Months passed; summer melted into autumn. Adelaide and Emory went to different high schools: He drove across the county to attend a private school, she took a slew of AP classes around the corner from her home. (She was often reminded how little intelligence her coursework required, comparatively.) At the start of their junior year, Emory befriended a new girl from San Francisco. Her name was Brianna, and she sat behind him in physics, and *Fuck, girls who know quantum mechanics are so hot,* he tweeted that afternoon.

Adelaide came home from her first day of classes. She pulled her hair into a ponytail, changed into pajama shorts, made a strawberry smoothie. She checked Twitter, just for kicks, and nearly choked on pink froth.

What the heck? she texted him. (Adelaide used much less colorful language at sixteen.) *Happy first day of school! My boyfriend is posting about how hot other girls are online!*

It's a joke, Adelaide, he replied. *Don't be so uptight. It's not attractive.*

Soon, Adelaide learned to nod and smile. She brought fresh-baked cupcakes to Brianna's house when Emory and his friends were invited over for a movie night. She bit her tongue so hard it bled when Brianna—*Bri,* he called her—greeted Emory by jumping into his arms. Brianna wrapped her legs around his waist as Adelaide stood a yard away, tasting blood, reminding herself to breathe.

Don't be so uptight, she told herself. *It's not attractive.*

On the drive home that night, Emory pulled off into a grassy expanse and suggested they lie in the bed of his pickup truck *To look at the stars.* He said this with one arm around Adelaide's shoulder, holding her hand, and the other sliding down her pants.

Please stop, Adelaide said. She grabbed his wrist with her free hand. *You know I'm not really comfortable with that.*

I swear, Adelaide, he said. He was silent for a minute, shifted the truck back into drive. *I'm trying to be nice and romantic. And you just . . . Are you, like, asexual or something? Are you a fucking starfish?*

Brianna moved back to San Francisco a few weeks later, and Emory returned to the spare room on weekends, and Adelaide started to wake up with his hands in her underwear, she thought? (Was she dreaming this?)

Then, one Sunday morning—as her mom left to pick up doughnuts—Adelaide stepped out of the shower and was suddenly pinned to the floor. Emory was on top of her, and his hands were inside her, and her mind went completely blank.

Adelaide? Eloise called from downstairs. She knew where they hid the spare key and often, blessedly, let herself into Adelaide's house. *Are you home? I brought coconut iced coffee!*

Emory leapt off of her and Adelaide met Eloise at the door, wearing a towel. She wondered what had just happened—if this was real, if the tiled pattern of the bathroom floor had left indentations on her cheek.

Are you all right? Eloise asked, placing the coffee on the counter. *You look a bit flushed.*

Just got overheated in the shower, I think, Adelaide said.

She was too ashamed to tell Eloise the truth. It would be years before that shame evaporated.

Adelaide's sisters flew down that December, both from Boston, to celebrate Christmas all together. Holly was newly engaged and working at the State House; Izzy was in her final year of a psychology program at UMass. She'd been in and out of boarding schools for troubled girls throughout her adolescence. Lately, though, she was doing better than she had in years. In decades, even.

But of course (of course!), it was impossible for the Williams women to gather without incident.

Adelaide wasn't sure how it happened, really; she just knew Izzy hadn't slept well, and the pharmacy was taking forever to refill her meds, and the server was rude at dinner, she guessed. And suddenly, Izzy was stomping her feet on the living room floor, screaming that no one understood her. That she wanted to kill herself on the spot. That no one—*No one*—knew what it was like to live inside her brain.

Deep breaths, their mom said. *Deep breaths,* Holly echoed. Adelaide, as usual, was silent. (She'd never known how to placate Izzy, only how to avoid taking up space.)

She texted Emory, asked if he could pick her up. Drive her around for a few hours, maybe? He was studying for a history exam at their friend Misha's, he said, but he could hang out with Adelaide for an hour or two.

That's fine, she typed back. I just need to get out of the house. Please.

Emory pulled up fifteen minutes later. She snuck out through the side door and into his truck.

Later, Adelaide would remember what happened that night. How she'd been crying, reaching to hug him. How he'd shushed her and called her "baby" before undoing his pants, slipping her hand past the zipper, forcing her tiny palm to move up and down his skin. There, in her driveway, while her sister howled inside.

Are you okay, love? Holly asked that night, crawling into Adelaide's bed beside her. They'd gotten Izzy to calm down an hour or so earlier—encouraging her to take a Xanax, to drink a warm cup of tea.

I'm fine, she said. *Don't worry about me.*

(But really? Really, she wasn't fine at all.)

Emory told Adelaide he loved her on AOL Instant Messenger, then again each night before she went to bed. Called her a cunt at a football game because she hadn't grabbed ketchup for his fries. He got her Sea-Monkeys for her birthday and a big bouquet of yellow flowers for Valentine's Day. Felt her up one afternoon as she lay there, silent, then said she had the tits of a chubby, preteen boy. He gave her T-shirts that he and his little sister had tie-dyed in their backyard. Told his friends he wished she'd wax, like his exes had. He invited her to his stepbrother's wedding at Clearwater Beach, where they snuck off from the reception and stretched out on the sand, tracing constellations with their fingertips in the night sky. Dumped a milkshake over her head while she was driving one day, just because. He helped her mom repaint the front door and plant hydrangea bushes in the garden. Held her head down as she gave him a blow job—after months of pleading, of telling her, *I'd do anything to make you feel good, and you won't do the same*—tears streaming down her cheeks.

He took Adelaide to prom, to Cumberland Island at sunrise, to meet his grandparents and the litter of baby kittens they'd found beneath their porch. And one night on Adelaide's couch—a pint of Ben & Jerry's melting on the coffee table—he pulled her pajama shorts to the side and slipped inside of her, without a condom or a question or consent. Her mind went blank again.

Did you just, she started to ask. *Did we just?*

Not everything has to be a big deal, Adelaide, he said.

She hated herself for doing it, for almost enjoying how it felt. *How was this even possible?* she wondered. How had he taken her virginity—

this bizarre piece of her identity that, at seventeen years old, she thought defined her virtue, her goodness, her purity—so quickly? So carelessly?

She cried the next day when it happened again on her bedroom floor, and the day after that in her pool in broad daylight. She cried with her cheek on the toilet seat, forcing herself to vomit, hoping she could purge all of this—the panic, the impurity, the self-hatred—from her body. She cried each night in bed, eyes open and swollen, wondering if she was capable of carrying this shame forever. Adelaide tried to convince herself that love involved compromise, and that was all this really was, right? Not rape, never rape. Just compromise.

A week before senior year began, Adelaide got a call from a girl on her lacrosse team, and *Do you want to meet for a coffee, maybe?* They met at a café downtown, and there was no easy way to say this, the girl explained, but she'd gone to pick up her schedule from school last week and seen Emory in the parking lot with Misha Stojanovic.

Oh, Adelaide said. *Oh yeah, of course. We're all good friends. I actually met Emory at Misha's birthday party last year.*

No, she said. *I don't think . . . They weren't just hanging out, Adelaide.*

What do you mean? Adelaide asked.

They were. Um. I don't know if they were having sex or just making out in her car or what, but—

Adelaide's breath became shallow, her vision blurred.

It was the last day she'd call herself his girlfriend, but Emory Evans would haunt her for years to come.

Five

Across the Atlantic, Rory Hughes arrived at Downing College in Cambridge on a crisp afternoon in September, unpacking old jumpers and new law books as the Red Hot Chili Peppers' "Under the Bridge" played from his iPod. Humming aloud, he unfurled posters and photos from his gap year, haphazardly pinning them to the wall: the Keith Haring print from an exhibition in New York, the Polaroids he'd taken on a road trip along the Côte d'Azur, the bright orange Penguin cover of *1984* he'd picked up at the ever-exotic Hatchards bookshop at St. Pancras.

Lovely poster, someone said. He turned around to see two young women in his doorway, both sporting bright Converse high-tops and even brighter smiles. *I love Orwell,* the girl continued. *I'm studying literature, as it happens.*

Her name was Nathalie Alban, and this was Diana, and they'd just moved in down the hall. Rory introduced himself, shook both women's hands, and sure, he'd love to get a pint with them, *Thank you for asking.* He grabbed his keys and followed the girls down a few winding staircases and onto a leather sofa at the Butterfield, where they drank IPAs and mingled with other new students. As more freshers squeezed onto the sofa, Rory's hand brushed against Nathalie's.

Sorry, he mouthed.

It's all right, she mouthed back, smiling.

Rory felt his cheeks flush. He hoped Nathalie hadn't noticed. (She had.)

The next few months were marked by moments like these—stolen glances, brushed fingers, flushed cheeks. Rory may or may not have memorized Nathalie's schedule, timing his tea breaks to hers. Nathalie may or may not have started to brush on extra coats of mascara and blush before popping down to their shared kitchen for a cuppa, tucking books into her rucksack that she thought he might like to read. At Christmas, she tied a ribbon around a new copy of *The Orwell Diaries*. It was a personal favorite of Nathalie's, one she thought he might enjoy over the holiday.

Rory thanked her, embarrassed not to have gotten a gift in exchange, and brought the paperback to his grandparents' house in Galway. It sat on his bedside table, ribbon waiting patiently to be untied. On a few occasions, he'd stumble into bed with a cute Irish stranger—one night a blonde, the next a ginger—and was it just Rory, or was George Orwell . . . judging him? He tucked the book into his drawer, hoping his guilt might dissipate if he couldn't see its cover. (It did not.)

On Christmas Eve—a bit tipsy from dinner and eager to escape the conservative news programs his grandparents had turned on—Rory untied the ribbon, started reading, and felt his heart catch fire. Perhaps it was the booze, or perhaps it was the Christmas spirit, or perhaps it was the hours he'd spent in the kitchen memorizing the freckles on Nathalie's face. But in that moment—groggy and heart-warmed and reading about George Orwell's life—it occurred to Rory that, maybe, he was falling in love.

Thanks for a brill term and this gift of a book, he texted her, sometime around one in the morning. Merry Christmas, you. xx

Around 7 A.M. on Christmas Day, Nathalie woke up and read the message, also groggy and heart-warmed. Merry Christmas to you, too, she wrote, realizing that, maybe, she was falling in love as well.

For the rest of the term, Rory and Nathalie—*Nat*, he called her— teetered in and out of a proper relationship. They would sit in the kitchen at all hours, discussing their classes and hometowns and *Isn't it a shame that Charles Dickens was such a sexist?* They'd go out to student bars like Life and Cindies, drinking shitty gin and tonics and letting their inhibitions hit the floor, hips swaying to songs from the late nineties. Sometimes they'd wake up in each other's beds, naked and hung-over and still, somehow, beaming from the night before.

But it was never official, never set in stone. They were just young, just freshers, just wanted to see what else was out there before *Settling down*.

Then came May Week.

Rory and Nathalie weren't the type for big parties and ball gowns, really, but this week felt different. It wasn't about the pomp and circumstance, the showiness and swish of dresses. No, this week was about tradition, about finishing their exams, about drinking until their heads spun and the sun rose. And Rory didn't want to spend it with anyone else.

He asked Nathalie to Downing's May Ball. She said yes.

The theme was Olympus, the space opulent and Technicolored. Nathalie's dress was a swirl of gold and white, her hair pulled half up in loose curls and tight braids, eyes brushed in golden shadow and lined in black.

You look like a Greek goddess, Rory told her, handing Nathalie a flute of prosecco.

That's the idea, she said with a wink.

Get your motherfucking groove on, Cambridge! the band shouted. *If they insist,* Rory whispered in Nathalie's ear. He grabbed her hand, spun her around the near-empty dance floor. Her drink splashed onto her dress, but she didn't mind. She shook her hair, spinning in and out of Rory's arms, the skirt of her dress flying left and right.

"Are there patterns in our skies?" the band sang. *"Are patterns only in our eyes?"*

Rory looked into Nathalie's eyes then—deep blue, with little specks of seafoam green—and, suddenly, there on the dance floor, the pendulum between love and friendship stopped swinging. She smiled, bounced her hips back and forth, and his heart skipped a beat. He was in love with this girl. *I'm in love with you,* he said.

Already had too much prosecco, Rory? she asked, laughing. *The night is young, mate.*

It's not the prosecco, he said, insistent. *I'm in love with you, Nat Alban.*

Well, I— He didn't let her finish that sentence. Rory kissed her then, more fiercely than he had before. *Come on,* he said, taking both of her hands in his. She didn't know what was happening, exactly, but she followed him. Nathalie would always follow Rory Hughes.

He led them out to the garden, to the fairground. There were twirling carnival rides, a giant screen playing old films. Somewhere, there was a hot tub; they could hear the splishing and splashing and giggles in the distance.

So, Nathalie said. *You love me?*

I love you, he said again. He wasn't drunk (not yet at least), but something was squeezing his heart, his mind, his vision. It was warping his perspective—like a fun house mirror or one too many glasses of champagne—making it impossible to focus on anything other than *Nat.* Beautiful, perfect, dusted-in-gold-and-white-and-moonlight Nat.

(One day, this will be just how he remembers her. When.)

So, are you my boyfriend now? she asked.

I suppose, he said. *If you'll have me.*

I suppose, she said. *If you'll have me.* She rolled her eyes, parroting him. But dammit, *Dammit. I love you, too, Rory Hughes.*

The rest of the night was a blur—all bright lights and white tie and blown-out speakers. They took shots of gin, then shots of espresso, slapping the bar and their cheeks to stay awake. Everything was over-the-top—extravagant and epicurean—but neither Rory nor Nathalie wanted it to end.

They danced to bad covers of Lady Gaga songs, grabbed a boat with friends from their halls at four in the morning. Rory wrapped his arms around Nat as they made their way down the River Cam.

Is this? Diana began to say, swinging her pointer finger at the two of them, a bottle of prosecco in her spare hand. *Are you? Is this a thing now?*

Apparently so, Nat said, kissing Rory's cheek as the sun came up.

Apparently so, Rory echoed.

The year was nearly over, and they were no longer just young, just freshers, just waiting to see what else was out there. No, they were in love now. Rory and Nathalie were in love. And everything was about to change.

Spring

London, England
2018

Six

It had been five days (five! days!) since Adelaide and Rory had sex. Five days since she'd woken up in his bed and he'd made her toast and kissed her forehead and asked where she'd been all this time, insisting he would never—*Could never*—disappear. And yet, somehow, he did. Adelaide had not heard a word since.

How the hell did I mess this up? she wondered.

She'd dropped him a note on Saturday after getting home, thanking him again for *A really nice time* and asking if he was free next Friday. All her exams would be done by then, and she could use a bit of celebrating. He didn't respond.

She felt like prey. Her body was his, her interest was known, the thrill of the chase was over—he'd consumed her and discarded the scraps and now, that was all she was. A mangled carcass of a girl.

The first few days she'd felt confused, almost paranoid. She checked her phone every ten minutes, thinking, *The next time I look down, I'm sure there will be a message.* When—several hours later—there was not, she began to think that something was wrong. Her texts weren't coming through properly, perhaps, or maybe he'd lost his phone. Or what if, *What if,* that summer cold escalated and he'd fallen truly ill?

What if he's lying in a hospital bed and you're over here, selfishly wondering why he's not planning dates? she asked herself. *Stop being so fucking self-absorbed, Adelaide.*

These theories were disproved when she refreshed their WhatsApp message thread and saw the word "Online" beneath his name and photo. The photo was of Rory as a toddler. Toddler Rory was wearing a sky-blue jumper and sitting, cross-legged, in some verdant setting. A park or garden in Galway or Shere, Adelaide presumed. It was a bit grainy, but you could tell Toddler Rory was smiling excitedly. Laughing, even. Toddler Rory was mocking her.

She was meant to be studying, so she set her phone to make a very loud chiming noise when a message came through and tossed it onto her bed, away from her desk. It chimed repeatedly—texts from her family, from her classmates, from Madison, asking if she should pick up toilet paper or Cadbury bars from Tesco. Now, the chimes were mocking Adelaide, too.

On day three, she walked out of the Tube station, sat on a park bench, and sobbed. Not quietly or discreetly; no, Adelaide sobbed in roaring, uncontrollable waves. People around her likely assumed she'd lost a parent or a friend—that someone had died, tragically and unexpectedly. It was an inappropriate amount of sobbing over a boy with whom she'd been on three dates, Adelaide knew, but she couldn't help herself. She sobbed anyway.

On Wednesday, day five, she finished her last exam and turned on her phone. When no messages from Rory appeared, she felt as though she was physically falling into the void. There was no repose in completing her tests, no sense of accomplishment or fulfilled purpose. Just emptiness. Finality.

She wandered into a Little Waitrose around the corner from campus and stared at the bottles of chilled rosé. Her eyes were watery. She had nothing to lose, she decided.

Hey, she texted. There's a chance I'm being oversensitive and reading into things, as I'm wont to do, but it kind of feels like we slept together and now you're ignoring me? Which isn't a great feeling?

A moment later, she heard the chimes.

Hi, he said. I'm sorry, no, that's not the case. Just busy with work is all. Hope exams have gone well. Are we still on for Friday?

Adelaide blinked, unclear on what, exactly, she was feeling. It wasn't as uplifting as relief, but not as heavy or complete as disappointment. This feeling teetered somewhere between the two, the center point on an emotional seesaw. She'd made plans with Celeste and Madison on Friday—certain she was not going to hear from Rory Hughes ever again—and now felt torn. She didn't want to cancel on her friends or set the precedent that she would hold her schedule open for this boy (for any boy). But she also knew that if she turned down this quasi invitation and, somehow, missed her opportunity to see Rory Hughes, she would implode.

Good to know, Adelaide said. And sorry work was hectic, I know the feeling. Hope it's eased up a bit? Made plans on Friday, as I'd assumed you were busy, but could do something later in the evening, if you're up for it?

She was rolling over, a dog doing parlor tricks. She hated herself, but she also knew she had to see this boy again. Had to, had to, had to.

He asked if she was free on Saturday, instead—he had tickets to a sketch show at Soho Theatre, and maybe she'd like to join? She accepted, bought a bottle of Côtes de Provence, and took the Tube home.

Sitting on the Northern line, Adelaide felt herself sink into the space between relief and disappointment. Her anxiety had ebbed, but not fully—there was no peace or warmth in this. She tried to collapse that space and push herself toward relief, toward excitement. Toward thoughts of what she would wear and whether red lipstick might be too much for a comedy show.

She opened the rosé and poured a glass the moment she got home. It was four in the afternoon, but *No hour's too early to be a happy hour,* she mumbled to no one in particular.

She told herself she was happy, that things were good. (Weren't they?)

Adelaide sat at a high top in a crowded tapas bar. It was 8 P.M. and she scrolled through her phone, waiting for Sam to arrive.

They hadn't seen each other in—*Gosh,* a year and a half? Two years? Not since Sam's last day at Endelman & Sloan, the public relations firm in Manhattan where Adelaide started her career and Sam had served as her director, her mentor, and a Jewish fairy godmother of sorts—delivering noodle kugel and stern reminders to *Look after yourself, Adelaide. You're skin and bones lately!*

The firm was made up of about fifteen women in their twenties, all whip smart and willing to work sixty-hour weeks in exchange for dismal paychecks. It specialized in business-to-business communications for companies in tech and finance, which meant the women of Endelman &

Sloan—E&S, they called it—spent their days writing bylines and pitching profiles on behalf of Silicon Valley and FiDi executives. In the evenings, they took tequila shots and shared cartons of salty Chinese takeout on the floor of the office, where they often stayed until eight or nine o'clock at night drafting press plans. Another one of Adelaide's colleagues had described E&S as "Satan's Sorority House on Spring Street." (She wasn't wrong.)

It wasn't the most rewarding work, by any means. Adelaide's college internships had all focused on writing and publishing and running around for budding literary magazines—sweating in little black dresses from H&M and dreaming of seeing her name on mastheads or in an author's acknowledgments. E&S was far from the realization of those dreams. But it was a job, an opportunity to build media relationships. And her colleagues? They made it all more than bearable.

About six months before Adelaide resigned and moved to London, Sam left the firm to work for a budding fintech start-up in Williamsburg. Several margaritas into her send-off, she'd squeezed Adelaide's hand and implored her to *Never doubt that you're smart and shrewd. You really are, you're a special one.* It stuck with her.

Sam walked into Brindisa and wrapped Adelaide up in a hug. She was wearing a cobalt-blue blazer, with a diamond solitaire and a new wedding band on the hand she'd used to squeeze Adelaide's years earlier. She quickly grabbed the waiter, ordering a pitcher of sangria for their table.

It's so good to see you again, Adelaide said. Sam returned her smile.

They talked about weddings and freelancing and Sam's boutique hotel around the corner. About the women from E&S with whom they'd stayed in touch (there were many), and those to whom they never planned to speak again (there were a few). Sam asked what dating was like in London, and Adelaide felt her cheeks flush, saying, *Well, there's this boy. It's still early days, but . . .*

Somewhere between pan con tomate and queso de cabra, Sam started to pitch Adelaide on a role at her tech company, Alliance, once again. It had outgrown its start-up title since Sam joined, with offices across the U.K., France, Switzerland. She needed someone to handle their international communications from London—*Someone who can balance our*

American tone with a European mindset, Sam explained between bites. Adelaide had been the first person to pop into her head.

And I know it's not super creative, she said. *I know it's corporate and techy, but I can pay you a ton of fucking money and you'll get to travel and I think this could be really great.*

Adelaide thought about the dismal starting salaries she'd seen listed from publishing houses on job boards. She thought about the countless applications she'd filled out to no reply, the stress of interviews, the challenges associated with landing a work visa—the uncertainty of it all. She looked at Sam and wondered what it might feel like to work for someone who had such faith in you, day in and day out. The answer was warm and confident and eager to accept.

All right, she said. *I'm in.*

Are you serious? Sam asked. *You're in? I thought it would take much more arm-twisting!*

Oh, Adelaide said. *You're right. Let's talk numbers. You can twist my arm then, yeah?*

They laughed, ordered dessert. Sam covered the bill and Adelaide walked her back to the hotel on Charlotte Street. They hugged goodbye and promised to be in touch—Sam would send her a note with more details in a few days, once she got back to New York.

Adelaide got on the Tube at Goodge Street. She thought about texting Rory her exciting almost-news, but decided against it, telling herself it was better to share this in person. Admittedly, she also didn't trust that he'd respond, but she couldn't think about that right now. She sent messages to her group chats with her family, with Madison and Celeste, and to Eloise. They all replied with confetti cannons and champagne emojis.

For the first time that week, Adelaide genuinely couldn't help but smile.

It was Friday night and pouring rain and Celeste bought the first round. Each of the girls' glasses was overflowing with foam, sloshing onto the table, onto their jeans. Nobody really minded.

They were at Adelaide's favorite pub—a spot in Bethnal Green with old portraits hung askew and cheese toasties soaked in truffle oil, one they'd stumbled into on a rainy Saturday in March. There were always dogs here, couples on dates, old Irish men arguing over rugby matches. The bartenders mocked her when Adelaide ordered Guinness with a splash of crème de cassis. She loved it all.

How are you feeling, Adelaide? Celeste asked.

Good, Adelaide said. *Really good, yeah. It's surreal, isn't it?*

They all nodded.

"Surreal" felt like the easiest way to describe this. She'd finished exams and lined up a job. Met a boy. She felt joy and optimism, appreciation and gratitude. But more than these, she felt the absence of other feelings—confidence, assurance, solace.

Years from now, one of Adelaide's colleagues would get a much-deserved promotion, and they'd drink prosecco in the office kitchen to celebrate. *You know that feeling,* her colleague would whisper, *when you've reached a goal, or a dream comes true, and you just don't really trust it? Like, you're waiting to hear it was all a mistake? That this was given to you accidentally?*

Yes, Adelaide would say. She knew exactly; it was what coursed through her veins at the pub that Friday evening.

Okay, okay, Madison asked, *I hate that this Rory fellow went radio silent for days, but let's assume it never happens again. Do you think . . .* She paused, took a sip. *. . . . when you're rich and powerful and engaged to Rory, you'll get married at a castle in England? Or at the Plaza in New York?*

Adelaide laughed, for many reasons. *Obviously both,* she said. She laughed some more and took a swig of her drink.

It's funny, she continued. *I never really thought about my dream wedding growing up. I thought more about my funeral.*

You always say that, you weirdo, Madison said. *Men should wear gray suits instead of black. And you want yellow flowers. And balloon letters.*

It's true! Adelaide said. *I'm glad you remembered. I have a vision.*

She did. Growing up, her Georgia town seemed to mourn a new teenager every few months—drunk-driving accidents, unintended overdoses, motorcycles wrapped around trees. More personally, she'd lost a number of extended family members and friends to suicide and malignant tumors. Through all of this, Adelaide had become surprisingly comfortable with the idea of Death.

She didn't do any sorts of drugs or extreme sports; she didn't even know how to ride a bike. But if Death was going to come for Adelaide, she wanted to maintain a degree of control. There were notes saved in her phone and on her laptop, plainly labeled IN CASE OF DEATH. As Madison said, she wanted men in gray suits (black felt too much like prom), bunches of yellow flowers, and metallic balloon letters that read, LOVE ONLY COMES IN WHOLE. She wanted egg salad and Chipwiches served, a mix of songs like "Drops of Jupiter" and "Pony" played in the background. She hoped this very odd send-off would leave its final mark on the people she cared about—an attempt to glue herself to everyone's metaphorical mantels and say, *This is exactly how I'd like you all to remember me. Just like this.*

Adelaide had once met a psychic—at the Jersey shore, of all places—who'd grabbed her hands and immediately said, *I don't know why you think you're going to die so young. You're not exactly jumping off cliffs, honey.*

Still, she'd expected Death; prepared for it, even. But she had not expected this. Adelaide could barely wrap her mind around how neatly the pieces of her life had begun to fit together: The job; the love interest; the perfect, rain-soaked city.

How lucky she was to exist in this reality. How terrified she was of this luck running out.

Seven

Adelaide woke up with a mild hangover and a craving for maple syrup. She had breakfast delivered from a local bakery—unwilling to put on real pants and walk ten minutes up the road—and stretched out in one of the recliners in their living room. It was pale gray and made of a suede-like material. She placed a box of French toast and an iced dirty chai on the armrest.

Soon after, Madison came out of her bedroom and grabbed an almond croissant from the table (Adelaide knew they were her favorite). They watched several hours of *Love Island* reruns before Adelaide stood up and got in the shower, washing the scent of truffles and hops from her hair. She put on sweatpants and an old sorority T-shirt and returned to her spot in the lounge to let her hair air-dry, content—for the first time in months, it seemed—to have absolutely nothing to do.

Adelaide had spent the last year juggling classes and freelance work, chasing down editors she admired on Twitter. She was rarely without her laptop and often sat in bed—hunched over its screen—until two or three in the morning, writing papers for class, poorly paid reviews for lit magazines at which she'd interned in college, book roundups for websites called Hustle or The Fix. (What she described as women's lifestyle outlets and her professors dubbed a waste of time.) On average, Adelaide clocked twenty hours of class time, thirty hours freelancing, and another five or ten hours on group work and pro bono projects each week. She loved writing. (*Remember,* she'd tell herself, eyes glassy from staring at her screen. *You love writing!*) But she was, in a word, exhausted. She was also infinitely relieved to be sinking into this chair—no assignments to complete, no red-lined Google Docs to taunt her.

The sketch show started at eight thirty that night, and Rory asked if she wanted to grab a drink an hour beforehand. Adelaide straightened her hair and put on red lipstick, then wiped it off; she was afraid it might seem as though she was trying too hard. She wanted to impress Rory Hughes, but without seeming like she wanted to impress him, you know? She dabbed clear petroleum jelly onto her lips instead, spritzed her hair with Flowerbomb.

At six forty-five, Adelaide poured some rosé into a water bottle and left the flat, feeling a different kind of nervous than she had before their first few dates. She hoped the alcohol might numb that apprehension; it didn't, really.

Rory was sitting in a booth with two glasses of wine when Adelaide walked into Soho Theatre. There was no tension in his smile when she approached the table, a pleasant surprise. (She'd feared he might resent her accusatory texts, her seemingly misplaced paranoia.)

You smell divine, he said quietly, kissing her cheek. It was like a spell; every concern Adelaide had been carrying seemed to vanish with a *poof.*

I got you a glass of chardonnay, he said. *Hope that's all right.*

That's perfect, she said. *Thank you.*

They talked about their weeks, about work and exams. Adelaide shared the news of her pseudo job offer from Sam, and Rory said he would demand their finest bottle of champagne to celebrate, slapping the table. She shook her head and chuckled. *Don't want to jinx it,* she said.

When he asked if she'd been to Soho Theatre before, Adelaide shook her head again, confessing she'd not seen much live comedy, just the occasional improv show at New York's UCB.

This is where Fleabag *started,* he said.

Fleabag? she asked. *Is that a sketch group?*

(The next summer, she would spend hours in the queue outside of Waterstones, dripping sweat onto the pavement and fanning herself with her hands. Phoebe Waller-Bridge would be signing copies of *Fleabag: The Scriptures* inside, with a limit of one signature per person, given the enormous demand. *Can you sign it to Rory?* Adelaide would ask.)

At quarter past eight, they shuffled down the stairs and into the theater, plastic chairs lined up in front of a small stage. There was no cur-
tain up, just a handful of track lights overhead. They gave off a bluish
glow.

Rory? a voice said. *Is that Rory Hughes?*

Diana Abrams, he said, standing up to greet a short woman with
curly blond hair. Adelaide's seat was at the end of the row, placing her between this stranger and Rory. She stood up to clear his path, wondering
whether she should sit down again. She didn't.

And Bubs as well, he said, shaking a much taller man's hand. *I didn't
realize you'd be here, mate.*

(*Didn't he call his roommate Bubs?* Adelaide thought. *Is that just how
he addresses all the men in his life?*)

She smiled, hooking one hand behind her back and twisting her finger
around the ends of her hair, unsure what else to do. Diana had on red
lipstick, she noticed. Adelaide wondered how much deliberation had
gone into her decision to put it on. Rory introduced them all—*Bubs. Er,
sorry, Brennan and Diana, Adelaide; Adelaide, Brennan and Diana*—and
she shook their hands. Rory explained that he and Diana had gone to
uni together before, coincidentally, landing at the same law firm where
Brennan was a senior associate. He was renting a room in Rory's flat for
a few months—*Saving up to buy my own place in Angel,* Brennan (Bubs?)
said. Adelaide nodded, still smiling.

Rory and Brennan began a sidebar conversation, and the woman
named Diana turned to Adelaide. She asked if she was American, how
long she'd been in the U.K., what she was studying. Adelaide tried to ask
questions in return. (*And where are you from in England? Born and bred
in Cambridge? That must have been such a lovely place to grow up!*) Adelaide noticed that Brennan was staring at her a bit; she wondered what
Rory was saying.

So, are you Rory's girlfriend, then? Diana asked.

Oh no, Adelaide said. *Not exactly.*

That's a shame, she said, her voice dropping to a whisper. *Rory Hughes
is the best.* Adelaide blushed.

And you and, um, Brennan, was it? she asked.

Bubs? Diana said. *No, no. We're just here as colleagues. As friends.*

The lights dimmed and they all took their seats. *Did you both call that man Bubs?* Adelaide asked. Rory whispered that Bubs's name was Brennan Uralla-Burke. *B-U-B,* he said. *Someone just started calling him Bubs one day, and I suppose it stuck.* Adelaide smiled again, thinking about how wild it was that Rory had unexpectedly run into his roommate and an old colleague at a basement theater in London.

The show began. It featured sketches about goofy, Swedish rock duos and a cat dancing across the stage. Halfway through, Rory reached down to grab Adelaide's hand, holding it as they both belly laughed. Between acts, he brushed her hair back and kissed her temple. It felt as though he'd rubbed liniment on her forehead, over her palms.

Adelaide still had the giggles when they left the theater. She laughed when Rory asked if she fancied a Nando's.

A cheeky Nando's? she said, forging an English accent.

Yes, Mary Poppins, he said. *A cheeky Nando's.*

She ordered chips and a salad. Rory mocked her for not getting chicken at a chicken shop.

I'm actually a vegetarian, she said, almost embarrassed.

Oh, he said. *You should have mentioned. I'd have suggested something else.*

No, this is perfect. She meant it.

He asked when she'd stopped eating meat, and how come. Adelaide lied, as she always did, saying it had more to do with her health than ethics. In reality, she was borderline anemic—her meat-free diet was likely detrimental—she just didn't believe in eating things with beating hearts. Saying that out loud made other people uncomfortable, though.

She changed the subject and asked to hear stories about his school days. She liked the way he described Canterbury, its rolling hills and stone buildings. He talked about how close he'd been to the boys with whom he'd boarded, how their socks would get mixed up in the wash and they would all jump into the River Stour at the end of each summer term.

It wasn't all boys, though, right? Adelaide asked.

Coed, Rory said, taking a bite from his fork. He chewed, swallowed. *I was very popular with the girls, of course, if that's what you're asking.*

Adelaide laughed, blushed a little. She hadn't intended for that to be a leading question. *Oh?* she said.

Only joking, he said. *I did have an American girlfriend, though, in sixth form. Ivy. She put on an English accent most of the time.*

An American? she said. *Wait, should I be putting on an accent right now?*

I like your accent as is, Rory said. He looked down. *It's very sexy.* She blushed a little more.

He didn't ask about her high school boyfriend. Adelaide was relieved.

Adelaide followed Rory home again, careful not to trip over the shoes by his doorway this time. He took off her coat and slowly kissed her chest, her rib cage, her abdomen as he unbuttoned her blouse. Adelaide felt the inside of his lips on her skin and wondered, honestly wondered, whether a better feeling existed in the world. It would be years before she knew the answer was yes.

Do you promise to stay for a proper breakfast this time? he asked, slipping off her tights. His mouth hovered above her hip bone. *Do you promise not to vanish for five days?* she thought.

If you insist, she said.

The next morning, Rory showered as Adelaide made his bed and tried to collect her hair into a neat bun. The sun shone brightly through his windows, and she heard him singing along to a Little Mix song on the radio, which made her smile.

Rory opened his door in a towel a few minutes later, all wet and pink. He stood behind Adelaide and kissed the top of her head, wrapped his arms around her waist—she felt little water droplets drip down her ear. She took his hand and brought it to her mouth, running her bottom lip along the inside of his forearm, curling her tongue around his thumb. Her back was to Rory, but she heard him exhale slowly, pleasantly. She imagined his eyes were closed.

You know, she said, turning to face him, *I haven't showered yet.*

What do you mean? he asked.

Just. She kissed his lips, the tip of his ear. Slid his hands beneath her

T-shirt. *If you wanted to come on me, anywhere on me, I wouldn't mind getting a bit dirtier.*

Adelaide had trained herself to say these types of things. She'd been trained, rather. Sometimes she wondered if, in saying them, she was surrendering to patriarchal subjugation—taking it all, very literally, lying down. Other times, she told herself it was an act of empowerment, of feminism—an unapologetic embrace of the sex-positive movement. The truth existed somewhere in the middle: She didn't say this because she liked having cum on her body, but because she liked the response these words would elicit. It made her feel as though she was in control.

Fuck, Adelaide, he said. She liked hearing her name in his mouth. *You're really something.*

They sat outside a café around the corner from Rory's building, both wearing sunglasses and enjoying the balmy morning. Adelaide had braided her hair to one side after showering; it felt damp and cool against her collarbone.

So, Rory said. *Tell me more about this job.*

Adelaide explained that she'd met Sam years earlier, working at E&S. It was always difficult to capture the firm's cultlike essence when speaking to anyone who hadn't lived it—which, she supposed, was also true of actual cults and harems. Some of the highest and lowest moments of Adelaide's life had transpired in that office; it was tricky to explain how much light and darkness could exist in the same setting.

She said that her initial goal had been to find a job in publishing—an editorial role, or something in marketing, maybe. At this, Rory's head snapped up.

Do you know anyone in that world? Adelaide asked, intrigued by his reaction.

Used to, Rory said. *But not anymore really, no.*

Anyway. She was glad to have something lined up, excited to work with Sam again. Alliance made technology for banks and financial institutions—*Not exactly my passion,* she said—but she was wary of turning anything she loved into work. While freelancing, she'd learned that writing became much less enjoyable when deadlines and strict SEO guidelines were attached. She feared the same might be true of books if she were to take a job red-lining and promoting them.

I believe in doing something you like, she said. *But not necessarily something you love.*

So, you like financial technology? he asked.

I like strategic communications, she said. *I like working with tech companies, like working with Sam. I like making enough money to pay off my loans and eat more than hard-boiled eggs for dinner. And I'll still get to write in this role. Just, not about books.*

Rory nodded, sipped his coffee. It occurred to Adelaide that she was speaking to someone who'd left a high-profile law firm to help produce films, to do something he loved.

Really, she said. *I like that they'll be able to sponsor my visa and I can live in this country. That's always been the goal, that's the bit I love. I would take a job as a chimney sweep if it meant I could stay in London.*

Would just have to brush up on your rhyming slang, he said.

Exactly! she said. *Will you teach me? Just in case this offer falls through?*

He taught her phrases like "brown bread" and "bees and honey," explaining that rhyming slang was likely the invention of Irish dockers, not Cockneys. The server brought out plates of avocado toast and bubble and squeak (Rory had asked for his recommendation, of course, though he'd been to this café at least two dozen times); Adelaide practiced her accent. Afterward, he walked her to the Tube station, looping his finger around her wet braid and kissing her goodbye.

Let's do something later this week? he asked. She nodded yes and bit her lip, fighting the urge to make a snide comment about his delayed reply time.

Let's, she said. *Can we plan something sooner rather than later?*

Can do, he said. He kissed her once more.

Adelaide stopped for coffee on her way home. When she opened the door, Madison was curled up on a chair watching *Love Island*. Just where Adelaide left her.

Have you been watching this whole time? she asked, handing Madison a latte. *I'm so far behind now!*

Don't worry, Madison said. *This is the recap episode. I've been waiting for you, mostly watching* Friends.

Bless, Adelaide said.

She plopped into the cushy recliner, coffee splashing onto her T-shirt. She blotted it with a napkin. Adelaide knew she should change and check her emails, send out some pitches, see if her dissertation advisor had notes on the proposal she'd sent before exams. But it was a sunny Sunday morning, and their windows were open, and there was nowhere else she needed to be.

Should we go to the park later, Mads? Adelaide asked. *Maybe have a little picnic?*

Madison nodded. *After the next episode,* she said. *And then you have to tell me about your date.*

They spent their afternoon at Waterlow Park and their evening at the Duke's Head. It was the fifth night in a row, Adelaide realized, that she'd been drinking—*But fuck it,* she thought, she was practically on vacation. They did shots of Irish whiskey with the bartenders and ordered plates of greasy, cheesy chips. She explained (in what was likely inappropriately explicit detail) how much she enjoyed her time with Rory Hughes.

I'm not going to lie, Madison said. *I don't love that he ignored you all week, especially after you slept together?*

Neither do I, Adelaide said. *It's weird.* She explained that yes, it was early days, but it felt like they had every element of a solid relationship— good chat, good sex, mutual interests. They were both ambitious, both fond of old Robin Williams films, both thrilled to send and receive pictures of fluffy puppies.

Part of me feels like he's got to be hung up on something else, Adelaide said. *Or someone else.*

That's a little presumptuous, Madison said. *Maybe he really is just busy with work, you know? Can we stalk him on the internet? See what he's been up to?* Adelaide shook her head. She'd tried to find Rory on every social network imaginable—there was nothing, save for a bare-bones Facebook profile and an out-of-date LinkedIn without a headshot. He was a digital recluse, and she was too terrified to ask him about past relationships outright.

Maybe he just needs more time, Adelaide said. They both shrugged.

The girls finished their pints and stumbled home around midnight.

Adelaide heard her phone chime as she crawled into bed. It was a text from Sam.

Hey! the text read. Just wanted to make sure you saw my email on Friday night? So sorry about the late notice, but wanted to check you were good to go into the office tomorrow morning? I can try to move some things around, if not!

Adelaide's heart dropped to her stomach; she sat up and quickly flipped her laptop open. She'd assumed, based on their conversations, that she would start work at Alliance after completing her dissertation and graduating from her program. Late August, maybe early September. But—as Sam's email now explained—*We'd love to have you really hit the ground running as soon as possible.* She'd asked Adelaide to come in on Monday morning (tomorrow morning) for an interview with Djibril, the head of the international marketing team. He would be traveling for the next few weeks, but blocked out time to chat with her at 10 A.M.

Oh my goodness, Adelaide texted. I'm so sorry! I hadn't checked my emails this weekend. Can absolutely go in tomorrow morning. Thank you for the text!

She chugged a glass of water and took a few ibuprofen, Googled the correct pronunciation of Djibril's name (*Gee-breel, gee-breel, gee-breel,* Adelaide recited). She mapped out how long it would take her to get to their office the next morning, set alarms for seven forty-five, eight, eight fifteen.

Adelaide sighed. Much like telling strangers they looked like Disney princes, accidentally drinking herself silly and still agreeing to a morning interview was, unfortunately, Something Adelaide Williams Would Do.

Eight

Miraculously, Adelaide made it through the interview. On time, on message, in an unexpected blend of French and English. (*Je suis rouillée,* she'd said when Djibril switched languages, mid-interview. *Mais je peux l'essayer*—I'm rusty, but I can try.) She'd shaken his hand and waved goodbye to the receptionist, walked out onto Tottenham Court Road. And then (then!), Adelaide pulled a rumpled Tesco bag from her purse and vomited into it. Right there. On the street.

I deserve a medal for this, she'd thought, wiping sick from her chin. She was right: She deserved a medal for this.

A few months later, once the contracts were signed and a rapport had been established, Adelaide told Djibril the full story over after-work drinks. Sitting at a booth in the Fitzroy Tavern—with its sticky, checkered floors and wood paneling—she recounted the late-night text from Sam, the vomiting on Tottenham Court Road, the sheer luck by which she'd been able to respond to his questions at all, let alone in French. He laughed (cackled, really) and clinked his G&T to hers—*Well, cheers to that, darling!*

Djibril was French Nigerian, with an unnaturally kempt beard and a Parisian accent that seemed to get thicker with each sip of his drink. He shared that he had broken up with his longtime partner, Louis, a few days before the interview.

You walked in and had this glow about you, this instant light, he said. *And I needed that light on our team!*

I think that glow was just hangover sweat, Djibril, Adelaide said, pressing her lips into a smile. *But either way, you are too kind. I'm sorry to hear about Louis, he's lost a winner.*

She asked how he was holding up. He shrugged, leaned forward. *All right,* he said. *Now, remind me. Are you seeing someone?*

Adelaide sighed. She was still, genuinely, unsure how to answer this question.

Was she seeing someone? Sleeping with someone? Spending many of her waking hours in a hormone-fueled reverie that featured that someone? Absolutely. But that same someone had a habit of missing text messages and failing to make plans more than a day or two in advance, of stretching Adelaide's patience like a petulant child.

I have, like, a person I see? she said finally. *If it were 2008, my Facebook status would say "It's Complicated."*

Mhm, Djibril said. He nodded knowingly. *Tell me more.*

She explained that his name was Rory. That he was beautiful and maybe her soul mate and also that she kind of hated him? They had been dating for about three months, though he often disappeared for four or five days at a time—ignoring texts, skirting plans.

But sometimes, he would show up with dim sum takeaway and say *Hey, you* when she opened the door to her flat. He would kiss her forehead and the tip of her nose, cover her eyes during spooky scenes and squeeze her hand beneath the covers when they watched movies in bed. (There was also the sex—*Ohmygosh,* the sex. For the first time in Adelaide's life, it was truly orgasmic.)

She showed Djibril a photo on her phone, one Rory had sent a few weeks before. He'd gone to the Lake District with his brothers one weekend and they'd thrown Rory—the youngest of four—into the water, fully clothed. The picture looked like something out of a summer catalogue: His hair was dripping wet, his shirt clung to his abdomen, a grin stretched across his face. Looking at it made her mouth go dry. The sheer image of Rory Hughes, quite literally, made Adelaide feel thirsty. It was ludicrous.

Mon Dieu, Adelaide, Djibril said. *You didn't say he looked like a Disney prince.*

So, she said, smiling. *Funny story.*

Adelaide got back to her flat around 8 P.M. She balanced her phone on the towel rack, playing Hall & Oates as she showered, glancing to see if she had any new messages between scrubbing her face, shampooing her hair.

She knew the pattern by now. Monday through Thursday were silent days, *Working days*. Friday nights, however, meant invitations for Popsicles along the South Bank or tickets to see that new Star Wars film at the Kino. They meant links to gallery openings, cheap West End matinees, brunch reservations the next morning. (*The Ivy Chelsea Garden? Eleven tomorrow?*) They had, at least—the last nine or ten Fridays. But Adelaide fell asleep with her phone in her hand that night and woke up with no new messages.

Happy Saturday, she texted around noon. Let me know if you want to grab lunch tomorrow, or maybe drinks one day next week?

No reply. Nothing Sunday, either. Pathetically or justifiably (or both), Adelaide's heart started to ache—this was a daunting breed of déjà vu.

You know that quote, Madison said, *the one everyone misattributes to Shakespeare?*

The one about claiming you love the rain and still carrying an umbrella? Adelaide asked.

No, Madison said. "*Fool me once, shame on you. Fool me twice, shame on me.*"

Adelaide shrugged, rolled her eyes a little. She knew she was being a fool this time. The trouble was, she didn't care. It was pathetic and pitiful and yes, foolish, but she just wanted to hear from Rory. An acknowledgment, a question, a word, even—anything from Rory.

A few months before meeting Rory Hughes, Adelaide had been reading *Call Me By Your Name* on the Tube when it hit her: She'd never really known love. Not like this, not like Elio and Oliver's. Nothing full, unconditional, romantic, apodictic. She'd started sobbing on the Northern line that afternoon and, just, never really stopped.

What if she was broken, she wondered. What if she'd been broken as a teenager and was now incapable of eliciting adoration, affection? What if her heart—or whatever thing existed inside of a person that made them worthy of love—was irrevocably damaged? She could charm strangers, and she could sleep with them, and she could remain cheerfully detached. But what if this was the reason that first dates never led to seconds? That one-night stands never asked for her last name?

For two weeks in March, Adelaide considered these questions in tears. Lots of tears. Warm, flooding, unable-to-go-to-class-or-do-work, must-eat-Shake-Shack-on-the-street kinds of tears. She'd not found an answer or resolution at the time, but she had found an artist in Shoreditch who tattooed a small peach onto her body. It was meant to be a reminder that she was, in fact, capable of regrowth. Of a love like Elio and Oliver's. Lately, though, it just reminded her of the first time she slept with Rory Hughes.

Rory fucking Hughes. This mirage of a person who took the shape of every childhood fantasy Adelaide had ever had: Tall and English. Handsome and well-read. Able to kiss the little peach on her ass and make her believe that here, maybe, was a human who could love her broken soul.

It was normal to feel hurt when a boy you liked disappeared, Adelaide knew. She'd felt that before. But this was different; it sank into her bones. It was proof, she thought, that she really was damaged beyond repair. And as five days of silence turned into six, into seven, into eight, Adelaide plunged deeper into this belief.

On Thursday, it had been eleven days since Adelaide last heard from Rory, and she was starting to feel physically unwell. She was resting her head against a pole on the Tube, playing Sufjan Stevens's "Mystery of Love" on repeat, when she thought she heard her name. She looked up to find that she'd started leaning on a very tall, vaguely familiar man. He had floppy brown hair and blue eyes. She took out her earbuds.

It's Adelaide, right? the man said. *Rory's mate? I think we met at Soho Theatre.*

Oh! It was Boodle, or Bobsy, or—*Bubs?* Adelaide said. Rory's old colleague and roommate. Adelaide didn't correct that he'd called her Rory's mate. (Goodness knew what the appropriate title would be, anyway. She couldn't exactly say, *Not his mate, no! Just the person he likes to have sex with sometimes, apparently!*)

I mean Brennan, she said. *So sorry for leaning on you just now. How are you?*

Bubs works, he said. *And I'm all right, yeah. Are you all right, though? You look a bit pale. I was getting concerned and then realized who you were.* His accent sounded different, she realized.

I'm fine, she said. *Just a bit light-headed. And confused about the concept of personal space, it seems. But thank you for asking. Also, are you . . . not English?*

Bubs chuckled. He was not English, no—at least not fully. He explained that he'd grown up in Ireland, England, and Australia—*My mum grew up on the Torres Strait Islands. We actually lived in the city of Adelaide for a few years, as a matter of fact*—which meant he had three passports and zero distinguishable accents.

I never quite know where to tell people I'm from, he said.

Neither do I! Adelaide said. *I'm just not sure which state I'm from, though. You've got three whole countries fighting to be your motherland.* He chuckled again.

They both got off at Tottenham Court Road (his office—Rory's old law firm—was just a few blocks down from Alliance's, as it happened). Bubs insisted on buying her a drink from the Mini Pret.

You really don't have to do this, she told him.

It's for my own reassurance, he said, handing her a bottle of lemonade. *Feel better, yeah? And have a good day, Adelaide. I'm sure I'll see you around.*

She stood there for a moment after he walked away, the condensation from the lemonade dripping down her palm. *For my own reassurance,* she repeated aloud. Adelaide took a sip, tucked the bottle into her bag, pressed a cool hand against the nape of her neck. She walked out of the station, making a mental note to call Rory before the day was up. For her own reassurance, she told herself. If nothing else.

That evening, after half a Xanax and a few deep breaths, Adelaide bit her lip and dialed his number. Her heart pounded as it rang.

Hiya, Adelaide? Rory answered. *Is everything okay?*

Hey, yeah, she said. *I just . . . Is everything okay with you? I don't want this to sound accusatory, but is there a reason you've kind of . . . disappeared?*

She heard him exhale at the other end of the line. *Well,* Rory started to say. They were working on a few big projects at work—summer was always a busy time—but there was something else, too. He had been in a long-term thing for about six years, he explained, and it ended a little over two years ago, and he wasn't quite sure how to exist in a relationship anymore. He liked Adelaide—*Really,* he said. *You're kind and beautiful and incredibly bright*—but he had a hard time with relationships. They made him nervous, and he tended to run. *Like a spooked gazelle,* he said.

Adelaide chewed at her nails as she listened, pacing her bedroom. It was the first time they'd ever discussed exes. She wasn't quite sure what she'd expected from this conversation, but it hadn't been this. Not exactly.

I'm so excited about you, she said. *I guess I wish you were excited about me, too.*

It's just, he said, *I haven't been excited about anyone in a very long time.* The words felt like acid poured over her heart.

Here's the thing, she said. Adelaide had her own sticky relationship history. She didn't want to go into details, really—not yet—but she struggled with hot-and-cold behavior. It was triggering for her. Unhealthy.

I don't need bells and whistles and weekend getaways, she said. *And I don't need to talk all day every day. But I need you to respond to my messages and make plans with more than twenty-four hours' notice. And, like, let me know what's going on in your head. At least a little bit.*

He understood, apologized. *And how about we go for a picnic in St. James's Park tomorrow?* he asked. *I'll bring a magnum of rosé, try to make it up to you a bit.*

A few hours after getting off the phone, Adelaide got an email from an old E&S client, the founders of a travel dating app. (*Imagine Tinder and Expedia had a love child,* Adelaide would tell reporters.) They were launching a new service, designed to help millennial couples plan luxury holidays on a budget—or something absurd to that effect—and they needed testimonials.

Not sure if this is an overstep, the email read. *But we know you've done some freelancing and we could really use your copywriting skills, as someone who knows our brand. Specifically, we need someone to write about couples' accommodations at a boutique hotel in Palma, Mallorca next month. Think you could give us a hand in exchange for a free getaway for you and a significant other one weekend?*

Well, fuck, Adelaide thought.

Rory was sitting on a big picnic blanket in front of the Duck Island Cottage—a bottle of Côtes de Provence in each hand—when Adelaide met him at seven the next night. His button-down looked like the one he'd been wearing when Adelaide first saw him at the boat race. She wondered if it was the same shirt, if he'd worn it on purpose.

They didn't have any magnums at the store, he said, kissing Adelaide's cheek. *But I thought two bottles and a couple of extra-long straws would do.*

He pulled a wine key from his rucksack, handed Adelaide a red-and-white-striped straw. They toasted, sipped from their bottles. Adelaide brought some chocolate chip cookies she'd baked that afternoon. She was disproportionately excited when Rory described them as *The best fucking thing I've ever put in my mouth.*

Besides you, he added with a wink.

They named the baby goslings in the pond—this one was Tom, because he just looked like a Tom—and debated whether ducks were inherently good or evil. (*Diabolically evil,* they decided.) They discussed the complexities of Margaret Thatcher's legacy, how much they missed Barack Obama, their favorite varieties of French wine and cheese. She told Rory about her coincidental run-in with Bubs. (*You know, he was there the day you decided I was a Disney prince?* Rory told her. *Huh,* Adelaide said. *The world really is small.*) Their conversation the night before did not come up, nor did the fact that Adelaide had been offered a free holiday for two in the Balearic Islands.

Abruptly, storm clouds started to swirl overhead. A few minutes later, it was pouring rain on Adelaide, Rory, and their half-drunk bottles of rosé. *Reckon that's our cue to leave?* Rory asked.

Adelaide nodded. She scooped up the takeaway container full of cookies, the gingham blanket. They could take the Tube, Rory offered.

Or, he said. *We could say fuck it, we're already drenched, and wind back to my place in the rain?*

Adelaide looked around, laughing. *Is this,* she said. *Are we in a Richard Curtis film?*

Shh, Rory said. *Don't break the fourth wall.*

They walked back to Rory's in the rain, paper straws disintegrating as they passed Westminster Abbey, the statue of Boadicea, Shrek's Adventure!

Wait, Rory said. *This may be the least English thing I have ever done, but.*

He took his phone from his pocket and started blaring "The Piña Colada Song," singing along in an exaggerated falsetto. Adelaide joined in at the chorus, shouting, *"If you like making love at midnight / In the dunes on the cape"* loudly and drunkenly and without a single goddamned care in the world. They played little air guitars along the river, shaking their wet hair like dogs. It was magic.

There was an urgency in the way Rory kissed her—in the way he picked her up and grabbed her ass, her hair—once they reached his flat. The windows fogged up in his bedroom; their wet clothes hung over the radiator. This, too, was like something out of a movie, Adelaide thought—dirty and tender and visibly steamy.

Suppose I should have opened these sooner, Rory said. He propped open the windows above his bed, then turned back to Adelaide. He ran his tongue along her collarbone, her bottom lip. *I quite like making you sweat, though.*

Adelaide had never really done drugs, but she imagined this was as close to ecstasy as she had ever, would ever, come. She wanted to know every part of him: Every taste bud on his tongue, every freckle on his body, every corner of his curious little Cambridge-educated, film-obsessed mind.

Tell me a secret, Adelaide whispered. She slid beneath his duvet and shifted onto her side to face him, her brain still swimming in oxytocin and pink wine.

Like, a sex secret? he asked.

No, she said. *Or maybe, I don't know. Just a life secret. What's something I don't know about you?*

He turned onto his back and looked at the ceiling, ruminating.

I'm an orphan, he said, several minutes later. Adelaide exhaled. She didn't say anything, just threaded her fingers through his.

Between deep breaths, Rory shared that his parents had gotten into a car accident when he was ten years old. They had been driving home from dinner one night, got a flat tire, realized there was no spare in the trunk. There weren't many cabs available at that hour around Shere, so they rang up Rory's "uncle" Trevor—his father's best friend—and asked for a lift. Trevor had been drinking, they later learned, but he'd said he could get them home to their boys that night and pick up a spare tire in the morning. *No problem.*

He'd driven off the road and into a ditch. The car flipped. Rory's parents died instantly, the boys were told, but their uncle walked away from the accident physically unharmed, save for a few scars and minor fractures. He'd spent years in and out of rehab and mental hospitals, riddled with guilt. But he was better now. He was clean, at least.

Holy shit, Adelaide said. It was far from eloquent, but she wasn't sure what else to say. *I know this is an odd question, but. How do you feel now? I can't imagine that's an easy story to tell.*

No, Rory said. *It never really gets easier, honestly. But it's okay. I'm okay now.*

He blinked and a few tears escaped his eyes. Adelaide wiped them away with her thumb, kissed the wet spot on his cheek.

I'm so sorry that happened to you, she said. He nodded, took another deep breath.

What about you, then? he asked. *What secret trauma are you harboring?*

I guess everybody has some hidden trauma, don't they? she said. *It's not at all comparable, I haven't lost my parents. But I've come quite close to losing family. Scary close.*

Adelaide described her sister Izzy's episodes: The screaming, sobbing, knife-brandishing fights she witnessed growing up. (Like Rory, she'd spent much of her adolescence at psych wards' visiting hours.) She told him about her parents' divorce, the times she'd had to talk her mom off of metaphorical ledges. She very deliberately did not mention Emory Evans.

At a point, Adelaide started to feel as though she had hijacked the conversation, burying Rory's heartbreak beneath her own. She hoped he wasn't thinking the same thing, that he knew she understood how vastly different their hardships had been.

Anyway, she said. *What brought you comfort, after it happened?*

My brothers, he said. *And my brothers' mates at school, who didn't really question why this eleven-year-old started living in their halls one day. My auntie Helen, Trevor's wife. Oh, and my other orphan friends. Harry Potter and Oliver Twist, old chums.*

Adelaide laughed a little. She kissed his cheek again, used her lip to gently trace his jawline.

I don't know if this is the right thing to say, she said. *But I'm glad I get to know you.*

I'm glad to know you, too, Adelaide, he said.

What she next thought—and absolutely did not say—was, *I love you.*

Adelaide had not fallen in love slowly, or carefully, or with intention. She had fallen in love the same way one slips at the grocery store, despite the CAUTION: WET signs lining any given aisle—quickly, accidentally, and fully aware of the mess into which she was getting herself. But it didn't matter. She'd loved Rory Hughes instantly and with a fervor that was all-encompassing, reality-altering, seemingly nonsensical. There was something so ineffably special about him. She never wanted anything, or anyone, to hurt him again. Ever.

Adelaide didn't utter a word of this aloud, though. She just asked to borrow his toothpaste and a dry T-shirt. She went to sleep, thinking, *Am I lucky or unlucky to have fallen in love with this person?* She would never really know the answer.

Adelaide woke up on Rory's floor, feeling sweaty and dehydrated. She was wearing a large Garfield shirt and underwear, no shorts. She reached for her bag and grabbed a Tic Tac, took a sip from her water bottle. Rory was stretched out in the middle of his bed—one pillow beneath his head, the other on the floor with Adelaide. She wasn't sure how she'd ended up there, but she lay back down, drowsily reading on her phone and waiting for Rory to wake up.

She dozed off, woke up again a few hours later as Rory stepped over her legs. He leaned down to kiss her forehead.

Morning, you, he said. *Sorry about the floor. You were thrashing around quite a bit in your sleep. I thought we'd both sleep better if I tucked you down here.*

He left the room and came back with two cups of tea. He handed one to Adelaide and joined her on the floor. They leaned against the edge of his bed and drank their tea, silent, listening to the birds chirp outside of Rory's window. It started to rain again.

It's supposed to rain all week, he said. *London summer, innit?*

Adelaide was too hungover to think through what she said next.

I, um, got an offer for a free holiday for two in Mallorca, she said. *If you, like, want a vacation.*

You what? he asked.

An old client needs someone to write about a boutique hotel in Palma, she said. *They offered to send me, plus a guest, to the island in exchange for copy. All expenses paid.*

Are you asking me to go on holiday with you?

I guess so, yeah, she said. *But I can find another random Englishman to take, if you'd rather not.*

Rory cracked his neck, smiled sheepishly.

Before

New York City and London, England
2015–2016

Nine

At twenty-two years old, Adelaide Williams was a disaster.

Not at a glance. At a glance, she was, arguably, very put together. Her hair straightened, her eyes lined, her shirtdresses perfectly pressed and business cards crisp in her faux-leather wallet. But look long enough and you'd find the dark circles beneath her eyes, the makeup-stained tissues in her coat pockets, the loose bottle of Xanax in her purse. (She'd often borrowed pills from her mom or sister before getting a prescription of her own in college. Bless that Xanax.)

She was sitting cross-legged on the office floor—laptop perched on the coffee table in front of her—half wanting the day to end, half wishing the hours might stretch on. None of this was out of the ordinary for a Thursday evening.

There are two things to know about E&S, her then-account director, Sam, had explained months earlier (just after Adelaide hit her first vomiting-and-sobbing-in-the-office-bathroom low). *There is always more work to do,* Sam said. *And there is always tomorrow.*

It was true. Though, for the first time in months, Adelaide wasn't wishing for more hours to wrap up her to-do list. She was just tired and cranky and in no mood for the date she'd scheduled that night. It was her first real date in six-plus years; her first real date since Emory Evans. And honestly? She was incredibly fucking scared.

Adelaide had made it through college remarkably unscathed. She'd lived alone with a fluffy, fostered cat named Peaches and avoided men, sex, and booze at all costs. (Okay, *Sure,* there was that night senior year when she was carted out of a frat party on a gurney. But by and large!) Then she'd studied abroad in London, moved to France, moved to Brooklyn. Somewhere along the way, she'd started to shed her Goody Two-shoes, Sandra Dee mentality and began to transform into leather-pants-wearing, cigarette-smoking Sandy. Though she'd yet to call anyone "stud."

Aside from telling the occasional stranger he looked like a Disney prince, Adelaide had seldom interacted with boys—any boys—since high school. She was still terrified of men, and of sex. But lately, that fear had started giving way to curiosity.

I'm considering downloading a dating app, she told Eloise one night, takeout containers spread across her bed.

Adelaide Williams on a dating app? Eloise said. She took a bite of lo mein. *Are you having a stroke?*

She was not, no.

It's just, Adelaide said. *I look at you and Nico. And I look at my colleagues getting ready for dates on Friday nights. And I don't know. I think maybe I can do that, too?*

Eloise cocked her head to the side. She lived by Lincoln Center, an hour or so from Adelaide's studio in Clinton Hill. They'd gone to different colleges—Eloise had attended the University of Florida, Adelaide moved up the eastern seaboard to go to Boston University—but they'd never lost touch, never lost their connection. Now, Eloise was preparing to start her first year of law school at Fordham and six years into a relationship with a boy named Nico.

They'd been dating since senior year of high school—almost as long as she and Adelaide had been friends. Originally from Mykonos, Nico had been a foreign exchange student; his host family in Georgia lived just next door to Eloise. He had a perpetual suntan, tortoiseshell glasses, and the capacity to read coffee grounds, which Adelaide made him do each time they saw each other. (*Be careful,* he'd said last time. *Boys are going to be trouble for you these next few years!*) Nico was superstitious, a firm believer in love at first sight—he'd told Eloise he planned to marry her at senior prom. Adelaide never doubted he would follow through.

Anyway.

Adelaide downloaded a dating app that night, swiped through her prospects, struck up a conversation with someone named Tyler. He lived in Park Slope, worked in advertising, and, *No, it's nothing like* Mad Men, he told her. He asked Adelaide if she wanted to grab drinks next Thursday; she agreed.

It was now six thirty, they'd be meeting at eight.

Want to do me a favor? she texted Eloise.

Always, Eloise replied instantly.

Want to come with me on my date tonight?

Was she serious? Eloise asked. Completely, she said. You and Nico can sit at a nearby table and then, when my date inevitably implodes 30 minutes in, we can all grab a late dinner together. Yeah?

All right, Eloise said. It's a deal. Lucky Strike at 8, right?

Lucky Strike at 8.

Adelaide finished work, applied a fresh coat of mascara, headed to Lucky Strike.

Her date, Tyler, was impossibly tall, with blue eyes and blond hair and an accent that suggested he was Not from around here, huh? (He was not.) He'd grown up in Peachtree City, not far from Atlanta, not far from Adelaide. He asked for her drink order, pulled out her chair—something about him felt both familiar and foreign, like landing on the tarmac in a new city or tasting your grandmother's cobbler at a swanky, modern restaurant. It was comforting and jarring all at once.

He is insanely cute, Eloise texted. Please don't let this implode in 30 minutes. Adelaide smiled.

The evening was like something out of a romantic spy comedy, she thought—Adelaide could feel them being watched. Not just by Eloise and Nico; by the bartender, their server, the couple to their right. Tyler had a magnetic energy, drawing everyone around him an inch or two closer. She could physically sense it.

They ordered fries and mayonnaise and second drinks. His friend was working at a dive bar up the street, he said, and *I'm sure he can get us free drinks, if you'd like another?* Adelaide did indeed.

She winked at Eloise and Nico as they left, and the moon was bright and beaming, and *My gosh,* the evening felt like a dream.

You're very tall, Adelaide said. *Do you ever walk into doorways?*
You don't get out much, do you?

Tyler's bartending pal poured shots of bourbon, on the house, because he could. Adelaide spilled half of the shot down her dress, because she was Adelaide. Though, something about this appealed to Tyler? He wrapped his arms around her lower back, laughing the way people only do after a couple of drinks, whispering, *I can't wait to get you out of that dress later* in her ear.

Slow down, cowboy, she whispered back. Her skin felt hot; Tyler bit his fist.

May I kiss you, Adelaide? he asked. She said he may. He tasted like honey and bourbon; his stubble tickled her chin. She could feel more eyes on them, but she didn't really care—his magnetism had pulled her all the way in. Tyler paused, bit her bottom lip. *Shall I grab us a cab?*

Oh no, Adelaide said. *I'm just going to take the C train home.*

Are you sure you have to take the C train home? Yes, she said. (Adelaide was still a bit wary of sex, but even more than that, she wanted to get a decent night's sleep and show up at the office in fresh clothes tomorrow morning. Besides, she was wearing wildly unattractive underwear.)

Can I see you tomorrow? he asked.

I suppose we can arrange that, she said.

Adelaide couldn't help but feel giddy as she ran through the details with Eloise via text message that night, then again with Sam on their way to a client meeting the next afternoon. They talked about where she and Tyler planned to go, what she planned to wear, the smooth-as-molasses sound of his voice.

She met him at the Ship on Lafayette Street at seven o'clock sharp. It was dark, crowded. Their knees bumped together beneath the table; he smiled in a way that made her cheeks flush.

What's that smile about? she asked him.

Just thinking, he said. He took Adelaide's hand, kissed the inside of her palm. *I'm thinking about everything I'd like to do to you right now.*

(My goodness.)

They wound their way through SoHo and Alphabet City, up to Mr.

Purple for cocktails and back down to Katz's Delicatessen for sandwiches. They hailed a cab and ate in the backseat, licking Russian dressing from their fingers as they crossed the Manhattan Bridge. *To Lefferts Place and Grand Avenue,* Adelaide said. To her building. Her front door. Her bed.

Sex felt different when you were in control, she thought. When you weren't a seventeen-year-old wearing polka-dot pajama shorts and teeming with guilt and fear. Adelaide liked the feeling of Tyler's hands on her body, in her hair. She liked the way he asked, *Is this okay?* or *Does that feel good?* Yes. For the first time ever, the answer was yes.

The next day and a half felt good, too. They ate bagels in bed, wandered through the city, held hands on subway platforms. He told Adelaide that *Indiana Jones* was his favorite movie, that he loved Audre Lorde's poetry, that he hadn't learned to ride a bike until he was fifteen years old. (Adelaide had yet to learn herself.) He liked scallion cream cheese and spontaneous karaoke nights—"Rocket Man" was his go-to song, he said.

Adelaide didn't want a boyfriend, nor did she really have time for one. But she wanted *Him,* wanted attention, wanted Tyler. On snow days and Sundays and always. And with the grains of salt with which statements like this must be taken, she was all but certain she was falling in love with this handsome stranger.

He went home on Sunday afternoon, returning to his apartment in Park Slope.

Let me know when you get home safe, Adelaide said.

Of course, he said. (He did not.)

Tyler turned into Samson, into Davy, into Jess. Sometimes the flings would last a night, other times they'd stretch on for a week or two. Three tops. They were always finite, always ended in disappointment and disappearances. In teary phone calls to Eloise, the words, *Of course you're not broken, baby girl. Put on your comfiest sweatpants. I'm coming over with tissues and wine and ice cream in thirty.*

Her colleagues and friends got flower deliveries, proposals, wedding bands. Adelaide, repeatedly, got ghosted.

It stung at first, Tyler in particular. But soon enough, the sting went numb, and so did Adelaide. She stopped giving men her last name or her real name (*Just call me Andy,* she'd say); stopped telling them stories from her childhood or her work week. She stopped asking about their favorite films and bagel orders. About what their friends were like. Adelaide learned to vanish before they could, to slip out of their apartments and flats in the dead of night before they'd even notice she was gone. She learned to beat them to the punch.

She redrew her boundaries—no hand-holding, no cuddling, no pillow talk. Just silly dates, superficial conversations, and sex. And it worked, until.

Until, two years later, when Adelaide met that Disney prince again: Rory Hughes. (And suddenly, insatiably, she craved commitment like candy.)

Ten

Back across the Atlantic, Rory and Nathalie were stepping off the plane in Ireland.

For nearly five years—through uni, through law exams, through moves to London and job interviews and holidays spent on the Amalfi Coast—Rory and Nathalie had been by each other's side. There were the nights they stayed up until five in the morning at garden parties and balls like Downing's, donning fancy dress and boating down the river as the sun came up. The days they soaked each other in Tesco cava brut after sitting their final exams (Nathalie finished with a first, Rory with a two-one—he was always a little bitter about that). There were the autumnal afternoons they spent wandering through Battersea Park or along the South Bank, subconsciously memorizing each other's scents, the patterns of their palms, the various crinkles in their eyes and smiles. They took Polaroids together, collected postcards, traded books.

And now, Rory was bringing Nathalie to Galway.

He introduced her to his grandparents, his extended aunts and uncles; they gave his brothers big hugs. She'd brought cookies and English lavender and they all loved her instantly, wrapping her up in their mismatched, Irish Catholic family. *I adore it here,* she told Rory.

I adore seeing you here, he said. *With every other living person I love.*

They sat on a grassy knoll, passing a bottle of Jameson back and forth. They looked out at the water, the vine-covered Menlo Castle.

Do you think we'll get married someday? Nathalie asked. The whiskey was warming her body, clouding her mind and usual filter.

I do, Rory said. He plucked a daisy, tied its stem around her ring finger. *Right there,* he said. He pointed to the castle. *I'm going to marry you right there one day, Nat Alban. I promise.*

She kissed him, looked at the flower on her finger. She imagined herself in a white lace dress, walking down the aisle to Rory on her father's arm, holding a bouquet of sunflowers and daisies just like this one. Maybe "Wild Horses" by the Rolling Stones would play. Maybe he'd cry when he saw her in a wedding dress. Maybe they'd have children—two girls and a boy—and an Irish hound named Winston. Their life could be full, their home happy.

Years later, it would take every ounce of self-restraint Rory had to keep from imagining this moment, from imagining what could have been. If. *If, if, if . . . It doesn't make sense . . .*

There was also the time Rory forgot Nathalie's birthday, then screamed at her when her colleague Joseph baked her a cake from scratch. (*It's his hobby,* Nathalie said. *Baking is his hobby. And if you're that bloody jealous, maybe you should have baked me a cake yourself!*) The night she phoned while he was on holiday in Lisbon, and it sounded like there were an awful lot of women giggling in the background. There were the days he'd go silent, ignoring Nathalie's messages for no reason in particular, just because he was busy and a lawyer and he could.

Out of school, Nathalie had landed her dream job at *The Times* almost instantly, quickly working her way from staff writer to associate editor to editor. Rory, however, had accepted a role at a soul-crushing corporate law firm by Tottenham Court Road where he often felt stuck. Stagnant. He was overwhelmingly jealous of Nathalie's love for her job, of her capacity to climb the ranks.

You know, she'd say, *you could do something you're passionate about as well, if you wanted to.* He rolled his eyes.

She suggested he see a counselor, and *Fuck, Nat, can you just give me a minute to figure out how I'm feeling before you tell me what to do?* She encouraged him to try pro bono work—to go to the States, to travel, to give film school a try. She then agreed, begrudgingly, when Rory chose to spend a full year swiping through Tinder in Birmingham, Alabama, and *Maybe it's best if we take a break for a little bit? Just while I'm in America.*

He left for the States six months after their trip to Galway, six months after he'd promised to marry her at Menlo Castle. Nathalie trusted that he'd come back, that he'd return to their relationship and her bedroom and their cozy postgraduate life in London. They were like magnets, after all. Drawn to one another, unable to stay apart for too long. (Weren't they?)

Rory returned on a drizzly afternoon in June of 2016. His bags were heavy, his body and mind jet lagged. Nathalie had offered to meet him at Heathrow, but *That's all right,* he'd told her. *I'd rather head to my brother's, take a shower, rest up a bit before we see each other.* He texted her when he landed, then failed to reply for another thirty-six hours. Sorry about the delay, he said, finally. Just readjusting to the climate and time zone this end.

It's fine, she said. It was always fine. Want to come over this afternoon? I've just got a new cafetiere, happy to brew some coffee.

Maybe tomorrow, he said.

The next day they'd meet; the next day they'd slink back into the same pattern they'd been in for so many years. Rory would tell Nathalie about his favorite little barbecue joint in Birmingham and the time he got chased out of a trailer park by stray dogs, warding them off with his jean jacket like a makeshift matador. Nathalie would make them coffee from her new cafetiere, show Rory the tattoo she got while he was gone: Magritte's pipe on her forearm, the words *"Ceci n'est pas une pipe"* just beneath.

How surreal, he said, arching an eyebrow. Nathalie rolled her eyes, knocked his elbow with her hand. *Enough, you,* she said. *It's just a reminder, really. Words, images, beings. Nothing is ever as simple as it appears.* He nodded, took a sip of coffee.

A week or so later, Rory dragged a giant suitcase into Nathalie's studio flat—temporarily moving in, feeling every bit like a derelict. Nathalie would make dinner, cover rent. Sometimes, she'd ask him to do the dishes or take out the trash. It made him feel like a child doing chores.

Eventually, he found a new place to live, a new job—producing indie films with a small studio, finally getting to do the thing that he loved. He thought it would solve the problem, that it would resolve the ache in his heart. But it didn't. *It's just,* he'd tell his brothers, his flatmates. *It's like something is missing. Something I can't put my finger on.* They'd shrug their shoulders, unsure what to tell him. Rory seemed to have it all.

Nathalie could sense it, too—the schism between them widening, just as it had when Rory went to Alabama. She wanted it to feel like uni again, like late nights and early mornings and pots of tea shared in their shitty student kitchen. Instead, their time together felt increasingly empty, increasingly quiet. They were comfortable with each other—now and always—but things didn't feel as easy as they once had. Their conversation was forced, their rapport stilted.

Perhaps they just weren't right together anymore, Rory began to think. The stars were misaligned. He started to cancel plans, to ignore messages. When Nathalie showed up at his flat with tea and scones and advance copies of hardcover books she'd snagged from work, he felt frustration instead of gratitude. *Can you just give me a week to myself, Nat?* he asked.

Of course, she said. *Of course. Blimey, I'm sorry for disturbing your solitude, Rory.*

Don't be like that, he said.

Like what? she countered. *Act like you don't appreciate any of the sodding effort I put in?*

I don't want to fight, he said.

You don't seem to want to do much of anything lately.

They went a week without talking, then slipped back into each other's lives, beneath one another's duvets, just like their school days. Things felt normal again, their chatter resumed. But Rory couldn't shake the feeling that something was amiss.

He wanted to love his life, specifically his life with Nat, but something just didn't fit. There was an enigmatic piece missing from this puzzle, he thought. And when she asked if he might want to look for a one-bedroom flat together in Waterloo when her lease was up, one afternoon in April— *Something with a full-sized refrigerator,* she said. *And a proper door on the bedroom. And a fireplace, maybe!*—he, well. He didn't say *No,* exactly. But he didn't say yes, either. Rory just nodded his head, made a sound like *Mhm*, asked if she wanted a cup of tea to change the subject.

Earl Grey, please, Nathalie said. Rory turned on the kettle.

Work was crazy. *Really,* he said. *It's mad.* That was why he wasn't much help in the flat search, why he turned down Nat's invitations to view this place off of Addington Street and that maisonette down Chaplin Close. She dutifully toured each location on her own, sending pictures and videos via WhatsApp, never questioning why Rory seemed so unenthused by floor-to-ceiling windows or the promise of a built-in washer *and* dryer (!). Then one evening, she interrupted his post-work drinks with a phone call declaring she'd found *The perfect place* in Marigold Alley.

It's got a view of the river and hardwood floors, she told him, speaking quickly at the other end of the line. *No fireplace, sadly. But it's got built-in bookshelves and all new furnishings and it's gorgeous. And an absolute steal, Rory! Did you watch the video I sent?* (He hadn't, no.) *Watch it when you have a second and let me know if I should put an offer in. I don't want us to miss out on this.*

Rory watched the video, as instructed, with one hand on his pint. Nathalie was right (of course she was): The flat was stunning, brilliantly located, and—at sixteen hundred pounds a month—such a bargain it was almost too good to be true. Instead of feeling excited or fortunate, though, Rory felt a pit forming in his stomach. An emptiness rather than fulfillment. It wasn't that he didn't want to say yes, it was just . . . He didn't know what. This was what he was meant to do, right? (So, why didn't he feel how he was meant to feel?)

He took a sip of his drink, then another. Go ahead, he texted. Make an offer. Let's do it.

Hooray! she replied. I'll let you know how it goes!

Their offer was accepted in under an hour, and Nathalie greeted Rory with hugs and squeals and a bubbling bottle of prosecco when he got to her place that night.

Cheers to a new home and a new chapter, she said. He clinked his glass to hers, forced a smile. He didn't say a word.

Is it possible to go month-to-month? Rory asked. It was the first sunny day they'd had in ages, light pouring through the windows of the estate agent's office in central London. The sunshine was making Rory feel overly warm; he tugged uncomfortably at his collar.

I'm afraid not, the estate agent said. *The minimum lease is twelve months. Will that be an issue for you two?*

Nathalie looked at Rory—she was trying to read his expression, to understand why he'd even asked that question. She turned back to the agent. *Twelve months should be fine,* she said. *But, I've just remembered something. Nothing to worry about, but do you mind if we step out for a moment?*

Not at all, the agent said. *In fact, I'll step out and leave you to it. Can I offer either of you a drink while I'm up?* Nathalie said, *No thank you* at the exact moment Rory said, *Water, please.* The agent chuckled, nodded. He stepped into the hallway and shut his office door.

Are you having second thoughts, love? Nathalie asked, looking at Rory. She was trying to sound sensitive, to sound understanding. *Of course not,* he said. He didn't make eye contact. *It's just, what if I were to start a new job? Or you start a new job? What if one of us is offered something incredible in, I don't know, Liverpool or somewhere?*

Are you thinking of moving to Liverpool?

No, he told her, exasperated. It was just—*It's of no import, I just wanted to check. I was a lawyer, wasn't I? I want to understand all of the options, find all of the loopholes.*

Right, Nathalie said. Right. (But why he was looking for loopholes at all?)

The agent returned a moment later, handing Rory a paper cup of ice water. Rory downed it in one sip; the cold made his head pound. *Well,* he said, picking up a pen. *Shall we?*

They went through all of the normal, exhausting motions of moving: Snagging cardboard boxes from Tesco, wrapping crockery in old newspaper, wondering if the chipped glasses they'd stolen from the Butterfield at uni were worth keeping. (Yes, Nathalie decided. *Absolutely.*) She stuffed her abundance of striped T-shirts and floral dresses and distressed jean jackets into duffel bag upon duffel bag; Rory was able to squeeze all of the belongings from his own flat into a single (albeit slightly oversized) suitcase.

Nathalie had a last-minute book event come up on the Saturday they were meant to move in, but *You'll be able to meet the movers, right, love?* Rory nodded. *Of course,* he said.

Great, she said. *I'll meet you at the new flat around one-ish.*

Her alarm went off at eight o'clock that morning; she was out the door by nine. Rory hit snooze once. Then again. Then a third time. And sometime around noon—when the movers started buzzing Nathalie's flat—he quickly shifted from drowsy to panicked.

He loved Nat, honestly. *You're the best,* he'd tell her. And he meant it. They'd just been together for so long (so long!). Shouldn't he know by now if she was the woman with whom he was meant to spend his life? The person with whom he was meant to build a home? *Wouldn't I know by now?* he asked himself.

Rory buzzed the movers in, opened the door, offered them glasses of water (which they politely declined).

There's been a bit of a change of plans, he told them, handing one of the movers his shiny new keys, heart pounding. *I have a work emergency. But feel free to take everything over to the new place. My girlfriend, Nathalie, will meet you there at one or so.*

The movers nodded, only mildly confused, and began to load up the van. Rory lugged his too-big suitcase down the carpeted stairs of Nathalie's building—*I'll take this one over myself,* he told them—and hailed the first black cab he saw.

To SW4 0AA in Clapham, he told the driver (his brother's postcode). *Please.*

Please, please, please. Anywhere but Marigold Alley; anywhere but toward his future with Nat.

L et the record show: Nathalie Alban was not a fool. She could feel Rory had grown distant again, could see he'd become particularly quiet during conversations about the future. He wasn't cheating on her, surely—*Rory would never,* she'd tell her friends—but something was off, this much she knew.

She just never expected this.

She never expected to arrive at the flat they'd leased together—its floors freshly polished, boxes stacked in the corner, river sparkling through the windowpanes—without Rory Hughes there to greet her. Had he gone out to grab groceries, maybe? Or toilet paper? Was he planning to surprise her with flowers and a bottle of wine, with a toast to their new home together?

No, she thought. Something in her gut told her no.

The movers were nearly done unloading boxes at this point; she tapped one on the elbow. *Excuse me,* she said. *I'm so sorry, it's just, did you see my boyfriend, Rory, earlier? I can't figure out where he's gone.*

Work emergency, I think he said, the mover mumbled. *He didn't tell you?*

No, Nathalie said. *But, but thank you for letting me know!*

She tipped the movers and thanked them again and wrinkled her brow, perplexed. A work emergency? On a Saturday? At a production company that was, at the moment, not shooting any films?

Nathalie only called him once. *Okay,* twice. It rang both times, eventually going to the voicemail she knew he never checked. She left a message at the beep anyway. *Hey,* she said. *It's me. I'm at the new flat now, and all of our stuff is here. Just wondering where you are?*

She sent the same message in a text, then followed up an hour later with a few more frantic question marks. No response. *Is he okay?* she wondered. *Did something happen?*

At five o'clock, she called his brother Daniel, who—fortunately—picked up immediately.

I'm so sorry to bother you, Daniel, she said. *It's just . . . have you seen Rory? He was meant to meet me at our new flat ages ago and I've not heard from him and I'm starting to get a little panicked and do you know where he is, or . . . ?*

Oh hey, Nat, Daniel said, trying to sound casual. *How are ya? Rory's with me, yeah. Got a bad migraine,* he said. *I'm sorry for not texting you to let you know sooner. He's just asleep now, but I'll have him—*

Call me when he wakes up? Nat interjected, heat rising in her chest. *Yup, great. Thanks, Dan.*

A work emergency. A migraine. No call, no text, no apology. What the hell was going on?

Nathalie walked through the flat, running her hands along the crisp leather of the sofas, the marble countertops in the kitchen, the plastic coating their new, undressed mattress. She sat down on the bed; the plastic made a squeaking sound beneath her. She placed her head in her hands and cried.

It wasn't meant to feel like this, was it?

A few days later, they made plans to meet at a pub by King's Cross station. Rory had all but vanished that week, and he owed Nathalie an explanation, she said. (Demanded, really.) It's been five fucking years, Rory, she texted him. We signed a lease together. You can't just ghost me like some stranger on Tinder.

Nathalie arrived early, grabbing a high-top table in the corner. They'd visited this pub a dozen or so times. It was the spot at which they'd book-ended trips to London while still studying at Cambridge, the place where they'd shared bottles of wine and pitchers of Pimm's and sloshy pints of lager before or after their train ride. *One day,* they'd say, conspiratorially. *One day, we'll live here. In London. Together.*

She ordered a glass of the house red and tried to push those moments from her mind. She was mad. She was confused. She was hurt and disappointed and a little bit scared. And she didn't want to forget that when she saw Rory Hughes—Nathalie wanted to remind him, for once (for once!), that his actions had consequences. That his aloof behavior could cause pain.

Rory walked in fifteen minutes later, wearing a jean jacket and sunglasses and looking so frustratingly handsome Nathalie bit her lip.

Hi, he said.

Hi, Nathalie said. Tears were already, annoyingly, prickling at her eyes.

The thing is, he could have stopped it all then. He could have wrapped his arms around Nat and begged for forgiveness and promised to show her the kindness she deserved. He could have worked to regain her trust—they both knew it.

But instead, he let it all fall apart.

Rory placed his hands on the table. *I'm sorry, Nat,* he said. *I just, I don't think we should move in together. It doesn't feel right anymore. This. It just. Nothing feels right anymore.*

Nathalie hardly even processed what was happening, she just burst into tears.

You promised me, she said. She stood up and placed her hands on his shoulders—half clinging to him, half pounding his chest. Her tears soaked through his shirt; the mascara left black marks. *This was supposed to be a forever thing. I've done everything right, haven't I? Everything.* She thought of their trip to Galway, the daisy he tied around her ring finger. *You promised.*

I broke it, he said, trying to hold her, his own eyes welling up. *All of it. I'm so sorry I broke my promise. I just can't do this. I can't.*

Summer

London, England
2018

Eleven

Their trip was booked for the third week of July.

Adelaide flew into Palma on an early-morning flight, about ten hours before Rory. She didn't go into Alliance on Fridays and planned to work on her dissertation from the balcony of their suite. Instead, she opened a complimentary bottle of Veuve Clicquot, stretched out on a lounge chair, and single-handedly ate a cheese plate for four.

Just landed, Rory texted around 9:00 P.M. Very hungry. Anything good on the room service menu?

Would you be horrified if I showed up with MacDo?

Definitely getting airport MacDo. Text me in the next few minutes if you want anything.

All right, heading to the hotel now. Hoping you're there and just away from your phone?

Rory was shown to their room thirty minutes later. When he walked in, Adelaide was splayed across the sofa in her swimsuit, snoring. There was an empty bottle of Veuve on the end table, a well-worn copy of *A Room of One's Own* fanned open on her chest. He laughed to himself.

Adelaide? he said, ruffling her hair a bit. *Adelaide, it's Rory. Wake up, you.*

He spoke quietly, gently, but it startled Adelaide. She jumped up. (This was not how she'd planned to greet him, but she was a bit too tipsy to care.)

Hi hello welcome to Mallorca! she said. *There is so much sun here!*

I can tell, he said. He chuckled, wrapped his arms around her waist. *You look quite bronzed, and incredibly good. And like you've been enjoying the champagne?*

She had, yes. Adelaide popped open a second bottle—the cork flying across the room—and poured Rory a glass. *Salud,* he said.

A delaide woke up at six the next morning and snuck to the bathroom to brush the soured champagne taste from her mouth. She undid the two braids in her hair, twisted the ends with her straightener, dabbed concealer over the dark circles beneath her eyes. She crawled back into bed and shifted closer to Rory, curling her body around his. He still smelled of fresh laundry and pine trees. Even here—even in this foreign, sun-drenched country in late July—he felt like Christmas morning to Adelaide.

Your hair is all curly, Rory said, running his fingers through her waves a few hours later.

Mhm, she said. *This is my humid holiday hair.*

Do you always travel with it? he asked. *Like in a little Dopp kit?*

She laughed and he kissed the tip of her nose. It wasn't a great joke, but it made Adelaide smile. She wrote it down in her notebook that morning, next to details of the hotel's bedding, the shampoo in the shower.

They ate breakfast—eggs Florentine drenched in hollandaise sauce, Sóller oranges, ensaïmada, and cappuccinos overflowing with froth and foam. (Rory said the spread was *Fit for a king.* Adelaide folded her napkin into a tiny paper crown and placed it on his head. *To match the occasion,* she said.) Rory asked their server how he recommended they spend the day; the man suggested they stroll down to the dock—maybe try Jet Skiing or go for a sunset sail. There were plenty of local skippers who could take them out on the water, he explained. She wrote this down as well.

Adelaide put on an impossibly small bikini, printed with red flowers and stuffed with padding that, deceptively, squeezed her flat chest into cleavage. (Had she gotten her first Brazilian wax the week before? She had. Had she screamed about the patriarchy throughout? Also yes.)

After they'd signed a few forms and waivers, a man who exclusively spoke Spanish took them out to a Jet Ski dock. It was about half a mile from the shore.

If I die out here, Adelaide started to say.

You're not going to die on a Jet Ski, Adelaide, Rory said.

Right, she said. *But if I did, what would you do? You should probably call my sister first. Holly, not Izzy. She's pragmatic. She can explain what happened to my parents, Holly can.*

Noted, he said. *Can we stop discussing your death now?*

She nodded. They climbed onto the Jet Ski.

Adelaide was a funny sort of feminist in that she believed, fiercely, in reversing and subverting stereotypical gender norms, but often subscribed to them herself. One night in May, for instance, she'd called Rory in a panic after finding a very large spider in the shower when Madison wasn't home to help evict it. (It did not make sense for him to come all the way out to Highgate to kill a spider, he'd explained. *I don't want you to kill it,* she'd said. *Just remove it. Please. I can thank you with ice cream and blow jobs—so many blow jobs!* He'd eventually agreed.) She was equally squeamish about driving this Jet Ski, preferring to ride behind Rory as he steered. But he insisted she try it—*Just for a few minutes,* he said—and shouted affirmations in her ear when she hopped to the front, looping them in bumpy figure-eight formations over the waves. It was equal parts charming and patronizing, she thought.

They returned the Jet Ski to its dock, jumped into the water. It was clear and warm and bright blue, like topaz. Practically iridescent in the summer light. Adelaide unclipped her life vest and stretched out on the surface of the ocean. Rory kept his on—he bobbed up and down like a lobster buoy, grinning in the sunshine, tethered to traps Adelaide couldn't yet see.

I love it here, he said. She hummed in agreement.

Dinner that night was her favorite.

They went to a tapas bar Adelaide's colleague Djibril had recommended, with high-backed chairs and saffron-infused cocktails. It was ritzy, sophisticated; Rory and Adelaide were in no such mood. They ordered stacks of small plates; licked brava sauce from their fingers; bought shots of aguardiente, the local grappa, for themselves and the waitstaff. (The first round was on Adelaide, the second complimentary.) Rory spoke in a faux-Southern drawl throughout dessert, which included chocolate mousse and churros and crema catalana. It all made her stomach ache—the food, the grappa, the silliness and laughter. She adored it.

After paying the check, they decided to have a dance party in their hotel room, just the two of them. Adelaide flailed rhythmically and did the Charleston; Rory wiggled his hips and arms from side to side in opposite directions (*You're flossing!* she said excitedly). They played the Spice Girls and sang aloud to "Wannabe." He picked her up and spun her around, the skirt of her black dress flaring out like a ballerina's in a music box. It made her feel a bit nauseous, but also deeply, deeply in love. She pressed her mouth to his, parting his lips with her tongue, tasting liquor and chocolate and a hint, she thought, of salt water. She wrote this in her notebook as well: How he tasted. Bitter, sweet, salty; delicious and acerbic.

Around midnight, Adelaide shimmied out of her dress, a bit embarrassed by the bloated puff of her belly. She put on a tank top that read THE FUTURE IS FEMALE and cotton shorts. Rory pointed to her shirt as she got into bed. *Good luck with that,* he said. *We've made quite a mess of things.* She rolled her eyes, playfully held up a middle finger.

They fell asleep watching reruns of *RuPaul's Drag Race* on Adelaide's laptop, her head tucked into the crook of his neck. She dreamt about Rory Hughes that night, sleeping in his freckled arms.

R ory suggested they go to an art museum. *Just for a bit of culture,* he said over breakfast. *We can look at, like, one or two arts each. We just have to choose wisely.* Adelaide giggled; she liked that idea.

They chose Es Baluard, a contemporary art museum not far from the hotel. The rooms were eclectic, filled with sweeping light fixtures, metal sculptures, paintings by Miró and Braque. Rory pointed to a ceramic plate. It had a face painted on it in black and green, a work of Picasso.

I think I'd like this to be one of my arts, he said.

To make a dove, Adelaide said, *you must first wring its neck.*

What the fuck? he asked.

Picasso said that, she said. *Pretty fucked-up guy.*

Adelaide found a few photographs by Diana Coca, self-portraits almost. The plaque beneath the black-and-white prints explained that, *Through narrative sequences, we find her semi-nude, fragmented body conceived as object and subject at the same time, as she uses herself as the territory for experimentation and subversion, with the desire of transforming the tension of what is concealed . . .*

These, she said. *I would like these to be my arts, please.*

There was a terrace atop the museum, overlooking the Mediterranean. It had a bar, where they drank cloudy lemonade, and a vacant rooftop, with the little stone turrets of a fortress peeking out at the sea. (Adelaide and Rory fucked in one, of course they did. He finished on her tongue.) She adjusted her sundress; they left the museum.

Can we stop in here? Adelaide asked, gesturing toward La Seu, the cathedral. It was enormous, Gothic—the kind of cathedral that exists all over Europe and is yet, somehow, remarkable. One-of-a-kind.

Are you sure we're allowed to go in? Rory asked.

What? she said. *With cum in my mouth? I think God's less bothered by sex than we all like to think She is. But if I burst into flames, remember: Call Holly first.* He nodded again, chuckled.

They shuffled inside between services, following other tourists stopping for photographs, abuelas stopping for afternoon prayers. They sat down in a pew and Adelaide looked up, straight up, at the ceiling. It was supported by slender pillars, like the tendrils of a melon or a spider's legs, and light cut through the stained glass at every angle, soaking the space in rainbow-colored light. She wasn't a particularly religious person, but there was such magic in houses of God, she thought.

Are you familiar with the aesthetic argument? Rory whispered.

Maybe, she said. *Plato?*

Plato, yes, he said. *And, more recently, an English scholar named Richard Swinburne. I saw him give a lecture once.*

It was the notion that God speaks through beauty, Rory explained. That beauty itself, be it natural or artificial, was evidence of a higher power, of a transcendent plane past our own. Symphonies and watercolors. Seascapes and starry skies. The laws of physics. Churches. Mosques.

They were all proof of something larger, something spectacular. It was its own form of religion, really.

I think that's what does it for me, Adelaide said, still looking up. *What gives me faith—the beauty of it all.* She believed in this: In beauty and grace and enchantment. In something bigger than herself. She looked at Rory—his bright eyes, the squiggly shape of his chin, the curl that hung just above his forehead. Sitting just next to her, all by design. She kissed his cheek. (Rory was strictly atheist, but he said he liked the thought.)

Adelaide left a few euro coins in the donation box as they were leaving, lit a votive candle.

May I ask who the candle's for? Rory said.

No one in particular, she said. *I just always like to light them in these big churches. As a thank-you.*

It was the last time he'd step into a church. Until.

T hey were sitting in front of McDonald's, waiting for their gate to be announced. Adelaide had ordered a Big Mac—no meat, no pickles. She stuffed French fries between the layers of bread and Mac sauce. (*I call it a fryburger,* she'd told Rory. *I think, in your country, it's called a chippy bun.* He looked fascinated, a little horrified.)

Are you happy you came? Adelaide asked. He thought for a beat before answering, which made her stomach churn.

I am, yeah, he said. *Are you glad I came?*

Very much, she said. *Though, I would have come with or without you, really.* She'd intended for those words to seem nonchalant, but they sounded cruel out loud.

Cheers, mate.

But really, she said. *Thank you so much for coming. I've had the best time.* She squeezed his hand across the table.

Their fingers stayed braided together as they walked to the gate, boarded the plane, took their seats in the very last row. They listened to Stephen Fry reading *Harry Potter and the Prisoner of Azkaban* throughout the flight, headphones split between them, hands still glued to each other's. They didn't separate until they landed at Stansted: Rory got in the line for British citizens, Adelaide spent an hour and a half in customs with everyone else.

Snagging the last express train back to London now, he texted from the other side of the terminal. Thank you again for a lovely trip. You're a special one. xx

Adelaide took the bus back to Baker Street and a cab home on her own, drowsy and suntanned and besotted.

Twelve

Two pizzas, garlic bread, a bottle of sauvignon blanc, and some apple slices. It had become a nightly ritual.

Adelaide and Madison would wake up around 8 A.M. Celeste would come over an hour or two later. They'd sit around the dining table in Highgate with their hair in messy buns—sharing cups of coffee, blasting Ariana Grande, typing with the fervor of three caffeinated twenty-somethings running up against a deadline. Which, with two weeks and ten thousand words to go in each of their dissertations, they collectively were.

Around seven, they would order dinner—*The usual,* Celeste would tell the pizza guy. They'd continue to thumb through textbooks and click-clack on their laptops with greasy fingers, half focus, and glassy eyes until about nine. Nine was always the point at which they reached delirium, pretending to break-dance on the hardwood floors and drafting fan mail to *Ms. Grande.* (*Not fan mail,* Madison would say. *Just, like, a letter from a new pen pal. The tone should be breezy. Breezy!*) Excluding the Mondays, Wednesdays, and Thursdays she spent at Alliance, or the odd Sunday she spent freelancing, this had become Adelaide's routine for the entirety of August.

By the start of the month, all of the girls had re-signed their leases and established plans to stay in the U.K. Adelaide would be a full-time communications manager come the tenth of September—Alliance's sponsorship license was already being processed. Celeste and Madison had accepted offers to teach years one and three at elite primary schools in Notting Hill and Westminster. Completing their dissertations was the only hurdle left to jump, the only blockade that sat between these women and their shared future in London. And so, for twelve hours a day, it was the only thing on which they focused.

Adelaide's dissertation was on the communications strategies of young female entrepreneurs and influencers, on the ways in which social media was transforming the marketing landscape. As her tan lines from Mallorca faded, she'd become so absorbed in the ventures of Emily Weiss, former *Love Island* contestants, and Caroline Calloway that, for the first time in months, she hadn't even realized it had been a week since she'd heard from Rory Hughes. Not until he texted her at ten thirty one night—well past the point of delirium.

Sorry I've been M.I.A., the text read. I didn't want to worry you, but I've been in hospital a few days now. Had some internal bleeding caused by a stomach ulcer, but all is on the up and up, it seems.

Adelaide nearly choked on an apple slice. *I think Rory is dying??* she said.

What? the girls shouted. *Ohmygosh, what's going on?*

Okay, okay, she said. *Not dying. But he had internal bleeding? And an ulcer? And he's at the hospital? And I don't know why I'm saying these things like they're questions, they are not! This all really happened.*

Adelaide licked garlic salt from her fingers and began to type a reply. She could head to the hospital right now, she said, with fluffy blankets and ulcer-friendly snacks and an ancient laptop with a DVD drive in case the Wi-Fi was shoddy and he wanted to watch films the old-fashioned way. Did he need anything else? Warm sweatshirt, Yorkshire tea?

She was already packing a bag when his reply came through—That's all right, he said. I prefer a bit of solitude when I'm ill. But thank you, you're sweet. She read it aloud, deflating.

Look, Madison said. *For all we know, he's vomiting blood and shitting himself right now. I wouldn't want my girlfriend, or whatever it is you are, to see me like that, either.*

Right, Adelaide said. Right.

It was selfish, she knew, but something about this stung. Not just his craving for solitude, that she understood (particularly if he was vomiting blood). No. It was the fact that he'd been in the hospital, *For a few days now,* and this was the first Adelaide had heard of it.

Before this evening, she'd thought they had reached a new level in their relationship (or *Situationship,* as she called it). She knew Rory was squeamish about titles and formal commitments, but. But Adelaide had wiped his tears. She'd seen his drunk dance moves and squeezed his waist on a Jet Ski and slept in his arms, on his floor, a dozen times. Maybe he hadn't told anyone he was in the hospital? Or maybe, she feared, Adelaide occupied such a small space in his mind that he hadn't even thought to let her know.

I think you're spiraling, Adelaide, Celeste said. *He was probably feeling so shitty he didn't tell anyone what was going on outside of his family. He might even feel emasculated by all of this. Or he genuinely didn't want to worry you. Who knows? But try to focus on the things you can control here, you know? That's all you can do, really.*

You're right, Adelaide said. *Of course. You're right.*

She squeezed Celeste goodbye, reminding herself that what mattered right now was taking care of Rory, of her friends, of her dissertation. Not nursing a wounded ego.

A delaide went to bookshops and Waitrose and all-organic health stores after work that Thursday, collecting items that Rory might need in the hospital. She stole a plush gray hoodie from Alliance (fintech companies had the coziest swag, she'd learned) and rolled it up like a scroll, squishing it into a gift bag with probiotic snacks, calming teas, a copy of *The New Yorker.*

Dear Rory, she wrote on Pomeranian stationery (of course she had Pomeranian stationery). *Hope this little assortment of goodies helps you feel a bit better. If ever you need a pep talk or probiotics (or both!), I'm just a phone call away!*

Adelaide signed her name with an *x* and tucked the note in the gift bag, walked from Waterloo station to St. Thomas' Hospital. Her plan was to leave the bag at reception—no contact with Rory, no interruption to his solitude.

Her plan led the hospital staff to believe she was dropping off a bomb.

Oh no, Adelaide said. *It's just for a patient named Rory Hughes. I can call him now and have him come down the moment I leave?*

Why can't you give him the package yourself, madam? the receptionist asked.

Excellent question, Adelaide said. *You see, it's like, we haven't been dating for very long and I think he's pretty sick and I didn't want to disturb him or anything. I was really just hoping to—* The nurse held up a finger. She was paging Rory's room as Adelaide sputtered. Fuck.

She paced back and forth in the lobby, feeling humiliated and selfish and immeasurably awkward, when the elevator doors pinged open and Rory walked out. He looked a bit gray and disheveled—his face unshaven, his curly hair matted—but his eyes still had the gleam of a cartoon prince. Her knees wobbled a little.

Adelaide, he said. *This is a surprise.*

I am so, so sorry, she said. *I was just hoping to drop this off, but I think the receptionist thought I was here to kill you or something. Anyway, I just put together a little care package of sorts. Here. I'll leave you to it, okay?*

Wait, Rory said.

He reached for her hand. For a glimpse of a second, Adelaide thought he was going to invite her up to his room. That she would be able to curl up in a chair by his bedside—stroking his hair, kissing his temple, squeezing his hand if and when he was in pain. Instead, he asked her to sit down in the lobby for a second.

It would be rude of me to rush you off, he said (in a tone that sounded as though that was exactly what he wanted to do). *So, tell me. What are you up to this week?*

Oh, Adelaide said. *Just working on my dissertation, really. Almost done. So, so close to being done. But more importantly, how are you?* He was feeling a bit better, he explained. Would likely be out of the hospital by Sunday at the latest.

That's great news, Adelaide said. *I'm so glad to hear it. I'll let you get back to using your energy to feel better. See you soon, I hope?*

She gave him a gentle hug and walked outside, passing Rory's roommate Bubs on her way. They nodded to one another. A small corner of her brain shouted, *Solitude my ass.* She hushed the thought.

Thirteen days, nine thousand words, and a few dozen cups of coffee later, Adelaide finished her dissertation. She submitted the physical copy, dripping sweat, with just fifteen minutes to spare on the thirtieth of August. Madison's dissertation was due the next morning, so Adelaide rushed home to play copy editor until midnight, when Celeste took a cab over and the girls popped a bottle of champagne Eloise had sent via courier, blasting "Successful" by Ariana Grande (who else?) at full volume. They did it! They were, almost, officially masters.

Rory had been home a little over a week now, but Adelaide hadn't seen him since stopping by the hospital. (She'd had too many words to write, too much space to give.) They were set to celebrate the end of the school year next week—Adelaide, Madison, and Celeste, plus Rory and Anurak (a boy Madison had befriended from her program and insisted she had no interest in dating—*Stop asking, you guys!*). It would be the first time Rory properly met Adelaide's friends, as Madison was often asleep or out of town when he came by the flat. They had a running joke that she wasn't even a real person, that Adelaide was secretly, shamefully, an heiress who simply pretended to live with another girl in an attempt to mask her embarrassing wealth and status. (*You see right through me,* she'd tell Rory, laughing. *I just want to be a normal girl!*)

Tonight, though, the girls were celebrating the end of a year of exams and literature reviews on their own—toasting the start of a fresh, full-time chapter in London. And holy shit, it felt good. They sat on the floor, passing around the champagne and taking swigs straight from the bottle.

I know this is cheesy, Adelaide said. *But where do y'all think you'll be in five years? And who do you think you'll be with?*

I don't think I want to be with someone in five years, Madison said. *I want to travel, continue to see the world, do my own thing. Teach in South America or Asia, maybe. I don't want to be tethered to anyone, or anything.*

I'd like to move around, too, Celeste said. *But I feel like you can do that with a partner, you know? Those things aren't mutually exclusive. Being with someone doesn't equate to being tied down, necessarily.*

The girls nodded, took another few sips. *What about you, Adelaide?*

I really don't know, she said, looking at the ceiling.

In five years, Adelaide would be thirty, which she used to assume meant she would be married with adopted children, a house, a Cavalier King Charles spaniel named something like Fitz or Willoughby. Lately, though, Adelaide's future seemed hazy. Unknown. She could see herself living in the U.K., or in Paris, or maybe back in a brownstone in Clinton Hill (her old neighborhood in Brooklyn). She could imagine working in tech or publishing or even for a politician, spending her days drafting press releases and tightening copy for Alliance, authors, presidential candidates. She wasn't sure whether she'd keep her hair long and straight or chop it into a chic, bouncy bob. (There was also, admittedly, a small part of her that questioned whether she'd live to see thirty at all.)

The only element that was clear and distinguishable was Rory Hughes. He was guarded and noncommittal, sure, but something inside of Adelaide knew this was it. He was it. The beginning and the end; the alpha and the omega and her soul mate—she was all but sure. This was the person with whom she was meant to live her life, no matter how short that life, or her hair, might turn out to be.

She'd lost the thread of the conversation, picked it up again when Celeste mentioned the book signing they'd be attending tomorrow night. The girls had plans to huddle in the basement of Waterstones for a Q&A with Wetherly May-Lewis, one of Adelaide's favorite authors. She'd written a memoir-cum-business-book about working for Barack Obama's presidential campaigns and the power of social media; about how brands and political figures have, and continue, to utilize social networks to peddle their agendas. The girls all read it for their pseudo book club. It was cited throughout Adelaide's dissertation, and Wetherly's European tour was perfectly timed to the end of her graduate program.

Well, ladies, Adelaide said. *It is two in the morning and I need my beauty sleep before meeting Wetherly tomorrow, but I love y'all. And I hope, in five years, we're still up at all hours, sharing bottles of champagne on the floor, drinking and talking about our future together.*

Cheers to that, the girls said. *Good night.*

Adelaide Williams had a theory. Well, she had many theories, but chief among them was the belief that people entered our lives when we needed them most. The important ones tended to, at least. Celeste and Madison, Sam and Eloise.

In her mind, the same was true of books. The words of Orwell, Plath, and Louisa May Alcott had made their way onto her school syllabi she most needed to read them, of this she was certain. And Wetherly May-Lewis's *A Modern Empire*—the cherry-red book she was set to have signed this evening—had undoubtedly been recommended by her sister Holly at the perfect time. It had inspired the subject of her dissertation, reignited her passion for communications.

During the Q&A, Adelaide raised her hand—and, embarrassingly, knocked her book onto the floor—to ask Wetherly what advice she might give to young women struggling to find themselves, to find their voices and paths.

Do the thing that sets your heart on fire, Wetherly said. *For me, that thing was writing. I woke up at four each morning and wrote, for years. And this book is the product of those hours, of that dedication. Writing was what set my heart ablaze, and now I get to do that full time.* Adelaide grinned, nodding graciously. She made a mental note to write these words in her journal later.

As she shuffled into the line for Wetherly to sign her copy—she'd dressed in cherry red to match—Adelaide bumped into a stranger, knocking *A Modern Empire* onto the floor once again.

Heavens, the woman said. *I'm so sorry.* She knelt down, picked up Adelaide's book, handed it back to her. Adelaide just stared.

When she was little, Adelaide read a story about a girl in the English countryside. She couldn't remember the name of the girl, or even the name of the story, but she remembered her description perfectly. She had *A button nose, rosy cheeks, deep dimples,* with *Jet-black curls* and *A smattering of freckles beneath bright blue eyes, like two aquamarines.* Adelaide developed an intense obsession with this depiction, with this coloring. She wanted to look just like this girl.

The easiest way to describe Adelaide was "cute." Perhaps "pretty," on a good day. She was petite and thin, relatively shapeless, with long hair that vacillated between dark blond and honey brown, depending on the season. Her eyes were giant—occasionally, they'd get little green specks in them, but mostly, they were light brown. Nothing like gemstones. Her nose was just a touch too big to be described as a button, her cheeks full and squishy and undefined. Sometimes, she would get a small dimple on the left side of her face when she smiled (never on the right).

Looking at the woman who'd just picked up her book, Adelaide saw everything she wished were true of her own appearance: A proper button nose, rosy cheeks, deep dimples at either side of her smile. Jet-black curls and a smattering of freckles beneath bright blue eyes, like two aquamarines. She was wearing a striped top with a floral miniskirt and Doc Martens, a tattoo of Magritte's pipe on her forearm—*"Ceci n'est pas une pipe."* She was uniquely beautiful; cool and sexy and cute all at once. Adelaide loathed and adored her instantly.

Oh my goodness, Adelaide said. *No, I am sorry! That was completely my fault.*

Not at all, the woman said, touching Adelaide's arm. *I love your dress, by the way. Sorry again about the bump just now, have a nice evening!*

The beautiful stranger walked away, leaving Adelaide with a curious feeling. She looked down. A business card must have fallen from the woman's purse in the kerfuffle; Adelaide picked it up, turned it over in her hand. *The Times*'s logo was on one side; the woman's email address and phone number appeared on the other. They were printed just beneath the words NATHALIE ALBAN, SENIOR EDITOR, BOOKS.

Thirteen

Freshman year of high school, Adelaide walked into English class and felt drawn to the desk in front of a girl with short, curly hair and a floral headband. *I'm Adelaide,* she'd said, placing her backpack beneath the chair. The girl waved one hand. *Eloise,* she said. This was how she'd met her best friend—by way of some cosmic pull. An unspoken order from the universe.

Walking out of Waterstones, with an editor's business card and a signed copy of *A Modern Empire* (*Send me your dissertation!* Wetherly had told her, jotting down her email address), Adelaide felt a similar pull. There was something about both Wetherly and Nathalie to which Adelaide felt connected. Deeply. *It's wild,* she said, turning to Madison and Celeste. *But I feel like that was all meant to happen.*

Meeting Wetherly? Madison asked.

Yes, Adelaide said. *And that* Times *editor. Like, what if we all work together on a project someday? I don't know. Maybe I'm having delusions of grandeur, but I have this weird feeling. Like it was fate that we bumped into each other. That I read Wetherly's book in the first place.*

It wasn't that Adelaide thought these women were destined to become her new best friends, as Eloise had. But she had visions of emailing Wetherly, of grabbing coffee with Nathalie. She could imagine asking them for tips on getting into media or publishing or politics. Maybe one day, Nathalie could review a book Adelaide wrote; maybe Wetherly could blurb it. She mentally drafted emails as they headed toward the Tube, back to Highgate—*Hi there! Know your inbox must be flooded, but . . .*

A delaide could barely concentrate the next morning. She bounced her knee, chewed at the fading gel manicure on her fingernails. She hit Refresh on her personal email inbox every few minutes, bursting with anticipation. With curiosity.

She'd spent the night before reading Nathalie's pieces in *The Times*, combing through every story and review with her name on the byline. Adelaide was in awe of the precision and beauty with which Nathalie wrote, the generosity and consideration injected into each of her critiques. How had Adelaide not read her work sooner? she wondered. How had she been writing about books for over a year and never once thought to check *The Times*'s coverage? Goodness knows. But she'd seen it now, and she was absolutely absorbed.

Hi Nathalie! she'd typed. *My name's Adelaide Williams, we bumped into each other at Wetherly May-Lewis's event the other night? (Literally!) Anyway. You dropped your card and I thought I'd get in touch . . .* The note continued, explaining that Adelaide was a freelancer, that she often wrote about books as well, and *I'm sure your schedule is crazy, but is there any chance I could treat you to a coffee or a cocktail in the coming weeks and pick your brain?*

Any reply? Eloise texted around 5 P.M. London time.

Not yet, Adelaide said. Eeeek.

She went to a spin class, took the Tube home, hopped in the shower. Adelaide was in her pajamas with her head flipped upside down, wringing her tangled and too-long hair with a towel, when her phone finally *ding*ed. A new email.

Holy shit! she shouted.

What?! Madison said, popping into the doorway. *Is everything okay?*

Nathalie? Adelaide said. *That* Times *editor from the other night? She emailed me back!*

Oh my gosh, Madison said. *What did she say?*

"*Hi Adelaide,*" she read aloud, her voice several octaves higher than usual. "*Thanks for reaching out! It's always lovely to hear from a fellow writer and bibliophile. You've caught me at the perfect time, as it happens.*" Adelaide took several shallow breaths. "*My diary's just cleared up tomorrow,*" *if you would like to meet for a coffee around Holborn? Say 6:00 P.M.? Apologies for the late notice, but my weekdays are rarely open. Let me know!"*

Oh my gosh! Madison said again. *I have goose bumps!*

Me too, me too!

Adelaide tossed the towel onto her bed, took her phone in both hands. *Thank you so much for your prompt reply,* she typed. She deleted the words, started again. *Thank you so much for getting back to me, Nathalie (and so quickly, my goodness)! I would love to meet for a coffee tomorrow. Let me know if the Hoxton sounds good? Very much looking forward to seeing you and chatting! Thank you again!*

She signed her name, hit Send, flopped on top of the wet towel on her bedspread. *Holy shit,* she said again. Had she heard from Rory Hughes or been even mildly productive at work today? No and not at all. But she had a meeting with a stunning, brilliant editor from *The Times* tomorrow evening. And something about it felt like fate.

A delaide sat at the Hoxton at five to six—knee still bouncing, manicure gnawed away. She told the server she was meeting someone, that she'd wait a few minutes before placing her order. *She should be here soon,* Adelaide said.

Nathalie arrived just after six, her curls pinned half back with a kimono clip. She wore a black smock dress and tights, the same Doc Martens from the other night. *Adelaide?* she said, approaching the table.

Adelaide stood up, outstretched her hand. *Yes, hello!* she said. *It's so nice to meet you! Properly, this time.*

Oh, no need for handshakes, Nathalie said, kissing Adelaide on both cheeks. *It's a true pleasure, my girl.* Her accent was light and feathery, a mesh of posh London and Estuary.

They sat down; Adelaide ordered an iced coffee, Nathalie a steaming Americano. They talked about authors and writing and *You loved* Conversations with Friends? *Just wait until you get your hands on* Normal People. *I read it in a single sitting.* It was so easy to speak with her, Adelaide thought. So easy to exchange ideas, to ask her opinion. Nathalie had such a lovely disposition, such an openness. She was warm, poised, a fierce feminist. She was categorically against Brexit and read only two books by straight white male writers each year, she said. (Though she loved Orwell—*How could you not?*)

Had the conversation not flowed so seamlessly, so effortlessly, Adelaide might have started to fill the gaps with more generic questions. She might have asked where Nathalie grew up, where she went to university. Had they not had so much else to discuss, Adelaide might have heard Nathalie say she went to Downing College at Cambridge and replied with a seemingly harmless, *Oh, that's where the boy I'm seeing went. What year did you graduate? Did you know a Rory Hughes?*

But the conversation never stretched to this point. Neither woman knew just how deep, how extensive their connection truly was. Not yet.

Eight o'clock rolled around, the sky a blend of peach and sapphire at that hour. *I have a review I have to finish by nine tomorrow,* Nathalie said. *So, I suppose I should get going.* She insisted on covering the bill—despite Adelaide's protests—and left her with a hug, another couple of kisses on the cheek.

Email me anytime, she said. *It's been lovely chatting with you, Adelaide.*

You too, Adelaide said. *Thank you so, so much. It's been an absolute pleasure, really.*

An absolute pleasure. Really.

Adelaide heard from Rory Hughes the next morning; he apologized for disappearing again. *Haven't been feeling well,* he said. *But very much looking forward to tomorrow night.* He was meant to meet Celeste and Madison—*At long last!* Madison said. *We can fully assess this mystery man!* They'd called ahead, booked a table at a pub in Dalston.

I still can't tell whether I love or hate him, Celeste said the next night, on the bus ride over. *Same,* Madison said.

Suppose we'll find out tonight, huh? Adelaide said. *But like, please be nice?* They nodded their heads.

Both Madison and Celeste knew that Adelaide had—a flare for the dramatic, should we say? Well, they knew she had a tendency to spiral and spin out, to take things to extremes. Adelaide once thought she'd failed an exam, for instance, and lost sleep for a full week, only to find out she'd passed with flying colors the following Monday. It was hard to gauge whether Rory was quite as dreamy, or quite as distant, as she often made him seem.

But they also knew Adelaide was a treasure. Truly, a person to be treasured. And they were unsure Rory Hughes had ever showered her with the affection and attention she deserved. He often forgot to respond to texts, went silent for days, had yet to ask her to go steady (*Or whatever the kids are calling it these days,* to quote Celeste).

There was a lot hinging on tonight. For all parties.

Rory was already at the Kingsland when the girls arrived. He picked Adelaide up and kissed her as soon as she walked in. *Congratulations on the diss,* he said. *I'm sure it's brilliantly written and cited and the board will love it.* She was beaming.

Rory, she said. *This is Madison and Celeste. They're both real people! Can you believe?*

He gave each of the girls a hug. *Lovely to meet you,* he said. *Adelaide has talked so much about you.*

You as well, they said.

Can we get you all something to drink? Rory asked. The girls asked for G&Ts, please, and Adelaide followed Rory to the bar. Madison and Celeste gave two thumbs-up and fanned themselves once his back was turned, mouthing the words, *So! Cayoot!* Adelaide couldn't stop smiling.

How are you feeling? Adelaide asked.

All right, yeah, Rory said. *I'll just be drinking cola tonight, though. Hope that's not a problem?*

Not at all, she said. *I'm just glad you were feeling well enough to come out.*

Rory asked how the book signing had been. Adelaide told him it was great, that Wetherly even offered to read her dissertation. She planned to send it to her in a few weeks, once she received her final marks.

I also bumped into this editor from The Times *as I was leaving,* she said. *Like, physically bumped into her. And I decided to make her my new best friend. And we got coffee this week. And I'm obsessed with her now.*

An editor? Rory asked, picking up two drinks. *From* The Times?

Mhm, she said. *Their books editor. Nathalie Alban.*

Rory dropped both glasses.

All right, mate? Adelaide asked. She gestured to the bartender and grabbed a handful of cocktail napkins, trying to mop up the spilled gin and ice, the mess of broken glass. Adelaide didn't use the word "mate" very often (or at all), but she wasn't sure what else to say.

Did you just call me mate? Rory asked.

Did you just shatter two glasses? Adelaide said. *What happened there?*

A few members of the bar staff swept the shards of glass into a dustbin. Adelaide muttered apologies and thanks, promised to leave a good tip.

Nathalie Alban, Rory said, *is my ex-girlfriend.*

Oh, Adelaide said. Shit. *The ex-girlfriend you dated for more than five years?*

Yeah, he said. *Yeah.*

I see.

Adelaide paid, carefully carried two gin and tonics back to their table. Rory waited at the bar as the other drinks were remade.

Do not react, Adelaide said, setting the glasses down. *But that editor I met? Apparently, she is Rory's ex-girlfriend. And I need to discuss this at length the second we leave. Please?* The girls nodded, awkwardly shuffled a bit.

Adelaide, Madison said. *This is Anurak.*

Adelaide truly had not noticed him sitting there. She felt embarrassed, incredibly rude.

Oh my goodness, she said. She leaned down to hug him. *I am so sorry! It's so good to meet you, hello. Can I interest you in a beverage of some sort?* Anurak laughed, gave Adelaide a friendly pat.

I was actually just going to grab myself a rum and Coke, he said.

Rum and Coke? Adelaide repeated. *I'm on it! You sit right there. So good to meet you, seriously. I can't wait to hear all about your life. Be right back.*

Thanks so much, he said, still laughing a little. Adelaide heard Madison whisper, *That's Adelaide. She's really something,* as she walked away. She wasn't sure if it was meant to be a compliment.

She rejoined Rory at the bar, returned with drinks for the rest of the table. (*Shall we?* he'd asked—clearly shaken by the mention of Nathalie, clearly trying to seem smooth.) They talked about their dissertations, their new jobs, the films Rory was working to produce, and his upcoming trip to L.A. Anurak explained that he'd moved to London from Bangkok last year to get his MA in education policy and international development, like Madison. He'd just accepted an offer to work for an education technology company—a consulting role for the next year, give or take. He planned to return to Thailand once the contract was up.

Adelaide and the girls described their trip to Menton earlier that summer: the sailboat on which they stayed, the shots of liquor they took with the skipper, the fireworks they watched from the port in Monaco. Anurak and Rory shared their own sailing anecdotes, discussing their favorite islands in the Andaman Sea, the way the stars seemed to drip into the water at night, sprinkling the ocean with white light. (Adelaide noticed that Anurak had his hand on Madison's knee beneath the table throughout this conversation. She shot Madison a wink when he wasn't looking.)

They laughed and toasted and joked with the bar staff, and for the rest of the evening, no one mentioned Nathalie Alban. Not in mixed company, at least.

Oh-my-goodness-gracious-I-cannot-believe-that-woman-is-Rory's-ex. Celeste said these words in one quick breath as soon as they'd closed the cab door. Rory went home on his own. He was still recovering from his hospital stay, he said. Madison left with Anurak, the boy in whom she claimed she was *Not at all interested.* Celeste, however, chose to follow Adelaide back to Highgate that evening. There was still too much to discuss, she said. (Bless her.)

Also-he-is-so-cute-and-so-is-Anurak-like-wow. Another quick breath.

I know, Adelaide said. *I know. My mind has been running in circles all night.*

I mean, Celeste said. *Whatever, you're cuter and stuff. And a boss bitch. But like, wow.*

First off, Adelaide said. *I don't think I'm even allowed to call myself a boss bitch. Second, she was gorgeous and we both know it, but like, it's not even about that. It's not a competition thing. It's just . . . crazy. And cosmic. And I can't make sense of it.*

Any of it. If Adelaide were a different person—someone who believed in coincidences, who trusted that events simply transpired with no greater design or meaning—perhaps she could have shrugged her shoulders and moved on. But that wasn't Adelaide. She believed in something more, in something purposeful, and she couldn't quite untangle the past few nights' events in a way that made sense. Not yet.

Why had she felt so instantly attached to this woman? Why had they physically collided, met for coffee, clicked and connected so instantly and tangibly? Why did this successful, beautiful creature have to be Rory's ex-girlfriend, the person who—through no fault of her own—was seemingly preventing Rory from falling for Adelaide with the same momentum by which she'd fallen for him?

For hours that night, Adelaide tried to learn everything she could about Nathalie Alban. The girls scrolled through her social media accounts—browsing old photos, reading captions and comments, sending screenshots to Eloise. There were pictures of Nathalie and Rory drunkenly riding the Tube, curled up by a fireplace in Cornwall, cuddling a puppy named Jem. (Had they adopted him together? Did Rory ever visit this dog?) Adelaide recognized one photo, a group shot, from Rory's dating-app profile—he, Nathalie, and a handful of friends held up bowls of strawberries and cream, pitchers of Pimm's.

(It now reminded Adelaide of the day she'd first approached Rory at the Oxford-Cambridge boat race. She wondered whether Rory had told Nathalie the story of the girl who'd hit on him without shoes on, calling him a Disney prince before stumbling away. More embarrassingly, she wondered if Nathalie had been there to witness the whole event. Did they laugh about it afterward? Had they mocked her for weeks?)

It's insane, Madison would say the next morning, once she returned home. (Adelaide wolf-whistled when she walked in wearing one of Anurak's T-shirts.) *Let's not focus on my clothing. Let's focus on the fact that Rory Hughes definitely has a type,* she said.

Maybe that's why he was hesitant about commitment, Madison suggested. Maybe he'd looked at Adelaide—*Deny it all you want,* Madison said. *But you're beautiful and bookish and ambitious too, Adelaide*—and seen too much of Nathalie. Maybe he wasn't hung up on Nathalie, but wary Adelaide might share her flaws as well as her strengths. And that scared him.

Maybe, Adelaide said. Maybe.

The next Monday was the first day of Adelaide's full-time role at Alliance. She wore hot-pink shoes to mark the occasion, though the day felt strikingly similar to every other she'd spent at the company thus far. She made a latte in the kitchen, answered emails, began drafting an opinion piece for their CEO. Adelaide pinged Sam around midday, asking if she had a few minutes to chat before their one-on-one that afternoon. She had a crazy story to tell her from the weekend, Adelaide said.

For you, Sam said, *I always have a few minutes. Can't wait to hear.*

Adelaide recounted the last week in a conference room, hunched over the speakerphone. The book signing, the run-in, the coffee date. And then: The dramatic reveal that Nathalie Alban was Rory's ex-girlfriend. *Believe it or not.*

You're joking, Sam said. She emphasized each syllable—*You're. Jo. King.*

I keep trying to figure out what it means, Adelaide said.

What it means? Sam asked.

Like, why it happened, she said. *I feel like there's got to be some larger reason, some meaning to this.*

Maybe it's another indication that you and that cartoon prince of a man are connected, right? By fate or God or whoever.

Adelaide cocked her head a little to the side. She liked this explanation.

(Months from now, Sam will remind Adelaide of this moment. *What if this is why?* she'll ask, her hands on Adelaide's shoulders. *What if you needed to meet her, to know her, to really understand?*

Adelaide will nod, teary-eyed, thinking, *What if, what if, what if?*)

Rory Hughes was going to L.A. for three weeks. He asked Adelaide if there was anything she wanted from the States—*Mac and cheese? Graham crackers? That horrible excuse for chocolate you call Hershey's?* She was all good, she said. *Thank you for asking.*

There is one thing, though, Adelaide said. *Promise not to charm the pants off any other Americans while you're there?*

There is only one American I fancy charming the pants off of, he said. *I think we both know that.* He leaned down, nibbled her earlobe, dropped his voice to a whisper. *Of course, I wouldn't mind getting a few photos of you with your pants off while I'm away.*

Adelaide didn't respond. She just kissed him, lightly nipped his bottom lip.

Consider it? he said. *For me?*

I'll consider it, she said.

Adelaide had never sent photos to men before, nude or otherwise. It felt like surrendering too much of herself, giving them too much control over her body. But Adelaide also knew she would do virtually anything Rory Hughes asked of her. *For me?* She would cross oceans, scale mountains, walk through hell for Rory Hughes. He could bend her will like a magician bending a spoon.

All right, she texted the next day. She knew he was at the airport—going through security, sitting at the gate. Ground rules: These photos are for your eyes only. And my face will be artfully cropped out, lest I run for political office someday! Deal?

Deal, he said. Adelaide attached four photos. Some in a black negligee, some in nothing at all. It marked the start of a new phase in their relationship. In their situationship, rather.

Soon, they were exchanging dirty messages at all hours. Soon, Rory Hughes was able to respond almost immediately. Adelaide loved it—the increased connection, the attention, the fresh tension between them. Though, a fraction of her mind was preoccupied. It asked if he'd had these types of exchanges with Nathalie. If he was comparing their bodies. If he still had her nude photos on his phone as well—perhaps he turned to them when he became bored of Adelaide.

More questions to which she would never have answers.

Winter

London, England
2018–2019

Fourteen

Christmas in London was a fairy tale. Giant baubles hung over the streets and strings of white lights stretched into the shapes of angels, hovering between the sky and the pavement in central London. It was the first time Adelaide had ever spent Christmas away from home. If she was being honest, she didn't fully mind.

Madison, Celeste, and Adelaide were still waiting for their Tier 2 visas to be approved, unable to leave the country. They sat in a pub on Christmas Eve—their favorite, the one in Bethnal Green that always smelled of truffles and spilled Guinness—holding hands and promising to meet back in a few short weeks, *Next time with work visas,* to toast their new immigration status. (Their visas would all be approved by the third of January, they'd soon find out.)

I feel like we're making a blood pact, Madison said.

We can do that later, Celeste said.

Back at Adelaide and Madison's, the three girls curled up on recliners and watched *Love, Actually* (at Adelaide's insistence). They had hot chocolate, misshapen cookies they'd made earlier. A small Christmas tree sat in the corner of the living room, dripping with gold ornaments and topped with a little star onto which Adelaide had pinned a picture of Beyoncé (*I'll call her Treeyoncé,* she said). It was the first Christmas Adelaide had spent away from home, yes, but she looked at Celeste and Madison—tucked beneath knit blankets—and found comfort in knowing she was still spending the holiday with family.

They opened gifts the next morning in their pajamas, watched more holiday films, made a feast for ten. Adelaide FaceTimed her parents and sisters, her sweet little nephew, and her Pomeranian, Puff. Her mom had sent Christmas crackers, which the girls popped over glasses of sparkling cider. They read the bad jokes from their crackers aloud—*What do you get when you cross Santa Claus with a duck? A Christmas quacker!*—and ate until their bellies were full. They wrapped the many leftovers up in tinfoil.

Rory returned from Galway two days later. Adelaide met him at his flat; she brought leftovers and bags full of presents. He was a fan of *A Christmas Carol,* she knew, so she'd gotten him gifts from the ghosts of Christmas past, present, and future. It was a lot to carry.

Months earlier, she'd asked the innocuous question, *What was your favorite Christmas gift as a kid?* He said his parents had given him Roald Dahl's *The BFG* the last Christmas they'd spent together, along with a VHS tape of the film. They'd read it to him as a child and said it was time that he had a new copy, all his own. He'd lost both at boarding school and cried for days, he said, frustrated by his carelessness, by his own tears.

Adelaide did the math. He was ten when his parents passed, twenty-eight now. She searched eBay for versions of *The BFG* printed in 2000, for VHS tapes of the cartoon from that same year. She wrapped both up in red-and-white-striped paper, tied a bow, and affixed a gift tag that read *From the Ghost of Christmas Past.*

From the Ghost of Christmas Present came a green knit sweater and *My Beautiful Dark Twisted Fantasy* on vinyl (Rory was, controversially, a fan of Kanye West; *His presence is the present,* Adelaide wrote on that gift tag). From the Ghost of Christmas Future: Tickets to a Pierre Bonnard exhibition—*The Colour of Memory*—at the Tate Modern that spring.

(There were very few things about herself in which Adelaide took pride. Her gift-giving skills were among the few.)

Rory opened the gifts in reverse order: He started with the future, worked his way back to the past. His eyes welled up when he opened *The BFG;* he couldn't believe she'd arranged this, that she remembered. Adelaide wiped a tear from his eye, biting her lip (a part of her couldn't help but smile). He gave her a number of gifts as well—a plushy stuffed Pomeranian (*Something to cuddle when Puff's too far*), a biography of Ruth Bader Ginsburg, a certificate for afternoon tea for two at the Wolseley.

They had sex—cozy, joyful, Christmastime sex—until. Until Rory began to come in Adelaide's mouth and grabbed hold of her ponytail, pushing her head down.

In a flash, she was seventeen again. She was in her high school bedroom and Emory was jerking her around. *I'd do anything to make you feel good,* he was saying. She could nearly hear his voice. *Why won't you do the same? Why are you fighting me?*

She swallowed, wiped her mouth. She started to cry.

I'm sorry, she said, hiccupping. *I'm so sorry, this is so embarrassing.* He shushed her, cradled her gently in his arms.

Shh, it's okay, he said. *I've got you, it's okay.*

A few minutes later, he asked what happened. Had he done something wrong? *No,* Adelaide said. Well, sort of. *I used to date this boy,* she said. She started to tell him about Emory Evans, but stopped herself. She wasn't ready to share everything.

I dated this boy in high school, she said. *My first real boyfriend. He was kind of, um, abusive. Not physically, he didn't hit me or anything, but emotionally. Sometimes sexually. When you pushed my head down it just kind of . . . sent me back.*

I'm so sorry, Rory said. *That must have been so triggering.*

Mhm. She nodded her head, her lips tightly pressed together.

He lifted her up a little, pulled her onto his lap. *I'm so sorry that happened to you,* he said again.

He waited a beat. *This is silly, but. Can I read you a poem?*

Adelaide chuckled and wiped her eyes. *Sure,* she said. He grabbed a copy of *The Poetry Pharmacy* from his shelf, turned to a dog-eared page. (Later, Adelaide would wonder if the book had been a gift from Nathalie, if she'd marked her favorite poems for him. But she wasn't thinking of that right now.)

She tucked her head into the crook of his neck.

"Everything Is Going to Be All Right," he read, *by Derek Mahon.*

It was New Year's Eve and London was sparkling and Adelaide Williams was the only person on the dance floor.

She'd promised Celeste and Rory a quiet night in—*Maybe just a quick pop to the pub up the road,* she'd said. *Nothing crazy.* But then there was a DJ, an old Robbie Williams song, a few shots of cheap whiskey.

Adelaide was wearing a pink dress and glittery heels, which she kicked off almost immediately. She slid around in her tights doing the sprinkler, the Charleston. Celeste and Rory watched from a nearby table, laughing. Adelaide threw an imaginary fishing rod in their direction, an attempt to reel them in.

This is all for you, Celeste said to Rory. *Think it's too late to flee and join Madison and Anurak at their friends' party?*

Oh no, Rory said. *You can't leave now, you're the one she's after.* Adelaide "caught" a woman at another table. *She's only got, like, five dance moves, anyway,* he continued. *And she's gone through three already. She can't last much longer out there.*

He was wrong. Adelaide roped Rory onto the dance floor when "Wannabe" came on, spinning him in circles and mouthing the lyrics with both of her hands on his face. He sang along, smiled back. She bought them all a second round of whiskey shots, a third, a fourth. At five till midnight, Rory hoisted her over his shoulder and carried her to Waterlow Park, where they shouted, *Happy New Year!* as fireworks lit up the night sky, leaving London in a purplish haze.

Happy New Year, you, Adelaide said, turning to Rory.

Happy New Year, you, too, he said. They kissed as Celeste watched the fireworks.

Adelaide called her family, trying to sound sober as she wished them a very early happy new year in Massachusetts. Her two-year-old nephew said that he was a lion, roaring. Rory growled back.

Is that the elusive Rory I hear . . . growling? her mom asked.

It is, indeed, Adelaide said. She laughed.

Rory carried her to bed around two in the morning, kissed her forehead.

Are you my boyfriend now? Adelaide asked.

I, he said. *Look, this year has been horrible, with my stomach and all. But you, my dear, have been a bright spot. You really are a bit of sunshine in my life.*

You didn't answer my question, she said.

I still don't really trust relationships, he said. *I don't even know if I'm any good at them anymore. It's been a while, you know? But I'll try to be a bright spot for you, too.*

He started to tuck Adelaide in, to turn off the light.

You're not going to sleep with me, bright spot? she asked. Since his hospital stay in August, Rory had seldom spent a night with Adelaide. Sometimes, awkwardly, he'd ask her to leave his flat around one or two in the morning so he could *Get a decent night's sleep.* She hoped tonight would be different, that the whiskey and New Year cheer might inspire him to lie down by her side. Rory kissed her forehead again.

Not tonight, he said. *Sleep tight, Adelaide. Happy 2019.*

(If only he'd known.)

At five in the morning, Adelaide's phone rang—it made the sound of an old-fashioned telephone. She picked up on the fourth ring.

Hello? she said, her voice sleepy and hoarse.

ADELAIDE! a voice yelped. *I need to FaceTime you immediately.*

Adelaide sat up straight, turned on her light. A few seconds later, Eloise's face appeared on her screen. She held up her left hand. The video was dark and blurry, but Adelaide could see there was a bright white diamond on her ring finger. Holy shit.

You're engaged! she yelped back, now wide awake. *Congratulations, oh my goodness! How do you feel? How does Nico feel? How did it happen? Tell me everything.*

Eloise told her the full story: The champagne they brought to the Brooklyn Bridge, chilly and bundled in coats and scarves. The fireworks that popped and sizzled over the skyline. The moment Nico got down on one knee, just after twelve, and asked her to marry him.

What a world, Adelaide said.

The sun was just starting to come up when they got off the phone. It was a whole new morning, a whole new year. Adelaide burst into tears. Happy and sad and exhausted and hungover and overwhelmed tears.

She was happy, of course she was. Her best friend was marrying the love of her life—a man who'd known and loved her for the better part of a decade. Someone who'd watched her grow from a shy, precocious teenager into an incredibly passionate, ambitious woman and adored her at every single stage in between. Whose love crossed oceans and seas. Adelaide knew few couples as well-matched as Eloise and Nico—in wit, in sense of adventure, in their shared appreciation for *Jeopardy!* reruns (Nico often said that Alex Trebek taught him English). But Adelaide's heart ached as it swelled.

She was afraid. She was afraid of the ways in which her relationship with Eloise might transform, of the chasms that might be created as Eloise shifted from *Girlfriend* to *Wife*. She was also afraid, secretly and selfishly, that perhaps she would never be loved like that. That no one— not even Rory Hughes—would ever drop to his knee on the Brooklyn Bridge, or anywhere else, and ask her to spend forever with him. (*Why would they?* she asked herself.)

Adelaide buried the thought. She had an obnoxiously large bouquet and a bottle of Nico's favorite ouzo sent to Eloise's apartment. She asked to have a couple of forget-me-nots included in the floral arrangement, just in case.

A few days later, a bouquet arrived at Adelaide's door as well—flowers folded from the pages of *Little Women*.

To my very own Jo March, the note read. *The woman who's loved and cared for me like a sister since high school, and the only person I trust to write a bang-up speech. Be my Maid of Honor? (There's only one answer, by the way.) All my love, Eloise*

PS: We're getting married in New York *and* Mykonos in August—no time like the present, they say!

Eloise was right. There was only one answer.

Fifteen

A delaide and Rory were born three years and six days apart. He would turn twenty-nine on the twenty-seventh of January; she would be twenty-six on the second of February.

(She'd soon learn that Wilhelm II was also born on the twenty-seventh—Rory shared his birthday with a man known for launching the world into war, into disarray. She shared hers with Josephine Humphreys, known for writing *Rich in Love*. What a coincidence.)

At one in the morning on the twenty-seventh, Adelaide was covered in flour and lemon juice—Rory had said lemon drizzle cake was his favorite. She'd never made one before, and her first and second attempts hadn't turned out as expected. They were too bitter, too sweet, too dense in texture. Now, the kitchen was showered in petals and peels of lemon zest—it looked like tiny yellow flowers were blooming across the countertops. Adelaide's white T-shirt was stained and smudged. Both she and the kitchen were a mess; both she and the kitchen were determined to produce a cake Rory Hughes would love.

On her third attempt, Adelaide decided to make cupcakes: Twelve with a slight variation to the recipe (the addition of a lemon pudding mix), twelve without. The pudding-mix batch was the winner, she decided, puncturing half of the cupcakes with a fork and pouring a syrupy drizzle on top. She would frost the remaining six with yellow icing in the morning, stick *HBD* candles into their tops. She planned to deliver his cake and gifts around lunchtime tomorrow. She had plenty of time to make this perfect. *Thank fuck*, she muttered to herself.

Adelaide Williams loved birthdays. All birthdays. She knew this was partly because of capitalism, sure. But more than gifts and Mylar balloons, Adelaide loved the idea of celebrating the day a person entered the world. How wonderful, she thought, that once a year, we had an opportunity to look at the people we love and say, *I'm so glad you're here. On this earth. Right this minute.*

To Adelaide, birthdays were a time for celebration, for reflection, for saying the kindest things you could possibly think to say about a person. And today, the twenty-seventh of January, Adelaide was going to tell Rory Hughes that she was in love with him.

Almost. Sort of.

Adelaide and Rory had been "dating," in quotes, for nine months. She'd yet to meet his friends or brothers, yet to enter an officially defined relationship, to fully win him over. But that was going to change today, she decided. His brothers were all in Manchester, but she was going to meet his friends at a pub this evening, and she was certain that if she gave him the most perfect twenty-ninth birthday, he'd turn to her and say, *You're it, Adelaide. You're the one.*

She planned to give him her original copy of *Call Me By Your Name*—a story he knew from the film, not yet from the page. It had all her annotations in it, all of the scribbles and underlines that indicated she'd loved a given quote or sentence. Like Rory, it was immensely special to her. On the back of page 165, she'd written him a note:

Rory, it read.

Goodness knows if or when you'll stumble upon this page, but it felt like the right place to tell you exactly what your existence has meant to me, lest I lack the courage to say this all in person. In quick sum: I fell in love with you instantly, Rory Hughes. (Seriously, consult my journal entries from April and May of 2018—they are . . . dizzying.) And as I write this, in January 2019, I am nauseatingly and joyfully and completely up-to-my-eyeballs in love with you. Richard-Curtis-style.

I'm in love with the shape of your chin and the curl that hangs above your forehead. With the way your eyes flash, your shoulders wiggle, and your voice cracks (just a bit!) when you're particularly excited. With the joy and comfort and longing that meld together and thump through each old story you tell. I'm in love with your dry wit and intellect. Your incurable enthusiasm. Your compassion. Your tenderness. The notes you jot in the books you read, the feel of your fingers combing through my hair.

Again, I'm not sure if or when you'll see this note. But—as you enter your thirtieth year on this planet—I wanted you to know the extent of your impact here, and the magical kind of adoration you're capable of stirring up in others. (Because I am certain it doesn't begin and end with little American me.)

So, thank you for being born, and thank you for letting me fall in love with you. It's been such a gift. Happy birthday and cheers to all that lies ahead.

Love (for real, though), Adelaide

She also got Rory an early-edition copy of *Les Misérables*—one of his favorites. She'd found it (after searching for hours) at one of the bouquinistes on Île de la Cité weeks earlier, on a weekend trip to Paris with Celeste. The book was gorgeous, leather bound, all in the original French. In his card, she promised to cover a flight to Paris or northern Italy—the setting of either novel, his choice—as a post-birthday treat.

She was so determined to make him love her. (How could he *not* love her, after all of this?)

The doorbell rang. Adelaide opened it, saw a man standing behind an enormous assortment of peonies. She assumed they'd come from her family or perhaps from Eloise—an early birthday gift.

To Mads, the card read. *I love you!!! So much!!! Anurak x*

Despite Madison's early protests and insistence that they were *Just friends,* she and Anurak had been near inseparable since they'd finished their graduate program last August. And now, they were in love. Openly, honestly, able-to-declare-it-with-bouquets-of-peonies in love.

Adelaide set the flowers down. She returned the note to its tiny envelope—*For Someone Special*, it said—and walked to the bathroom. She kneeled on the tile floor and leaned over the toilet seat and threw up for several minutes. It felt like hours; everything inside of her came out. She started sobbing, heaving, trying to breathe.

This, her brain told her. *This is what you could have if you weren't so goddamned broken. This is what Rory would feel for you. If only you were someone else, someone better. Someone like Madison or Nathalie or anyone but exactly who you are.*

The thing about Adelaide is that she felt everything. Truly, everything. She cried during documentaries, while reading books, when royal babies were born. She cried when she was happy and when she was sad and when the world felt like it was all just too much and her face was on fire and the only way to cool it down was to cry, cry, cry, cry, cry. It often felt selfish and irrational. She knew she was so lucky, so blessed. That there was no reason to cry. It didn't matter; she would cry anyway.

Adelaide thought about the mess in the kitchen, the note written in *Call Me By Your Name*. She thought about how desperately, pathetically, ardently she was fighting to be loved by Rory Hughes—no doubt because her past had taught her that love meant sacrifices, that it meant she had to fight. (Ages would pass before she understood what it meant to fight for good love. True love.) She wanted to rip her own beating heart from her chest, to toss it onto the bathroom floor and watch her blood spatter like wet paint.

Instead, she took a Xanax. Washed her face. Called her mom. Told herself there was no time, no space, for her to be acting like this. She wrapped up Rory's books, his cupcakes, in white ribbon and Saran wrap. She frosted her first and second cakes, too—put them in a takeout container for the man who often sat outside her Tube stop.

Lemon cake, she said, placing the container in his hands. *They're far from perfect, but I hope you like them!* The man smiled. It was his birthday today, he said, as a matter of fact.

Well goodness, Adelaide said. *I owe you a gift! Can I get you anything from the corner store?*

I'd love a lotto ticket, he said. *This feels like my lucky day.*

She picked up a few scratch-offs, a lotto ticket, a bottle of water. She gave them to the man, left him a one-pound coin. (Adelaide never saw him again, so she would never know he won two thousand pounds that day. That he believed she was an actual angel.)

She took the Tube to London Bridge and walked to Rory's flat, knocked on the door.

Happy birthday! she said when he opened it, surprised. He was still wearing his pajamas. *I'll see you later tonight, but I wanted to drop this off now! I hope you're having the best birthday!*

Thank you, you, he said. He gave her waist a little squeeze. She half hoped he would invite her inside; he did not.

You are just the loveliest thing, he texted once she'd left. Thank you so much for these gifts and these cakes. We'll have to plan a trip to Italy soon, won't we? See you tonight. xxx

She smiled.

Adelaide woke up with the lights on, her jeans off, and one hand in a bag of salt and vinegar crisps. It was three in the morning. The day had been a roller coaster; the night was a blur.

She'd met Rory at the pub around eight. He introduced her to his friends James and Sarah and Jeff. *This is James, and Sarah, and Jeff,* he'd said. *My mates from uni. Everyone, this is my girl—this is Adelaide. Not from uni.*

(Adelaide would replay this moment on a loop all evening. This almost, sort of declaration that she was . . . not *his girlfriend,* per se. But *his girl.*)

She bought a pint of Guinness and black with a shot of bourbon. Adelaide had never added liquor to this drink before, but she wanted something strong. She didn't particularly enjoy the taste, but it made everything feel a bit cloudier. In a good way. At one point, someone called Adelaide *Nathalie* by mistake. She ordered two more pints.

An hour or so later, Rory's roommates arrived. Adelaide was relieved to see Bubs—someone who might remember her name, she hoped. He shook Rory's hand, patted his back, sat down next to Adelaide.

Adelaide, he said. (Thank goodness.) *What are you drinking?*

Guinness and black, she said. She didn't mention the shot of bourbon.

You know, he said, *in Dublin, my grandfather calls that a Girly Guinness.*

That's some patriarchal bullshit, she said, too heady to stop herself. She paused. *I'm sorry. That was rude.*

Not at all, he said. The right corner of his mouth lifted in a small smile. *I'll get a round for the table.*

He came back with a round of proper Guinness for Rory and the others, plus a Guinness and black for Adelaide. She downed it. Then "Footloose" came on.

Whoa-my-gosh-I-love-this-song-my-sister-played-Ariel-in-high-school. No one understood what she said.

Adelaide left her shoes at the table, sprinted to the dance floor, began kicking her feet out in front of her like Kevin Bacon. Rory joined her after a minute or two. (Later, she'd realize he was trying to prevent her from humiliating herself, from dancing alone for too long.) She spun him around and grabbed his face, just as she had on New Year's Eve. She could feel his friends watching, judging; she didn't really care. Rory played along.

It's your birthday, Adelaide said. *And we're dancing and we're alive and isn't this magic?* She was very, very drunk.

You are very, very drunk, Rory said.

Barely, she said. The song ended; the last-call bell rang. *Is it last call? Do we get to go home and have birthday sex now?*

Not tonight, Adelaide, he said.

Friends surrounded Rory and started singing "For He's a Jolly Good Fellow," which Adelaide thought was funny. She said good night, kissed them all goodbye.

Shall I call you a car? Rory asked.

Adelaide said no, she'd take the Tube. Neither of them was sober enough to recognize it was Sunday, that the Tube wasn't running at this hour. She realized outside of the station and started to call a car—her phone was dead.

This is also when it hit Adelaide that she'd had four pints of Guinness and had not gone to the restroom, not once, all evening.

She wandered around Covent Garden, twisting her legs, trying to find a black cab to hail. The pubs were closed, the streets empty. Somewhere between Seven Dials and Tottenham Court Road, still searching for a cab, she lost her will. Adelaide Williams peed her pants (Peed! Her!

Pants!). On the street, in central London. Like a small child. Six days before her twenty-sixth birthday.

Finally, a cab arrived. She told the driver she slipped in a puddle. It hadn't been raining.

Adelaide's birthday fell on a Saturday. She rented a cozy, thatched-roof cottage in Somerset for the weekend, just after Rory's birthday, to celebrate. Celeste and Madison came along. Madison brought Anurak as her plus-one; Adelaide brought Rory. (He'd gone out with coworkers the night before and nearly missed the train. He made it to Paddington with moments to spare.)

The group played drinking games and Cards Against Humanity, taking turns sipping from an acrid bottle of Jose Cuervo. They ordered pizza and ate it on the floor, talking about everything from who was most likely to get arrested for having sex in public (a toss-up between Celeste and Adelaide, they decided) to the social costs of late capitalism. They sang "Happy Birthday" and cut into a giant rainbow cake that Adelaide's sister sent to the cottage. Adelaide ate her slice sitting on Rory's lap, his arms around her waist.

(The beds were old and creaky. Everyone heard Adelaide and Rory have sex that night, then again the next morning. Anurak first assumed the sound was someone pumping water from a well. They would joke about it for years.)

For several days, Rory had been teasing Adelaide. He asked if she was free the weekend after her birthday, and what were her favorite scents, and did she have any allergies he should know about? (Penicillin, for the record.) He told her he was planning a surprise getaway—a trip just for the two of them. *Someplace special,* he said.

Do you think he's planning a trip to France? she'd asked Madison and Celeste. *Grasse, maybe? Or even Budapest? Somewhere with perfumeries galore?*

I don't know, Adelaide, they'd said. *It doesn't quite seem like his style, honestly,* Madison had offered, shrugging her shoulders. She gave Adelaide a sympathetic half smile.

More than the presents her family had shipped over, or the giant card from Eloise, or the gift bags fluffed with tissue paper that Celeste and Madison had brought to the cottage, Adelaide was eager to see what Rory Hughes had gotten her. What on earth was this charming boy planning? (And did it, perhaps, possibly, involve him finally asking her to be his girlfriend?)

Shh, he said the next morning, just as she started to wake up. *Close your eyes again.*

A moment later, Rory told her to open her eyes. He handed her a silver envelope, the name *Adelaide* written across it in fresh, blue ink. Inside was a Groupon for one night at a spa hotel in London, the words *Happy birthday! Let's get massages! From Rory xx* scribbled at the bottom of the page.

Okay, sure. It wasn't a trip to Grasse or Budapest, nor was it a declaration of love or commitment. But it was kind and thoughtful and sure to be enjoyable. *A spa trip with a dreamy Englishman?* Adelaide thought to herself. *How insanely lucky am I?*

They went for a country walk on Sunday morning, got a roast at the pub. Adelaide fell asleep on Rory's shoulder on the train ride home. One of his hands held hers, the other combed gently through her hair. It was her favorite birthday in forever. *Twenty-six is going to be just fine,* she thought.

How little she knew.

They sat in lush hotel robes and ordered room service.

Rory had forgotten to book their spa treatments in advance, unfortunately. *Oh,* she said, trying to mask her disappointment. *No worries, it's fine.* (*How does one forget to book treatments at a spa hotel?* she asked herself. *How does one so consistently fail to show up?*)

He'd given her a back rub himself, instead, spreading the tiny lotion from their hotel bathroom across Adelaide's shoulders. Everything felt a bit easier now.

Tell me a story, she said, eating a French fry.

What kind of story? Rory asked.

Anything, Adelaide said. *Tell me more about your time in Alabama.*

Rory told her the story of a girl named Harper, someone he'd met on a dating app and then, coincidentally, stumbled upon in real life. This wasn't the kind of story Adelaide had in mind.

It's kind of the opposite of how we met, Rory said. *Although, Harper and I never ended up going on a date. I think my accent might have scared her off.*

That's impossible, Adelaide said, another fry in her mouth. *Your accent is the sexiest thing in the world.*

Only to you, he said with a wink. *And every drive-through attendant I met in Alabama.*

She giggled, but something didn't add up. Hadn't he gone to Alabama, like, four years ago? Was he even single when he met Harper? she asked.

Yeah, Rory said. *Nat and I broke up for a while when I left, then got back together.*

Interesting, she thought. Since Adelaide met Nathalie—*Nat*, Rory always called her Nat—she'd come up almost weekly. It was as though Adelaide had willed Nathalie's presence into the relationship. Like a perfectly beautiful, perfectly charming version of the Babadook: This physical manifestation, not of grief, but of all of Adelaide's relationship fears.

You mention Nathalie quite a bit, Adelaide said. *But I still don't know what happened between you two.*

It wasn't particularly complicated, Rory said. They'd been together for ages, off and on, and when it came time to take the next step in their relationship—*To think about moving in and all that comes after moving in*, as he put it—he simply wasn't prepared. *It wasn't right*, he said. *And once you shut that door on youth, you can't really reopen it, you know? I don't know if I ever want to do that, really. I certainly didn't at the time.*

Do what? Adelaide asked.

You know, he said.

No, Adelaide thought. *Say the words.*

I really don't, she said.

Get, uh, married. I don't know if I want that.

Adelaide ate another few fries, took a long sip of water. She didn't say anything else.

Want to watch a film? Rory asked. She shrugged, waited a beat. *We're so mismatched*, she said.

Rory put down the remote, turned to face her. *What do you mean?* he asked.

I mean that you're here next to me, saying you're unsure if you ever want to get married. I, meanwhile, am knee-deep in love with you, Rory, and you seem to have no fucking idea because you're so hung up on the last person you dated and, apparently, didn't even want to stay with.

He was silent, but his eyes had softened a bit. He exhaled. *Adelaide,* he started to say. (What the hell had she just done?)

I'm sorry, she said. *I have no idea where that came from.*

Adelaide, Rory said again. *You are such a special thing.*

Not enough of a thing, she said, petulant.

You are, he said. *It's me, not you. But I can tell you, I'm not hung up on anyone or anything, that couldn't be further from the truth. I've considered you my girlfriend for months now.* For months?

He picked her up, tugged at the tie of her robe. *Months?* she said. *What the hell? You can't just suddenly tell me I'm your girlfriend and seduce me like this.* But he could. He hushed her, kissed each of her eyelids, her shoulders, her breasts. He traced her thighs with the tips of his fingers.

The sex was slow, gentle, methodical; it was lovely and comfortable. But Adelaide felt uneasy.

Rory was her boyfriend—finally (finally!). And she guessed she should feel happy? In some ways—in many ways, really—she did. Adelaide was lying next to the man of her dreams, both of them wrapped in Egyptian cotton sheets, at the most stunning London hotel.

But there was also something that was just so unnerving about all of this, wasn't there? About the way her emotional security seemed to be an afterthought for him. The manner with which he'd so abruptly brushed off the importance of commitment. The fact that he could not, would not say he loved her, too.

The hardest part about falling deeply, knowingly in love for the first time—the first time outside of hormonal, teenage love, that is—is suddenly realizing you're alone in this place. That you're sitting in the most spectacular setting and no one is there to admire it with you.

Rory had been there; he'd experienced true love as an adult. He knew this land, this Eden she'd entered. And he'd moved on, searched for greener pastures.

Adelaide shuddered. She was getting everything she wanted; why didn't she feel that way?

Sixteen

It was mid-February, half term. Madison was in Scotland with An-urak, Celeste was in the States, and Rory Hughes was thirty minutes late for dinner.

About once a year, Adelaide would prepare a Southern feast. She'd get her grammy's cookbook from the shelf—a collection of photocopied, handwritten recipes that practically spoke with a Georgian accent—and pick up fresh green beans from the grocer, tubs of Crisco and Ritz crackers from the American store. She'd slowly bake beans in a homemade barbecue sauce, cover casserole dishes of macaroni in a cheesy béchamel (topped with crumbled crackers and baked at 170). She would fold sour cream into chocolate cake batter, whipping semisweet chips into buttercream frosting as it rose in the oven. She'd brew sweet tea, buy orange and grape Popsicles, make it all truly feel like summertime, even in the dead of London winter.

It was delicious in flavor, disastrous in its capacity for coating counters in grease and flour and stray greens. But Adelaide had the kitchen to herself this evening. And she couldn't wait to share this, all of this—her food, her roots, her extraordinarily un-English way of making tea—with Rory. (She'd even fried some chicken, battered in Rice Krispies, just for him.)

He was meant to arrive at seven; it was now seven thirty. Adelaide set plates on the table, laid out silverware, folded spare napkins into flopsy little cranes. She placed the mac and cheese and chicken back into the oven, just to keep the dishes warm until he arrived.

Sorry to do this, he texted around eight. But feeling quite unwell this evening. Can I get a rain check?

It was the type of thing that should have been fine. It would have been fine, really, had he given any warning. Had it been the first time he'd canceled plans well after the time he was meant to arrive. Had he not said he was *Getting ready to head out* nearly two hours ago. Adelaide was left with dishes to wash, chicken she couldn't eat.

I'm so sorry you're not feeling well, she said. I can wrap this up and bring it over, if you want? We can just eat from your bed, if you like?

No, that wouldn't do, he said. He wasn't *Up for company.* But she could drop it off tomorrow night, before the football? She could even watch the football with him, he said, in a gesture of goodwill. (Neither Rory nor Adelaide enjoyed it when she watched football with him.)

She had calls until nine tomorrow night, she explained.

After? he said.

Was she overreacting, or was this—once again—remarkably unthoughtful? Careless, even? *Thanks for dinner, dear! You can bring it by after work and watch me watch football, dear!* Was she meant to be June Cleaver? To prepare food, brush off his incapacity for maintaining commitments, spoon-feed him as he watched sports matches from his sofa?

Deep breaths, she said aloud. She counted them. In. And out. In. And out.

Adelaide cleaned up the kitchen, scrubbing grease and flour from the butcher block countertops. She put the food in little takeaway containers in the fridge, took a shower, put on a romantic comedy. Almost instantly, she started to cry.

This was not how the evening was meant to go—this was not how anything was meant to go, really.

Three years, nine months, and two hundred minutes earlier, when Adelaide first met Rory Hughes at that boat race (albeit briefly), she believed him to be a prince. *Her* prince. There was something about him that spoke to the part of Adelaide that grew up watching Disney films, that had memorized every lyric from every song in *Cinderella* (and often performed them all for her family).

Two years, twelve days, and three hundred and three minutes after that, when they met again—a chill in the air, fairy lights and expectations hanging above them—she could practically hear the refrain: *So, this is love / So, this is what makes life divine. This was it*, she thought. *This was love.* She was certain.

But it wasn't. Love was challenging, complex, unforgiving, yes. But love was also meant to feel easy, comfortable, not. Not whatever it was Adelaide felt—something akin to her heart being grated, slowly. Fresh cuts emerging each time Rory refused to adhere to plans, to say he loved her, to call her his person or his partner or his favorite.

Adelaide was imperfect, she knew this. She was stubborn and awkward, easily drunk, at times manic. She was opinionated and argumentative, too emotional about current events and old films. Obsessive about making the bed. But, particularly in this relationship, Adelaide had been overwhelmingly kind, patient, caring. Yet, she continued to feel as though she was not enough, as though she would never be enough to earn the love and respect of this prince, Rory Hughes.

Perhaps he wasn't a prince at all, she thought. Perhaps he was yet another dragon she needed to slay, another hurdle to overcome on her own journey to self-actualization. Or love. Or something. And, perhaps, the only way to find the meaning of this relationship was to let it end.

So, for the first time in nine months, four days, and one hundred and eight minutes, Adelaide Williams considered letting this whole mess of a fantasy go.

A delaide dropped leftovers at Rory's the next night, after work. She didn't stay to chat.

Is something the matter? he texted.

A little, she said. But I'm also underwater with work right now. Maybe we can catch up in a few days?

Sure thing, he said. Thanks for dinner, it looks delicious.

(In a few days, he'd tell her he thought the meal made him sick, that it had all been a bit too rich for his highly sensitive stomach. But in a few days, the world would be ending, so it wouldn't really matter what he thought of her cooking, would it?)

It was Tuesday, the twenty-sixth of February. The sky was gray, rainy. Adelaide straightened her hair, listened to a news podcast as she put on eyeliner. They were just discussing politics, but her eyes became misty.

It's almost like she knew.

She read *The Year of Magical Thinking* on the train, tearing up again at Joan Didion's prose. She sat through a few morning meetings, drank three cups of coffee before noon. In less than a week, the executive team would be flying in from New York for two events—the first Alliance had hosted in Europe—and Adelaide was responsible for ensuring *All content goes off without a hitch!* (An expression Sam and Djibril had been using a bit aggressively of late.) The first event would be in London on Monday; the second, two days later in Paris. Sam had arrived on the twenty-fifth to help with planning.

Adelaide sat in a conference room—*The war room,* they called it—with Djibril, Sam, and her fourth cup of coffee. She was wearing a sweatshirt with Alliance's logo on the sleeve, her hair now tied back in a ponytail. They were finalizing the events' agendas when her phone started to vibrate on the table. *It's Rory,* Adelaide said, confused. *One second.*

She stepped out to the stairwell, her heart racing for no known reason. She hit the little green Answer button and knew, inexplicably—before he'd uttered a word—exactly what he was about to say.

Adelaide? Rory said. His voice was strained. Wounded, almost. She asked if everything was okay (though she knew the answer was no).

This is a bit hard to say, he said. *But. Um. But Nathalie died yesterday.*

There's another version of this story. One in which Nathalie lives, and the world continues turning. Maybe she and Rory find their way back to each other one day. Maybe they just get together for lunch in a few years—both married, awkwardly twisting their rings, asking what the other's been up to all this time. *How's the job? Any kids? How's your mum?* Maybe, in this story, Adelaide and Nathalie get coffee once again—discussing their favorite books some more, their cosmically tangled past.

But tragically, this story exists in a universe where Nathalie Alban does not live. And everything—absolutely everything—falls apart. Because young women with promise, with kindness, with ambition and swarms of adoring family and friends . . . they're not meant to die suddenly at twenty-seven. They're meant to live. Nothing makes sense in a world where they do not live.

*O*h *my gosh,* Adelaide said. *I am so, so sorry, love. You don't have to answer this question, but. Can I ask what happened?*

She was in an accident, Rory said.

I'm so sorry, she said again. Her mind immediately went to his parents. *Where are you right now? Can I come over, or do you want some time to yourself?*

Rory was at home, he said. His brother Daniel was over now. But if Adelaide wanted to stop by later, that might be nice. *Of course,* she said. *I can be there at the drop of a hat. Just say when.*

Thanks, he said.

Adelaide hung up, sat down on the steps. In a very dark corner of her mind, a voice asked how many people he'd called before her—how many people he'd already turned to for comfort. She silenced it. Semantics didn't matter right now, supporting Rory did. Why the fuck was she even asking this question? *Be strong,* she told herself. *Be strong, be strong, be strong.*

She couldn't. Sam found her a few minutes later, the sleeves of her sweatshirt soaked in tears.

Nathalie, she said. *Rory's ex-girlfriend. She—she died.* It felt perverse to say those words out loud, like Adelaide had no right to speak her name. Sam scooped her up, took her to the bathroom, wiped smeared mascara from her cheeks with toilet paper.

It's okay, she said. *It's okay.*

It's not okay, Adelaide said, tears still streaming. *I don't know how to do this. I don't know how to make this okay.*

*L*ater, people will wonder why Adelaide was so torn up; why this stranger's death impacted her so greatly. *Why were you so saddened by this?* they'll ask. Adelaide will never be able to pinpoint the answer.

The truth is that Nathalie's death broke her heart. She'd felt a connection to this woman, a kinship. There was something about them that felt the same. Something kindred—a rope that had been tied around both of their waists and looped them together in the universe. At points, Adelaide had wondered if, perhaps, this whole thing—this whole love affair with Rory—had been a map. Not to a prince, but to Nathalie. She'd wondered if they were meant to be friends; if they were meant to sit over cocktails and coffees, to share anecdotes about their exes, to swap paperback books and floral dresses.

Had Adelaide imagined this, the connection between them? She supposed she'd never know. She would never know what made this woman feel so inexpressibly special to her: The light that had been Nathalie Alban was extinguished. And yes, this broke Adelaide's heart.

Imagine if you'd known her, Adelaide thought. Met her more than twice; really, properly known her. Imagine her friends, her sisters, her parents. Imagine the people who'd kissed her good night, driven her to uni, held her hair back after drunken nights out and squeezed her at school reunions and called her before big interviews for a quick pep talk—they couldn't have her anymore. The world couldn't have her anymore. And the fact that people like this just fell out of our universe—just stopped existing—was so scary, so cold. Adelaide didn't know how to handle it.

She told Djibril the news, left the office, worked from a coffee shop not far from Rory's. (*Without a hitch,* she reminded herself, struggling to send perky emails.) She sent a pizza to Rory's flat, waited for his text.

My brother just left, he said around five. If you're able to come by.

I'll be there in 10, Adelaide said.

For the rest of her life, Adelaide would remember the look on Rory's face when he opened the door. She would remember what it felt like to hug him, to stand up on her tippy-toes and envelop him in her arms. Because hugging someone in that moment, feeling their shoulders shake, their tears damp against your chest—you never want to let go. Literally and metaphorically and ever. You want to hold them as long as this life will allow you, to protect them from every possible pain in this world, to pretend you'll never have to grieve their absence.

Because if we knew, if we honestly knew the price of love was grief, we'd never do it. We'd never succumb in the first place. And once we do—once we fall in love, against our better judgment, with something or someone—we never want to let go. No matter how many dinners they miss, how many texts they ignore. None of it matters. And none of it mattered. Adelaide was never going to let go.

Seventeen

It doesn't make sense.

Rory continued to repeat these words. Like an incantation, almost. If he said them enough, the curse would be broken. Nathalie would return to this world. *It doesn't make sense . . . so restore her to the universe. It doesn't make sense . . . so let her live. Please.*

Adelaide brewed two cups of tea in Rory's kitchen. The steam rose in wispy curls. *It doesn't make sense,* she echoed, taking the tea bags out, adding a splash of milk to each cup. Nothing about this made sense.

She asked if he wanted to watch *The Princess Bride.* For a fraction of a second, he began to smile. *How did you know?* he asked.

Adelaide knew because she'd been paying attention. She knew because she knew Rory Hughes—the infuriating, cartoonishly handsome, and now completely broken Rory Hughes—too well not to know *The Princess Bride* was his favorite film to watch while sick. Or, more aptly, his favorite film to watch when he wanted to feel better. And she wanted him to feel better. Desperately. She wanted to make him feel better.

They sat on his bed, both holding their tea, both breathing a bit laboriously. They watched *The Princess Bride,* then *The Lion King,* then *Singin' in the Rain.* Adelaide petted Rory's head, held his hand in hers. *I'm here,* she'd whisper when he began to cry. *I'm so sorry. I'm here.* Sometimes, the words would spill together—*I'm so sorry I'm here,* she'd say. *I'm so sorry it was Nathalie instead of me,* she'd think.

Rory's phone was hot to the touch, constantly vibrating with messages from friends, family. He would step out to take quick calls and come back weeping—still heartbroken over the news, but honored that her cousins, her friends, her colleagues had thought to call him. His breathing got heavier, harder, with each phone call. (*Would a small bit of Xanax help?* Adelaide asked him. *Oh golly, no,* he said. *I'm not American. I don't just mask things with pills.*)

During the third film, his phone pinged with a message from Nathalie's mum. Her words belonged to Rory, not to Adelaide, but he read them aloud anyway. *We are heartbroken to have lost our girl,* she said. Adelaide's heart broke again. She blinked back tears, feeling like she was trespassing in a space where she did not belong.

Around nine o'clock, once the sun had fully set (what business did it have rising on a day like this anyway, Adelaide wondered), she combed her fingers through Rory's hair until he could barely keep his eyes open. She'd offered to stay the night, but both she and Rory knew he slept better on his own. She kissed his forehead, pulled the duvet above his shoulders, slipped a note she'd written earlier, at the coffee shop, beneath his pillow.

> *Rory,* it said. *My heart is broken for you. And for Nathalie. And for all those who loved her—a community made up of everyone who'd ever met her, it seems. I have no doubt that you'll all continue to spread her light and energy here on earth, but please know that I'm here for you, now and always, when you need to feel a little light yourself.*
>
> *Love, Adelaide*

She took the teacups from beside his bed, washed them in the kitchen.

Hey, Bubs said.

Hey, Adelaide said.

I know this can't be easy, he said. *But I'm really glad you're here for Rory right now.*

Of course, she said. *I just . . . I can't imagine.* After all, she thought, *They've lost their girl.*

Bubs nodded. She placed the cups on the drying rack.

Is there anything I can do for you? she asked, wiping her hands on a tea towel. *Do you need a pizza, a cold beer, a cake? I'm sure this is a rough time for you all as well.* He chuckled a little.

All good this end, he said. *Thanks, Adelaide.*

Sure thing. Have a good evening.

She walked outside, down a few flights of stairs, out into the night. She burst into tears.

It's okay, Madison said, once she got home.

It's not okay, Adelaide said again. She collapsed in their doorway, her tears warm. It would never be okay.

There was too much work, an impossible amount of work. Adelaide blew her nose and brewed another pot of coffee around 11 P.M. She opened her laptop, tried to compartmentalize.

She couldn't.

She went to sleep sometime after 4 A.M., woke up three hours later. The sun shone through her window, and for a moment, Adelaide forgot what happened; she forgot she lived in a different world now. Remembering felt like firing a gun in the wrong direction, wishing you could catch the bullet.

Adelaide sent an email to Djibril and Sam with the decks she'd edited overnight. She planned to work from the coffee shop again until Rory woke up, spend a few hours with him, make it back to the office by three for presentation run-throughs. *Was that okay?*

Of course, Djibril messaged. *See you later today. Let me know if you need me to cover you. Bless him,* Adelaide thought. She didn't want to let him down.

Are you all right? the barista asked, sweeping crumbs from a nearby table. Adelaide was sobbing. Not light tears—true, heaving sobs. She hadn't realized how much noise she was making until this barista spoke to her. She felt doused in waves of fresh guilt.

Fuck you, Adelaide, she thought to herself. *How dare you cry over this person you barely knew. How dare you waste other people's concern, their kindness, on your tears.*

All good, she said to the barista, sniffing. *Thanks.*

Around 10 A.M., she called her sister Holly. She needed comfort, words of wisdom—some reminder that things were going to be okay. (Holly was a young mom—surely, she'd be awake at this hour in Massachusetts. And surely, she'd have answers for Adelaide. She'd always known how to calm her during Izzy's episodes.) With each ring, more guilt poured over her. Never again would Nathalie's little sisters be able to call her, to seek her counsel. The scales of the universe felt so unbelievably off-balance.

Holly picked up after the third ring. *Hi, love,* she said, her voice delicate. It was still so early there.

Adelaide could barely speak. She tried to say *Hi;* it sounded like the cry of a wounded animal.

Oh, Adelaide, Holly said.

I don't know what to do, she said, finally. *I don't know how to pull myself together. Or make this okay.*

Holly explained that grief reverberates; that Adelaide was on the outer edges right now, feeling every pulse, every pound of heartbreak. *The closer you go into that circle,* she said, *the stronger you have to be. Cry now, but try to be a pillar for Rory. Hold him up.*

Adelaide nodded, the phone held to her ear, tears damp and hot on her cheek. *Be a pillar,* she thought to herself. *Hold him up.*

She bit her lip, trying to seal the sobs inside her mouth. She swallowed, wiped her eyes with recycled napkins, sent a few more Slacks and emails. She tried to breathe deeply, slowly. She counted her breaths. In. And out. In. And out.

Rory texted around ten thirty. He was up. Can I bring anything over? she asked.

A juice would be great, he said.

Adelaide grabbed every flavor of juice offered at this coffee shop—carrot and ginger, orange, apple, cucumber and spinach, blackcurrant. She placed them all at the till, lined up like a rainbow.

Lot of juice, the barista said. *Like a little rainbow.* Inexplicably, Adelaide began to cry again. *Are you sure you're all right, hon?* the barista asked.

I'm sure, Adelaide said. *I'm sorry, just having a rough morning is all. Thank you for asking, though.*

She was lying.

Rory answered the door to find Adelaide with tearstained cheeks and five bottles of juice balanced in her arms. He almost laughed.

She set the juice on his kitchen counter, turned around to hug him. *I got every juice they had,* she said. *I hope they're all right.*

Thanks, he said.

This morning, he'd learned that Nathalie had been named deputy editor the day before she died. At twenty-seven, she was the youngest deputy editor at *The Times.* He wiped his eyes with the back of his hand.

She was remarkable, Rory said. *In every way, to every person. She was just so good. I don't want to live in a world without her.*

I know, Adelaide said. *I'm so sorry. I wish you didn't have to.*

I guess I'm just lucky to have known her, he said. *I mean, my life has been irrevocably made better because of her. All of the books I've read,* The Orwell Diaries. *Did you know she gave me my first copy over Christmas at uni? It's all because of her. I just. I don't even know how to describe this.*

It occurred to Adelaide then how complex Rory's grief was, how layered. For the duration of their relationship, Adelaide had understood that she was playing second fiddle—first to a faceless, nameless ex, and then to Nathalie Alban. *The* Nathalie Alban. A woman who was not just successful, graceful, beautiful, it seemed, but truly full of success, of grace, of beauty. Despite his claims to the contrary, Adelaide knew that Rory still harbored love for Nathalie Alban, that she owned pieces of his heart Adelaide would never be able to reach.

And now, she was gone. And Rory was forced to grieve the love of his life once again, a person he'd lost long before she left this earth. She was no longer a partner, not even a friend. She was—well, he didn't know what, exactly. Nor did Adelaide. It was impossible to pinpoint what he'd lost; it was such a complicated breed of mourning.

How do you mourn a person you've not spoken to in more than two years? A person who kissed your forehead when you were sick, who baked cakes on your birthday, who slept by your side, off and on, for more than five years? How do you mourn a person whose breath you once listened to over the phone, late at night, when you'd both run out of things to say but just wanted to feel close to one another? How do you make sense of the fact that that breath has ceased; that this person is gone; that they're no longer at the other end of the phone line, the city, the planet?

How do you keep your feet on the ground knowing your world is now one person—one brilliant, effervescent, incredibly kind, loving person—lighter? You can't. And so, you grab hold of the nearest thing, the nearest being, in hopes that they will tether you to this side of existence.

For Rory, that tether was Adelaide. He held her hair in his fists, breathed in the scent of her perfume—floral and rich, orange flowers and bergamot. He wiped his tears on her sweatshirt—the same one she'd worn yesterday, with Alliance's little logo on the sleeve—grateful she could stand when it felt like his knees might cave. Grateful to have a pillar.

Adelaide felt Rory's weight on her shoulders, both literally and metaphorically. She rubbed his back, kissed his wet cheeks. He continued to cry. Adelaide didn't know how to pacify him, how to fill the Nathalie-sized hole in his heart and make the world feel warm again. But she had to, she told herself. *You have to make this better.*

She pulled back a moment, her arms on his shoulders. She looked at his watery eyes. *I know we have different perspectives on faith,* she said. *And I know I didn't know Nathalie at all. I met her over coffee. Once. That was it. But even I could tell that there was something magical about her, that she had this sort of . . . energy. And that energy doesn't leave earth. It's still here, I promise you.*

I know, he said. *But it feels so cold here without her.*

It's so cruel, she said, pulling him into another hug. *That grief comes part and parcel with love. It's just so unfair.*

They watched old Disney films, documentaries about the moon. They got pasta for lunch. Adelaide hated herself for having to run out once the bill came, sprinting to the station to ensure she wasn't late for her meetings that afternoon.

Adelaide sat down on the Tube and some valve inside her turned, releasing every tear, every ounce of hurt she'd been holding in for the past several hours. She played Maggie Rogers's "Give a Little" through her earbuds, at full volume, trying to drown her own emotions in the song.

(When she was growing up, music had always offered an escape from the tumult of her home.)

At the office, she quickly washed her face, manically reapplied eyeliner in the bathroom. *Can you tell I've been crying?* she asked Sam, walking into the conference room.

Not at all, Sam said. *But if you need to step out for a moment, just tug your ear twice and I'll ask you to run and grab everyone a cup of tea.* Adelaide smiled at her.

It's a plan, she said. *Thank you.*

At six on the dot, Adelaide slipped out of the office and met Rory again. They went to the movies, saw a film with an actress Adelaide thought looked a great deal like Nathalie. Was she seeing things? she wondered. Had Rory also noticed the resemblance?

They went back to his flat afterward. Adelaide offered to stop by the grocery store on their way, to make some comfort food. *Mac and cheese?* she asked. *Fried chicken? I can even try to find some green tomatoes and fry them up.*

That was okay, Rory said. He wasn't particularly hungry, and it all sounded too rich for him, anyway. The last Southern meal she'd prepared had given him a bit of a stomach ache. Adelaide bit her lip. *Oh,* she said. She made him a strawberry smoothie instead, combed his hair with her fingers on his bed, washed the blender once he'd fallen asleep.

Thanks again, Adelaide, Bubs said, passing by the kitchen.

Sure thing, she said.

By the way, he said. *I stole some of Rory's leftovers last week. That mac and cheese was incredible.*

She smiled weakly, went home. Sobbed. Worked overnight. Slept for a few hours. Woke up, remembered, wished she could turn back time. All over again.

The next two days followed this pattern. Adelaide spent her mornings with Rory. Her afternoons at the office. Her evenings watching films, petting Rory's hair, lulling him to sleep. *I'm so sorry. I'm here.* She worked until 4 A.M. and woke up at seven, running on adrenaline, little food, and a dangerous amount of caffeine.

On Friday morning, Rory had a doctor's appointment—a quick check-in to see if he'd developed any more ulcers (he had; they prescribed a new medication)—so she worked the full day at the office. They were less than three days from Alliance's first event. The executive team was flying over that afternoon, on-site run-throughs were planned for the weekend. Adelaide checked items from her to-do list, trying not to cry. She still wanted to be a pillar, not just for Rory, but for Alliance.

She was on a conference call with the Paris office—pretending she could understand more than half of their quick-fire French—when she saw a text from Rory.

Afternoon's taken an interesting turn, he said. I'll explain later, but I got a few calls from Nat's mum and her best friend earlier. I'm off to her home to see the family. Should be back late this evening.

Excuse me for one second, Adelaide mouthed to Djibril. She got off the call, left the room, almost fainted on the bathroom floor. She threw up bile, laid her head on the cold linoleum floor.

Get it the fuck together, she told herself, willing her body to sit up, the room to stop spinning. It wouldn't, it wouldn't; nothing would stop. Adelaide couldn't make any of it stop.

Her fear was this: Rory had gotten a call because Nathalie still loved him. She'd always loved him, of course she had. She'd kept every birthday card he'd ever given her, pressed every rose from Valentine's Day. Her friends, her family, they simply could not lay her to rest without letting Rory know; they couldn't bury her with secrets untold.

This wasn't the truth. (If it was, at least, Adelaide never knew.) The truth was that Nathalie's mum had called Rory because she loved him. He'd broken her daughter's heart, yes, but he'd also spent five-plus years by her side—at graduations, at little cousins' baptisms, at her grandparents' funerals. Her mum simply wanted to see Rory, to check in on him, to hold his hands and say, *I can't believe this is all happening, but I'm glad you're here.*

Nathalie's best friend had called with different, more painful news—Nathalie and her surviving boyfriend, Peter, had picked out rings and chosen settings several weeks earlier. They'd moved in together just last month, planned to get engaged that spring. Peter was meant to give her eulogy, and her friend wanted Rory to know the full extent of their relationship. She didn't want him to be blindsided.

He told Adelaide all of this on Friday night, over boxes of Chinese takeout. (They'd overordered dinner at the office earlier; she brought the leftovers to Rory's around nine, her stomach in knots.)

How do you feel? she asked.

I don't know, he said, though he seemed a bit more at peace. Adelaide imagined it must have felt a bit like cleaning a bad scrape. It stings, but at least the flesh will heal. You know the person you loved found happiness, that their family still cared for you, that you'd not fully decimated their heart while it was still beating.

Still, none of this could bring Nathalie back.

His roommates came in, put on another movie—one from the *Fast & Furious* franchise. Adelaide squeezed onto the corner of the couch, feeling awkward. Invasive, somehow. She left as the credits began to roll, just before they started the next film in the series. Rory walked her to the door.

He gave her a hug and murmured something, three syllables, very faintly. Just into her hair. *I love you,* she thought. She heard Rory say, *I love you.*

Hm? Adelaide asked.

Oh, Rory said. *I just said thank you.*

During

London, England
2019

Eighteen

It wasn't meant to happen like this. Nothing was meant to happen like this.

She was so healthy, so kind. She was so cautious and privileged and loved and cared for—so many of the things that are supposed to mean you live for decades upon decades. For a century, even.

He could picture it: Her name in the local paper, smile shining above a candlelit cake. NATHALIE ALBAN TURNS 100 THIS WEEK. She would celebrate with friends, with family. With her grandchildren and great-grandchildren, her nieces and nephews. That's what was supposed to happen, at least. Before.

Before everything went wrong. Before everything was broken. Before Nathalie Alban died on a dark, rainy evening and the world as Rory knew it ceased to exist.

It doesn't make sense.

Rory Hughes knew grief (arguably better than most). But this feeling was different—extraordinary in the worst way. This was shocking and gutting and confounding and all-consuming and, just, *Holy shit.* It really, truly did not make sense.

He'd seen the news on Facebook, of all places. One of Nat's sisters had posted a status. *I'm devastated to share that my sister—my silly, joyful, always-right big sister Nathalie—was killed in a car accident last night.* She'd included a picture: the pair of them hugging and smiling at Nathalie's Cambridge graduation, her robes black and white and lined with fur. Rory had taken the photo.

He'd run to the bathroom then, started to vomit, but nothing would come up. *Thank fuck I hadn't eaten porridge yet,* he'd thought. *Thank fuck?* a voice shouted in his brain. *How can you be thankful for anything right now?*

He'd wiped his mouth, his eyes. Called his brother Daniel, the only other Hughes boy in London. *I'll be over in an hour,* Daniel had said; he wrapped his little brother in a bear hug as soon as he got to the flat.

Daniel had made toast, eggs. Rory didn't eat. Instead, they'd sat in bleary silence, daytime news buzzing in the background, eggs going cold on the coffee table. It stretched on for hours.

Rory texted the rest of his family, his roommates and old hallmates. He told them what happened, the horrible, horrible news. Sometime around noon, Daniel turned to him and asked, *Have you spoken to Adelaide?*

Oh, he thought. *Adelaide.* Her name hadn't even crossed his mind.

Rory called; Adelaide answered. He told her about Nathalie. Her voice was so full of empathy, of care. She sent a pizza thirty or so minutes later, making him feel nauseous all over again.

You don't deserve this, the voice shouted. But what was it, exactly, that he didn't deserve? Was it the grief, the agony? Or Adelaide's sweet concern?

Hours later, she'd shown up and thrown her arms around him. So earnestly, so carefully. *You don't deserve this,* the voice said again. Rory tried to ignore it, to avoid focusing on the implication. He didn't really want to know what it was he didn't deserve.

She'd been there every morning, just after he woke up. Every night as he fell asleep.

Had it been awkward, he wondered, for Adelaide to comfort him as he mourned the love of his life? The woman who—as a bright-eyed Cambridge student—he thought he'd one day marry. The woman to whom he still, honestly, thought he'd find his way back someday. The one who'd picked out rings with another man, breaking his heart in so many different, unique, and devastating ways. Had it been uncomfortable to wipe his tears and pet his hair and hear Nat's mother's words? *We are heartbroken to have lost our girl.*

He couldn't know, would never know. But honestly, did he care? Adelaide was there, and that was all that mattered. It was all he needed: Just, someone to be there. Someone to hold his hand and echo his disbelief—*It doesn't make sense.*

And then, somehow, those other words had spilled out of his mouth. *I love you,* he'd said, wishing her a good night. Did he, though? Or did he just love that she was with him?

He wasn't sure. But *Fuck,* nothing was meant to happen like this.

D aniel took him to Manchester that Saturday; their older brothers, Cameron and Arthur, picked them up at the train station. They patted Rory's back, ruffled his hair.

We love you, mate, they said. *We're so sorry this happened. Nat was a great girl.*

The best, Rory said. The absolute best.

They drove to Arthur's house, parked out front, walked to a pub around the corner. It was empty, save for a teenager working the bar and a stack of dusty board games in the corner. Arthur's wife, Stella, met them at the table—she had pitchers of beer and plates of fish and chips waiting for their arrival.

I'm so sorry, she said to Rory, arms outstretched. *Nat was the loveliest.*

The best, Rory said again, leaning into her hug.

They sat in silence at first—pretending to watch a cycling race on television, awkwardly nursing their beers. Rory's brothers weren't sure what to do, really. Whether they should distract Rory, or wallow with him, or remind him of the time they made Nat laugh so hard, sangria came out of her nose. They didn't know what he wanted, what he needed. So, they did what too many of us do in the face of grief: Nothing.

He texted Adelaide, asked what she was up to. Oh, she said. Just stuffing a million and one swag bags for this work event on Monday. I'll save you one if we have extras! She sent a picture: Her floor covered in puffs of white tissue paper, piles of gray Alliance hoodies, packages of fancy sunglasses.

(She didn't include herself in the photo, her red-rimmed eyes and splotchy cheeks. She'd been sobbing all morning. Every ounce of her was on fire, every ounce of her was afraid. Of what? Adelaide didn't even know. *I'm so sorry,* she'd said, calling Eloise at 6 A.M. Eastern time, tears sliding down the phone screen. *My family wasn't answering and Madison's not home and, can you talk? Of course she could,* Eloise said. *And don't you ever apologize. "Sorry" is not a word that exists in this friendship, okay?*)

How's Manchester? Adelaide texted.

Rory looked at his brothers, all silent at the table. It's good, he said. Good to be with family. And it was. Genuinely, it was. But a part of him wished he were curled up in bed, a film on his laptop, Adelaide's long blond hair wrapped around his fingers.

Then Stella asked if anyone fancied a game of Cards Against Humanity. The guys hesitated, nodded.

Sure, they said. *Why not?*

Here's the thing: If you're bereft and grieving and brokenhearted, and you're presented with the opportunity to say, *My name is Peter Parker. I was bitten by a radioactive spider and now I'm covering myself in parmesan cheese and chili flakes because I am pizza . . .* You must— must!—take it.

Less than ten minutes into the game, the Hughes were all in tears. The best kind of tears. The joyful, out-of-control kind.

They played for hours. First at the pub, then back at Arthur's house, gathered around his kitchen table. He ducked out for a few rounds to make dinner, chopping potatoes and rosemary as Stella roasted a chicken, watching his younger brothers cackle like a pack of hyenas. *What is George W. Bush thinking about right now? Many bats.*

It reminded Arthur of the night of his parents' funeral, the way their grandmother had taught the boys to play old maid with that yellowed deck of cards she always carried in her purse. Sitting on the living room floor, mum and dad's wedding photos still framed above the fireplace, the boys shifting uncomfortably in their overstarched suits.

It upset Arthur at first, this attempt to distract them. *It's not about distracting you,* she'd told him. *A linbh—my child—you'll never forget this pain. But I want you to remember that you can still feel joy, too. That you can still laugh and smile like the wee rascals you are.*

Arthur looked at his brothers again now, relieved that Rory could still laugh, still smile. He exhaled, tossed the potatoes in salt and olive oil. *Remember this*, he thought. *Remember that you're still allowed to feel joy.*

Daniel slept on Cameron's couch; Rory took Arthur's guest room. They all met up at a different pub the next day, one with a beer garden out back and a killer Sunday roast, Stella promised. Adelaide texted Rory that morning, wishing him a good day, asking what his plans were.

Near the end of their meal, a server arrived with a dessert sampler— decadent chocolate cakes and mousse and custard-drenched apple crumble. *Is this the Hugheses' table?* he asked. They nodded, confused. *This is for you, compliments of an Adelaide Williams?* Rory smiled, rolled his eyes. They all tucked in.

You didn't have to do that, he texted Adelaide.

It's the least I can do, she said. I have to run to the venue tonight and set a few things up, but let me know if you need a pal when you get home from the train station, okay?

So, Cameron said, dipping his spoon in the mousse. *This Adelaide? She's a good one, I take it?*

The best, Rory said.

The best. He'd said it without thinking, without even realizing. But she wasn't the best, not really. She couldn't be. It was Nat; it would always be Nat.

Not Adelaide.

Nineteen

Adelaide got to the event venue—a swanky hotel in Bloomsbury—just after four o'clock that Sunday, a few minutes later than planned. She was wearing jeans, a too-big sweater, an Alliance beanie, hardly any makeup. The company's CEO greeted her with a high five she almost missed—*Look at the elbow,* she told herself—and complimented her hat. She was mortified. How had she forgotten the executives were rehearsing on-site this evening? How could that possibly have slipped her mind as she was getting ready?

You look like you've been working some late nights, Adelaide, the CEO said. He was among the only Black leaders in the fintech space—tall, bright, unbearably cool. She laughed nervously.

Oh, she said. *Events, you know. Here for the midnight oil. Or something.* Words were hard right now.

Something like that, he said, giving her back a pat as he began to walk away. *Heavy is the head that wears the director's crown, huh?*

Adelaide caught Sam's eye then, giving her a funny look. *Director's crown?* she mouthed. Had she misunderstood?

Hey, Sam said. She gave Adelaide a quick hug, pulled her aside. *He's a little confused, but. Here's the thing.* There had been talks that week of opening a role for an international communications lead—a position with a bit more autonomy than Adelaide currently had, one that would cover comms in EMEA as well as emerging markets across Asia-Pacific. It would involve travel to Sydney, Singapore, Seoul. It wasn't quite director-level, Sam said, but it was close. *And obviously you were the first person who came to mind. I just, I know there's a lot going on right now, in and outside of work. I didn't want to stress you out.*

Whoa my gosh, Adelaide said. *Yeah, no, that would be incredible. I'd love a role like that.*

We've got a few months before we even plan to pull the job description together, though, Sam said. *So like, futile as this is to say knowing you, try not to think about it too much? Don't put any extra pressure on yourself.*

Of course, Adelaide said. *Of course. No pressure.*

Great. For now, can you give me a hand getting the stage set up?

They rolled out a gray carpet, dragged cushy blue lounge chairs and a small coffee table to the center of the stage. BBC Radio 1 blasted over the speakers, and the executives paced the room, reciting their presentation points at a whisper. Adelaide took her hat off; she and Sam both pulled their hair back, wiped sweat from their brows.

They spent the next few hours placing Alliance-branded notebooks and pens on tables, checking floral arrangements, adjusting the lighting. They practiced stage changes for fireside chats, individual presentations, panel discussions. The speakers ran through their decks and questions and talking points. *Don't forget to vary the three P's,* Adelaide would say. *Pitch, pace, and projection.* They'd nod, give her a thumbs-up.

The execs went to their rooms around eight that night; Adelaide, Sam, and Djibril combed through the decks one more time over glasses of wine and truffle fries, literally crossing the *t*'s and dotting the *i*'s with their graphic designer.

She was exhausted and sweaty and starting to go cross-eyed, yes. But for the first time in days (in weeks?), Adelaide was also starting to feel as though she was in her element.

The next morning was the best part.

Everyone took their seats, the lights dimmed. "DNA" by Kendrick Lamar boomed through the ballroom, and massive screens at either side of the stage played a video about Alliance—featuring testimonials and rocket ships and a voice-over describing advancements made with machine learning and blockchain (which, admittedly, Adelaide still struggled to understand). It was all very over-the-top, very *fintech conference-y.* But still. It gave Adelaide goose bumps.

She'd written the script for this video, sourced the clients who would soon be speaking, invited the trade reporters who were sitting at a table in the front row. In tandem with Sam, Djibril, and the events team, she'd helped make this moment happen. It felt good to have brought it all to life.

To life, she thought, and the world stopped. It was warm inside, but Adelaide started to shiver uncontrollably, grabbing her blazer from the back of her chair at the tech desk. She pulled it over her shoulders; her hands were all clammy, the room suddenly cast in a fog.

Are you okay? Sam mouthed. *All good,* Adelaide mouthed back. But she wasn't. She tried to focus on the presentations and chats, to cheer on Alliance's leadership team with a smile. But Nathalie Alban was dead, and that horrible fact sat at the forefront of Adelaide's mind for the rest of the day. Through content, through happy hour, through clinked glasses and more pats on the back and *Thanks for the hard work, Adelaide—see you in Paris*es.

It was suffocating.

I'm coming over with a tray of hors d'oeuvres and a pitcher of something called the Alliance Spritz, she texted Rory. She was trying to sound chipper, to bring warmth. Spoiler alert: It's Aperol.

I hope there are mini quiches, he replied.

What is this, she typed. 1984? (Totally kidding! There are so many mini quiches!) He smiled at his phone.

Adelaide appeared at his doorstep thirty minutes later, tray and pitcher in hand, heels hooked on her pointer finger. *There was no way I could make it up the stairs in these,* she said, tilting her head toward the pumps. It was not unlike the day they'd first met. The moment she'd called him a Disney prince with pitchers in her arms, no shoes on her feet—*I'm so sorry. I just. I had to tell you . . .*

They sat on his bed, eating teensy quiches, blini topped with crème fraîche and quinoa caviar. They split the pitcher of Alliance Spritz, put on another Disney film. Adelaide was meeting the CEO for one more reporter meeting in the morning, then boarding the train to Paris for their next event. She had to shower, to pack, to double-check the French decks. It was important, all of it was important. But it felt so insignificant, so small, considering.

She looked at Rory—a bit tipsy, giggling for the first time in over a week—and curled up in the crook of his neck. She still felt it all: the weight of his grief, the relief at having wrapped one event, the fresh promise and *No Pressure!* (but really, very much pressure) of a promotion—the coalescence of good and bad and. Well, of everything. But for a split second, it almost felt bearable.

She closed her eyes.

A delaide had fallen asleep, of course she had. (She was so tired. *My gosh*, was she tired.) Rory looked at her snoring body—hair spread out around her shoulders, tickling his arm a little; her eyelashes fluttered.

Adelaide, he said, nudging her elbow with his own. *Adelaide. Wake up, baby.* (He used to call Nathalie "baby," too. The word tasted sour in his mouth now.) She snapped awake a second later, seemingly surprised to be in his bedroom.

Fuck, she said. *I didn't mean to doze off. What time is it?* It was ten after midnight, he told her. They'd fallen asleep watching another film; Rory had just woken up to brush his teeth, change his clothes.

I hate to ask this, she said. *But do you mind if I stay the night tonight? I'm afraid it's too late to take the Tube and I've had bad experiences with cabbies at this hour.* Most of the time it was fine, of course. But every now and then, on her way home from Rory's, she'd get a driver who asked what a *Little girl* like Adelaide was doing out so late.

Being a bit naughty? one had said to her. *No,* she'd told him. *That's not it.* Thinking about it made her feel nauseous.

There's a night bus you can take, he said. *The stop's not far from here, just a ten-minute walk or so.*

It's after midnight, she said. *And it's raining.*

It's a safe area.

Adelaide sat up from his pillow, nodded her head. *Right,* she said. *Got it.* It was hard not to sound bitter, but she tried her best. She gave him a kiss on the cheek. *I'll see you after Paris. Sleep well.*

She walked out of his bedroom then, tiptoed down the stairs. There was a light on in their living room. *Adelaide?* Bubs asked. She popped her head through the doorframe.

Yup, she said. *What are you doing up so late?* He was working on a pro bono brief, he said. Got a bit caught up in all of it, lost track of time.

You're not leaving now, he said, checking the time on his phone. *Are you?* Adelaide shrugged her shoulders.

Rory usually sleeps better when I'm not here, she said. *And he's had, you know, a tough week. I shouldn't have dozed off up there. I'm just a little run-down, I think. Not from him, of course. Just, like, in general? From life? But not like I need sympathy or anything. Fuck, you know what I mean. Anyway. I'm going to catch the bus.*

Don't worry, Bubs said. *I know what you mean. I think February gets everyone a bit run-down, and you've had a rough go of it lately, eh?* Adelaide nodded. *Give me a minute to grab my coat and I can drive you home, all right?*

Oh, she said. *No, you don't have to do that.* (Though it was cold, and raining, and honestly? Honestly, it'd be quite nice to have a ride home.)

Don't be silly, he said. *It's no trouble at all, and you shouldn't be out in this. I'm sure if Rory were awake, he'd not want you trudging through puddles and waiting for the bus so late.* Adelaide nodded again; she didn't correct him.

Bubs ran up the stairs. He came down in a navy-blue rain jacket a few minutes later, turned off the light in the living room. *Here,* he said, handing Adelaide an umbrella. *I'm parked just around the corner.*

They walked out the door, rain sputtering from drainpipes. Bubs led them down the stairwell, around the corner, into a silver Mitsubishi. Adelaide nearly opened the door to the driver's side; she still hadn't adapted to the fact that they drove on the left. *Old habits?* Bub asked. He winked.

So, Adelaide said. She shook out the umbrella, closed the door, buckled her seat belt. *You said you were working on a pro bono brief?*

Mhm, he said.

Tell me more, she said.

I primarily do immigration law, he said, pulling up to a traffic light. *And a few years ago, I thought I could maybe make myself useful, what with all this bloody Brexit business and the Windrush scandal kicking off.*

Adelaide nodded. She tried to wrap her mind around his accent, the lilt and brogue and drawl of it; she could sense the miles traveled in the sound of his voice.

I started volunteering with a migrant group, he continued. *Picking up a few cases a year. I was working on one for a woman from Sierra Leone just now. She came over as a student with pretty severe post-traumatic stress disorder. Had a panic attack during exams, failed out and lost her visa. The government's kept her in a holding pattern ever since.*

Oh my gosh, Adelaide said. *This is probably a silly question, because I'm, um, not a lawyer. But is there anything I can do to help?*

Bubs explained that they were always looking for volunteers to serve as conversation partners, people to practice English with men and women who'd recently arrived in the U.K. Adelaide made a note with the name of the organization in her phone, mentally promising to send them an email next week.

I know it's late, he said. *But can I take you on a quick detour?*

Um, Adelaide said. *Sure?* (Was this where he murdered her?)

Bubs turned down a side street in Angel, rows of terraced houses with white doorframes and wrought-iron fences on either side. He pulled off in front of one. It had a bright red door, a bit of wiry ivy climbing up the brick. Number sixteen.

That one, he said, pointing, *will be my house in about two weeks' time.*

No way! Adelaide said. *You already bought a house? Didn't you, like, just move in with Rory and them?*

This past summer, yeah, he said. He grinned, put the car back into drive. He explained that he'd needed a place to stay for a few months, just as he saved up the final bit of his down payment. He knew Rory had a room open; it all made sense. *And now he's mine.*

Well, congrats! Adelaide said. *That's so exciting! And, um, are houses gentlemen now?*

Technically, no, Bubs said. *They're gender neutral, I suppose. But people are always calling boats "she" and "her," aren't they? Bit fucked up in my opinion. Just because you own something doesn't make it female.*

Right, Adelaide said. *Right. Gender's a social construct, anyway.*

Exactly, he said. She smiled. Then she remembered.

It happened like this; it came in waves. Adelaide would get distracted by work, by films, by conversations. And then she'd remember: Nathalie Alban was dead. Nothing was okay.

Her eyes filled with tears; she bit her lip. *Not now,* she thought. *Please.*

Not now. It was a fruitless thought. Tears started to run down her cheeks; a sob caught in her throat. Adelaide sniffed. *Sorry,* she said, feigning a yawn. *Just super tired, I guess.*

It's all right, Adelaide, Bubs said. *I get it. It's been a really, really shit week. And you've got a tough job in all this.*

She sobbed harder then, tears flowing uncontrollably. It made Bubs think of his little sister, of the way he'd watched her cry after she'd fallen off her bicycle on the cobblestone in Dublin, completely unfettered. He had the impulse to reach across the console and grab Adelaide's hand, to smooth her hair and remind her that she was safe. *It's all right,* he wanted to say again. But that wasn't appropriate. (And things weren't really all right.)

There are tissues in the glove box, he said. *And Adelaide? Remember, feel whatever you need to feel. There's no right answer here.*

Yeah, Adelaide said. She grabbed a tissue, wiped her eyes. *Yeah, thank you. Seriously.*

Bubs turned on the radio, spinning the dial until it reached a classical-music station. *Good?* he asked.

Perfect, she said.

They listened to "Clair de Lune," then "Danse Bohémienne," then something Adelaide couldn't quite place. Neither really spoke; Adelaide just sniffed on occasion. *Sorry,* she'd say. *Don't apologize,* Bubs would reply. He pulled up to her building about fifteen minutes later, wished her a good night.

Thank you so much, Bubs, Adelaide said. *For everything. Can I give you gas—I mean petrol money, or . . . ?*

Oh please, no, he said, waving her away. *Just have a good one, Adelaide.*

You too, she said. *A good one.*

Spring

London, England
2019

Twenty

Nathalie Alban was buried on the twenty-sixth of March, just over a month after her death. She was laid to rest in a graveyard in Cambridge, next to her grandparents (she'd always been their favorite). Rory spent the night of the funeral at a friend's home near the church. Adelaide gave him an embroidered handkerchief for his pocket, sent flowers anonymously to the service—yellow chrysanthemums. She sat on her living room floor that night with Celeste and Madison, all in tears.

What a legacy to have left, Adelaide thought. That three strangers sat around through the earliest hours of the morning, crying over a person they'd never known, wondering how to make the world the least bit better in her absence. It was telling of Nathalie's mark on this earth, of her impact.

Adelaide, as we know, was not afraid of Death. But she struggled with this particular death, with Nathalie's. There was no relief here, no end to suffering. There was simply a woman whose body stopped pumping blood, whose heart stopped beating, whose lungs stopped breathing air. Inexplicably. Adelaide still struggled to make sense of it, to find meaning.

I think, maybe, that's the beautiful thing, Celeste said. *That she never had to hurt, to suffer.*

Perhaps she was right. Adelaide never knew Nathalie, not properly, but she knew certain chunks and details of her life. She knew that she'd just been promoted, just moved in with the boy she planned to marry, just chosen an engagement ring. She knew she had a chocolate Lab named Jem who'd surely greeted her, every morning and every night, with fierce loyalty and slobbery kisses. If one were to cram Nathalie's life into the pages of a book, Adelaide trusted this chapter would have been an incredible note on which to end. She was, and would forever be, vivacious and vibrant, filled with reasons to celebrate herself and others. Frozen and memorialized with her warmth, her ambition, her beauty, her light all burning bright as ever. Without prolonged suffering or bitterness. Nothing but frenetic energy, boundless potential, and love left behind.

Still, absence bears weight. Loss is heavy—oxymoronically heavy. And it sits on our hearts completely unforgivingly. Even trusting Nathalie's life had closed on a remarkably high note, Adelaide could feel the weight of it all. She could sense the gravity that was crushing Rory.

It had not eased in the last month; thus far, time had refused to heal this wound. *Not yet,* it said. *Feel this a bit longer,* it said. And Adelaide, the very tired pillar, was beginning to crumble beneath the pressure.

She'd brought Rory books, cups of coffee, endless offers of hugs. She'd sent milkshakes and dumplings when he ignored her messages, when he *Needed a night to himself.* She watched movies in his bedroom, took long walks along the river, bought him cones of Mr. Whippy with a log (always with a log). Tried to smile, to kiss his nose, to bring joy.

But sometimes, she was ten minutes late for dinner because work meetings ran over, or she'd check her email while they watched a film. (She was still up for that promotion and eager to prove her worth. And yes, Alliance's Paris event had gone off without a hitch, thank you for asking.) She'd step outside to call a bakery in Mykonos, to check the schedule for the train from New York to Boston, to ask tailors on the Upper East Side about last-minute alterations. She was drowning in maid-of-honor duties and work and feelings of her own inadequacy, all while trying to be a pillar. Because goddamnit, she wanted to be a pillar. For everyone. But she was starting to fall short, as Rory often reminded her. *Late again,* he'd say. *Can you be present for once and just watch a film with me?* he'd ask. *Nat was able to climb the ranks without letting work swallow every weekend. There's no reason you can't do the same.*

It started a few weeks before the funeral; some switch flipped inside of him. He was still aloof, still unreachable at times. But he was also, suddenly, demanding of Adelaide.

It led to a mix of emotions she'd never before experienced—one that was near-impossible to articulate for fear of sounding selfish or bitter or self-aggrandizing. For fear of taking up too much space. Adelaide liked being needed, and she liked taking care of Rory, and she knew how to offer comfort and solace when he was depressed. (This was a skill she'd mastered throughout her own life.) But she didn't know how to navigate the bitterness and resentment that followed.

From his grief-stricken vantage point, Adelaide wasn't planning enough holidays. Wasn't offering up enough positivity. She was flaky and dismissive and why didn't she know how to kayak, anyway? Everything she did was suddenly wrong, and it was all being starkly compared to Nathalie: Her love for the Rolling Stones and pink rose gardens. Her interest in reading *Wuthering Heights.* Her appreciation for the curl that hung just above his forehead (*Nat liked my hair long, too*).

Goddamnit, she was trying.

On the twenty-seventh of March, the day after Nathalie Alban's service, Adelaide and Rory made plans to meet at the movies at eight o'clock. One of Adelaide's friends, Dayita, was visiting from the States—a stopover in London for one night only. Adelaide was convinced she could meet Dayita for dinner and make it to the film on time. *No problem,* she thought. She could do it all.

She left work at five forty-five, rushed to the restaurant, made it (miraculously) by six fifteen. She and Dayita shared a burrata, a carafe of Frascati. They got plates of pasta covered in shaved truffles, shared a tiramisu for two. When Dayita asked how life had been treating her lately, Adelaide shrugged. *Can't complain,* she said. (It was best not to address it all, she thought. And besides, Adelaide was known for being fun! Bubbly! She didn't want to be a burden.) The check was paid with extreme efficiency at seven thirty, and Adelaide kissed her friend on both cheeks and apologized for rushing off before heading to the theater. She was there with ten minutes to spare.

The trouble is, she went to the wrong theater. There was more than one cinema by the Barbican, evidently, and Adelaide circled the block trying to find Rory—asking her phone, Barbican staff, random pedestrians for directions.

I'm so sorry, she texted. *I've been running in circles for ten minutes and my phone doesn't seem to know where your pin is. Can you tell me the cross streets?* He read her message, didn't respond.

She finally arrived, sweaty and breathless, five minutes into the previews. She squeezed into Rory's row, straightening the skirt of her dress as she sat down.

I'm so sorry again, she said.

It's fine, he said. He didn't offer her popcorn, a sip of his drink. She turned to face the screen. Neither one of them reached for the other's hand.

After the film, a sweet Pixar movie, they walked out of the theater single file. The sky was dark now, the air a bit humid—it had been a surprisingly warm day. Adelaide tried to take Rory's hand as they walked to the station. He pulled away. *My palms are all sweaty,* he told her.

I'm sorry again for being late, Adelaide said.

It wasn't that, Rory said. *I was just a bit irritated.*

With me? Adelaide asked.

Well, yes, he said.

He was irritated because he needed joy and light and a bit of sunshine today, he explained, after a month of darkness. *Especially after yesterday.* He wanted Adelaide to be there for him, to actually show up for once. *But then you made plans with your friend,* he said. Adelaide opened her mouth, closed it. *And you were late, and all agitated, and you made no effort to make conversation during the previews.* She bit her tongue. *And it just . . . it wasn't quite what I needed.*

I see, Adelaide said. She began to tear up. *I'm really sorry I couldn't offer what you needed.*

Oh, don't do that, he said. *Don't make me feel like shit. I feel bad enough as it is. Nat's in the ground now, and my stomach's been acting up, and I don't need your guilt trip, Adelaide.*

You're right, she said. She wasn't sure what else to say.

They walked in silence to the station, gave each other a quick peck good night. *What are your plans this weekend?* she asked him. *Can I plan a little surprise? Try to make it up to you?*

I'm free, he said. *No need to do anything fancy, though.*

Nothing fancy, she said. *Got it.*

It's *not fancy,* Adelaide said, taking Rory's hand on Saturday afternoon. *But it's not not fancy.* She was leading them to the Parlour at Fortnum & Mason, a lush department store in Piccadilly.

When Adelaide was younger, she spent a year of her life just outside of London in a small town called Beaconsfield. Her father, a human resources director, was helping his company open a new office in the U.K. Trips to London were a rarity, a treat, but they always included a stop at Fortnum & Mason. She, her mother, and her sisters would pile into a train car in floral tops and bouncy skirts. They'd order ice cream dripping with fudge sauce, scones covered in jam and clotted cream, cups and saucers filled with fruity, herbal tea. The girls—aged eight to sixteen—would all mimic English accents, drinking with their pinkies straight out.

It's silly and frivolous, she told Rory. *But it's also delicious and so much fun.* He gave a weak smile.

They walked through the doorway, past counters of chocolate truffles and Turkish delights, up the stairwell to the first floor. The Parlour had undergone several iterations and changes since Adelaide's childhood, but it was still painted in pastel colors. It felt like walking into a schmaltzy memory. A candied fever dream.

They sat down, chose the Knickerbocker Glory to share, broke the meringue topping with long silver spoons.

What do you want your legacy to be? Rory asked. Adelaide hesitated. She was afraid of questions like these, of questions that unequivocally evoked thoughts of Nathalie. *Kindness?* he asked again.

I guess so, Adelaide said. *But I'm not sure if it's really all that kind to do nice things in the hopes that you'll be remembered for doing nice things, you know?* He nodded. *What about you?* she asked.

He didn't answer, just stared ahead. Undoubtedly thinking of Nathalie.

Smart, I suppose, he said, a few minutes later. *I want to be remembered as smart, intellectual. And well liked.*

Well, Adelaide said. *For what it's worth, I think you're both of those things. That and handsome,* she added with a wink. *Exceptionally handsome.*

He grinned at her; her heart swelled. It had been so long since she'd seen him properly smile.

She paid for the sundae and they wound their way out of the Parlour, out of the store, over to Green Park. Just past its gate, at a nearby hotel, they could hear the early rumblings of a wedding reception. There was a couple taking photos in the garden, tuxes and tails and silky dresses mingling over canapés. Adelaide stuck her nose through the fence.

Remember that time you wedding crashed? she said to Rory. *What if we put on dress clothes, met back here, and tried our luck at sneaking in?*

Oh, Rory said. *That'd be such fun.*

Let's do it, she said. *Why not? YOLO or whatever.*

He couldn't, he told her. *Makes me think too much of uni,* he said. *Too much of Nat.*

Of course, she said. *Of course. Back to your place it is?*

H as it been mentioned that Adelaide and Rory hadn't had sex in a month?

Adelaide and Rory hadn't had sex in a month. Not since Nathalie died, not until this evening.

They returned to Rory's flat and stretched out on his bed—no film to watch, no tears to cry. Not now, at this moment. Adelaide turned to Rory. She kissed his cheek, brushed her lip against his jawline. *Adelaide,* he said. It was so quiet, so faint; the same way she could have sworn she'd heard him say *I love you* all those weeks before. (She'd not heard him say it since.)

Rory, she said.

He turned and pressed his lips to hers. Gently, then with force. It felt like they were doing all of this for the very first time, exploring each other's bodies anew. It felt different. But then, they were different now, weren't they? Mourning is transformational.

Adelaide moaned with complete sincerity, her nails digging into Rory's back. It was so comforting to be this close to him again, to know she still had the capacity to make him feel good. That she could move her body in ways that made him say, *Fuck, Adelaide. That feels so good, Adelaide.* She could make him thank deities he'd grown prone to cursing, wince with pleasure rather than pain. For once. Thank the lord.

Was it like this with Nathalie? she wondered. It was a twisted thought.

How did you do it? Adelaide had asked over FaceTime a few days earlier. Her mom was on the other end of the line, bouncing Adelaide's nephew—Holly's son—on her lap. She set him on a playmat beside her. *Do what?*

How did you take care of all of us, of Izzy especially, when you were struggling yourself? Adelaide paused, started to backtrack. *I mean, not to suggest that I'm struggling. It's just, where did you find the strength?*

Remember the book A Wrinkle in Time? her mom asked.

Of course, Adelaide said. *It's one of my favorites.*

Mine, too, she said.

She reminded Adelaide of the scene in which the character Charles Wallace—the protagonist Meg's little brother—has essentially been possessed by an evil, disembodied brain.

Right, Adelaide said. *IT.*

The only thing Meg had that IT didn't, her mom reminded her, was love. That was ultimately how she saved him; how she restored order. *I love you, Charles. Oh, Charles Wallace, I love you.*

You have to love fiercely, and unselfishly, and with intention, her mom said. *It's the only way.*

Now, she lay by Rory's side, naked and breathing. He traced the profile of her body with his finger. *That was truly incredible,* he said. He brushed her lips with his thumb, touched his nose to hers. She closed her eyes.

I love you, she said. She opened her eyes. *So fucking much. I don't know if now's the right time to say that or not but I just. I needed to say it. Again. I love you, Rory.*

Sometimes, she wished he treated her more delicately, with more kindness. But he was mourning and hurting and Adelaide understood.

And also, she loved him. Really, truly, honest-to-goodness loved him. Fiercely. Unselfishly. With intention. And—though she was certain he would always love Nathalie just an inch or two more—she suspected he loved her, too. Which made the words that followed all the more devastating.

Oh, he said. *I don't. Um. I don't know what to say. Do you want to watch a film before you head home?*

Oh, Adelaide said. *Sure.*

Adelaide followed a number of writers online. If she liked their novels, their memoirs, their essay collections, she tended to like their quippy tweets and photos of their dogs, the fresh bouquets of hydrangeas they'd just picked from the garden. Generally, she expected that their posts would make her laugh or smile. She did not expect that—on her way back from Rory Hughes's flat that evening, after hearing that he did not, in fact, love her—swarms of her favorite writers would share photos of Nathalie Alban, emblazoned with the words *#TeamNathalie*.

It had nothing to do with Adelaide. *It has nothing to do with you,* she told herself, chastising her own self-obsession. But my goodness, did it feel pointed. Literally, pointed. As though they were two points in a young adult love triangle: Team Nathalie versus Team Adelaide. (And how could she compete with a literal angel?)

There were nods to Nathalie's writing skills, her unmatched capacity for mending broken sentences and sewing words into beautiful paragraphs. There were photos of her eyes, her curls, her smile. *That megawatt smile,* the one she'd flashed at Adelaide all those months before—picking her book off the floor, meeting her for coffee. There were notes about the singularity of her kindness, her enthusiasm, her joie de vivre. There were shirts and bookmarks and buttons all declaring they were *#TeamNathalie,* fundraising pages to which Adelaide anonymously donated. It was everywhere; she was everywhere.

We lost the best kind of person, one post read. *My hope is that we can all carry a bit more Nathalie in us moving forward.*

But Adelaide could not. She was physically incapable of carrying an ounce more of Nathalie Alban inside of her—she already occupied every corner of Adelaide's heart and mind. *Be more like Nathalie,* her brain would shout. *Why the fuck aren't you more like Nathalie? Maybe Rory would love you, if only you were more like Nathalie.*

Another voice, slightly quieter, asked this question: *Why should you get to live when Nathalie couldn't?*

Adelaide didn't know why.

Twenty-one

This is unbecoming, Adelaide thought. She rinsed her mouth, splashed some water on her face. It was the twelfth day in a row that she'd vomited, the tenth time she'd done so in her office bathroom.

She wasn't pregnant—she'd been on birth control since she was sixteen. No, vomit was one of the many ways her body tended to react to stress: Her mind would scream that she needed a break, a few more hours of sleep, a proper meal. When Adelaide ignored these signs, her body would revolt and, inevitably, she'd find herself kneeling on a bathroom floor. (It had been a weekly occurrence at her last firm, E&S. She and an old colleague used to hold hands beneath the stalls as they stress-vomited. *Traumatic bonding,* they'd joke. It wasn't really that funny.)

It was deeply unhealthy, she knew, but there was just so much going on. She was still gunning for that promotion to international communications lead, working late evenings and early mornings to show her dedication to Alliance. Just next week, Eloise would be flying in for a quick spring break visit to London, the wedding celebrations in Mykonos and New York a few months away. For the first time in ages, Adelaide had picked up a few freelance projects—speed-reading books and speed-writing reviews for editors she'd not worked with since grad school. (They'd gotten in touch that spring, short-staffed and eager for round-ups of new releases and forthcoming beach reads. The word "no" had seemed to vanish from Adelaide's vocabulary. *Besides,* she'd say. *Writing is soothing.*) And, of course, she was still striving to support Rory. To hold him up.

Are you sure you can handle all of this? Djibril had asked one night, pouring Adelaide a glass of white wine from the office fridge. They'd both been working late.

Oh, Djibril, she'd said. *You underestimate me.*

Had he, though?

I t was Sunday, Holly's birthday. Adelaide sent flowers to her sister and a bottle of cabernet sauvignon. Her nephew gave Holly a finger-painted rainbow. She texted Adelaide pictures later that day; the painting was very cute.

In theory, Adelaide was spending the day volunteering with refugees. After hearing about Bubs's pro bono work, she'd joined a program that paired established, native English speakers with women who'd recently fled to the U.K., often from war-torn environments. This morning, she was meant to be helping the women practice their conversational English with a few other volunteers in Notting Hill. There were only two women in need of practice, though, and about ten like Adelaide who were eager to help. She felt a bit slimy about it all, as though she wasn't really doing good, simply making herself *think* she was doing good. If asked, she could say she volunteered with refugees—but was she making a true difference? Or just striving to check an invisible *I'm a Good Person* box somewhere in her mind?

Maybe these questions were making Adelaide's stomach churn. Or maybe it was the Sunday scaries? Regardless, Adelaide barely made it through the three-hour conversation session—nausea washed over her every twenty minutes in unbearable, frothing waves. Near the end, she politely asked for directions to the restroom and rushed down the corridor. She vomited up coffee and bile; the acidity stung her throat. Something about this was different, she thought. This didn't feel like stress.

Had it not been her sister's birthday—had she not seen that finger-painted rainbow—Adelaide might not have gone to Boots at all. She didn't have a regular period, so what else might have inspired her to pick up a fancy digital pregnancy test, *Just to be safe*? Goodness knows. Sometimes, she wished she'd never stopped.

She got home, fixed some toast, took the test. She watched as the little hourglass flipped up and down. Adelaide expected this time to go slowly—to stretch out—but it felt like it only lasted a few blinks. *Pregnant*, it said.

Okay, Adelaide said aloud. *Okay, okay, okay.*

Her chest tightened and she got tears in her eyes, but she didn't cry. Didn't break down. This was going to be okay, she told herself. It was all going to be okay.

The odds were one in two-eighty-two.

Adelaide had endometriosis. She had a relatively mild case, but even so. She'd been on birth control for a decade to help curb the symptoms—a contraceptive injection she got every three months. It was more than 94 percent effective in preventing pregnancy, and her odds of conceiving were slimmer anyway, doctors said. There was a 30 percent chance she might not be able to have children at all. (Adelaide first heard this news when she was seventeen. It had done little to mitigate the fear that she was, in fact, broken—destined to be alone.)

Throughout high school and college, Adelaide had almost exclusively held jobs that involved children. She was a CPR-certified babysitter, a day camp counselor, a nanny, an au pair. The summer before she left for Boston University, Adelaide took a job at a frozen-yogurt chain—she was the only employee who offered to work every children's birthday party, to lay the rainbow and chocolate sprinkles out with little silver spoons. She'd cared for newborns whose mothers had reluctantly reached the end of their maternity leave, for precocious three-year-olds who knew more about dinosaurs than she did, for prepubescent French boys who refused to unglue themselves from video-game controllers and take a shower. Her big, beaming eyes often attracted babies in supermarket aisles and on crowded trains—she always smiled and waved and cooed. Adelaide Williams loved children, truly; she'd just never believed she would be able to have one of her own. And yet.

And yet, she was pregnant. At twenty-six. With a baby. *Baby*, she said. *Baby baby baby baby baby.*

Adelaide? a voice called from the hallway. It was Madison. *Are you all right?*

Adelaide stuck the pregnancy test in the waistband of her jeans and buried the box in their bin (which was only a little disgusting). She washed her hands, dried them with a hand towel, walked out of the bathroom.

Yeah, she said. *Sorry about that. Sometimes I talk to my own reflection. Psych myself up, Mulan-style, you know?*

Sure, Madison said. She gave Adelaide a funny look.

Adelaide called her doctor the next morning before going into work. She wanted to go in for a blood test before she told Rory. She wanted to be certain this was happening before she said, out loud, to anyone but her own reflection, that this was happening.

We don't usually take appointments this early on in a pregnancy, the receptionist said (Adelaide guessed she was eight weeks or so along). *But we have a few openings next Friday, if you really want to come in. I can squeeze you in that morning. Around eight A.M.?*

Perfect, Adelaide told her.

Adelaide mapped out her expenses. She'd been paying off her student loans fairly aggressively, but if she reduced a couple of those payments and bought fewer gin and tonics each week, she could support this child almost entirely independently, especially if she landed this promotion. (*Bless Alliance,* she thought. *Bless Sam!*) She could afford a small two-bedroom in Highgate, see about working from home to save money on childcare. Maybe she could hire an au pair, she thought—someone who could help with the baby just as she'd helped a family with four boys in Paris.

She was terrified of Rory's reaction, but also. Also, also, also, a small part of Adelaide thought he might be excited, too. He'd be shocked at first, of course, but he was nearly thirty years old. And he loved babies! He might not love Adelaide, but he cared for her. Hopefully, he would care for this baby as well. And maybe, perhaps, potentially, Adelaide would give birth and he'd fall fully in love. Drop to his knees, wrap his arms around baby and mother, form a perfect little unexpected family. *I can't believe I didn't realize sooner,* he'd say. *Of course I love you, Adelaide. Of course!*

(It was irrational, a fairy tale. But Adelaide couldn't allow herself to consider the alternative. Fantasizing was a matter of self-preservation.)

His mother's name had been Anne, which would make a good middle name, Adelaide thought. Maybe the baby would have her eyes, even.

She liked Nora as a first name, like Nora Ephron. Or maybe Sylvie could be cute, like Sylvia Plath. *Nora Anne,* she said. *Sylvie Anne.* Perhaps Victoria, like the queen, or Catherine, like Parr—they could call her Torri or Kate, for short.

(Would he want to name her Nathalie? Adelaide hoped not.)

She browsed teensy tiny outfits for teensy tiny newborns, filling and abandoning shopping carts with items she desperately wanted, but knew she didn't yet need. She was nervous, of course she was nervous. But again, the fantasy was a means of protection. Everything would be okay if she remained joyous, delighted; if she pretended the sheen of sweat on her forehead was simply a pregnancy glow. So, Adelaide chose to be excited.

And she truly was excited. To have a baby. How mad.

It was raining when Eloise landed that Wednesday. Because London. Adelaide had a day of meetings and couldn't meet her at the airport, but she'd left her keys in a little envelope beneath the doormat. She placed fresh towels, a bar of Cadbury chocolate, a preloaded Oyster card on her bed—little somethings to ensure Eloise felt welcome, she hoped.

Eloise was waiting at the flat when Adelaide got home from work that evening, chilly and wet from the rain. It was the first time they'd seen each other in nearly two years; they all but leapt into each other's arms.

I'm so happy to see you, Adelaide said, rocking back and forth. *So, so, so happy.*

I'm so happy to see you, my Adelaide, Eloise said. *You Londoner, you!*

They went to the pub for dinner, ordering goat cheese tarts, juicy burgers. *And two pints of your finest IPA,* Eloise told the bartender. *Please, sir!*

Make that one, Adelaide corrected. She turned to Eloise. *I'm just, um, feeling a little dehydrated tonight.*

Or you're pregnant. She said it quietly, deadpan; Adelaide's eyes flashed. *The hell, Eloise?* she said.

Holy shit, Eloise said, her own eyes flashing. *I knew it. Oh my gosh, I knew it!*

It took Adelaide a beat to process what had just happened. *I knew it.* She knew it? How on earth did she know it? This was the first time they'd seen each other, properly seen each other, in years. And it wasn't that abnormal for Adelaide not to drink. Was it?

What the hell? Adelaide said again.

They paid for their meals, grabbed a wooden spoon with the order number, made their way to a booth in the corner.

To start, Eloise said, sliding onto the seat, *you are both the best and worst secret keeper I have ever met. I could tell something was up when we talked, like, a week ago.* Adelaide just stared. *Then you started saving all these little outfits and ideas to that secret Pinterest board for Holly's baby shower. Which was, what? Two and a half years ago? And I thought, All right, either Holly's having another baby. Or Adelaide is pregnant.*

Fucking Pinterest.

But none of that even matters right now, Eloise said. *How are you doing? How are you feeling? Tell me everything.*

Welp, Adelaide said, *I'm pregnant. With a baby. Which is a crazy fucking thing to say out loud.*

She'd wanted to confirm it with a doctor first, to let Rory know before sharing it with her own family, her friends, her colleagues. But also, *Oh my goodness.* Adelaide had been carrying so much. For months now. It felt so good, so freeing, to drop this particularly heavy news onto Eloise's lap. To have someone to help her carry it.

She told her about the morning sickness (which had yet to ease), the test from Boots, her appointment on Friday morning. Their food arrived.

Can I come on Friday? Eloise asked, picking up her burger. *Can I hold your hand in the waiting room?*

Please, Adelaide said. *Please. And then you have to help me figure out how on earth to tell Rory.*

Of course, Eloise said, her mouth full. *How is the elusive Rory, by the way?*

He was all right, Adelaide said. *As all right as one can be,* she supposed. *Given the circumstances.*

Maybe this was just what he needed, Eloise said. *A baby?* Adelaide asked.

Yes and no, Eloise said, another bite in her mouth. *A whole new life to focus on. Literally. Something to bring him joy and light, even as he continues to grieve.*

Right, Adelaide thought. Right. Maybe this was just what he needed.

The story was simple: Eloise and Adelaide had been sailing off the coast of Greece with their friend Barbara. (*Why Barbara?* Adelaide asked. *Why not?* Eloise said.) It was late, the sky a velvety blue. Barbara had told them she was going above deck to look at the stars. And then, she, just, never came back. They'd called her name, placed ads in the paper a few days later. Nothing. They were suspicious of the skipper, they said—thought something nefarious might be going on there.

This was the mystery they shared with the faux detectives at Evans & Peel the next night, a speakeasy in Earl's Court with decadent gin cocktails and a very silly front. Patrons had to present "detectives" (in quotes) with a "mystery" (in quotes) before they could enter the bar. It was campy and ridiculous and loads of fun.

Rory was meant to meet them at eight; he was running a bit behind schedule. Sorry, he texted at five past. Be there soon. Just faffing around.

Tell them you're looking for Barbara, Adelaide texted.

Barbara? he asked. She didn't explain. He arrived twenty minutes later.

Hi-hello-I'm-Eloise-it's-so-good-to-meet-you, Eloise said, immediately embracing him. *Can we get you a drink? A snack? Do you want to tell me your entire life story? I'm here for all of it.*

I can see why you two are mates, Rory said.

He asked their server for her recommendation, ordered a cocktail. The girls got a second round (Adelaide's was virgin, of course). They shared anecdotes from high school, from law school, from New York and Cambridge and Mallorca. Eloise told Rory that Adelaide was voted Miss Congeniality their senior year.

Oh, Rory said. *That I know.*

I bring it up every chance I get, Adelaide said. *But! Did you know Eloise was voted Most Likely to Rule the World?* (He did not.)

Adelaide sat back. She watched Rory and Eloise chatting—two of the people she loved most in the world—and it felt so natural, so comfortable. He was brilliant with new people, and Eloise was brilliant with everyone, and *Fuck,* she thought. *I'm going to have a baby with that man.*

Rory kissed Adelaide at the end of the evening, hugged Eloise goodbye. They walked him to the Tube, said good night once more.

Eloise and Adelaide looked at each other. *I know it's late,* Adelaide said. *But. Do you want to go on another adventure?* Eloise grinned. *It's like you read my mind,* she said.

They were both, undoubtedly, exhausted, but Eloise had just five short days in London. She would then fly to Mykonos, back to New York. She was working for a district court judge this summer, with two weddings to plan in less than four months. But here, now—between school and work and weddings—her sole responsibility was exploring a new city with her oldest friend. There was no time to waste, really. She looped her arm through Adelaide's. Off they went.

There was something about London, about its energy, that felt like a current beneath Adelaide's skin. It coursed through her veins. Maybe Eloise could sense it, too, Adelaide thought, with their arms laced together. Maybe Eloise could look at the pink flowering trees, the light reflecting off the Thames, the buildings—skyscrapers of glass and steel, ancient churches cast in stone—and feel this electricity as well.

They walked down to the river, across Chelsea Bridge, through Battersea. *I can't believe we're here,* Eloise said. *Can you imagine what our fifteen-year-old selves might say?*

Adelaide could imagine. She could see herself at fifteen—eyes wide and rimmed in eyeliner—dancing alone at homecoming. She could see herself meeting Eloise in English class and reading *The Picture of Dorian Gray* until three in the morning on the day of their exam, suddenly entranced by the story. She'd be thrilled to know that a pseudo-grown-up Adelaide lived in London, wouldn't she? That she'd landed bylines in publications she adored in high school, never once voted to elect a straight white man for president (not yet, at least), and was still, blessedly, friends with Eloise, all these years later.

They'd be in awe of us, Adelaide said. *But.* (But, but, but.) *I wonder what pure fifteen-year-old Adelaide would think about the fact that I got knocked up out of wedlock.*

Oh, come on, Eloise said. *I feel like Young Adelaide would love to know that Adult Adelaide is having the baby of a gorgeous Cambridge man with an English accent. No?*

Maybe, she said. They were quiet.

Rory was handsome and charming, yes. But in truth, Eloise had no idea what to make of him, let alone what Young Adelaide would think.

She understood that he'd had a tough childhood, an especially tough year. He'd had a tough existence, so far, really. But she also knew that Adelaide had a tendency to make excuses for the shitty men in her life, to rationalize their poor behavior.

There was something about Nico that Eloise had felt early on—this sense that they were a team, a unit, no matter what. She knew Nico would always be there. To catch her, to comfort her, to celebrate her. And, for nearly a decade, he'd only strengthened that perception. He was always on her side, Eloise thought. Always.

Is Rory really on Adelaide's side? she wondered. Would he be there— stay there—once the baby came? She couldn't be certain. But she also didn't dare suggest this to Adelaide. Not now, at least. Not with everything happening.

Just remember, she said. *You run yourself ragged for other people, Adelaide. You deserve someone who's going to show up for you, too. Yeah?*

I guess so, Adelaide said.

She shivered; Eloise squeezed her hand. Maybe it was just the night air.

Twenty-two

What if you planned a weekend away? Eloise suggested. She was holding Adelaide's hand, just as she'd promised, in the waiting room of the doctor's office that Friday morning.

Adelaide was biting the nails on her other hand, bouncing her knee. *Maybe,* she said. *Maybe.*

Think about it, Eloise said. *You and Rory can go away to some fabulous place. Like Bath, like you're in a Jane Austen novel. Or France. Or Italy! You can have dreamy dinners and take long leisurely walks and it'll be a total escape from the city. And then—*and then!—*you can tell him you're expecting his child in thirty to thirty-six weeks, respectively.*

It wasn't a bad idea, actually. (She still owed him that birthday trip, anyway.)

In a few hours, the blood test would confirm that Adelaide was, indeed, pregnant. Ten weeks pregnant, to be exact. She'd send Rory a cavalier text, at Eloise's insistence, that simply read, Hey, you. Happy Friday! Do you have any interest in going away for the weekend? Maybe around Easter? (He did. Thank goodness.)

She and Eloise would spend the next few days flitting around London, the evenings browsing resorts and bed-and-breakfasts in Somerset, Paris, the Italian lake district. They'd search for openings around Easter weekend, restaurants with sun-soaked terraces, spas with availability. (*Yes hello do you offer prenatal massages?* Eloise asked one hotel. *I suppose showing up for a prenatal massage is one way to break the news,* Adelaide said, chuckling.)

On Sunday, they found a remarkable deal at a villa in Lake Garda—a room with a view, all meals included. Adelaide formally booked it thirty minutes later. She sent the confirmation to Rory.

We're going to Italy! she said. He replied with a sunshine emoji. *See,* Eloise said. *It's all coming together. Now, what's the plan for tonight?*

Eloise had no interest in bridal showers and bachelorette parties. They were too pedestrian, too much effort, too celebratory of capitalist ideals, she said, to really be enjoyable. *They're all about commodifying sex and friendship,* Eloise would say. *And I don't love doing either of those things.* Even so, Adelaide wanted Eloise to have just one night that was frivolous and extravagant and required a hot pink veil. She surprised her with a miniature bachelorette party on her last night in London— Madison and Celeste (neither of whom knew anything about the baby) met them with party poppers and feather boas. And who was Eloise kidding? She loved it.

She'd only had one, maybe two tequila shots, but she professed her love for Adelaide with slurred words and long hugs on the dance floor at Tonight Josephine. *I don't know what I'd do without you,* she said. *I love you more than anything. More than coconut iced coffee and Audrey Hepburn films and frothy pink cocktails and any boy who has ever existed.* It was all true.

Okay, Eloise whispered. *You're tied with Nico. But don't tell him I said so.*

The pair of them sat down at a table; Madison and Celeste continued thrusting to "Jumpin', Jumpin'." Adelaide turned to Eloise. Her head felt like a balloon about to pop.

I have to tell you something, she said.

Anything, Eloise said.

I'm scared. Adelaide paused, closed her eyes. *I'm scared I'm going to raise this baby all by myself and Rory Hughes will never love me and I'll spend the rest of my life comparing myself to Nathalie Alban and falling short and Team fucking Adelaide will never, ever win.*

Eloise reached for Adelaide's hands. *Baby,* she said. It was unclear whether she was calling Adelaide "baby" or simply speaking the word aloud. There was, in fact, a baby.

I know, Adelaide said. *I know.*

Eloise didn't say anything else. She just wrapped her arms around Adelaide's shoulders, tucked her chin over her head. Their eyes filled with tears; Eloise blinked a few into Adelaide's hair. It reminded them both of high school, of sitting in Adelaide's car and crying because Emory Evans had broken her heart. Because Nico had flown back to Mykonos.

I love you the most, Eloise said, her arms still enveloping Adelaide's. She took her face in her hands, looked straight into her eyes. *I'm sure Nathalie was wonderful,* she said. *I'm sure every good thing that's been said about her is true, and I truly do feel for those missing her. But you have to trust me when I tell you two things. One: Your mark on my life, on so many people's lives, has been nothing short of profound, okay? And two: Even before Nathalie's death, Rory had chosen to be with you. And I have faith he's going to continue to choose you, and this baby, every day moving forward.*

Adelaide blinked. She wiped a few tears with the back of her hand, smiled awkwardly at the server who'd come to check on them (*We're fine,* she mouthed, giving a thumbs-up).

She wanted to believe this: That Rory had chosen her, would continue to choose her. That he was, almost literally, on her team. And a small part of her did, trusting this was all part of their mess of a love story—their very tangled journey to happily ever after.

Thank you, she said. *I love you the most.* She grabbed Eloise's hand, led them back onto the dance floor. They did the sprinkler, Eloise took more tequila shots (*Gotta drink for both of us,* she whispered). Adelaide giggled, chugged some water.

But what if he's not on your team at all? she thought.

Eloise flew out on an early flight the next morning. Adelaide hugged her goodbye, carried her bag to the car, promised to see her so, so soon. She curled back up under the covers, dozed off again.

Then, sometime around 8 A.M., she woke up in a pool of blood.

"Pool" was a strong word. But this was more than Adelaide had bled before, she was sure. It was thick. Clumpy, almost—with clots that looked like small, dark jellyfish. Adelaide gathered and washed her sheets, washed her body. She asked to work from home, called the doctor again. (*Can you come in at noon? I know it's a while to wait, but we're slammed today.*) She went in at midday, took a blood test, had an internal. *No,* they said, she was no longer pregnant. *Yes,* they said, it looked as though she'd had a miscarriage, early stage.

One in two-eighty-two. This baby was exceptional, statistics-defying, a miracle. Why couldn't Adelaide have been a better host, created a better home, for this little being? This miracle. She grabbed the doctor's hands and wept.

She wasn't sure how long she waited there, holding the doctor's hands, feeling the folds of her knuckles in a way that, under any other circumstances, would not have been appropriate. Was it a few minutes? A full hour? She didn't know. But eventually, Adelaide let go. She left the office, wiped her tears. She got a fully caffeinated latte, took half a Xanax, texted Eloise.

I lost the baby, she said. No punctuation, no commentary. Eloise would call immediately. *Do you want me to fly back from Mykonos? I can be on the next flight out.*

Oh no, Adelaide would say. *It's fine. I'm fine. I promise.*

Three days later, she flew to Italy with Rory. Like nothing ever happened.

T he thing about Adelaide is that she felt everything. Truly, everything—except the things she most needed to feel.

In high school, she lost a good friend to suicide. Adelaide cried briefly when she heard the news, and again at the funeral, and at no other point. *I just trust he's in the right place,* Adelaide said. *That he doesn't hurt anymore.* It wasn't untrue, but it wasn't the Full Truth. The Full Truth was that Adelaide buried this kind of hurt so deep in her bones she could barely feel it.

She buried this miscarriage, too. Tucked it away. She told Rory her endometriosis was flaring up—that was why she was bleeding so much, she said. They had sex anyway. Adelaide threw up afterward, the bathroom door locked. *I'm so sorry,* she'd say, crawling back into bed. *This is not the time to get sick, is it?*

It's really not, Rory would say. *But I'm sorry you're feeling so ill.*

Rory had called ahead, requesting a room with two single beds at the villa, which broke Adelaide's heart just a bit. She insisted they push the beds together, and *You have to tell me secrets to bridge this gap in intimacy,* she said.

All right, he said. He told her that when he was little, he'd dreamt of being a famous writer. He still had this idea for a story about a man named Mr. Burns, or Mr. Berner, or Mr. Bernstein—he could never quite decide, so he could never write it. *But it would be great,* he said. *I know it. I used to tell Nat about it all the time.*

His name doesn't matter, Adelaide thought. *Call him "TK." Write about who he is, about what drives him, about what happens to him. The name can come later.* She didn't say this out loud, though. She didn't want to challenge him.

What about you? he said.

I've got nothing, Adelaide said. *You know all my secrets.*

Even through the lens of buried heartache, Lake Garda was among the most beautiful places Adelaide had seen in real life. She and Rory ate pasta drenched in cream and cheese and freshly ground pepper, drank entire bottles of La Chiamata Trebbiano. They took the ferry across the lake, visiting different little towns each day; Adelaide insisted on holding her hands out at the bow of the ship and yelling she was *King of the World!* She was abruptly interrupted one day when an older Italian man came up to smoke. She and Rory could barely stop laughing.

Are you going to paint me like one of your French girls after this? Rory asked.

Only if you're lucky, she said.

They took steamy baths in an enormous clawfoot tub. He read "The Turn of the Screw," she read *Beloved.* It was perfect and idyllic. (Until Adelaide began bleeding, the water blooming red like a scene from *Jaws.* But anyway.)

They got coffee at a little café on the water, called their families on Easter Sunday—the second to last day of their trip. Rory showed

Adelaide a sparkly graphic his grandmother had emailed. It was a Bible verse from Matthew, surrounded by animated bunnies and daffodils. Adelaide cooed.

That's sweet, she said.

She's as Irish Catholic as they come, Rory said. *Very sweet, but very fond of Donald Trump.*

Your Irish grandmother is very fond of Donald Trump?

Well, he explained, she was very fond of any pro-life politician. She'd had a number of miscarriages early in her marriage and they'd shaped her political perspective. *That's interesting,* Adelaide said. She shifted in her seat. *Truthfully, I'd think that might lead one to believe less firmly that life begins at conception. I'd find more comfort in thinking I lost a vessel, not a soul.*

Yeah, he said. His tone was curt. *Not sure you can really presume what she experienced, eh?*

Adelaide bit the inside of her cheek. *You have no fucking idea,* she thought.

Summer

London, England
2019

Twenty-three

Adelaide brought Rory a daisy, a few months later, in a little purple pot. She found it at Columbia Road that morning. It had been sitting at the corner of the table, away from the other plants. It needed a home.

It's a little sad and scraggly, she said. *But hey, so are we.*

It's perfect, Rory said. His eyes flashed at Adelaide. *Daisies were Nat's favorite. Thank you.*

He placed it on his windowsill, just above his bed. They sat beneath it, cross-legged, talking about how they couldn't believe it was August already. How this spring and summer seemed to be slipping through their fingers like flower petals. Like sand.

What if we planned another trip? Adelaide asked. *We could drive to the Jurassic Coast for the weekend, or go over to Paris on the Eurostar? And you're still welcome to come to Mykonos or New York for Eloise's weddings, of course. Even if you just want to hang out on the beach or in a hotel room. For a little change of scenery.* (She was talking so quickly, but she couldn't quite slow down.)

Maybe, Rory said. *Maybe.*

Why don't we look at places to stay in the Marais? she suggested. *Just for kicks?*

He pulled out his laptop, jiggled his finger across the mousepad, entered his password. There were tabs open to personal websites and fundraising pages, to Nathalie's obituary in *The Times*. There were threads of text messages, lined up in a row on the left side of the screen, the words "*Nat*" or "*Nathalie*" appearing more times than Adelaide could count. His screen seemed to shout her name.

I know, one message read. *You just have to focus on the good. Nathalie would*—He closed the tabs, but it was too late. The dam had burst. The room began to spin.

Maybe we could go camping? he asked, casually.

We can't go camping, she said. *We can't do this anymore.*

Adelaide, he said. *What are you talking about?*

She stood up. Her face felt like it was melting. *I mean, this.* She gestured at herself, at Rory. *I feel like I've been aiming at a moving target and I just, I can't hit it. I think you need a friend right now. I think you need me to just be your friend and also I don't even know how to camp! I had such a hard time in Girl Scouts!*

What the fuck, Adelaide?

It should be noted that Adelaide had barely slept in months, not since Nathalie's death. She would lie awake, her lights out, playing whale sounds from her laptop, *Harry Potter* audiobooks from her phone, clutching a bottle of cheap chardonnay. She'd pray that something, anything, would soothe her. (Nothing could.)

She'd been passed over for the promotion at work last week—*You're just under a lot of pressure right now,* Sam and Djibril said. *And we don't want to add to that.* She'd excused herself to cry in the bathroom. (But how could she cry over missed work opportunities when Nathalie was dead? Nathalie, who'd surely secured every promotion for which she'd ever applied. The youngest deputy editor at *The Times.*)

There was also the huge (joyful) fact that Eloise was getting married in two weeks. Adelaide was thrilled. Absolutely, she was thrilled. But she needed to get eyelash extensions, dress alterations, to clear up the stress blemishes on her chin and the dark circles beneath her eyes. What if she showed up, a messy shell of herself, and let sweet Eloise down on her wedding days?

Oh. *Oh,* and somewhere in the depths of her mind, she remembered that morning. Her sheets soaked in blood. The miracle of a baby she'd loved and lost in a matter of weeks.

She was just so fucking sad.

In the time they'd been seeing each other, Rory had only ever seen

Adelaide cry at movies and *Friends,* when Rachel got off the plane. She hid this part of herself, the part that lay down in the shower and sobbed and tried to make the world make sense and couldn't. But it all began to tumble out now—the stress, the frustration, the missed dinners, the grief. The words fell from her mouth before she could stop them. *I'm living in this shadow and I don't know how to make you love me. What the fuck else can I do to make you love me?*

She wasn't just speaking to Rory anymore. It was absurd—Adelaide had been afforded every imaginable privilege in life—but now, she felt she was speaking to God. Everything hurt. Everything. What else could she possibly do?

I've only had one boy love me, Adelaide said, her eyes welling up. *The same boy who held my head down and stuck his cock in my mouth. Who poured drinks over my head while I was driving and told me my tits were too small and still broke my heart when I was seventeen and—*

Stop fucking telling me this, Rory said. *I don't need to hear this.*

That's the problem, Rory, she said. *I am carrying all of this. Every day. And it's heavy, and it's hard, and—rationally or otherwise—it impacts the way I view and perceive your actions. You refuse to introduce me to your family. You ignore me for days at a time. You make it so crystal clear that I will never, ever be a fraction as wonderful as Nathalie. And it all makes me feel really, deeply fucking unlovable.*

That's so unfair, Adelaide, he said, exasperated. *You don't think I'm carrying any weight right now? You think I don't have enough on my fucking plate? I lost my parents when I was a kid and my stomach's perpetually on fire and now the woman I once thought I was going to marry is dead and . . . Do you want me to just say I love you when I don't? To placate you? Because I'm not going to do that. Not because I'm heartless, because I'm careful. And prudent. I understand how short life is, Adelaide. But I'm not just going to say things I don't mean.*

I know, she said. *I don't want you to lie. I just. I want it to be true. I want you to love me. It's increasingly difficult that that's not true.* He said nothing.

I'm sorry, she said. *I'm losing my mind and I'm sorry. Maybe we just need a few days to breathe and reset and figure this out.*

You're throwing this at me at nine o'clock on a Sunday night? he said. *You show up with a potted daisy and now you want to take a fucking break?*

Just a few days, Adelaide said, rubbing her eyes. *Just a few days.*

They stared at each other then, their chests rising and falling. Neither spoke.

Can I give you a hug good night? Adelaide asked, after a minute.

Not if it's the last time, he said.

It's not, she said. *I promise.*

She hugged him, his body limp in her arms. She hated herself for everything she'd just done, for unloading like that, adding to his never-ending list of burdens. She hated herself for breaking. *So much for being a pillar,* she thought. *So much for holding him up.*

She left his flat, heard the door slam shut.

*Y*ou'd think it would feel lighter, she told Madison and Celeste. *To let all of that out. It doesn't. And also, holy shit, I'm sorry that all I've been able to talk about for the last year and a half is how desperately I want some boy to love me and how sad I am when he doesn't.*

Hush, Celeste said. *That's what we're here for. And we've talked about plenty of other things. Remember the royal wedding? We talked about that for, like, a month straight.* Adelaide chuckled weakly.

Madison was quiet, she made Adelaide an iced tea. Adelaide imagined she must be feeling slightly uncomfortable in this conversation— her relationship with Anurak had been wonderfully easy, it seemed. Free of deaths, late-night arguments, ignored texts, and unreturned *I love you*s. They spent nearly every night together, cooking elaborate dinners in the kitchen, making floury messes that Adelaide—the obsessively tidy Adelaide—often cleaned up.

I hate to change the subject, Madison said. *And I'm so sorry you're feeling this, Adelaide. But I have to tell you something.* Adelaide and Celeste held their breath. *I'm. I can't sign our lease again this year, Adelaide. Because I'm, um, and I don't want to make a big deal of this.*

You're what? Adelaide asked, a bit more aggressively than she'd intended.

I'm moving to Thailand, she said. *Bangkok. With Anurak. Just for a year, but we're moving this September.*

The timing of this announcement was horrible, Adelaide thought. But then, what timing wouldn't be? She suspected Madison had known for months. That she'd been sitting on this news and waiting for a moment of calm—the eye of the metaphorical storm that was this year—to let them know. There hadn't been a break.

Maybe she'd already told Celeste, Adelaide thought. Maybe they'd been struggling to know when, and how, to break the news to Adelaide. Weak, fragile Adelaide. It was odd that this was, apparently, the right moment.

But this was good news, wasn't it? Of course. It was good news. *Smile*, Adelaide told herself. *Rejoice!*

Wow, Adelaide said. *Oh my gosh! I'm sorry if that took me a second to process. What exciting news!*

Yeah, Madison said. *I mean, again, it's not a big deal. Just a year. But I'm excited.*

As you should be! Adelaide said. Her voice sounded like aspartame—artificially sweet.

The next day, she bought a fizzy bottle of prosecco, a bouquet of fresh flowers. She wrote a note in a cheeky little card that read, *Hate to see you leave, Love to watch you go.* She was happy for Madison! Really. She promised.

But sure, beneath the surface, Adelaide felt like her legs couldn't move fast enough. Like the water was coming, coming, coming, and she could barely keep her head up. Her life raft was, almost literally, floating away. How was she meant to survive?

M*adison is moving*, she told Rory a few days later. (Of course she saw Rory a few days later. She'd texted him two days ago—I'm sorry for everything: Dinner on Friday?—and they glazed over their argument as though it never happened, patched a Band-Aid over the gaping wound. She didn't have the willpower to stay away. Not now, not with everything else changing.)

To Thailand, she added.

She's moving to Thailand?! he asked.

With Anurak, she said. *For the year—she'll be working in school administration over there, covering a maternity role in mid-October, I think. But yeah, they're moving in September.*

Wow, Rory said. Adelaide took a bite of pasta; she nodded.

They were sitting at the bar at Padella, side by side. Their knees knocked together as they spoke.

So, he said. *Where does that leave you?*

That's the question, she said. *I think I'm going to look for my own place. I'm hoping that'll be easier than finding a new, random roommate? And tidier? But I've got to try and find a place before Eloise gets married.*

Right, he said.

She had viewings lined up throughout the week, she explained—in Highgate, Bermondsey, Bloomsbury. *All over London, really,* she said. *Any place with wood floors and one-bedrooms that aren't a million pounds should do.*

What about Celyse? he asked.

Celeste? she corrected. *She's got a gorgeous studio in Islington and no desire to move, understandably. But if I do nothing but view flats and wedding prep after work for the next few weeks, I'm sure I'll find something.* He nodded.

She hadn't realized she'd hoped Rory might offer to view the flats with her until he didn't. *He's got enough on his plate,* she reminded herself.

They finished eating and paid the bill. They walked through Borough Market, down along the river. It was chilly for an August evening; Adelaide pulled a yellow cardigan from her bag, tucked her arms through its sleeves.

Should we talk about the other night? she asked.

I don't see a need to rehash it, Rory said.

Mmkay, she said. *I just. I wanted to apologize.*

Something had broken inside of her, she explained, when Nathalie died. *I know it makes no sense,* she said. *My only real connection to her is through you, through your past. But it broke my heart. I think of her mom and her sisters and her friends every single day.* But there was more, Adelaide explained. There were layers of fear, incredibly selfish fear, on top of this grief—*Fear of the comparisons you must be making in your head. Fear of the Nathalie-sized hole in your heart that I know I can never fill.* It made Adelaide feel insecure, pushed her to act out. *And I'm sorry about that,* she said. Her eyes were misty now. She wiped them with the sleeve of her cardigan.

Rory gave her a hug, kissed her hair. *You're so kind,* he said. *Let's get you home.* They took the Tube back to Adelaide's. Nothing else was said.

I *always mean to ask you,* Rory said. He was taking his jacket off in Adelaide's bedroom, pointing at a small shelf by her doorway. *You're always talking about the books you're reading, but . . . where are all of your books?* There was a hint of accusation in his tone.

Unlike Rory, she didn't have a wall of cubbies stuffed with books and mementos—books and mementos, she'd learned, that had largely come from Nathalie Alban. Adelaide just had a small stack of novels on her nightstand: a copy of Wetherly May-Lewis's *A Modern Empire;* a few Virginia Woolf, Toni Morrison, Sylvia Plath books displayed between melting candles and potted orchids on a shelf. (Not because she liked these authors especially, though she did. But because she wanted to be the type of person who had *Mrs. Dalloway, The Bluest Eye, The Bell Jar* on her bookshelf.)

I gave away a bunch of books when I moved here, she said. *And I mostly read on my phone these days, to be honest.* He gave an almost imperceptible scoff.

But I used to have this dream, she continued. She bought her own copies of all the books she'd had to read for high school English classes— all annotated, their margins filled with colorful ink and thoughts from tenth, eleventh, and twelfth grade. She had this vision of a little house or flat in the city. With huge bookshelves, all filled to the brim—*Shelves so high you'd have to use one of those sliding ladders to reach the ones up top.* She thought these books, and her notes, would follow her everywhere. *But then you move once, twice, three, four times,* she said. *And you decide that paperback copy of* The Scarlet Letter *probably isn't a necessity after all, you know?* Most of her annotated books were now floating around Goodwill stores in Georgia, charity shops in Boston and Brooklyn.

There was another reason, too, one she didn't give. Adelaide's memories from high school existed only in fragmented pieces. Some were crystal clear: Gluing feathery lashes to her eyelids before senior prom, tightening the straps of her heels at baccalaureate. The day she and Eloise finished their last AP exams, celebrating with a dance party in the parking lot, blasting Hall & Oates's "You Make My Dreams Come True" from the stereo of her Volkswagen Beetle. She could still feel the sun on her bare arms, taste the greasy drive-through fries and milkshakes they ate, grinning, that afternoon.

But there were also chunks of time that were tainted, memories her brain tried to block off in an effort to protect her. As a result, there were very few souvenirs from high school that Adelaide wanted to hold on to. Her junior prom dress, the pink Converse high-tops she'd gotten on her sixteenth birthday, and that copy of *The Scarlet Letter* all became flotsam, thrown overboard in an act of self-preservation.

Now didn't feel like the time to bring that up, though. Rory didn't want to know those details.

Maybe in your next place you can have great big bookshelves, he said.

Maybe, she said. *I'll just need to fill them now, won't I?*

She needed more books, she thought. And she needed more happy memories.

Twenty-four

Adelaide arrived at Heathrow in a tizzy.

She'd viewed three flats that morning (all of which, coincidentally and disappointingly, smelled of feet) before haphazardly stuffing her suitcase with formal dresses, a steamer, a variety of heels. Her hair was unstraightened, pulled up into a sweaty bun. She was wearing an oversized T-shirt from high school—OBAMA '08, it read—with little holes in the sleeves, a small grease stain by her navel. At the airport!!!!! she texted Eloise. Eeeee!!!!

She put up an out-of-office, bought a coffee for the flight, landed in Mykonos a few hours later. Nico's older brother, Baz, picked her up. They'd met only a few times before. He was going to be the *koumbaros,* the best man. *What have you got in here?* he asked, putting her suitcase in the trunk. *A dead body?* Adelaide tried to laugh.

Nico and Eloise were sleeping, he explained—*Napping off the jet lag*—but he was happy to take Adelaide around the island now, if she liked. *Absolutely,* she said. She would love to.

It was almost dusk, and the sky looked like a scarf unraveling—half blue, half lavender, cut with the deep orange stripes of the sun. Adelaide took a breath. *Not bad, eh?* Baz said. *Not at all,* she said.

Adelaide had seen the Mediterranean from the Côte d'Azur, the Italian Riviera, the Balearic Islands (how lucky she was). But nothing quite compared to this. The sea seemed to reflect the fading colors of the sky, waves lapping the shore in hues of blue, purple, orange. The air was thick and salty, her hair unfurling from its bun in wisps and waves. It felt so good to be here, to be away from everything.

Baz showed her the windmills and the cobblestoned streets of the

Old Town, waving to bartenders with whom he was familiar. One offered Adelaide shots of ouzo, on the house. *You've got to have one for me,
too,* Baz said. *I'm driving.* She swallowed both shots, the liquor burning
her throat. She winced, they all laughed.

Welcome to Mykonos, the bartender said.

Eloise and Nico were just waking up when they got back to the house,
drinking coffee on the porch in their clothes from the plane. For
Adelaide, seeing Eloise felt like coming home from metaphorical battle, opening the door in your tattered uniform to find everything has
remained just as you left it. Not a speck of dust has accumulated. Everything is the same, everything is okay. It's safe now.

You're here! Eloise shouted.

I'm here! Adelaide said. *And y'all are getting married!*

They all exchanged quick kisses, long hugs.

It's so good to see you, Adelaide whispered to Nico. *But, like, you're
stealing my best friend.*

Please, he said. *We both know you're her number one. She still lists you
as her emergency contact half the time and you live on a different continent.*
He winked at Adelaide; she grinned.

Eloise showed Adelaide to her room. She explained that her mom
and aunts were flying in the next morning for the rehearsal. (Eloise's dad
passed away when she was a toddler. Her mom, Joanne, had brought her
up on her own; she was among Adelaide's favorite people.) Most of the
guests at this ceremony would be Nico's relatives, though, *So expect lots of
dancing and "Opaaa"s and ouzo,* Eloise said. Adelaide nodded.

What can I do to help you right now? she asked.

Nothing tonight, Eloise said. *Tonight, we get souvlaki wraps and just
enjoy that you're here in Mykonos. We both need a night to unwind, I think.*

I think so, too, Adelaide said.

What happened next was unexpected. She hadn't intended to stay out
this late, to drink this much, to find herself on a crowded dance floor at
three in the morning with Baz and his boyfriend, Haralambos. (They
called him Bobby.)

Eloise and Nico were home in bed now. *Are you sure you don't want to come back with us?* they'd asked around ten. *No, no,* Adelaide had said. *I'll stay out.*

And here she was: drenched in sweat, still wearing her old campaign T-shirt, singing aloud to songs she hadn't heard in a decade. The three of them danced and laughed and tiptoed home at four in the morning, whispering loudly as they chugged water in the kitchen, the others asleep upstairs.

For the first time in months, Adelaide was not thinking of Nathalie Alban or Rory Hughes, of miscarriages or finding a flat or her overflowing email inbox. No, she was thinking of how good the morning breeze felt on the back of her neck and the bliss of drinking cold, crisp water. She was thinking of how much she adored every person in this house, most of all the jet-lagged bride upstairs. She was thinking that this little island was magic, and maybe she should move here one day, retire on Mykonos.

Her brain was going a million miles an hour, but she was thinking that sometimes, actually, it's quite nice to be alive.

Celeste texted her the next morning. A friend of hers was moving out of a one-bedroom in Pimlico next month and the landlord was looking for a new tenant as soon as possible. Gorgeous flat, she said. Herringbone floors, nice living room and bedroom. I can stop by and take some pictures this afternoon, if you want?

Adelaide wiped the sleep from her eyes. It was 8 A.M., her head was pounding, but Yes, please, she texted. That would be amazing. Thank you so much!

She took a few ibuprofen from her bag, swallowed them dry. Nico was in the kitchen when she came downstairs. *Coffee?* he asked. She nodded. *Please,* she said.

Do you want me to—

Read my grounds? she asked. *If you're up for it, abso-fucking-lutely.*

I was going to ask if you wanted a frappé, he said. They chuckled. *But sure, I can read your grounds.*

She loved that he had this talent, this capacity for fortune-telling. Adelaide drank her coffee quickly, poured the sludgy remains into a saucer.

She let her cup sit there for a few seconds, facedown, as instructed. Then Nico lifted it up, looked inside.

He had a rule, she knew. He never revealed the bad (*It just leads to anxiety,* he'd say); Nico only shared good news. But looking in her cup that morning, Nico saw so little that was good. He wanted to see trees, ribbons, gateways—shapes that indicated Adelaide was going to find happiness, enter a new era. Instead, he saw knives, broken rings, scissors—all indicators of damaged relationships, of physical harm.

It's blurry this morning, he lied. *But it looks like you might have a fall. Be careful on the stairs, Adelaide.*

Insightful, Nico, she said. He laughed a little, brewed more coffee.

Nico would tell Eloise later that day, after dinner, washing dishes. *I'm worried about Adelaide,* he'd say.

I know, Eloise would say. *She's had a rough few months.*

No, he'd say. *I'm afraid for her future.*

He'd tell her then, what he saw in the cup—the end of her relationship, the pain, the danger.

You're wrong sometimes, right? Eloise would say. *Maybe it was just blurry. She has to be safe, I'm sure. She has to be.*

I am wrong sometimes, Nico would say—fearing that, this time, he was exactly right.

But that would all come later. For now, he brewed another *briki* and chatted with Adelaide, asking what she thought of the island, of his home, of her first night in Mykonos.

I love it here, she told him. He tried to smile.

E loise and Nico were married, two days later, in a small church overlooking the sea. Adelaide understood very little of the ceremony, but she wept throughout. (Mostly happy tears.) She held two bouquets of wildflowers in her hands, unable to wipe her eyes.

They'd stayed up stuffing bags of Jordan almonds the night before, sharing anecdotes from the last year, laughing too hard because it was late and they were exhausted and everything made them giggle. Nico and Eloise went to sleep around ten (in separate rooms—*Tradition,* they said). Adelaide, Baz, and Eloise's mom stayed up a few hours later, ensuring the favors were all prepared, the *stefana* crowns packed away safely. Adelaide washed her face, brushed her teeth, went to her room around one in the morning. She found Eloise awake in her bed.

Sorry, Eloise said. *I couldn't sleep. It felt spooky being on my own.*

Never apologize, Adelaide said. She crawled into bed, shimmied beneath the covers. *How are you feeling, dumpling?*

Eloise felt good, she said. Nervous, but good. *It's crazy,* she whispered. *I know nothing's really changing, but we'll be married tomorrow. Like, I'll be a wife.*

It is crazy, Adelaide echoed. *It's wonderful.*

You know you're still my number one though? Eloise said.

Oh, I know, Adelaide said. *I made Nico say so himself.*

The girls laughed, sinking deeper into the mattress. *Good night,* they said, closing their eyes. *I love you,* they said.

Now, Eloise was married in a flowy white dress. With the sea breeze in her hair, the *stefana* atop her short curls, a ribbon and vow connecting her to Nico for eternity. *Na zisete!* the guests cheered. *May they have a long life!*

Adelaide sent Rory pictures from the reception: The happy couple, herself in a pale blue dress, the *kalamatiano* (during which everyone danced around Eloise and Adelaide as they giggled at the center). *Wish I could send you some baklava and ouzo,* she said. *But for now, enjoy these pictures!*

He didn't respond.

She landed in New York a day later, hungover and beaming from the magic of the night before. Eloise and Nico's second reception was the next weekend. Adelaide would be working from Alliance's New York office for the week, sharing a desk with Sam, watering Eloise's plants while she and Nico enjoyed a brief interlude of a honeymoon in Santorini. In a few days, Adelaide's parents would be coming into the city for the celebration, and she and her mom would take the train up to Boston just after (Adelaide wanted to quickly see her sisters, her nephew before flying back to London).

She hadn't heard from Rory in more than a week, not since she first landed in Mykonos and he'd wished her a good trip. Should she be worried? *No,* she told herself. It was fine, it was fine. The photos from the wedding likely stirred something in him—thoughts of weddings he'd attended with Nathalie, trips they'd taken. She'd leave him be.

Adelaide splurged on a cab from JFK to Eloise's apartment—a shoebox of a one-bedroom on the Upper East Side, filled with green plants, Beatles records, evil eyes. It smelled of vanilla candles, of Eloise's lavender perfume. To Adelaide, it smelled like home.

She unpacked her bags, hung up her dress for the second reception— this time in a deep navy, not unlike the color of her senior prom dress. (*That's why I love it,* Eloise had told her. *It's like déjà vu in a dress.*) The party would be held at the Stephen A. Schwarzman Building at the New York Public Library. Adelaide watered the plants, took a quick nap, ordered takeout from a Thai restaurant down the street. She wrote and rewrote and rewrote her toast for the next weekend. It had to be perfect, she told herself. Everything had to be perfect.

*E*loise *and Nico,* she said, a coupe glass in her hand. The room was bathed in candlelight, the tablescapes dripping with fresh eucalyptus. Her hair was pulled to one side, soft curls draped over her shoulder. *I've always had this theory. This theory that people come into our lives when we need them most. Not when we least expect them, and not when we try to will them into existence—no, when the universe knows we need them. More than ten years ago, I sat in front of this dreamboat of a girl, in freshman-year English class, named Eloise. The universe knew I needed a true best friend, and there she was: sitting just behind me with a purple backpack and a floral headband and a heart of pure fucking gold.* Shit, she'd not meant to curse there; she apologized. There was a rumble of laughter. *Now, I don't want to be presumptuous,* Adelaide continued. *But I trust the same is true of both Nico and Eloise—that the world threw them together, one next door to the other—because it knew these two were meant to be. That they needed each other, and that the rest of us needed them. Together. As a team. Never in my life have I met a couple who is better matched, who is full of more love or grace or kindness than these two. I don't know what I would do without you, and I will forever be grateful that the world thrust us all into* *each other's lives because it knew. It knew we were meant to stand here one day and say: To Eloise and Nico! Congratulations! You're married! Na zisete! May you have a long, happy, wonderful life. I can't wait to see what else the universe has in store for you both.*

The room raised their glasses, Eloise wiped her eyes. *Thank you,* she mouthed. *I love you the most.*

I love you the most, Adelaide mouthed back.

A few minutes later, her phone began to vibrate beneath the table. It was a text from Rory. (It had been nearly two weeks since she'd heard from him; she'd texted that morning to say she was getting a bit concerned. Will naked photos get your attention? she asked, half jokingly.) It was one in the morning his time.

Sorry for the delay, the text read. Hit a bit of a low this end. Hope you're having a good time.

She stepped out to call him a moment later—just after Baz's toast, before the dancing began. He didn't answer; she called again. Going to try to get some sleep, he texted.

She sent breakfast the next morning, croissants from PAUL. He missed the delivery. In Manchester, he said. Visiting his brothers.

Oh, shoot, Adelaide said. Well, I hope your roommates enjoy the croissants! I'll bring you some myself once we're both back in London.

That's all right, he said. Nothing else.

Twenty-five

It was Saturday morning and London was uncharacteristically warm.

Adelaide had just signed the lease on her new flat—the one-bedroom in Pimlico that Celeste found. The couches were frayed, the floors dusted with dog hair, but they'd promised a full cleaning and new furnishings before she moved in next month. *No problem*, the agent said. Adelaide signed the contract on the spot.

Now, she was walking to Notting Hill Carnival, dripping sweat, carrying a container of cookies she'd baked and a copy of *Fleabag: The Scriptures* she'd had signed by Phoebe Waller-Bridge the day before. (Adelaide had not seen Rory in nearly three weeks, before Eloise got married. She hoped the cookies and signature from his favorite comedian—*To sweet Rory*, it read—might lift his mood.) She found him on the curb outside of the Electric Cinema, arms draped around his roommates—nothing to lift but his drunk, slouchy body from the ground.

Adelaide! he shouted. She'd never heard him say her name like that, with such enthusiasm.

Rory! she said. *Rory's roommates! I brought y'all cookies! And a surprise!*

She made Rory close his eyes, placed the book in one hand, a cookie in the other. It was large and doughy—chocolate chip, stuffed with an Oreo.

There's a motherfucking Oreo in here, Rory said, his mouth full. He swallowed. *And there's a motherfucking signature in this book! You're a motherfucking genius.*

And you, Adelaide said, cupping his face. *You are drunk, my dumpling.*

He kissed her then—brought his sweaty mouth to hers, parted her lips with his tongue. His roommates and passersby watched from the pavement, but neither of them minded. For a moment, nothing else existed; Adelaide felt only light. She reentered the universe she'd found that first time he kissed her—last April, on Lower Marsh Street. Before she fell in love, before Nathalie died, before everything was different and broken and wretched.

This was the danger of Rory Hughes, she realized. There were moments in which he was absolutely perfect—she couldn't imagine ever floofing the hair, tracing the chin, running her tongue along the bottom lip of another man. There were parts of them that clicked together like puzzle pieces. (But there were also parts, jagged edges, that didn't align at all.)

They took cheap tequila shots from makeshift bars along the sidewalk; danced in the street; got covered in red paint, yellow paint, blue paint. They ate more cookies and sang aloud to Lizzo and giggled as they boarded the Central line of the Tube—coated in primary colors and sweat—other passengers staring.

Adelaide and Rory showered at her flat, scrubbing shampoo from each other's hair. How intimate, Adelaide thought, to wash the sweat and paint and grime from another person's body. To watch them become the cleanest, purest version of themselves. She kissed his shoulder, wiped the suds from her mouth.

I missed you, she said.

I missed you, too, he said. He ran his fingers through her wet hair and kissed her again.

He agreed to spend the night, just this once. Side by side in her bed, his fingers still twisting through her hair, Rory invited Adelaide to Surrey the next weekend, to his little hometown of Shere. He desperately needed to get out of London, he said. To get some fresh air. (He did not mention that it was Nathalie's twenty-eighth birthday—that the things from which he was desperately fleeing were memories of pub nights, frosted cakes, special dinner reservations at rooftop restaurants. That he was using Adelaide as an escape.)

They were hosting a farewell party for Madison that weekend, she told him—a soirée, they were calling it, on Sunday night. Adelaide was hesitant to go away. She needed to be there.

We can be back in time for the party, he told her. *Please, Adelaide. I need this. I don't think I'm asking too much.*

Of course, she said. *Of course. As long as we're back in time, I'm in.*

In the meantime, she continued, *I have a very intense craving for buttermilk ranch. Do you ever get that? Just, like, a crazy intense craving for ranch dressing?*

Rory was lying next to her, his eyes on the ceiling. *I do not,* he said.

She sat up, straight up. She was literally salivating, and her hands were shaking a little, which was odd. *I need some,* she said. *Like, right now. This instant. Buttermilk ranch. Where can we get it at this hour?*

She was searching for delivery options when Rory reminded her it was almost ten at night, that now was not the time for this buttermilk ranch over which she was suddenly obsessing.

Maybe he was right, but it wasn't what she wanted to hear. She wanted him to sit up, too. To say, *Anything for you, m'lady* in a goofy accent and search Deliveroo with her. She wanted him to be silly and stupid and look for ranch and be on her team. Just a little bit. Just a lot a bit. (Maybe even more than she wanted the fucking ranch.)

But she was being a bit over-the-top, wasn't she? It was just ranch, and he was just sleepy, and they'd had the loveliest day, after all.

Tone it down, Adelaide, she told herself. *Don't be too much.*

Adelaide bought confetti-filled balloons and Bombay Sapphire, swept the floors and dusted their shelves on Friday night. She placed an order at the florist up the street—poofs of white peonies she would pick up on Sunday, just before the soirée. She packed a bag for the weekend, baked rhubarb muffins. *I'll be back by four on Sunday,* she told Madison. *See you then,* Madison said. *Have fun!*

Adelaide waited to meet Rory at Waterloo. Precariously and cautiously, she balanced her phone, two iced lattes, a copy of *The New Yorker,* and a rhubarb muffin in her arms. (Maybe Rory would be hungry, she thought.) He arrived three minutes before their train was meant to leave; the pair of them rushed through the station, leapt onto the carriage. Coffee spilled down her T-shirt. Adelaide cursed under her breath.

Are you kidding? he asked. *You're soaked in coffee now.* She didn't understand why he was frustrated, exactly, until he explained they'd be meeting his brothers, their partners, and his aunt Helen and uncle Trevor (the man who'd killed his parents, Adelaide remembered) upon arrival.

You hadn't told me that, she said, now frustrated herself. She'd hoped they might meet Helen and Trevor while in Shere—it was the reason she'd made rhubarb muffins (Rory had mentioned rhubarb was Helen's favorite)—but she'd not realized they were on their way to meet his entire family. Adelaide hadn't been sleeping particularly well again, and she was wearing a baseball cap over unwashed hair, ripped jeans, a ratty T-shirt that was now drenched in coffee. She changed her clothes in the train bathroom and tried to tie her hair back halfway, to hide the grease at her part.

Better? she asked, returning to her seat. *Better.* Rory nodded. She tried to mask her nerves with excitement, positivity, thoughts of telling jokes and listening to his brothers' laughter. He was letting her meet his family. His whole family! And everything was going to be fine.

There's something you should know about Trevor, Rory said then. He looked down at his hands, twisted his palms up. *He's a bit, I'm not sure what the word is. Off, I suppose. I think he's still struggling to find himself without alcohol.* He paused. *He can be a bit awkward at times.*

I totally understand, Adelaide said.

Really, Rory said. *Be sensitive to it, all right?*

Of course, she said. *I'll be sensitive. But, respectfully, if there is anyone I know how to speak to, Rory, it's people in pain. Or, people struggling to find themselves, I guess.*

It was true. Adelaide was not exactly well-versed in small talk. Her brain didn't work like other people's, she suspected, and it made friendly social interaction difficult at times. She'd once, for instance, had a lengthy conversation with one of Rory's roommates about the night she spent as a go-go dancer in college, and how, *Sure, I would absolutely be a stripper if I lost my job.* She wasn't trying to sound sexy or cool; she genuinely did not know how else to fill the conversational space.

It had become a joke of sorts among her friends. Adelaide was fun, sure, but she wasn't the life of the party—that was Madison, Celeste. Adelaide was good at making friends in a *Let's contemplate our own mortality in the corner* sort of way.

When she was in kindergarten, Adelaide had approached another little girl on the first day of class. The girl was born a twin, but she'd lost her sister the year prior to pneumonia. Somehow, Adelaide had recognized something was amiss. She'd approached this young girl, wrapped her tiny arms around her waist. Adelaide could sense that she was hurting, she'd later tell her parents; she could sense she needed a hug. It was spooky, almost—her capacity for identifying pain.

She'd long believed this was part of the reason she'd connected with Rory Hughes as well: Adelaide could tell he was hurting, and she knew how to guide a lost soul. How to navigate a crisis. Not always, and not perfectly, but with a greater deal of empathy and compassion than most four-year-olds, teenagers, twenty-six-year-olds possessed.

Rory pursed his lips. *I suppose you are quite good at that,* he said. *Thank you for being mindful.* She gave a gentle nod.

They arrived in Shere an hour or so later. Rory's brother, Daniel, picked them up at the station.

It's so good to finally meet you, he said.

It's so good to meet you, too, Adelaide said. *I can't believe we haven't met before!* She shot a quick look to Rory. He shrugged.

Daniel drove them to Trevor and Helen's, a little old farmhouse on a stretch of green land. There were baby chicks in the yard, small rabbits, a light blue door. It was breathtakingly pastoral—a Thomas Kinkade painting come to life. Helen opened the door. *Come in, you lot,* she said.

Though she had no children herself, Helen had the distinct energy of a mother in a children's novel, Adelaide thought. A blond Mrs. Weasley, perhaps, or Marmee in *Little Women*. Adelaide went to hug her, then quickly pulled back. She stretched her arm out instead.

I'm Adelaide, she said, taking Helen's hand. *It's so good to finally meet you.*

And you, darling, Helen said. *Come in, come in. I've just made a pot of Earl Grey.*

Helen ushered them inside, through the back door, into the garden. She offered them tea from a kettle in a striped knit cozy, biscuits she'd made earlier that morning. *I made muffins as well,* Adelaide said, taking them from her bag. *Rory mentioned you like rhubarb.*

Well, aren't you a treat, Helen said. *Boys, can you grab some plates and napkins for us?* Rory and Daniel obediently walked to the kitchen. Helen leaned a few inches closer to Adelaide.

I've heard from his brothers that you've been fantastic in all of this, Helen said. *Thank you so much. It can't have been an easy thing to go through, but I'm so glad he's got you by his side. I don't think he would have survived it otherwise.* Tears pricked at the edges of Adelaide's eyes. She hadn't expected this.

Oh, Adelaide said. *It's been no trouble for me. My heart's just been broken for him.*

I know Rory, Helen said. *And I know it's not been no trouble, dear. Thank you. Truly, thank you.*

(Would she hear the full story in a week's time? Would she blame Adelaide when it all fell apart?)

The boys returned, their hands full of mismatched plates and paper napkins. Cameron and Arthur—Rory's other brothers—arrived less than an hour later. Cameron with his girlfriend, Gracie. Arthur with his wife, Stella.

Gracie's accent was different, Adelaide thought. American, but with a tinge of something else. *Where are you from?* she asked, shaking Gracie's hand, kissing her cheek. *Boston,* Gracie said. *Well, Quincy specifically. Just like you, I hear.* Adelaide grinned.

She'd never considered Boston her hometown. It was just the place she'd gone to college, the place her family now lived. But there was a singular kind of comfort, Adelaide thought, that came with realizing your roots were intertwined with those of a stranger. (Particularly a stranger in a foreign land.) She asked Gracie about Quincy, about how long she'd lived around Boston. Gracie was born and bred there, she explained. She'd graduated from Boston College about three years before Celeste. They hadn't known each other, but Adelaide was certain their paths must have crossed on the quad at some point. *What a coincidence,* she thought.

They'd actually just flown in from Boston last night, Gracie said. They'd been visiting the States for her parents' anniversary party.

Oh my goodness, Adelaide said. *How are you coping with the jet lag?*

Just fine, Gracie said. *I have a few sleeping pills to get me through.*

Oh, perfect, Adelaide said. Rory rolled his eyes.

Americans and your pills, he said.

The afternoon stretched on in the garden. Everyone drank tea, shared anecdotes, ate biscuits and scones and rhubarb muffins with dollops of clotted cream. Trevor arrived around five that evening—he'd been doing landscaping work all afternoon, Helen said. Adelaide greeted him with a handshake.

Are you American, too? Trevor asked.

I am, she said. *I feel like I should apologize?*

Couldn't get an English girl, could you, Rory? he said, turning away from Adelaide.

I tried, Rory said. *None of them would have me.*

(Was Adelaide being overly sensitive again, or was this a cruel thing to say in her presence? She felt it was.)

Helen quickly changed the subject, asking Trevor how his afternoon had been, how the jobs had gone. It was fine, he said. Everything had been fine. Adelaide watched them interact, looking for indicators that Trevor was—in Rory's words—*A bit off.* She found none, unable to help but wonder if, perhaps, Rory was projecting.

The sun began to set then, showering the garden in yellow light. It was golden hour: The boys' cue to head to the pub, it seemed. Rory and his brothers stood up, dusting crumbs from their laps. *All right, then,* Arthur said. *To the White Horse? Helen and Trevor, always a pleasure.*

The White Horse was a large Tudor-style house with beveled glass windows and a hearth at the center. Adelaide walked to the bar, offered to buy the first round for everyone.

You don't need to showboat, Adelaide, Rory whispered. It sounded more like a hiss.

Showboat? she asked. She giggled a little, it was such a silly word. *Are we eighty and playing bingo and I'm too into the game?*

I'm serious, he said.

I'm not trying to showboat, Rory, she said, firmly this time. *I'm just trying to be gracious.*

He subtly rolled his eyes again, but helped her carry the pints back to the table. She felt like a child who'd had her hand slapped. She wasn't sure what she'd done wrong.

The day had been going so well, she thought. She'd bonded with Gracie, with Stella, with Helen. Trevor had liked her muffins, left her with a pat on the back and a kiss on the cheek. But there was the joke about English girls, the frustration at her apparent showboating, the small reminders that Adelaide was imperfect. She was so imperfect.

It returned later that night, the slapped feeling. Washing her face in the sink of their bed-and-breakfast, she heard his words over the running water—*Do you think we have much in common?* he asked. She turned off the tap, patted her face dry.

I think so, she said. *I think we have similar interests and values, no?* He was quiet. *What makes you ask that?*

Oh, nothing, he said. *Just wondering.* Though Adelaide was almost certain he'd been comparing her to his brothers' partners, to their relationships. She was growing fatigued of the constant comparisons. Perhaps they'd be better off friends, she thought again.

He suggested they play *The thirty-six-question game*—something his brother suggested, apparently. Adelaide had heard of this before, though she'd thought the questions were designed to lead to love. Either way, she agreed to play along. *Sure,* she said, crossing her legs at the foot of her bed. (Rory had requested a room with separate beds.)

Okay, he said, reading from his phone. *Given the choice of anyone in the world, whom would you want as your dinner guest?* They both said Barack Obama. Rory chuckled, apologized. He was so sorry, you see, because their dinners were on the same night and *President Obama has already said he can come to mine.*

Can he stop by my dinner party for dessert? Adelaide asked. Rory shook his head no. *He's busy,* he said. Adelaide laughed. It was a good start.

Do you have a hunch about how you'll die? he asked later. *Oh no, let's skip this one.*

For what in your life do you feel most grateful? he continued. *For me, it'd be my brothers, Helen, my grandparents.* Not Adelaide, never Adelaide. She exhaled.

My family, she said. *Eloise. Celeste. Madison. Sam at work. And you, of course.* He lifted his chin a touch, though he did not smile.

Your house, containing everything you own, catches fire, he read. *After saving your loved ones and pets, you have time to safely make a final dash to save any one item. What would it be?* Adelaide thought for a moment.

I have this pair of cameo earrings, she said. *They were a gift from my mom. They'd been a gift from her mom. I lent them to Eloise for her wedding; she wore them as her Something Borrowed. I'd probably save those.* She paused. *What about you?*

My copy of The Orwell Diaries, he said. There was no hesitation.

He would not save *Call Me By Your Name*—in which the sappiest, most earnest love note Adelaide had ever written was jotted on the back of page 165. (Had he even read it? She didn't know.) No, Rory would save the last piece of Nathalie he had, the last piece within reach. Of course he would.

Adelaide understood, she really did. But it felt like such a waste. All of those words, those books, that love. All of it felt wasted on someone who didn't want it, someone who would let it all burn.

I'm tired, she said, feigning a yawn. *Can we maybe finish in the morning?*

I t was the first of September, what would have been Nathalie's twenty-eighth birthday. Her friends, her sisters, her boyfriend were gathering at a pub in south London, toasting with pints of cider in her honor. Adelaide and Rory were touring a sculpture garden in Surrey, taking turns guessing the names of various pieces, the inspiration behind hunks of metal and glass. (His brothers returned home the night before; Helen and Trevor were at church.)

It's so dark in here, Rory shouted. He was standing in a large wooden box of sorts, allegedly built to be a bat house at human scale. *Come in,* he said. *Check it out.* He pulled Adelaide through the entrance then, pushing her body against one wall of the box, his hands immediately unhooking the button of her jeans.

This was why they could never be friends, she thought to herself. Because even if she'd entered this sculpture garden as Rory Hughes's friend, she inevitably would have found herself in this spooky, defunct bat house with her pants at her ankles, his hands in her hair. *You feel so good,* she whispered. *You, too, baby,* he said. It was all so good, too good.

She fixed her hair, her jeans, rehooked her bra beneath her shirt. They managed to catch the train back just in time, dozing off and on as they rode back to London, Adelaide's fingers laced through Rory's as fields of yellow flowers passed in a blur. She'd have an hour to pick up the peonies, once they arrived, for Madison's party. But she wouldn't remember that fact.

It was a series of unfortunate events, really, that led Adelaide to this moment. It wasn't her fault, you see, because the train was delayed. There were leaves on the track. It was the train's fault, honestly. And the leaves!

(At least, this is what she'd try to tell herself. What she'd try to tell Madison.)

I'm so sorry I missed most of the party, she said. *Seriously, Mads. I'm so sorry. How can I make it up to you?*

It's fine, Adelaide, Madison said. *It was just a little get-together. No big deal.*

She'd fallen asleep on the train ride home, her head on Rory's shoulder. He ran his fingers through her hair, held her hands on his lap. He didn't think it was worth waking her when the conductor announced the train was stopped, that there were leaves on the track up ahead, debris they had to clear. He hadn't realized how much time had passed, how late they'd be getting into London.

Then she boarded the wrong Tube at Waterloo, started heading in the entirely wrong direction, went three or four stops before she realized, dazedly, what she'd done. Adelaide arrived three hours into the soirée—no peonies, no real excuse.

It's fine, Madison said again. She didn't make eye contact. *Let's just drop it, okay?*

But it wasn't fine, and something inside of Adelaide twisted. Had she misplaced her priorities? she wondered. Had she placed Rory Hughes's needs above those of her friends?

Actually, Madison said. *One more thing, then we'll drop it for real. I've been holding my tongue for months now, but Rory? He doesn't fucking love you, Adelaide. He doesn't show up for you.* She was tying a knot in the garbage bag, still avoiding eye contact, but her words knocked the wind out of Adelaide. A gut punch. *I know that's hard to accept,* she continued. *I know that's a tough pill to swallow, but you've got to stop putting him above everything else in your life, okay? Enough already. It's enough.*

Adelaide bit her cheek, nodded her head. Madison left for Anurak's. She sobbed in the shower—so hurt by Madison's words, so desperate to believe they weren't true. (So ashamed to know that they were.)

This would all come after, though. After Adelaide kissed Rory goodbye at the station. Just quickly, a peck on the lips beneath the Solari boards. Nothing special, passionate, exceptional. He had a bit of a headache, he said. Couldn't come to the soirée. *But I'll see you next week?*

She said yes, gave him one more peck, waved goodbye. She had no idea it was the last time she'd ever kiss Rory Hughes.

Twenty-six

Adelaide knew. Well, she didn't *know*. She had no idea what was coming, really. But she knew that her relationship with Rory Hughes had to end, that theirs was not a love story in which the music swells and crescendoes as the credits roll. No, theirs was a story that would end with—with what, exactly? A thud? A fight? An abrupt fade to black?

The answer was heartbreak, she'd soon see. It would end in heartbreak. But she didn't know that yet; not exactly. For now, she only knew it was the second week of September and oh my goodness, there was so much going on.

The girls would move out of their flat next week, Madison would move to Bangkok on Tuesday. They'd brushed past their fight, thankfully, but they both had boxes to pack, frames to bubble-wrap, off-brand booze in the pantry to consume. Alliance also had a few executives speaking at conferences that week, all of whom were in town from New York (Sam had flown in, too). Their administrative assistants milled about, asking Adelaide when she might have those talking points ready and *If you could print out directions to the conference venue, that would be great, thanks.*

Of course, Adelaide would say, adding scribbles to her to-do list. She hadn't succeeded in checking anything off.

One assistant was named Raven. She was tall, slim—with long black hair (*Black as a raven,* she said. *It's where I got my name*) and blue eyes. She had the same coloring Adelaide had envied in Nathalie. Even so, the women had bonded on Adelaide's last trip to New York over their shared love of Maman in Flatiron and reality shows about real-estate agents. She apologized for the million requests this week, promising to take

Adelaide, Sam, and Djibril to drinks on Wednesday afternoon. *To make up for the madness,* she said.

At five fifteen—Adelaide's inbox still overflowing—they walked to the Fitzroy Tavern. It was the same pub she and Djibril had frequented last summer—gossiping about colleagues, about their relationships, about that boy with whom Adelaide had just fallen in love, Rory Hughes. The floors were still checkered and sticky, the walls still covered in wood paneling. They sat down at a corner table, ordered four gin and tonics. *Cheers,* they said.

Raven asked what dating was like in London; Adelaide and Djibril rolled their eyes.

English men are something else, Adelaide said. Though, she wasn't sure what she was implying, exactly.

I've been scrolling through dating apps this week, Raven said. *Thinking about planning a few nights out.*

Why not? Adelaide said. She understood the appeal of getting dinner with a man you'd see once and never again.

Raven took her phone out then, opened a dating app. They looked at the prospective men, giggling over their drinks as they swiped. And then it happened—a new photo flashed on her screen. It looked like something out of a summer catalogue: His hair dripping wet, his shirt clinging to his abdomen, a grin stretched across his face.

It was a picture of Rory Hughes. And Adelaide was going to throw up.

This is how it ends. With a photo from Rory's dating profile, the realization that he had been browsing for something better, prettier, smarter than Adelaide. It ends with her heart racing, aching. Her eyes filling with tears, her throat with sobs. With the reminder that no matter how fervently she'd fought for a place in his heart, how desperately she worked to win him over, it was never going to be enough. She was never going to be enough for Rory Hughes. *Why wouldn't he look for something better?* she asked herself.

(The reality, of course, is that Rory was looking to patch up a Nathalie-sized void. No person was big enough to stretch across that hole in his heart and hold it together—though Adelaide really did try. But even this knowledge couldn't make it all hurt any less.)

What happened next is unclear, even in retrospect. Adelaide remembered leaving the table, rushing to the restroom. (*Did I excuse myself?* she'd later wonder. *Did I apologize for my abrupt exit?*) She remembered dialing Rory's number, hearing it ring, hearing it stop—At work, he texted. Can't talk right now.

Why the fuck did my colleague just find you on a dating app? she replied. She remembered seeing him type, then stop. Type, then stop.

She remembered a knock on the door, Sam coming in to sit on the filthy bathroom floor with her, wiping her tears. *Seeing you like this breaks my heart,* she said.

Adelaide did not remember leaving the pub, exactly, but she remembered walking outside, feeling the breeze, feeling her heart pound. She remembered getting on the Tube and seeing Bubs. His face concerned, hers hot and stained with tears.

Adelaide? he'd said. *Golly, are you all right? Do you want my seat?* She remembered feeling embarrassed, but she didn't remember how she replied.

It wasn't him, Rory said. There was a mistake. Okay, well, maybe it was him, but he'd just downloaded it for a few days this summer. When we were on a break, he said. That was all.

A break? Adelaide thought. What break? she asked him.

Last month, he texted. When you said you needed space.

I told you I needed space for a few days because I was falling apart, she said. And you got on a fucking dating app.

Later, Adelaide will wish that she'd gone to his flat. That she'd let him kiss her hands, her wet eyelashes, say, *I'm so sorry. I didn't mean to hurt you. It was cowardly and foolish and I wish I'd never done it, Adelaide.* But she did no such thing. There was no big fight, no dramatic end. She simply called him, once the workday fully ended and her tears had temporarily dried, and said, *This doesn't need to be a long drawn-out conversation. I wish you the best, but I'm done now. This is done.*

He would challenge her. He would say he'd had a terrible year, that he'd been suffering for so long. *No,* she would say. *I'm not buying the victim narrative right now. You intentionally betrayed my trust and I can't come back from this.* She couldn't. Adelaide truly could not come back from this.

She'd lent him copies of *The Little Prince* and *Tuesdays with Morrie* months earlier, asked that he mail them to her new address as soon as he could. *Of course,* he said.

I hate this, she said. *But there will always be a huge shelf in my heart for you, I promise. Goodbye, Rory.*

You too, he said. *I don't want to say goodbye.*

She took a deep breath and hung up the phone.

A delaide tried to do with this pain what she'd done with the rest of it—to bury it, deep in her bones. Undetectable, she thought. But it didn't work this time. There was too much hurt down there. Too much heartache and not enough room. It rose up in waves, usually when she was alone. She'd go to the stationer for more boxes or the grocery store for cleaning supplies, and she'd emerge, inevitably, with her arms full and her face wet, tears falling so fast they felt like running water. The threads of her life were being pulled apart, one by one—career ambitions halted, friends moving across the globe, across the threshold from single to married life. She'd wanted to hold on to the thread that was Rory Hughes, no matter how frayed. And she couldn't, not now.

My goodness, she was so sick of this.

She was sick of crying over Rory, over the pain he'd intentionally and unintentionally inflicted. His lack of text messages, of commitment; his grief, his resentment, his unborn child. She was so sick of wasting her friends' empathy on these tears. But goddamn, all she could sense right now was a cavern in her chest, an emptiness. The kind of void that felt like it could only be filled with Rory. Just hugging Rory.

Was this what he'd felt for Nathalie, she wondered, all this time?

C eleste came over that weekend, wrapping Adelaide in her arms. *Are you okay, baby girl?* she asked. Adelaide insisted she was fine. *Totally fine,* she said. The girls ordered their usual: Two pizzas, garlic bread, a bottle of sauvignon blanc. They took shots of mysterious liquor from the pantry and blasted Ariana Grande from tinny speakers as they rolled up clothes, wrapped coffee mugs in newspaper. Adelaide put on an oversize sweater and a pair of white knee socks (no pants, she was too sad for pants). She was grateful to have her friends here, grateful Madison hadn't said, *I told you so.* They pulled their hair up into high ponytails and danced around to "Thank U, Next." Adelaide had no idea that in two days, she was going to try to kill herself.

It hit her that night, in a room full of boxes and overstuffed duffel bags: The timeline was off. She and Rory fought in early August, at least five weeks ago—surely, if he'd deleted his dating profile once they'd reconciled, it would be hidden by now. No? It was 2 A.M. Adelaide sat up, luminated by her phone screen, furiously searching for answers.

Profiles that are inactive for more than fourteen days will be removed from the application, one article explained. *More than seventy-five percent of profiles shown have been active in the last three days, or seventy-two hours.*

Fourteen days before she'd found his profile on Raven's phone, she and Rory had been dancing on Portobello Road, soaked in paint and sweat and sunshine. They'd watched the meld of colors swirl in her shower drain like tie-dye, kissing each other's noses, washing suds from each other's bodies. Three days before, they'd sat in a garden with his family, Adelaide laughing at his childhood anecdotes, grabbing his brothers' arms as they joked about the performances Rory used to give from the bathtub. *No way,* she'd said, her cheeks sore from laughter. *No way.* It made no sense.

She wasn't even angry; she was just so heartbroken.

Adelaide wrote it all down—the details of the article, the moments they'd smiled at each other in the last fourteen days. She would call him in the morning, she decided. Confront his dishonesty in the light of day.

In high school, Adelaide's mom told her that relationships ended in one of two ways: You break up, or you don't. But this wasn't entirely true, Adelaide now knew. There were ways to break up without breaking down, without crumbling, without losing every ounce of yourself. There were ways to break up without having to question how much of your relationship had been built on falsehoods and feigned promises. There had to be.

These were her thoughts at 2 A.M., 3 A.M., 4 A.M. Around five thirty, the sun began to bubble up in the sky. She wished she could weave together some metaphor about her love for Rory behaving like this sunrise—piercing through the dark, slowly and poetically, clouds melting away like candle wax. But their love did not rise, or set, naturally or gradually. Anything but.

Adelaide made a pot of coffee, poured some into a paper cup. It was white with gold polka dots, something she'd picked up for Madison's birthday party last year. She twisted her hair into a bun and packed her last few items into a suitcase, Maroon 5's "Sunday Morning" playing at lullaby volume in the background. (It soothed her.) Around eleven that morning, she took a breath and dialed Rory's number. He ignored the call. *I don't want to say goodbye,* he'd said, just a few days earlier. She wondered if this, too, had been a lie.

What if it was all a lie? she asked herself. What if none of it was ever real, ever reciprocal? What if their relationship hadn't just been ephemeral, but fabricated?

Hey again, she texted him. I went back and forth about sending this in a text. And rationally, I trust it's better to let things lie than ignite an argument. But when have I ever behaved rationally, you know? She hit Send, began a new message. "Profiles that are inactive for more than fourteen days will be removed from the application. More than seventy-five percent of profiles shown have been active in the last three days, or seventy-two hours." Fourteen days before Raven found your profile, we were soaked in paint and sweat while dancing in the streets. Two days before, we were fucking in a sculpture garden and I snored on your shoulder on our way back from Surrey. It doesn't even make sense. I don't know why I sought out this information or why I'm sending this note to you now. Can't resist scratching at a very fresh scab, I guess. I just feel so sad. And I hope we can both strive to end things when we need to end them in the future.

In true Rory Hughes fashion, he never responded.

I t was Monday, moving day, and there was something else at play. There was the sting of the breakup, the impending crash of eight months without sleep, the loneliness that was closing in from every direction. And then, beneath it all, was the hurt in Adelaide's chest. The constant pang of envy and guilt and heartache over Nathalie Alban.

The perfect Nathalie Alban.

Adelaide picked up the keys to her new flat. She spoke with the landlord, in person, for the first time—a woman with a thick German accent and little tact. *Is it all right to put nails in the wall? And do you have information on the electricity and utility providers?* Adelaide had asked. *No,* the landlord said. *And I'm sorry, what is it that you do? I've never had to explain this to someone before.*

She looked at the new couches that came with the flat, sitting perpendicular to one another in the living room. One was a light gray, the other a deep charcoal. *Fuck,* she thought. Looking at them made her skin feel itchy. She'd taken the day off, but there was still work to do, too. So much work to do. (She'd fallen so far behind.) And soon, there would be movers to meet, boxes to unpack, dishes to stack in the cabinets.

But this is when Adelaide stops caring about all of that. This is when her mind starts to scream that nothing is okay. That the dishes don't matter and the couches don't match and her landlord's a bitch and there is work, but no purpose, and her friends are moving on and Rory Hughes is probably fucking hot strangers and she can't keep a baby and Nathalie Alban is dead, and Nathalie Alban is dead, and Nathalie Alban is dead.

Stop thinking it, she told herself. *Stop thinking those words.* She sat on the undressed mattress in her new bedroom, scrolled through Twitter, tried to distract herself. But there was no escaping any of this, was there? She saw that the London Book Awards had named an entire category after her—the Nathalie Alban Award, Recognizing Excellence in Young Editors. It hit her like a punch in the mouth.

This was a different kind of envy. One Adelaide couldn't directly communicate to anyone, really: She was jealous that Nathalie got to die.

It was sick, she knew. Warped. Twisted. But it was the truth. Adelaide had all but accepted the fact that her life would be full of lukewarm celebrations and successes. Maybe she'd get married, but probably not. Maybe she'd have a child, but it would be expensive and complicated to get pregnant, to stay pregnant, and what if motherhood overwhelmed her? Maybe she'd get promoted. Maybe she'd one day work in publishing or politics. Maybe she'd pay off her credit card debt and student loans and buy a house—but she would never be extraordinary. Never special. Her memory would fade with friends and relatives, her name would never appear in print or neon lights or at the London Book Awards.

The only way to bypass having to be extraordinary, Adelaide knew, was to die young. To leave others with the impression that you would have made the most beautiful bride, the most loving mother, the most adorable neighbor with a garden full of peonies . . . had you only had the chance to live.

And so, she decided to stop living. She knew she would not be mourned by thousands, that her name would not become a hashtag on Twitter. She knew a few people would miss her. But they'd be okay; it would all be okay. And it was kinder to stop her heart than allow it to continue beating, pounding, aching in her chest. She just needed a few pills. Where were her pills?

After

London, England
2019

Twenty-seven

Rory Hughes had expected to spend the evening helping Adelaide unpack. Carrying boxes upstairs, placing her few books onto shelves, eating pizza on the floor, maybe, if the furniture hadn't arrived yet. Instead, he was reheating a chicken-and-vegetable casserole from Tesco, watching reruns of *Crashing*, remembering the afternoon he and Adelaide had watched it in her bedroom and she'd laughed so hard she spit red wine all over the duvet.

He'd found it a bit immature at the time, like she must have been exaggerating. But no, he thought now. She was too genuine to feign laughter like that. Too good. *Fuck,* she was good.

The only problem was, he didn't love her. She was good, yes, and kind, and so cute it made his knees feel a little wobbly—her frame small and delicate, her smile bright. She was clever, too, he knew. Too clever sometimes. He liked her so much. But he didn't love her. He never really wanted to.

What he loved, truthfully, were the perks that came with dating a woman like Adelaide. The sex, the cupcakes, the little surprises she sent to his door—*Adventures in the Screen Trade*, takeaway dinners, a new wallet when his fell apart. He wanted her generosity, her caretaking. But he also wanted stability, and Adelaide Williams couldn't offer that.

He'd done it to cheer himself up, to stroke his ego a little, after their argument in August. He'd never seen Adelaide like that—with tears in her eyes, such strain in her voice. She'd been so high and so low that summer, so dizzyingly unpredictable. It wasn't what he wanted, what he needed. Not with everything else going on. So, he'd downloaded an app that night. Just for the hell of it, just to see.

And then, he couldn't stop.

He added that picture from the Lake District, the one Adelaide said made her physically thirsty. Girls were fawning over it, over him. Suddenly, he got to exist in a universe where he wasn't sad and grieving and broken. He wasn't something that needed to be cared for. He was something girls wanted to join for drinks, for dinner. Something they wanted to fuck. (A few blunt matches had specifically said as much.)

He hadn't done anything, though. Not really. He'd talked vaguely about plans with some of these women—going to a cocktail bar or a pub, maybe—but nothing firm. Nothing that ever really felt like cheating. Rory had not intended to betray her trust, as Adelaide put it. He'd just wanted to remind himself that things could be good and easy and light sometimes. He wanted to re-create that feeling he'd had the first time he'd met Adelaide, the first time he'd seen Nathalie. Not quite like lightning in a bottle, but the early hint of a spark, of heat. A gas stovetop clicking to life before catching the flame.

Rory thought about sending her dinner that first night, after everything happened. After she'd told him they were done over the phone. He knew she tended not to eat when she was upset. It was another habit that rubbed him the wrong way, the fact that she rarely seemed to eat around him. She was so stressed, she'd say. Too stressed for dinner.

She'd passed out in the shower one day because of it, sometime around April. She'd called him in a panic—Madison wasn't home, everything was spinning, she just wanted some company. *Please.* And when he'd asked what she'd eaten that day, she'd said, *Coffee.*

What the hell? he'd thought. *Who does that?* He'd made her some pasta with butter, just to get something in her system. She'd looked so weak eating it. So small.

He wanted to feed her now, too. To bring her noodles slick with butter and say, *Here. I'm sorry. Please eat.* But Rory knew if he sent food, she'd likely wrap it up, deliver it to someone outside of Tesco or the Tube. Pretend it had never been hers at all.

He'd told his flatmates the truth. Sort of. He said he'd downloaded a dating app while they'd been on a break, that a colleague of Adelaide's had found his profile and she'd freaked out, ended things. *I don't remember you two taking a break,* one flatmate said, an eyebrow raised. *I didn't really want to talk about it at the time,* Rory told him. He wasn't lying.

He'd not expected anyone, least of all Adelaide, to realize he'd been on the app far longer than three days. He had never meant to hurt her. Honestly. She was so fragile, so gentle. It felt like killing a mockingbird. How was he meant to face that? he wondered. How was he meant to explain it all to Adelaide when he could barely make sense of it himself?

Rory's work phone rarely rang at night, if ever. But it started to ring this evening, a few days after he and Adelaide had broken up. An American number—was she calling his work phone now? Was she that determined to say her piece?

Hello, he answered. *This is Rory.*

Rory? a voice said. *Great. This is Eloise, Adelaide's friend? We met this summer?*

Right, he said, trying to keep his tone steady. (*Please let her be safe,* he thought. *Please, please let her be safe.*) *How are you? Everything all right? Is Adelaide all right?*

She's all right, yes, Eloise said. *But here's the thing.*

They'd met at that cute little speakeasy, she remembered. Rory had been running late, and Eloise could sense Adelaide was bothered by it, though she wouldn't explicitly say so. Adelaide still wanted her to love him, Eloise knew. To see an ounce of what she saw in him, a glint of that shimmering light.

Eloise understood immediately. Rory Hughes was the encapsulation of every fantasy Adelaide had ever described: He was tall and charming and English, exactly the Disney prince she'd made him out to be. She smiled, greeted him with a hug, asked him about his life, his job, his favorite memories from law school. Adelaide went to the bathroom, asked Eloise if she cared to join. *No,* Eloise had said. *I'm fine, thank you.*

She'd turned to Rory then, once Adelaide had turned her back and walked a few paces away from their table. Her tone was suddenly serious.

Listen, Eloise said. *I feel obligated to tell you that Adelaide has a heart of gold, and if you hurt her, I will fucking destroy you.* She grinned and he laughed a little. Genuinely, but uncomfortably. *I'm half joking, but I'm also telling it straight. Take care of her, yeah?*

Of course, he'd said. Of course he would, he'd never dream of hurting Adelaide. *She's so good,* he said.

She is, Eloise echoed. *Glad that's settled.*

Adelaide returned from the bathroom a moment later and Rory kissed her cheek, placed his palm on her knee. She squeezed his hand. Eloise smiled, crossing her fingers that Rory Hughes had told the truth. That he really wouldn't hurt this girl. Her girl.

R*emember,* Eloise said now, months later.

Adelaide had texted her from the hospital earlier. Just a heads-up, she'd said. Checked myself into A&E for suicidal thoughts. Will keep you updated. As though she'd gone in for a checkup and was running late for lunch.

Remember when I said if you hurt Adelaide, I'd destroy you?

Rory was silent on the other end. She waited for him to answer.

I do, he said, finally.

Obviously, I'm not going to do anything real or tangible right now, she said. *But I am going to very sternly tell you that if you go near her, ever again, I will lose my shit. I will send my husband to your door if I have to, and I hope the fact that I've called your work number is a clear enough indication that I am dead fucking serious about this, Rory. You are not to contact her, you are not to show up at her door, you are not to download an Instagram account and anonymously like her photos. You are to stay the fuck away from Adelaide Williams. Is that clear?*

Again, he was silent. *Yes,* he said after a beat. *It's clear, yes.*

R*ory hung up, shaken by the interaction. Eloise had been lovely when he'd met her. Gracious, silly, with a mischievous giggle like Adelaide's. She'd joked about "destroying him" if he hurt Adelaide, but in the way any woman might jokingly defend her mate. He'd expected it, almost.

He'd not expected this.

He wondered what Adelaide had told her, what she'd said to Eloise that prompted this phone call. Before their breakup, he'd had a feeling their relationship would end sooner rather than later. But he'd hoped they could end things on a friendly note, with the potential for coffee, lunch, the odd favor. He'd burned that bridge, he now knew. He was not to contact her again. Adelaide was not his anymore.

Rory felt a sudden wave of nostalgia wash over him. He missed her so much now, even more than before.

It's interesting, isn't it? How easy it is to care for something once it's no longer ours.

Twenty-eight

delaide stayed in the hospital overnight. *Just so we can keep an eye on her,* she heard the nurses tell Celeste. She'd insisted she was fine on her own, but Celeste snuck back to Chelsea and Westminster early the next morning, ensuring Adelaide woke up to company and warm croissants from Le Pain Quotidien. *A treat from me and Mads,* she said, handing Adelaide a dirty chai, a bag of pastries. *Don't worry, I didn't tell her the full story. But either way, she sends her love.*

Two days before, they'd been packing their rooms, taking shots in the kitchen. Thinking about it felt like déjà vu.

A nurse popped her head through the door a moment later. Adelaide's sweatpants were covered in flakes and croissant crumbs; she tried to brush them off.

Hi there, she said. *Adelaide Williams?*

That's me, Adelaide said. She gave the nurse a small, half-hearted salute.

The nurse wanted to talk through Next Steps, she explained. Figure out the best course of action for Adelaide moving forward. All parties advised against a stay at a psych ward—something Adelaide was deeply relieved to hear—but they agreed that she needed support, at least for the time being. The National Health Service had a group that provided daily check-ins. They could come to Adelaide's home, or Adelaide could stop by the local hospital. *Whichever you prefer,* she said.

That sounds good, Adelaide said. *I can go by the hospital, that'll be fine.*

She'd emailed Sam and Djibril the day before, typing paragraphs with her thumbs from the hospital bed. She was candid, explaining that she was experiencing a pretty major depressive episode and would likely need a week or two off from work. Alliance was relatively flexible in these situations—the benefit of working for a tech company with unlimited sick days, really. *No trouble at all,* they'd said. *Take all the time you need.* She imagined her colleagues must have been watching her deterioration for months now, wondering when she'd fully fall apart.

Now, she thought. The answer was now.

The nurses had her fill out a few forms, sign a few papers, and then, she was free to go. She would check in with NHS staff at ten tomorrow, but Adelaide still felt like a wounded bird told to fly. She wasn't quite sure how.

Celeste went home with her, helped her start to unpack. She took Adelaide's Xanax, her cough medicine, her copy of *Little Women.* (*The name Laurie is too close to Rory,* she said.)

A bouquet of yellow roses arrived at her doorstep that afternoon, bundled in cellophane. *A little something to remind you of sunshine and friendship,* the note said; they were from Eloise. Adelaide found a vase in one of the boxes they'd yet to unpack. She felt something warm in her chest, just subtly. It was odd—she'd had the capacity to feel joy before, to feel gratitude. Even after Nathalie's death, the miscarriage, the breakup. But it felt like that muscle had gone limp now. Like she could flex and stretch and strain, but not fully feel a sense of positivity. She'd never experienced this before.

The girls called Madison, who did not yet know the full circumstances of Adelaide's hospital stay (they'd told her it was dehydration, a bit of stress). She was at the airport with Anurak, waiting to board their flight to Bangkok, waiting to start a new life in a new foreign land. *Good luck,* they said. *Safe travels! Send so many pictures!*

Oh! Adelaide said. *And check the front pocket of your suitcase when you can.* She'd snuck some Polaroids of the three of them into an envelope, wrapped them with a Cadbury bar and a packet of English lavender seeds in a white ribbon. A little souvenir.

Will do, thanks, guys! Madison said, her voice thin over speakerphone. *And take care of yourself, Adelaide!*

I will, Adelaide said. She tried to say it with conviction.

They ordered Shake Shack for dinner—Adelaide's mom's treat. (She had texted her parents individually from the hospital. Sorry to send this via text, but . . . Fortunately, if any family understood the complexities of a suicidal episode and the healing power of fast food, it was the Williamses.) The girls ate crinkle fries, portobello burgers, strawberry milkshakes on the mismatched couches. They watched *What a Girl Wants,* a film neither of them had seen since they were eleven, maybe twelve.

Celeste decided to stay the night. She borrowed a T-shirt from Adelaide, a pair of sweatpants that were comically short on her five-ten frame. They pulled fresh sheets onto Adelaide's bed and stuffed her duvet into a yellow cover. It was bright and warm and smelled like fresh laundry, which was nice (albeit slightly reminiscent of Rory Hughes). The girls crawled beneath the covers.

Thank you for being here, Adelaide said.

Of course, Celeste said. She reached for Adelaide's hand, gave it a firm squeeze. *But don't you ever think about leaving this earth again, okay? It's not even an option. We have to be here to hold each other's broken pieces. Deal?*

Deal, Adelaide said. She closed her eyes. Tears she'd not known were forming ran down her cheeks.

Celeste had called in sick the day before, but she woke up early that morning, crept out of the flat for work around 7 A.M. She wore yesterday's slacks, borrowed a bulky sweater from Adelaide's dresser. She left a sticky note on the coffee machine—*The world is your oyster,* it said. *See you after school! I love you!*

Adelaide woke up an hour later. This bed was king-size, larger than her bed in Highgate had been. There was so much space here, she thought. She imagined herself as a million broken pieces scattered across the yellow duvet—divided and spread out, struggling to come together, to feel whole. How unfair, she thought. That she'd helped Rory piece himself back together, and he'd never even know she fell apart.

She smiled at the note on her coffee machine, made a café au lait. She showered, played Lizzo from her phone in the steamy bathroom. She wished she had the energy to sing along.

There was a buzz at her door. *Package for Adelaide Williams,* a man's voice said. It held her copies of *The Little Prince* and *Tuesdays with*

Morrie—the books she'd lent Rory—both wrapped in brown parchment paper. There was a note tucked between them. *No matter what,* it said, in Rory's scribbly handwriting, *I'll always think the world of you.*

She wanted to rip it up, light it on fire, stomp the ashes with her bare feet. Instead, she held the note to her face, almost kissing it. She hoped it might smell of his cologne, that it could somehow collapse the space between them, this single piece of paper. It could not.

Adelaide went to the hospital that morning. And the morning after that. And the morning after that. She spoke with different nurses each day—some men, others women. Some short, others tall and slim. Like string beans, her mother would have said.

They all had different perspectives on what it was Adelaide needed. Some felt she needed talk therapy, others suggested cognitive behavioral therapy, others brought up SSRIs. Some said this would pass soon, which made Adelaide's skin feel hot. There was a part of her that wished she physically harmed herself. That her self-hatred might manifest itself in cuts and bruises, that she could show them to the hospital staff and say, *Here. Look how hurt I am. Look at the damage I've done.*

It was all so difficult, she felt, and Adelaide didn't know how to explain why she wanted to decorate her flat with peonies and plants and color-coordinated stacks of books while simultaneously wanting her life to end. She wanted to be here, on this earth—to squeeze her friends' hands on their wedding days, to kiss their babies, to send care packages to her family for their birthdays. But she also just wanted to die. To leave. If she felt more secure in her faith—safer in the knowledge that heaven existed, that she was guaranteed entry—she would have done it. She would have left. But she didn't want to go to hell or the Bad Place or that island in *Lost.* Right now, she just wanted to not live and be safe.

On Saturday—her fourth day checking in with the NHS—a nurse suggested Adelaide meet with a psychiatrist and have a full evaluation done. There was normally quite a waiting list, he explained, but they might be able to squeeze her in quickly on Monday, if that would work?

Yes, please, Adelaide said.

By Monday morning, she was brilliant at sitting in waiting rooms.

She waited patiently, one earbud in—playing "Rhapsody in Blue"—her head tilted down as she read from a book of poetry on her lap. Today, it was Mary Oliver's *A Thousand Mornings,* though she'd also brought the works of Sylvia Plath and Emily Dickinson. She was trying to memorize their words, to sew them inside the pockets of her mind.

Adelaide Williams? a woman asked. She had horn-rimmed glasses, a clipboard in her hand. Adelaide raised her hand, walked toward the woman, was shown to another all-white room with two chairs and a small desk in the corner.

I'm Dr. Grayson, she said. *A psychiatrist with the NHS. I've been looking forward to meeting you.* Adelaide appreciated these words, though she knew they weren't fully true. *I want to talk about what's been going on lately, but first, I'd like to get a sense of your history. Can you tell me about your family, your childhood?*

Adelaide started from the beginning. She explained that she'd grown up in a loving but tumultuous environment. That her sister, Izzy, struggled with bipolar disorder, her mother with depression, and *It didn't exactly help that we moved around a lot.* Later, Izzy would go to boarding school, Adelaide's other sister to college, and her parents would get divorced. It all led her to become a bit angsty, she said, to become an especially irritating ten-year-old—*Not very popular with the cool kids at school.* She was bullied so severely she dropped out of primary school at the age of eleven. She was homeschooled for a year or so, then moved to St. Marys, Georgia, with her mom—a town known for its horses and Confederate-flag enthusiasts. She dated a boy in high school, Emory Evans, who abused her both emotionally and sexually. *Though I didn't realize it at the time,* Adelaide said. *I thought it must have been normal, I guess. And anything that wasn't normal I just kind of blocked out or repressed.* It all came back when she was about nineteen, twenty, she said. She became terrified of men, *All men,* and avoided them for years—well through college, through her au-pairing job in Paris. *Then I moved back to the States and started working in New York and it's like this switch flipped in my brain,* she explained. *All of a sudden, I could sleep with men, so that's what I did. I slept with, like, a lot of men.* She then moved to London, slept with more strangers, met Rory Hughes. Fell in love, fell into mourning over ex-girlfriends and embryos.

And here she was, a year and a half later, her heart once again obliterated by a careless boy.

She exhaled. *That was so much,* she said to the psychiatrist. *I'm sorry for unloading all of that.*

Not at all, Dr. Grayson said. *This is all important to hear. To understand what we're dealing with.*

She asked Adelaide a handful of questions—how often did she feel high, elated, excited? For how long? How often did she feel low? How extremely did she experience such emotions? Adelaide thought, answered. Thought, answered.

She remembered the darkness she'd found last March, reading *Call Me By Your Name* on the Tube, feeling so irrevocably damaged she could hardly get out of bed the next day, the next week. She remembered, just a month later, feeling wholly rescued by Rory Hughes—overjoyed by his entrance into her life, convinced this man was her ticket to happiness, to freedom from suffering.

Beyond Rory, though, she thought about the pattern her life events seemed to follow: Highs followed by lows followed by highs followed by this. The lowest possible low.

Very extremely, she said. *It's like . . .* She stopped, wondering how best to frame this. *I'm either on or I'm off, alight or dark. There's no in-between.*

It sounds, Dr. Grayson said, *like you may have manic depression, or bipolar disorder.*

No way, Adelaide said. Though, she'd truly never considered it. Suddenly, unexpectedly, something made sense.

Autumn–Winter

London, England
2019

Twenty-nine

Bipolar disorder. She let the words roll around inside of her head. *You're bipolar,* she thought to herself.

It had never even felt like a possibility. Her sister was bipolar, and Adelaide was not her sister, and thus. Thus nothing, it seemed. Mental illness was a shape-shifter. It could appear in different forms, with different presentations, and still bear the same name. She spoke with a second doctor, who confirmed that yes, it seemed Adelaide had bipolar disorder, type two. It was almost comforting to have a name for this, for whatever it was going on inside her mind. It felt like naming the beast, so to speak, was the first step in learning to placate it. (And she so desperately wanted to placate it.)

The light had gone out in Adelaide's life the day she swallowed those pills. But together—with doctors and therapists and friends and family—she was building a staircase, placing proverbial candles at each step. Relighting the way.

The first step was medication—a combination of drugs called olanzapine and sertraline, Dr. Grayson recommended, to start. She gave Adelaide an envelope of sample pills, suggested she take them in the morning. *You should start to feel the effects after five days or so,* she said. Adelaide graciously accepted, made plans to return to work the following week, convinced that these pills were the magic potion. That soon, she would be healed.

Adelaide returned to work on the last day of September. The final remnants of summer had left weeks before, the leaves in Hyde Park now a crisp golden hue. She'd gotten a manicure that weekend—*Black, please,* she'd said. *For the spooky season.* It really was a new season in

Adelaide's life, a new era. She could be happy now, she told herself, admiring her shiny, black fingernails. She was better.

(She wasn't. But that would take a few days to discover.)

Meekly, nervously, she crept into the office with the dexterity of a person trying not to wake a sleeping baby. There was a little white orchid waiting on her desk, a note from Sam that read, *Boys are fools! Welcome back, xo.* It made Adelaide smile.

Djibril took her to coffee, asked how she was feeling, if she was ready to return to work. *Ready as I'll ever be!* she said, forcing a smile. *Well,* he said. *We're glad to have you back.*

She spent the day sifting through emails, thanking coworkers who stopped by her desk to say they were glad to have her back as well. She'd been out just two weeks, but she knew they were curious about her quick departure; she was sure they'd heard rumblings of what happened from Raven, from Sam, from Djibril. *Were you off on hols?* one colleague asked. *Spiritually,* Adelaide said. He didn't ask what that meant, exactly.

Adelaide was accustomed to working late nights, but today she closed her laptop at five thirty, locking it in the cubby beneath her desk. *Oh,* Djibril said. *I nearly forgot—this came for you while you were out.* He handed Adelaide a small, relatively flat package. *Thanks,* Adelaide said, unsure what could be inside. She opened it to find a Moleskine notebook she'd ordered. It was black, with the letters *RBH* embossed in gold on its cover (for Rory Bernard—she still chuckled at the fact that his middle name was Bernard—Hughes). She'd almost forgotten about this.

Before Raven found— Before everything ended with Rory Hughes (she was trying not to rehash the rest of it), Adelaide had purchased theater tickets, made dinner reservations, found silly local festivals for the months of September, October, November. She'd mostly canceled the reservations, requested refunds, removed the reminders from her phone's calendar. But she'd nearly forgotten her plan.

She was going to jot the upcoming plans in this little diary in brightly colored ink. She was going to give Rory Hughes a collection of events and moments, finally, to which he could look forward. *I feel like I let you down this spring and summer,* she was going to tell him. *I wanted to make sure I didn't let you down this fall.*

Adelaide made it out of the office and onto Tottenham Court Road before she started to cry, holding the Moleskine to her chest. She looked at her shoes, her hot pink flats, and reminded herself to place one in front of the other. *Keep moving forward,* she mumbled. *Forward forward forward.*

She bumped into a stranger, then—her head still down, eyes bleary. She looked up and started to apologize.

It was Bubs. (For fuck's sake.)

Bubs! she said, quickly wiping her eyes with her sleeve. *How are you? I am so sorry that I am literally always running into you on the worst days. I promise I'm not perpetually a blubbering mess. Sort of. Maybe not.* She was rambling.

I've never once gotten that impression, he said. *How are you? Everything well?*

As well as can be, she said. She shrugged a little. *But, how are you? How is life?*

It's good, yeah, thanks, he said. *Listen, I'm just running to meet a client, but I'm going to write down my number, all right? Call me anytime you're having a rough day and need a pick-me-up, yeah?*

He pulled his wallet and a small pen from the pocket of his jacket, jotted his personal number onto the back of a business card. He placed the card in Adelaide's palm. *Here,* he said. *Have a good one, Adelaide.*

It would be months before she realized he was flirting.

It started on Wednesday, the second of October, two days after she'd returned to work. Adelaide woke up and, suddenly, everything was terrifying. Fucking terrifying. She was afraid before she'd even opened her eyes.

She was hot. Sweating, she noticed. But she was convinced that if she touched the radiator, if she tried to turn the temperature down, the dial would melt her skin. Had she had a nightmare? she wondered. Was she still dreaming?

Is it okay if I work from home today? she messaged Djibril. *Um,* he responded. *Sure. Is everything okay?*

No, she wanted to say. *Everything is hot and melting and my skin is on fire and I'm so fucking scared.*

I think so, she said instead. *Just want to check in quickly with my doctor.* Adelaide tried to lie back down, to close her eyes and sleep a little longer, hopeful she could shake off this waking nightmare with a bit more REM. But the world was no less frightening with her eyes closed. If anything, the darkness made it worse.

She stood up, walked to her kitchen, brewed a pot of coffee. She found comfort in the sound of scooped grounds, the drip of the machine. *It's okay*, she said out loud. *Everything is okay.* She sat on the couch with her coffee, a quilt wrapped around her body, though she was still so warm. She wanted to feel cocooned in something, held together. She turned on the television, but the noise was too much, the light too bright. She turned it off and sat in silence, shaking as she sipped from her mug. *Everything is okay*, she said again.

At exactly eight o'clock, Adelaide dialed her doctor's office, requesting an urgent appointment. *We can have a GP call you at twelve*, the receptionist said. *Will that do?*

Yes, Adelaide said. *Yes, thank you.*

She sat—shaking and waiting and struggling to get an ounce of work done—for four hours.

It was likely the medication, her doctor explained. One of the drugs she'd been taking was an SSRI—a selective serotonin reuptake inhibitor—which sometimes led to adverse side effects in patients with bipolar. *I see*, Adelaide said. *How long until this stops? I need this to stop.* It would take a few days for the drug to leave her system, the doctor explained. *Maybe give yourself a week or so,* she said. *And then we'll try something new. In the meantime, try to take it easy. Just do what you need to do to get by. Lots of deep breaths, yeah?*

Adelaide nodded, though she knew no one could see. *Yes*, she said. *Thanks for your help.*

And Ms. Williams? the doctor said. *You may want to take a few weeks off from work while we get this sorted. Reduce as many external stresses and pressures as you can.*

Adelaide nodded again, biting her lip. *Okay*, she said. *Okay.*

She would take four weeks off on short-term disability leave, it was decided, at half pay. Adelaide hated herself for having to make these arrangements.

She spent the first few days in bed. She was too afraid to cook, so she ordered takeaway to her door, the containers piling up in her garbage bin, the charges multiplying on her credit card. The messiness made her skin itch, but the thought of going outside, of carrying that trash bag, felt impossible. It was all so impossible.

The trouble with this specific breed of pain, she thought, was that she'd not lost herself. The qualities that had long been integral to her character and being, the desires that had always existed within her—to be successful; to be a good friend, daughter, employee; to be healthy and presentable and desirable—they all still existed. They pulsed through Adelaide with the same regular rhythm and pace. She still *cared*. But she'd lost her ability to fulfill these duties, to check these boxes. And that fact fueled her self-loathing like gasoline on a fire. She wanted to be good. No, she wanted to be great—but she couldn't be. She physically could not do it. Hell, she could hardly wash her hair, get her mail. How was she meant to become anything close to the person she wanted to be when she could barely make it outside?

A few days later, the world stopped melting. Everything started to cool, to feel a bit steadier, more solid. Adelaide was magically, mercifully, able to squeeze in another conversation with Dr. Grayson, who recommended a drug called aripiprazole this time—a mood stabilizer that would hopefully help Adelaide feel more grounded, more at ease in the world. It would take up to two weeks to set in, she said, but Adelaide was fine with that. She didn't feel fully like herself, but she was no longer terrified to take out her trash. Things were okay.

She took the pills at night, just before bed, and—for the first time in what felt like years—she was able to sleep. There was no magic potion, Dr. Grayson had said, no singular salve for her pain, but this felt like a start.

The next step on Adelaide's proverbial staircase was therapy—cognitive behavioral therapy, specifically. It would be months before she could see a therapist through the NHS, but even on half salary, Adelaide was blessed with the financial capacity to seek treatment privately. Soon after starting aripiprazole, she met a therapist named Margaret—

Meg, as she'd introduced herself—who, like Adelaide, was an American living in London. She cursed like a sailor, called Adelaide "Sugar." She was full of light, energy, moxie. She was perfect.

They spoke once a week in Meg's office. The walls were layered in light green wallpaper with a white, botanical print; sandalwood candles were always burning. It was comfortable there, Adelaide thought. It felt safe. Inviting.

I don't know, Adelaide said one afternoon. *I don't know how to balance my mental health needs with my obsessive need to please, you know? I don't know how to be a good friend or partner and set boundaries, how to be a good employee when I just bounced on all of my work for weeks. But also, fuck me, my problems are so small.*

Your problems are not small at all, Meg corrected. *You completely emptied your tank on someone who fucked you over and that is a horrible feeling that you are absolutely allowed to feel. You're running on empty, Adelaide. But we're going to figure it out, okay? We're going to find a way to refill your tank.*

Okay, Adelaide said. *Yes, okay.*

Her sister Izzy had a mantra, one Adelaide had learned decades earlier: *Pain is pain is pain.* It was important to recognize your privilege, yes. To show gratitude, to count your blessings. But it was also important to acknowledge and accept your pain, to understand that no matter how large or small your problems, your losses, your wounds—they are yours. And you're allowed to feel them. The hardest loss will always be your own.

Adelaide tried to remind herself of this. Her grief was not as acute as Rory's, but it was hers. Her experience seeking help was marked by far fewer obstacles than the average person's, but it still had not been easy. Adelaide—the girl who felt everything—had to remind herself that it was, in fact, okay to feel. That it was okay to fill her lungs with air, her tank with fuel, her brain with the chemicals it needed. It was okay to go to hell and back, to carry every ounce of light and darkness inside of her. It was okay to love herself fiercely, a little selfishly, and with intention.

It was all okay.

Thirty

She'd started to do yoga, because what else does one do after a mental breakdown?

Meg had recommended it. It was a fresh challenge for Adelaide, she said. A test for someone who struggles so much with centering herself, with finding calm. Adelaide left the studio one night feeling grounded in a way she'd not felt in years, if ever. Like something in the universe was pulling her closer to its orbit, hugging her tight. She took a sip of water, checked her phone, closed her eyes for just a second. And then she saw Bubs. Again. She said it aloud. *Again.*

He was wearing a gray suit, a deep blue tie loose around his collar. It looked like the top button was undone. Ordinarily, she would have avoided him—their offices were nearby and they used to ride the same Tube line, yes, but they'd run into each other too many times for it to feel like coincidence, she thought. She was wary he might think she was following him (or was he following her?), but no matter. Something about this evening made her approach him anyway—her face shiny with sweat, her hair tied into a high ponytail.

Bubs, she said. *Hey, how are you?* She went to give him a hug, he awkwardly patted her back.

Good, he said. *Just thinking this evening was too lovely to waste on a Tube ride home.* He scratched the back of his ear with two fingers. *Care to grab a drink outside the Fitzroy?*

I have some rough memories at the Fitzroy, she said. *Maybe the Marquis? Works for me,* he said.

She would stay for one pint, she told herself. Maybe two.

Okay, three. *But this is the last one,* she told Bubs (she'd barely had a drink since early September). *I'm a lightweight these days.*

He nodded his head, lifted his hands a little. *No pressure,* he said.

They talked about the cases on which Bubs was working, the Cavalier King Charles spaniel mix Adelaide planned to adopt that January (he was going to be named Fitz, she said, *Because Fitz Williams is just a great name*). They shared stories about their sisters and their moms and agreed that "Don't Stop Believin'" is both the best and worst karaoke song there is. It was easy, friendly. Free of tension.

So, Bubs said. *Hate to bring this up, but I've heard through the grapevine that you and Rory broke up?*

I had no idea there even was a grapevine, Adelaide said. *I didn't realize his friends knew my name, to be honest. But anyway, yeah, we broke up. Nearly two months ago now.*

I'm sorry to hear that, he said. (He was lying.) *Should I ask what happened, or . . . ?*

Adelaide explained the situation as diplomatically as possible. *Oh,* things had been deteriorating for some time, really. They'd been drifting apart, it seemed, since that August or so, she said. Adelaide didn't mention the resentment she could feel, the gap between them that widened with each ignored text, every *I love you* met with empty air.

And then, she said, *a colleague of mine found his profile on a dating app.* She sighed, took a sip of her drink. It still hurt to think about, like lifting a bandage to find a cut hasn't yet scabbed over. *It was kind of the nail in the coffin.*

Look, Bubs said. *Rory was a stand-up colleague and flatmate, but that's some shite, that is.* Adelaide nodded, looked down at her drink. *I'm sure you've heard this a dozen times from a dozen people, but you don't deserve that, Adelaide. You deserve so much more.*

Thanks, she said. She shrugged a little, swallowed the last of her pint. *On that sorely depressing note, should we head out?*

They walked outside. *I'm going this way,* Adelaide said, pointing toward Oxford Circus.

And I'm going to Tottenham Court Road, Bubs said. He took a step, waved one hand in her direction. *See you around, Adelaide. Take care.*

You too, she said.

There was now a trade-off, Adelaide knew, that existed in her life. She'd used to think that, one day, things would just be good. Stay good. That she would feel settled at work, settled with a partner. That she would adopt a dog in London and save enough money for a zone-three flat and sink into a life of comfort, of relative ease. Lately, though, she'd learned that the good, light, joyful days were often followed by darker moments. There were no more hiding spots for her sadness, no more places where she could tuck away and ignore catastrophe. She was relearning how to experience full joy, full calm, full happiness, but her mind also now knew how to access full hopelessness, complete self-hatred. At times, it bounced between the two like a pinball.

Sometimes, things felt okay. Riding home on the Tube after drinks with Bubs—her body stretched, a few pints in her bloodstream—things felt normal. Good, almost.

But these times, the good moments, were often short-lived.

The next day, Saturday, Adelaide sat on her couch. She bundled herself in blankets and watched old sitcoms and thought about making a grilled cheese, but decided to order pasta from a little Italian place instead. She spilled red sauce on her white quilt and cursed under her breath. She muttered an apology, out of habit, though she knew no one could hear her. Something about all of this made Adelaide feel supremely lonely.

She washed the quilt with some white T-shirts and socks, pulled them all from her dryer a few hours later. The quilt was still stained, but now it was warm, too. It smelled, aptly, of fresh laundry. Of Rory Hughes.

How frustrating, Adelaide thought. So many things that never should have belonged to him had become his: The scent of laundry detergent. The perfume she'd worn on their first date. The flavor of Colgate toothpaste she'd once tasted on his tongue. They were his now, wholly. And she wanted them back.

The thought brought her to her knees. Kate Nash was singing "Merry Happy" from a speaker on her table—she'd been listening to old pop songs as she folded laundry—and Adelaide began to cry. *"Yeah you make me merry . . . but you obviously, you didn't want to stick around."*

(Later, she will forget. She'll forget what it was like to be this heart-broken, this unwell. To sit on her floor with her back against the charcoal couch, wiping her eyes with freshly laundered shirts, then cursing again when, stupidly, she'd smudged them with mascara. You forget what it feels like to have fallen apart once you've pieced yourself back together, what the scars feel like once they've healed. You know, vaguely, where they were, how the fresh cuts had stung, but you can't run your finger over the surface anymore and say, *Here. Here's where you hurt me.* The pain will eventually dull. But not yet.)

"Wannabe" came on a moment later, and Adelaide imagined dancing with Rory in their hotel room in Mallorca, then again on New Year's Eve. She touched her waist, remembering the grip of his hands on her body, the feeling of his face beneath the pads of her fingers. Adelaide closed her eyes—she could all but feel him, right there, in front of her.

Stop it, she said aloud. *Don't let that motherfucker steal the Spice Girls from you.* He'd taken enough already.

Adelaide wiped her eyes on the T-shirt once more (it was already smudged now, anyway). She texted Celeste. In the mood for a night out? she asked. Or a night in?

Be over in an hour, Celeste replied. See you soon.

Adelaide needed a night out, they decided. Some drinks, a bit of dancing. A top that left her shoulders bare and a pair of black jeans that were just a touch too tight. *Is red lipstick too much?* Nah. Not tonight.

They went to the Roxy, a club Adelaide frequented when she studied abroad and had not set foot inside since. It was sticky and full of students—not the type of place sensible twenty-six-year-olds would mingle. *But tonight's not about being sensible,* Celeste said. *Tonight's for buttery nipples and maybe grinding with a stranger to Nelly songs from 2001.* This was just the place.

They knocked back shooters, shared pitchers of cheap booze. They spoke with English accents and introduced themselves to strangers by fake names, because they were drunk and it was silly and why not? Adelaide, now Lula Mae, met a boy named Townsend—a financier from

Texas who was *In town on business,* he said, his drawl syrupy and Southern. They sang "No Scrubs" to each other, giggling like high schoolers at a homecoming dance. She liked feeling his hands on her hips, in her hair. He blew lightly on the back of her neck and sent goose bumps down her arms and *Ohmygosh,* this really was just what she needed.

My name is actually Adelaide and this is my real accent and I need you to kiss me right now please, she said.

Hell, he said. *Well, all right.* He grabbed her waist, picked her up off the dance floor, shoved his tongue in her mouth. It was slobbery, unromantic, but *Fuck,* it felt good. Celeste cheered from the corner, a fresh pitcher in her hand.

He came home with her, of course he came home with her. They stumbled into her flat around three in the morning, unzipping their jeans in the hallway like overeager teenagers. He had an insulin pump in his side, which Adelaide was terrified of somehow disrupting. (It was fine.)

Wait, she said. *Do you have a condom?*

I don't, he said. *Don't worry, baby.*

I am worried, baby! she yelped.

Adelaide sat up, tucked her hair behind her ears. She spoke—with the speed and diction of an auctioneer—about the importance of safe sex, the fact that she'd never completed her HPV vaccine because *I got a very bad rash,* she said, *and I don't want to perpetuate the stigmatization of STIs, but did you know, in some cases, that can turn into cervical cancer if you're not careful?*

You're great at pillow talk, Townsend said. He laughed a little—a low, gravelly sound.

What? she said. *Is this not what you expected when you agreed to come home with me?*

She found a condom in an old wallet in her dresser drawer, one she'd carried in New York, the faux leather worn at the edges. They had sex—the easy, mechanical sex of two drunk strangers—and then. Then, Townsend asked what drove Adelaide in life, and when she said, *People, I guess. The good ones,* he started to cry on her pillow.

I'm sorry, he said. *Shit, this is embarrassing. It's just, my sister. She passed away a few months ago. She was one of the good ones, and—* Adelaide bit her lip, petted his hair with one hand. She said it was okay, cry it out, she was here.

Internally, she cursed the universe and tried not to laugh. It was a horrible thought, but honestly. *What were the fucking odds?*

Thirty-one

Eloise and Nico's flight landed at 10 A.M. on the morning of November twenty-seventh. Adelaide had returned to work just a few weeks prior—more permanently this time—but she'd scheduled the next couple of days off anyway. She wanted to meet Eloise at the airport in a jaunty cap, a sign for THE DEMOPOULOSES in her hands. Her colleagues were likely frustrated by her repeated absences, she knew. But Adelaide was learning that, sometimes, her needs trumped others' minor irritations.

Eloise walked out in a maroon Fordham sweatshirt, her hair pulled into a lopsided bun. She rushed toward Adelaide, suitcase dragging behind, and wrapped her up in a hug, knocking the cap from Adelaide's head.

I'm so happy to see you, Eloise said into her hair.

I'm so happy to see you, Adelaide said, emphasizing the final word. *You have no idea. Where's Nico?*

He just went to the bathroom, Eloise said. *But I couldn't wait to give you a hug.*

Nico walked out a few minutes later, his hair also elegantly disheveled. He wrapped Adelaide up in a hug as well, picked her up off the ground.

My favorite faux sister-in-law, he said. *How's it going?*

Oh, Adelaide said. *The usual, you know. Nothing major since we last saw each other.* She winked at him, trying to make light of her breakdown. A very Adelaide thing to do.

They took the Gatwick Express back to Victoria, walked to Adelaide's flat in the rain. She brewed a pot of English breakfast tea as they showered, handed a cup to Eloise as she stepped out of the bathroom—her hair in a towel, the mirror foggy with steam. *Nico passed out on your bedspread*, she said. *I'm sure he's snoring in his towel as we speak.* Adelaide laughed.

Which means, Eloise continued, *you and I get our own little catch-up time while he dozes.* She sat down on one of the sofas, patted the space to her right. *Come. Sit. Tell me what the fuck's been going on.*

Adelaide sat down, sighed lightly. *Well*, she said. *There are three things I know for sure: I fell in love, and then I broke, and now I'm trying to piece myself back together.* They'd become the central facts of her life, at least for now. *Sometimes*, Meg would remind her, *things need to fall apart before they can come together in their rightful place.*

Eloise nodded, took a sip of her tea. *How's the piecing together going?* she asked.

It's weird, Adelaide said. *Right now, I feel good. Completely, totally good. I'm sitting here with my best friend in the world, and my fridge is full of Thanksgiving groceries, and—*

That reminds me, Eloise said, holding up one finger. *I have a can of pumpkin and a can of cranberry sauce in my suitcase. Don't let me forget.*

Perfect, Adelaide said. *That's perfect. Like, see? Things are good. You're here, and Nico's here, and you brought American treats. You two are spending your first Thanksgiving as a married couple with silly little me in silly little London, and I should be immeasurably grateful. And I am immeasurably grateful.*

But, Eloise said.

But, Adelaide continued. *But my brain has been to this incredibly dark place now. And that darkness is always kind of lingering at the periphery. No matter what. No matter how much light is in my life.*

Sickness feels different when it takes place inside your head, Adelaide thought. When the illness flows through the chemicals of your mind rather than clogged sinuses or broken bones. No illness is ever really linear. But the thing is, once you've gotten so sick you nearly kill yourself, your mind knows where it can go. It knows that no recesses are out of bounds or off-limits.

Maybe, Eloise said. *And I'm no therapist. But maybe, the darkness isn't such a bad thing. Maybe it's a reminder that you're capable of turning the car around, you know? You're capable of rerouting from a very dark, scary path back to the light. You know how to go to that dark place now, but you also know how to come out of it.*

You sound like Meg, Adelaide said. *In the best way. She always says I have to learn to live with the darkness instead of fearing it.*

Exactly, Eloise said. *Exactly. But it can't be easy, can it?*

Not at all, she said.

Adelaide started to tear up then, for no reason in particular. She was scared, maybe? Or relieved to have someone who understood her right there, in front of her, sitting cross-legged in sweatpants on her couch. Eloise wiped a tear from Adelaide's cheek. *I love you the most, you know,* she said. *And I'm here to help battle that darkness with you.*

I know, Adelaide said. *I love you the most.*

Adelaide had given her bed to Nico and Eloise. She was happy sleeping on the couch, she'd said. She wanted them to have room to curl up, to stretch their legs, and she would have felt too guilty making Nico sleep on a pull-out. (Not to mention, they'd had so much wine the night before, she hardly knew where she was sleeping, anyway.)

Around 7 A.M. on Thanksgiving morning, Eloise crept into the living room. She was already dressed, her hair pulled up into another lopsided bun. *Adelaide,* she said, tapping her shoulder. *Wake up, throw some clothes on. We're going for a walk.*

Adelaide would bookmark this memory for years to come. Being woken up by your best friend was something reserved for grade school sleepovers, naps on vacation, mornings that followed nights of drinking and exhaustion and daze. *Wake up, throw some clothes on* were not words to which Adelaide often woke up. They were special. This was special.

The girls poured milky coffee into travel mugs, bundled up in coats and scarves, and stepped outside—the morning crisp and fresh and dewy. They walked to the Tate, then down along the river, weaving past morning joggers and children in dark blue uniforms on their way to school. They talked about Eloise's last year of law school, her finals in a few weeks, how it felt to walk around campus with a wedding band on her finger. *It's strange,* she said. *I feel this renewed sense of purpose as Nico's wife. Like, I want to do right by him more than ever, you know?* Adelaide nodded. (Though in truth, she didn't really know, no.)

They passed by Parliament, the scaffold-covered Big Ben, Westminster Abbey. The sky would fill with rain clouds in a few hours, but for now, it was clear and blue, speckling buildings in the kind of bright morning light that only really exists before 9:00 A.M. They stopped at Waitrose on their way back, grabbing a mixed bouquet of flowers for the table, fresh whipping cream, three bottles of red wine (to make up for the two and a half they'd finished the night before).

Nico was still asleep when they got back to the flat. They brewed another pot of coffee and began plotting their Thanksgiving menu, sitting on Adelaide's kitchen counter, whispering about sourdough stuffing and pumpkin pie. Eloise insisted on preparing an entire turkey that Adelaide wouldn't eat; they watched an old video of Julia Child and Jacques Pepin stuffing and roasting a turkey on *Cooking in Concert* for inspiration. (Adelaide very nearly put the raw bird on her head. *We can spook Nico!* she said. *Or you can wear it and do a little jig, like Monica on* Friends! Eloise refused.) By ten thirty or so, when Nico stumbled into the kitchen, they were on the floor, laughing like little kids over goodness knows what.

I hate to interrupt, ladies, he said, his glasses a bit crooked, his hair a messy brown mop atop his head. *But look what I brought.* He held up a *briki* in one hand, a plastic bag of Greek coffee in the other. *Anyone care to hear their fortunes?* Both girls raised their hands.

It had been three and a half months since Nico last read Adelaide's grounds. Since he'd seen knives and broken rings and scissors—all hints at danger—in her cup. This time, he saw the faintest shape of a hoe and a horse—promises of hard work and (could it be?) romance.

That cup is a liar, Adelaide said. But it wasn't, not really.

They made mashed potatoes and creamy mac and cheese, sweet potatoes topped with vegan marshmallows. They made stuffing, brussels sprouts, cranberry sauce, an oxymoronically massive little turkey Adelaide was sure her friends would never finish eating. (They did.) Celeste came over around four, giving Adelaide and Eloise hugs, shaking Nico's hand for the first time. She brought more wine, chocolate pecan pie. The table was brightened by flowers and candlesticks, their glasses dangerously full of Côtes du Rhône. *To old friends and new beginnings,* they toasted before tucking in.

Should we go around and say what we're thankful for? Celeste asked, halfway through dinner.

Absolutely, Eloise said. *You start.*

Celeste was thankful for her job, for her students, for the NHS. *And all of you,* she said. *I'm thankful to be here, and I'm thankful to Miss Adelaide Williams for bringing us together, and I'm thankful Eloise made this bird so I didn't have to.* They chuckled a little.

Nico was thankful for good friends and good food and his *Happy wife, happy life.* (Eloise rolled her eyes at that.) Eloise was thankful for the earned miles that allowed her to book this trip and for *Sweet Adelaide, sweet Nico, and the sweet London family we've found in you, Celeste.*

This is a little dark, Adelaide said. *But I'm thankful you all kept my heart beating this year, literally and metaphorically. And I'm thankful we're all here, together, right this minute.*

Hear, hear! they said.

Now, Adelaide said. *Time for pie?*

W*ould you rather,* Eloise began, *be covered in fur or covered in scales?* Adelaide and Nico shouted *Scales!* in tandem.

No way, Eloise said. *I'd be covered in fur. All the way.*

Same, I think, Celeste said. *Fur would be so cozy. But, hm. Maybe not. I'm on the fence.*

I'm Greek, Nico said. *I like the heat and the sea. And Adelaide is basically a lizard person. Team Scales,* he said. He gave Adelaide a high five. *Team Scales,* she said, too.

They were three bottles of wine and ten rounds of Would You Rather? into the evening; Adelaide's living room was now blurry at the edges. *Would you rather be a reverse centaur, or a reverse mermaid? Would you rather have spaghetti for legs, or muffins for hands? Would you rather be able to teleport or fly?* Each had led to spirited debate.

Around eleven, they quieted down and sprawled out on Adelaide's couches, Eloise's feet dangling off the edge of an armrest. *I should make my way home,* Celeste said. *It is a school night.* She stood up, then leaned back down to give everyone hugs goodbye. She blew kisses as she walked out the door.

It was another one of those nights when things felt safe and good and okay.

Nico had plans with an old friend from Greece; Eloise and Adelaide had a date the next afternoon. Despite the gloomy weather, they walked arm in arm to Fortnum & Mason—a sacred spot to which Adelaide had not yet introduced her friend.

My mom and sisters and I used to come all the time when we lived over here, she told Eloise. *It was such a treat.*

I can't wait, Eloise said.

Adelaide hadn't been since her visit with Rory that summer, since the afternoon that made everything dark feel bright again. Being back in the building—its counters still stacked with Turkish delight, its shelves still lined with tea—didn't feel joyful and comfortable anymore. It felt tainted by the memory of Rory Hughes.

Another piece of Adelaide to which he'd laid claim.

Everything good? Eloise asked.

Yeah, Adelaide said. *Yeah, it's just. It's like I'm seeing everything through Rory-tinted glasses right now.*

What do you mean?

Adelaide tried to explain it. How the scent of fresh laundry and the minty flavor of toothpaste and now the confectionary charm of Fortnum & Mason were intrinsically associated with Rory. *It's like he owns them,* she said. *It's like I can't even cross that land anymore. Metaphorically, you know.*

I know, Eloise said. *I mean, I don't, but I do. And I guess I could say let's turn around and let Rory ruin this like he's ruined the enjoyment of brushing your teeth. But you know what I'm going to say, instead? Fuck him. Fuck this boy, let's make some new memories that are entirely ours. Entirely yours.*

They went up to the Parlour and ordered warm scones, gooey sundaes, steaming cups of tea. They talked about life in New York and London, speaking of everything except Rory Hughes. And together, they started to rewrite Adelaide's memories.

Thirty-two

Adelaide spent Christmas with her family, wrapped in blankets at her sister's home in Massachusetts. She decorated stocking-shaped cookies with her nephew (that were largely, hilariously phallic) and snuggled her dog Puff, telling him about the pup she planned to adopt in London who would soon become his long-distance best friend, she promised. They opened presents and sang carols, and for the first time in Adelaide's memory, Izzy turned to her and said, *Remember, Adelaide. You're allowed to take up space, too.* There were no fights that year, no blowouts or screaming matches. For once, Adelaide didn't feel the need to shrink down, to make herself smaller.

After Christmas, Adelaide took the Amtrak down to New Jersey. She spent a few days with her dad, who gave her hugs and encouragement (and even more presents, like candles and sweaters and ankle socks with hedgehogs) before she boarded a plane back to London, just in time for New Year's Eve.

It felt different this year, New Year's did. Maybe because Adelaide was drunk? (Like, very drunk.)

She was wearing a black sweater with gold sequins, her hair pulled into a high ponytail with a silky black bow. She'd landed around 10 A.M., come home to nap for a few hours, then popped to life and started to get ready for Celeste's New Year's Eve party. She'd lined her eyes in black pencil, smudged gold shadow across her lids, straightened her hair over and over and over again before tying it up and back.

It was just a few friends at Celeste's flat: Adelaide, some colleagues from work. They had cheese plates and cupcakes, wine and more wine. (One colleague also brought a pitcher of eggnog that was, she explained, a potent family recipe. Adelaide had more cups than she could count.)

I have three resolutions this year, Adelaide said, holding up three fingers and closing one eye. Her words were only slightly slurred. *One,* she said. *Get a dog.* Celeste nodded; she was set to adopt him next week. *Two, get back on the dating horse—I mean, the apps. The metaphorical horse, you know.* They laughed. *And three, don't be such a fucking disaster in 2020.*

Cheers to that! Celeste said. *Cheers to 2020!* (Neither of the girls even knew the word "COVID" at this point.)

They danced to old David Bowie songs, played charades and Celebrity as a group. They lit sparklers and waved them in the air as midnight approached, counting down from ten to nine to eight to the new year—a year that would not be remembered by breakups and hospital visits, she hoped. They screamed *Happy New Year!* and Adelaide kissed her friend's cheeks, grateful to have had both Celeste and Madison (whom they FaceTimed) by her side throughout the mess that was 2019. (The mess that she was in 2019, specifically.)

I love you girls, she said, before stumbling into Celeste's bathroom and falling asleep on the rug.

Ten, maybe twenty minutes later, Celeste scooped her up and carried Adelaide into her bed, where she bundled her in a duvet and tucked her in for the rest of the party. Celeste crawled in next to her around three that morning, gently pushing Adelaide—who was splayed like a starfish across the mattress—to one side.

I can't believe I got this drunk, Adelaide mumbled. *We're barely an hour into 2020 and I'm already a mess. Why am I like this? Why do you even like me?*

I don't just like you, Celeste said, petting Adelaide's hair. *I love you, my girl.*

You do?

I do, she said. *Drunk or not drunk. Asleep on my bathroom floor or wide awake. I love you, Adelaide.*

I love you more, Adelaide said.

Adelaide woke up with a hangover and mascara smudges on her cheeks, the silky bow askew in her hair.

This is 2020, Celeste said, half sarcastically. She handed Adelaide a cup of coffee, steam rising from the mug. *Welcome to your new life.*

Oh my gosh, Adelaide said. *Welcome, indeed.*

She took a quick shower, helped Celeste clean up the plastic champagne flutes and glass bottles that were scattered across her studio. She borrowed a fresh sweater from Celeste—one that nearly touched her knees, given their height difference—and walked to the nearest Tube stop, the air fresh and biting all at once.

For a second, she thought she saw Rory Hughes standing on the platform beside her. It wasn't him, of course—this man hardly resembled him at a second glance. Still, Adelaide's stomach started to churn, her eyes to water. It was an entirely new year, a fresh chapter, but something felt so unfinished in their story. She'd kissed Rory at Waterloo station and broken up with him over the phone and never seen or heard from him again. He'd disappeared with a *poof*. With an abrupt fade to black.

She had this theory, remember? The one that the most important people entered our lives when we needed them most? She'd thought it applied to Rory Hughes (for a time, she'd even thought it was true of Nathalie Alban). How could she have been so wrong?

Maybe you weren't wrong, Meg would tell her the next afternoon. She took a sip of tea (Meg always drank tea during their sessions, without exception). *Maybe you need to flip this theory on its head. Maybe you were meant to enter his life at the time he needed you—you—most.*

What do you mean? Adelaide asked, leaning forward. She'd never really considered that the theory worked this way, that she could have a significant impact on others' lives.

Think about it, Meg said. *I don't want you to believe you were a martyr meant to save him from himself, but think about the compassion you demonstrated. Think about the donations you made to that girl's memorial fund. The books you gave him, the times you left his flat in the dead of night so he could sleep more soundly. Think about the sacrifices you made and the kindness you showed him at a fundamentally challenging time in his life. Maybe he wasn't meant to enter your life, per se, but you were meant to enter his.*

Adelaide paused, thought. She was imperfect, she knew this all too well. Yet, when Adelaide looked back at their relationship—when she added up all of the good moments and bad (the times she was late to dinner versus the moments she left milkshakes at his door after a rough day), Adelaide knew. She knew! There was no equation in which she was not overwhelmingly kind. She had been more good than bad, by every measure. She had been enough.

She left Meg's office, zipped her coat up to her chin. It was the second of January, and holiday cards were on sale at the local stationer's. She picked up a box at half price. The cards had red postboxes on them, dusted with sparkly snow.

Dear Rory, she wrote. *I'm still heartbroken, of course I am. But I also wanted to wish you a belated happy Christmas and an even happier New Year. I've always believed that the most important people enter our lives when we need them most, and I hope—with every ounce of me—that we entered each other's lives at just the right moment. Thank you for introducing me to* Fleabag *and Crabbie's Ginger Beer. Here's hoping the highs soar even higher (and the lows become a bit easier to bear) in 2020.*

She signed her name with an *x,* tucked the note inside an envelope. She wrote his address, stuck a stamp in the upper right corner, walked outside to put it in a postbox that was not, in fact, dusted with snow.

There are parts of our hearts we give away. Not lend, but sacrifice entirely. And there are some people to whom we give these pieces, knowing we'll never really get them back. It felt like Adelaide had been holding on, with all her might, to the chunk of her heart she'd given to Rory. *No,* she said. *I still need it,* she said.

But there was no use. It was his now. It would always be his. And, with the gentle *thunk* by which her letter landed in the postbox, Adelaide felt like she'd finally let it go.

It was Saturday. And if Adelaide were one to write *Dear Evan Hansen*–style letters to herself each morning, today's would have started with an emphatic *Dear Adelaide Williams, Today is going to be a good day.* Because today—the very crisp fourth of January—Adelaide was on her way to adopt a fluffy Cavoodle of a dog, and she was going to call him Fitz, and he was going to love her forever.

She could barely sleep the night before; she just tossed and turned and peered out her window at the moon. Was Santa coming? It felt like Santa was coming.

Adelaide sang show tunes in the shower. She straightened her hair, as she always did, and treated herself to an iced latte on her way to the shelter in Battersea. It made her fingers go numb in the winter air, but Adelaide didn't mind. The sun was shining, and the clouds were parted, and yes, today was going to be a good day.

Hi there, she said to the receptionist. *I'm Adelaide Williams! I'm here to pick up my dog! I'm going to be his Forever Home!* The receptionist laughed politely at Adelaide's enthusiasm. *How exciting,* she said. *Have a seat right here. We have a few more forms for you to fill out, I'll go grab them now.*

Adelaide took a seat and pulled out a copy of *Heartburn* as she waited. She flipped to the bookmarked page where she'd left off, but she could hardly follow its sentences and paragraphs. Just a few forms and minutes stood between Adelaide and Fitz, and her mind could focus on little more than the thought of his floofy ears and pink nose and *I hope he likes the doggy bed I picked out.*

A few minutes later, a woman in a purple T-shirt and jeans walked out holding Fitz. There was a red collar around his neck, the leash looped around her left hand. The woman handed Adelaide his fluffy, wriggling little body, a blend of white and ginger and brownish curls, and Adelaide bit her lip. It felt like someone had handed her a sunbeam, her body and spirit instantly warmed by his presence.

Fitz, the woman said. *Meet your new owner, Adelaide.*

A pleasure, Fitz, Adelaide said. Her voice choked on the words. *I'm sorry,* she said, turning to the woman. *I'm a little emotional.*

Totally understand, the woman said. *I just need to go over a few house-keeping things and then you two are free to go off and live happily ever after.*

Adelaide smiled.

Celeste came over a few hours later, eager to meet sweet Fitz in real life. He'd immediately peed in the corner of Adelaide's living room, but she didn't mind. She cleaned it up with paper towels and antibacterial spray, grinning as she tossed the soaking towel into her garbage can. She had a dog now! Adelaide Williams had a dog all her own.

The girls took turns holding Fitz between sips of hot chocolate. He was so chill, Celeste said. So gentle and docile and sweet. Adelaide nodded—already, embarrassingly, wondering whether she would soon become the type of person who called him "My son." (The answer was yes, absolutely.)

All right, Celeste said. *So, box number one of 2020 is checked. Get a dog: Done.* Adelaide nodded again. *Next up: Get back on the dating horse, as you so charmingly put it the other night.*

Adelaide wrinkled her nose. *One thing at a time,* she said.

Hand me your phone, Celeste said. *What if we made an account right now? Ripping the Band-Aid right off your dating wounds, so to speak.*

Almost instantly, they'd redownloaded the dating app where Adelaide first met Rory Hughes—their early conversations still saved in a chat box. Her photos were outdated now, nearly two years old at this point. *But you look the same,* Celeste said. *We'll update those later. Let's see who's out there.*

It was funny when she thought about it, really. Bizarre. Absurd. This had all started with an algorithm designed by a few guys trying to get laid in Silicon Valley. It hadn't been the stars, the gods, the fates. An algorithm on a dating app had placed Rory Hughes in her life, then just as easily snatched him away.

Now, here she was. Playing with fire once more.

It was then that Adelaide ran into Bubs for the dozenth time. Not in the basement of a comedy club or on a crowded Tube car; not in Rory's living room or on the corner outside of her office. It was on a dating app—the same dating app where she'd met Rory Hughes, the same dating app that had split her life in two.

She looked at his profile—her thumbs hovering above his face, his goofy smile. She let her fingers slide across the screen, wondering what on earth she'd just done.

Spring

London, England
2023

Epilogue

She'd see him again, of course she would. Years later, she'd pass him in Green Park—Adelaide would be running with Fitz (she ran now!) and he would be bent down, tying his shoelaces. She'd watch him smile at Fitz, puckering his lips, making a kissy noise. There would be a thick silver band on his left ring finger, she'd see—it would sparkle a little in the sunlight.

He would stand up, keep walking, never notice who was holding the leash. Adelaide would feel her stomach twist, bile rising in her throat.

Guess who I saw today, Adelaide said to Brennan once she got home. (She called Bubs Brennan now.)

Who? he asked. He kissed her sweaty forehead, handed her an iced coffee.

Guess.

Princess Charlotte? he said. *George? Louis? Any member of the royal family? A ghost? Perhaps a royal ghost?*

Ghost is close, she said. *Rory Hughes.*

Oh, Brennan said. *Shit. Did you talk?*

They hadn't, no. Brennan was visibly relieved.

I noticed he had a ring on, though, Adelaide said, trying to keep her voice even. *He must be married now.*

Yeah, he said. *I saw Diana posted some photos, our old colleague. He married a woman named Ivy, I think. Someone he knew from sixth form.*

He married Ivy? she asked. His first girlfriend—the American who'd spoken with a faux English accent. *And you didn't tell me?*

I thought it, um. I thought it might upset you.

He wasn't wrong, Adelaide thought, remembering the way her stomach twisted inside out at the sight of Rory's ring. But he wasn't quite right, either.

So much had changed since she'd last seen Rory's face. She was still in London, yes, but now lived in Brennan's flat in Angel—it had a little garden for Fitz, an old fireplace Adelaide filled with pillar candles and topped with fresh orchids, a plush king-sized bed they shared each night. (Brennan sometimes complained about her thrashing around, but he'd never asked her to sleep on the floor.) She also still worked with Sam and Djibril at Alliance, though she'd been applying for jobs on the campaign trail for a few months now, determined to help a female candidate clinch political office in the States. (She had a few connections from undergrad.)

Madison and Celeste had both left England: Madison and Anurak were living in Singapore together—she was now head teacher at an American school, he was working for an investment firm that funded educational tech start-ups—and Celeste had spontaneously run off with a French financier-slash-DJ last October. They shared a flat off of Canal Saint-Martin in Paris; she taught at a nursery school for the children of diplomats. Naturally.

Eloise and Nico were living in Brooklyn, where she worked at a small criminal justice NGO. She was pregnant with their first child, a girl to be named Mia Lucille Adelaide Demopoulos, bound to live up to each and every letter of her name.

Adelaide thought about these women, about her family and sweet little nephew and the baby with whom she'd soon share her name. She thought about how her heart swelled each time she spoke to them over the phone, how she never hung up without saying, *I love you.* She thought about the way falling for Brennan felt like curling up by the fireplace, drinking hot tea, warming her bones and her heart and her soul with each metaphorical sip of his company.

She knew that not all love felt the same, of course, but she tended to experience love (be it romantic, platonic, or familial) in all-consuming, dizzying proportions. For her friends. For her family. For fictional characters and adopted dogs named Fitz and now, for Brennan Uralla-Burke. She dove in headfirst. It was the only way she knew.

Rory Hughes didn't love like that. His heart functioned very differently from her own, she realized. Rory's love existed in the past tense, not the present. He'd essentially married his high school sweetheart—it had taken decades of hindsight for him to realize that she was the person with whom he was meant to share his life, likely because Rory never imagined the future. But Adelaide? Adelaide had envisioned their life together almost instantly. She fell fully in love with him, as she always did. Jumped in without hesitation. It was chilling and exhilarating, like swimming outside in winter: an icy rush. But it was also painful and numbing and impossibly cold. It was never a comfortable kind of love, no matter how desperately she tried to bring warmth to their relationship.

She trusted that now, in retrospect, Rory Hughes might recognize that he did love Adelaide. That she would always own a small piece of his heart, just as Nathalie did (and just as he would always own a small piece of hers). But she'd never really know if this was true. There was still so much Adelaide did not—does not—know.

Adelaide doesn't know, for instance, that Brennan has a ring box and two train tickets to Paris tucked in his sock drawer right now. She doesn't know that, in just four short weeks, he's going to wake her up at six in the morning and insist she get ready for a mystery adventure. That he'll already have their bags packed and a proposal in Montmartre planned at midnight. That Celeste will be waiting to surprise her in their hotel lobby the next morning with mimosas and croissants and so many flowers and hugs. (In this moment, not even Brennan knows that he'll spoil this plan entirely the night before they're meant to leave for France. That he'll look at Adelaide over boxes of Pizza Express takeaway and say, *Fuck it, I can't wait to start this life with you*—running to their bedroom, grabbing the ring, proposing right there on the floor as Fitz steals their crusts.)

She doesn't know that she's going to get a call from the office of a certain female presidential candidate. That just a few days after getting engaged, she'll be asked to join the campaign's communications team, playing an infinitesimal role in the election of the first woman to become president of the United States. (Nor does she know that she'll quickly gain ten pounds living off Jack in the Box biscuits in South Carolina, telling Brennan she's *Sweating for the wedding* in an entirely different sense.)

She doesn't know that—two years from now—they will get married in an old English manor house, covered with wisteria and fairy lights. That Brennan will wear a crisp navy suit and they'll both get tears in their eyes when she walks down the aisle, mouthing *Holy shit* to each other and giggling. She doesn't know that she'll write her own vows, calling Brennan a dream, comparing him to a nap in the sunshine—warm and comfortable and the closest she's ever felt to real magic. (She won't say the next bit: That she once thought Rory was the sun. That she'd flown too close, like Icarus. She knows better now.) Brennan will write his own vows, too. He'll tell Adelaide she is perfect, promising to love every ounce of light and darkness inside of her, no matter what. He'll pledge to buy her flowers every Monday, just because. His mom will fan fragrant smoke around each of them—an effort to ward off evil, to surround the couple with only good.

She doesn't know that after this indelibly special day, there will be days that feel uniquely, unconquerably difficult. That there will be more pregnancies lost, more deaths to grieve, more unrest and hurt and suffering and incredibly heavy baggage to carry. She doesn't even know these days will exist, but somehow, she knows she'll survive them as well. (Just as she has every other hard day.)

She doesn't know what it will feel like to hold sweet baby Mia Lucille Adelaide for the very first time, counting her tiny fingers and tiny toes, pinkie-promising to be her very best friend forever and ever, whispering secrets about Eloise and their bachelorette weekend in London all those years before. She doesn't know that she'll also squeeze Madison and Celeste on their wedding days—on tropical islands and along the Côte d'Azur—feeling the sweat in their palms, insisting that yes, they smell fantastic, and no, their eyeliner hasn't smudged at all.

No, she doesn't know all of this just yet. All she knows is that she's alive and loved and breathing. She's here. And everything is going to be okay.

Acknowledgments

All of my love and gratitude goes to Melissa Edwards and Sallie Lotz, my infinitely wise (and infinitely patient) agent and the world's most wonderful editor. Thank you for making my dreams come true, and thank you for reminding me not to settle for crumbs when there is cake and champagne to be had. I'll never know what I did to deserve your combined generosity and guidance, but I will forever (and ever, and ever!) be grateful.

So many thanks to Sarah Cantin, Jen Enderlin, Lisa Senz, and everyone at St. Martin's Press—from production to sales—for your enthusiasm and belief in this story from the very beginning. To Olga Grlic, for designing this stunning cover. To Henry Kaufman, for your counsel and song recommendations. To Terry McGarry, for your shrewd copyedits. To Addison Duffy and Olivia Fanaro at UTA, for seeing potential in these pages. To Ben Fowler, Anna Carmichael, and Rachel Clements at Abner Stein (and to sweet Emily Patience!) for your tremendous help across the pond. To Mary Moates, Alexis Neuville, and Brant Janeway for promoting the hell out of this book. It truly takes a village, and I am over the moon to have you all on *Adelaide*'s team.

To my parents, Beth and Brian Wheeler, who have supported me in absolutely every sense and through every endeavor. Thank you for always telling me I could, and I would, and that things would get better. You were right all along. To you, I owe everything.

To my sisters, Kate Haranis and Tori Wheeler, thank you for exemplifying success and resilience in their purest forms. To my sweet nephews, Clark and Dean, thank you for giving me hope beyond hope. And George, thanks for keeping us all in check.

To Torri and Stephanie Macarages, my favorite reader and the miracle of a woman who shaped her into one of my very best friends. To Megan Daglaris, my Megster (and my Cosmo), the first person to show me what true friendship looks like. To Elyse Crescitelli, the reason I'm still on this earth. I'm so glad we're here to hold each other's pieces; thank you hardly begins to cover it.

To Emma Leighton and Emily Glaser, who perpetually said yes to *Jeopardy!* reruns, Deliveroo orders, and "London Bridge" dance parties. And to Lucy Cross and Allison Schoner, two (of the many) women who helped dry my tears, build my furniture, and mend my heart. Thank you for living with me, and walking with me, through the highest highs and lowest lows. You all feel like home.

To Iain Naylor, who entered my life at the wildest, most perfect moment and threw his support behind this book in unimaginable ways— thank you for being my happy ending. I'm so absurdly lucky to love and be loved by you. (And I'm so grateful *that sassy little minx* found us both!)

To Alyssa Lodge, who made my words bloom by illustrating the gorgeous flowers in the earliest copies of this book and on my inner arm. *Je te remercie beaucoup.*

To my greatest pals and most passionate cheerleaders, many of whom are my Sigma Kappa sisters: Caroline, Alex, Sophia, Miranda, Katie, Caitlin, Jenn, Carly, Christina, Anna, Raychel, Samantha, Angie, Allyson, Ramya, Katerina, Laurie, Rachel, Becca, Nicole, Vasavi, Ashwin, Camille, and Nik. Thank you for spending hours by my side in various coffee shops, tapas bars, and text chains as I worked to bring this to life. Huge thanks (and hugs) to Lisa, Alyssa and Amanda, and the extended Wheeler, Kinney, and Phillips families for the additional encouragement and champagne toasts as well.

To my colleagues and mentors over the years—Jaime, Samir, Lori, Emily, Caroline (the list goes on). To Lexie Hewitt, a lifesaver in the truest possible sense. And to the women of Powell, who collectively got me through my time in New York. Thank you for the endless inspiration and understanding. I adore you all.

To Lily Herman, Hannah Orenstein, Beck Dorey-Stein, and each of the brilliant, bolstering authors who provided blurbs—thank you for your early edits, sage advice, and cosmic motivation. It means more than you know. (Oh, and shout-out to Bad Bitch Book Club for always hyping me up!)

To my wonder-working therapist, Janet, thank you for caring for me through this period and for giving me the tools to better care for myself. And thank you, Sandhya, for helping me find the magic potion. If you, too, are struggling—to write a book, to get out of bed, to dig deep down inside yourself and want to *live*—please know, clichéd as it is, that light exists at the end of the tunnel and help awaits. Resources are very much available, and I felt it important to include a few at the end of this book (see the next page).

And, finally, an honorable mention to LK. In the words of Charles Dickens, *Since I knew you, I have been troubled by a remorse that I thought would never reproach me again, and have heard whispers from old voices impelling me upward, that I thought were silent for ever . . . A dream, all a dream, that ends in nothing, and leaves the sleeper where he lay down, but I wish you to know that you inspired it.* It hasn't ended in nothing. Thank you, you.

Mental Health Resources

National Alliance on Mental Illness (NAMI), NAMI's Compartiendo Esperanza
nami.org

The Trevor Project
thetrevorproject.org

Black Emotional and Mental Health Collective (BEAM)
beam.community

Asian Mental Health Collective
asianmhc.org

Substance Abuse and Mental Health Services Administration (SAMHSA), SAMHSA's Circles of Care: Creating Models of Care for American Indian and Alaska Native Youth
samhsa.gov

The Jed Foundation
jedfoundation.org

To Write Love on Her Arms
twloha.com

1. In *Adelaide*, mental health is an integral part of the narrative. How does Adelaide's relationship with her own mental health transform over the course of the novel? Which relationships are most important to supporting Adelaide's mental health throughout? How did your understanding of mental health change (or not) after reading the novel?

2. The novel's structure shifts in both timeline and viewpoint, featuring snippets of Adelaide's and Rory's past relationships—as well as Rory's perspective— throughout. How does this structure shape your reading experience and inform your understanding of the characters overall? Does it enhance or detract from your ability to empathize with them?

3. Adelaide attempts to rationalize and excuse Rory's behavior on a number of occasions. Why does she do this? What does it say about her character, and about his? Were there moments in the novel when you felt compassion toward Rory? Why or why not?

4. In chapter one, Adelaide notes "she'd never known that a metropolis could become a booming, integral character in your life" before living and studying in London. Would you say that the city of London is a booming, integral character in *Adelaide*? What role does the setting play throughout the story, and how does being an American in London shape Adelaide's outlook and behavior? Is there a place in your life that has become an integral character?

5. How is the character of Nathalie presented in the novel? What does Adelaide's perception of and response to Nathalie suggest about her own character, and does it suggest anything more broadly about how women respond to—and even mythologize—other women, particularly in the context of dating and past relationships?

ST. MARTIN'S GRIFFIN

6. Continuing from the previous question, how do Adelaide's relationships with other women throughout the story—from her sisters to her close friends to her colleagues—shape and inform the development of her character? How did the novel's emphasis on female friendship serve the narrative as a whole?

7. Dating apps play a key role in driving the plot of *Adelaide* forward. Why do you think this is? What does it imply about modern dating culture?

8. Adelaide is twenty-six years old when the novel opens, yet in many ways this is a coming-of-age story. In what ways do you agree with this statement? What does she have to learn and reckon with in this new stage of adulthood? And what does this indicate about the nature of coming-of-age stories in general?

9. Flowers are often present throughout *Adelaide*. What themes do they symbolize and represent at various points in the novel? Do these themes change and evolve as the story progresses? If yes, how so?

10. The idea of fate also comes up throughout *Adelaide*. Why do you think this is? How does Adelaide's interpretation of fate inform her decision making and even distract her from the rest of her life? Is fate in the eye of the beholder? Why or why not, and how does *Adelaide* support your own interpretation of fate?

11. The end of the novel hints at both resolution and uncertainty. From your vantage point, what does it say about Adelaide's story? And how does it make you feel about your own? What emotions did the ending of *Adelaide* make you feel?